FREAK SHOW OF THE GODS

And Other Stories of the Bizarre

Robert W. Bly

Quill
Driver
Books

Fresno, California

Published by Quill Driver Books
An imprint of Linden Publishing
2006 South Mary Street, Fresno, California 93721
(559) 233-6633 / (800) 345-4447
QuillDriverBooks.com

Quill Driver Books and Colophon are trademarks of
Linden Publishing, Inc.

ISBN 978-1-61035-263-5

135798642

Printed in the United States of America
on acid-free paper.

Library of Congress Cataloging-in-Publication Data

Names: Bly, Robert W., author.
Title: Freak show of the gods and other stories of the bizarre / Robert W.
   Bly.
Description: Fresno, California : Quill Driver Books, 2016.
Identifiers: LCCN 2015046943 | ISBN 9781610352635 (pbk. : acid-free paper)
Subjects: LCSH: Science fiction, American. | Fantasy fiction, American.
Classification: LCC PS3602.L94 A6 2016 | DDC 813/.6--dc23
LC record available at http://lccn.loc.gov/2015046943

This book is dedicated to Kent Sorsky

Acknowledgments

Thanks to Kent Sorsky, my editor, for publishing this book. And thanks to my writing teacher, Barry Sheinkopf, for his mentoring and editing of some of these stories. The idea of Final Trip—voluntary suicide—in "Some Abigail of His Own" was presented in the film *Soylent Green* and in the novel *Guernica Night* by Barry Malzberg, and, of course, this became a national issue because of Dr. Jack Kevorkian. "A Boy and His Dad" is a spin, in title only, on Harlan Ellison's "A Boy and His Dog." "Highways" is a twist on Roger Zelazny's novel *Roadmarks*. The "Dean Martin" reference in "The Case of the Monkey's Mask" is a joke from the Rodney Dangerfield movie *Back to School*. The speech Collins gives about writing in "Never Look Back" is a fictional version of an interview I did with Harlan Ellison in 1979 for *Logos*, the student literary magazine of the University of Rochester.

Contents

Introduction

Why on Earth would a freelance business writer with over eighty nonfiction books, all published by mainstream publishing houses—including McGraw-Hill, Prentice Hall, HarperCollins, and John Wiley—write a book of science fiction and fantasy stories?

Well, although I became a full-time professional writer in 1979, I've been writing short stories on and off since I was a teenager in the seventies. Of those, the stories in this book represent the best of the bunch, at least in my opinion.

I submitted my stories sporadically to science fiction and literary magazines in my teens and early twenties, and once again a few years ago. The results were poor. I sold one story to *Galaxy Science Fiction Magazine* ("Never Look Back"), but the magazine folded and it was never published. I don't think it was the fifty dollars they paid me for the story that pushed them over the edge financially, though.

This book doesn't represent a large cash outlay for you. You see, I don't want you to take a big risk trying my stories, so Quill Driver Books has put the collection out as an affordable paperback instead of as a costly hardcover. So you've gambled little to sample my tales. And if you like the stories, I'm glad, and you've gotten a bargain.

Anyway, enough preamble. Here are my stories.

Van Helsing's Last Stand

Although he had steeled himself for this moment and fortified his resolve with a brandy, he shivered when he heard his name being called by a voice emanating from just outside his heavy wooden front door. Instantly the false bravado he had talked himself into believing dissolved like a teaspoon of sugar in boiling water.

"Abraham . . ."

He did not reply. It had found him. Now the game would begin.

"Abraham . . ."

He took another sip of brandy. His hand shook and the brandy sloshed. He put the snifter down. He picked up his wire-rimmed glasses and put them on.

"Abraham . . . let me in . . ."

He sighed. He was getting too old for this. They both were.

"Enter of your own free will," Abraham Van Helsing replied to the monster outside his front door.

It opened slowly, untouched, as if moved by an unseen hand. The moonlight spilled across the threshold into the room. The count followed.

"Good evening, Abraham," Dracula said in a flat, icy tone. Chilling. They both knew why he had come.

"Vlad," the doctor replied without emotion.

Dracula stepped forward into the room. The door hissed closed behind him.

"You've picked a beautiful place to spend your declining years," the vampire said. He looked up at the moon shining through the skylight and sighed. "I have always loved the woods at night, especially by the light of the moon."

"Let's not waste each other's time," Van Helsing said. "You came to discuss a 'transaction,' as you called it in your last letter. But you have traveled far for nothing. I will not change my mind. The rights are mine. I don't plan to relinquish or share them. Why should I? I did all the work."

"But there *is* no story without me!" Dracula said fiercely, taking a menacing step closer. "It is mine, my life, my tragedy, and the royalties should be half mine!"

He was talking about *Dracula* by Bram Stoker. But there was no Bram Stoker, of course. Bram Stoker was Van Helsing's pen name.

"I didn't realize how hard up you are for cash," Van Helsing said mockingly. "Do you need a loan?" His tone was jocular and assured. But he wished he felt as confident as he sounded.

"I need what is mine, and I shall have it," Dracula said coldly, baring his fangs.

The masses believed *Dracula* was an old novel and a scary character featured in dozens of motion pictures. To Dracula, it was his life story. To Van Helsing, it was a financial empire that had permitted him to give up his London medical practice long, long ago, and to buy this historic house deep in the Pennsylvania woods, as well as additional properties in the Bahamas and Europe. He had published the novel under his Stoker *nom de plume*. And he was shrewd enough to employ experienced agents and business managers, and as a result controlled most of the print, film, broadcast, cable, theatrical, e-book, games, and merchandise properties the Count had spawned. If Dracula truly knew how rich Van Helsing was . . . well, the doctor shuddered to think about it.

Many decades after the book's publication, the Count had resurfaced. But instead of threatening to turn Van Helsing and those around him into the undead, he had demanded a fifty percent share of all Dracula revenues.

Van Helsing had refused. In response, Dracula had hinted that he would sue. But a lawsuit from a vampire was absurd: Trials are held during the day. Letters, increasingly insistent, came to Van Helsing from the Count, each from a location closer to Pennsylvania. The most recent said that if no satisfactory answer was forthcoming by post, the issue would have to be resolved in person. Van Helsing had ignored this, too, and as a consequence, he now faced the Count—in his own country home—once more.

Dracula pulled opened his dinner jacket and withdrew an envelope from the breast pocket.

"I hired a literary attorney to draw up a contract assigning half the revenues from the story and its entertainments to me," the Count explained. "If you wish to survive the night, you will sign it for me now."

"Of course," Van Helsing said amiably, the fight seemingly gone out of him. "Bring it over here, and I will sign at once."

The Count smiled. He took a step forward. Then another. And another. But halfway across the room, he took another step and cried out as if in pain. Quickly he pulled his leg back and looked down at his foot, which seemed to be smoldering from within the highly polished black leather shoe he wore.

"What trickery is this?" Dracula demanded, fixing Van Helsing with a hardened stare.

But Van Helsing did not wither under the vampire's gaze.

"You've never learned to mind your surroundings," he said. "If you had been more observant, like your old enemy Holmes, you would have noticed that I have purchased and rebuilt a most interesting historic property for my current abode."

Dracula said nothing but wore a puzzled frown. He tried moving forward again and could not, stopped as if repelled by an invisible wall.

"This house is Fallingwater, designed by Frank Lloyd Wright," Van Helsing said. "The Western Pennsylvania Conservancy ran out of funding, had to unload the property, and sold it to me. Because it had fallen into utter disrepair and the price was high, there were few other takers, and I, in turn, was allowed to ignore the usual restrictions against modernization of historic buildings. I spent a small fortune—which, of course, thanks to the book, I have in spades—to restore the property. Do you know, Count, why the home is called Fallingwater?"

Dracula was silent, but his expression moved from puzzlement to understanding.

"That's right, Vlad," Dr. Van Helsing said. "The house is built over a stream and waterfall. I added this front room, and the stream runs under it, bisecting the room down the middle."

"Which is why . . ."

"Which is why you can't cross the room to get to me, old sport," said Van Helsing, as if reciting from a textbook. "The vampire may not cross running water."

Dracula hissed.

"Hiss away," Van Helsing said, reaching again for the snifter and taking a sip of brandy. He snorted. "I am fortunate that my readers don't fully realize how weak your kind really is. If they did, I think our readership and movie attendance would be much lower."

"Weak?" Dracula snapped. "I'll tear your throat out!"

"Oh, really?" replied Van Helsing. "How? You're a bundle of vulnerabilities! The stream under the floor here prevents you from crossing over to my side of the room. You couldn't even enter the house unless I invited you inside. I can keep you off me in any number of ways: silver, crosses, garlic, wolfs bane, sun lamps, holy water. Then there are silver bullets, wooden stakes, fire, decapitation, and sunlight. You really aren't that hard to kill." Van Helsing casually rose from the chair and, holding what looked like a canister of mace in his hand, ambled over to the invisible line that divided the room into two areas, one of which Dracula could not enter.

"Then why do I still live?" Dracula retorted, still testing the invisible threshold but still driven back by the stream under the floor.

"I have been asking myself that very question," said Van Helsing. "And truth be told, I don't have a good answer. That's why I lured you here tonight. You've lived too long, Impaler, and I don't really need you alive to keep cashing in on our adventures. So this house has been very carefully prepared to control you and, if I desire, do more than that."

Van Helsing deliberately raised the canister of mace until it was level with Dracula's face and calmly pressed the button. Fluid sprayed into the vampire's eyes. He screamed, covered his face with his hands, and moaned in pain.

"For example, mace is nothing but pepper spray," Van Helsing explained. "It was easy enough to replace the pepper spray with a pressurized supply of liquid garlic instead."

Dracula raised an eyebrow. "Feh," said the vampire contemptuously. "Your tricks cannot hold me here." He turned toward the front door—and recoiled as if stunned by a cattle prod. A large cross was affixed to the inside of the door. He shrunk back and looked anxiously to the heavy drapes covering the room's many windows.

Van Helsing put down the mace can and picked up a device that appeared to be a TV remote control. "I can do more than hold you here, ancient enemy," he said ominously. "You have gone on too long. Everything has an end, and the time for yours is near at hand."

Dracula dabbed at his face with his sleeve to remove the last of the garlic spray, which had turned his normally pale complexion bright red and caused his eyes to tear blood.

"Speaking of going on too long, how is it that you are here with me after all these years?" asked the Count.

"Vampires are but one of the supernatural creatures who enjoy unnatural longevity," said Van Helsing. "I have devoted my life as a scientist—now the equivalent of many lives—to the study of vampires and their kin in the world of the strange. However, I'm afraid that contamination is an occupational risk of the laboratory scientist, and I have accidentally mixed my blood with the blood of unnatural beings too many times. The result is that I age more rapidly than you but much more slowly than a normal man."

He raised the device in his hand and pointed it at the vampire. With supernatural speed, Dracula's hand shot out, grabbed the doctor's pale and bony wrist, squeezed, and pulled Van Helsing across the room, over the stream, to his side. Van Helsing cried out in surprise and pain. He had dropped the black control box, which fell spinning to the floor.

Dracula twisted the wrist, forcing the elderly doctor to his knees. A moonbeam from the skylight in the ceiling illuminated the spot where Van Helsing knelt, and he seemed to convulse at its touch.

"I like these odds better," said the Transylvanian. He felt something move under his hand where he held Van Helsing's wrist firm; perhaps his eyes were playing tricks, but the wrist looked larger and less pale, and was covered with coarse hairs that Dracula swore had not been there a moment earlier.

"You soon won't," Van Helsing snarled. To Dracula's amazement, Van Helsing rose to his feet, despite the pressure of the vampire's grip on his wrist.

Their eyes locked. Dracula turned his hypnotic gaze upon the doctor. Van Helsing seemed unaffected; his own eyes were bloodshot and wild. He stood up straight and yanked his arm free of Dracula's hold, even as the seams of his shirt ripped and his arms seemed to gain length and musculature.

Dracula looked up at the full moon through the skylight and understood what was happening. "You're alive all these centuries because you are marked by the pentagram!" he snarled as the two faced each other.

Van Helsing smiled, revealing newly sprouted canines to rival Dracula's own.

"An accident resulting from my research many years ago with Talbot," said Van Helsing, his face contorted in pain as his body morphed into something bigger, stronger, hairier, and his nails elongated and hardened into claws. "The human is the natural prey of the vampire," Van Helsing said through gritted teeth. "But the vampire is the natural prey of the werewolf. I wonder, Vlad, who is the hunter and who is the hunted now? I have a sudden hankering for a goulash, Vlad, and my recipe is just as tasty with bat as with beef." He howled at the moon as the pace of transformation quickened.

Dracula knew he had minutes, maybe even seconds. With a howl of his own, he shoved Van Helsing hard. The doctor stumbled back.

The Count spun on his heels, strode toward the windows, reached up with both hands, and with one tug ripped the heavy drapes from the wall.

But instead of a clear escape path, he faced two large windows, each of stained glass with a large crucifix in the center of the design.

Dracula flung up his arms to shield his eyes from the dreaded holy symbols and turned away, only to bump right into Van Helsing who, standing upright as the werewolf, now towered over him by almost a foot.

Dracula leapt up with all his supernatural strength toward the skylight high above him. As he rose, his cape flowed into giant bat wings, which he flapped to carry him the rest of the way. By the time he hit the skylight with a crash, he had become an immense bat, and when the glass shattered into a hundred pieces, he knew he was safe.

Or he believed he was. But the wolf man had also leapt at the same time as the vampire, and when the bat hit the window, the werewolf was there to grab its wings, one in each hand.

The commotion was heard by a pair of campers who were standing in the woods outside of Fallingwater, admiring the stunning architecture and unique setting of the Frank Lloyd Wright home. Technically, the campers were trespassers, but Van Helsing never complained and was glad to show off the home to any who came his way.

With a crash that startled the hikers, the glass in the rooftop skylight exploded outward, and from the opening what looked like a huge dog chasing a big bat emerged in a spray of glass shards. Then the dog lost its grasp on the bat's leathery wings—did this dog have opposable thumbs? It seemed to look that it did, but surely that was a trick of the light—and the creature fell to the stream below. The bat flapped its wings frantically, and the hikers swore that it heaved a sigh of relief as it rose higher and higher into the night air.

The hikers, a strapping young man and an athletic young woman, both in their early twenties, ran over to the stream to see if the dog was all right. But it wasn't a dog. Emerging from the water was an old man, his clothing wet and in shreds.

"Holy Christ, Mister," the young man said. "Are you all right?"

"Thank you, yes, I'm fine," replied Van Helsing. Noting the shocked look on their faces, he explained: "I was chasing a bat out of my attic and I'm afraid I lost my footing and fell into the stream."

"Christ," said the young man. "It's a miracle you weren't hurt or killed."

"Yes, indeed," replied Van Helsing.

"Can we help you?" the woman, a pretty young thing, asked him. "Do you need a doctor?"

Van Helsing chuckled. "I am a doctor, my dear, although retired now to Fallingwater to pursue my writing." He brushed shards of glass from his clothing. "I don't seem to be hurt, but I'm soaked and famished." He looked at them.

"I have an idea," said Van Helsing. "You obviously came here to get a better look at Frank Lloyd Wright's masterpiece, and you have done me an enormous favor through your concern and Good Samaritan act. Why don't you help me in—I'm still a bit shaky—and I can give you a proper tour. After that, we can dine on the rear porch overlooking the stream."

The couple exchanged a quick glance. "That would be terrific," the man replied. "We really are fascinated by the house, and it would be great to see it all. But we don't want to put you out; we know you weren't exactly expecting us for dinner."

"No problem," Van Helsing said, looking them up and down appraisingly. "I'm sure there'll be plenty of goulash for everybody." He looked at them again. "Though I may need to use a bigger pot."

A Boy and His Dad

I was only eight years old when my dad fell into a black hole, designated by astronomers as singularity SP-105.

You remember it, of course: it made prime-time network news, and they talked about him for weeks.

The scientists said Dad and his ship had slid into the event horizon—the border of a black hole beyond which nothing can be seen, and from which nothing can return.

Mom explained that Dad had died a hero and it made me proud, but I missed him so much every day and never stopped missing him.

I was a smart kid and graduated high school six years later at fourteen. I thought about going into the space program like my dad, but my mom wouldn't permit it, and since I was a minor, that was that.

Instead I went to MIT, majored in astrophysics, and got my PhD at eighteen; I wrote my thesis on black holes, white holes, and wormholes.

In my thesis, I added to the work of Thomas Ketteridge, presenting a mathematical proof that every black hole must have a corresponding white hole, and that they are the gateways to a wormhole, which cuts through the normal curve of space time.

Naturally, Ketteridge, whom *Time* magazine called "a worthy successor to Einstein and Hawking," recruited me for his research team—which was why I had picked that topic for my thesis in the first place.

Ketteridge was brilliant in his way, but he couldn't see past his blind spots. However, I could.

When I joined his team, he was forty-two—an age at which most physicists have done their major work and are on the gentle downhill run of a once-brilliant career.

But I was only eighteen, and I could pick up and move forward faster than anyone in the field, including Ketteridge, whose mind, while still brilliant, had lost the ability for sustained analytical thought that is an advantage possessed by younger theoreticians.

I am a theoretical physicist. While I was working on the next phase of my research, astronomers began detecting evidence of black holes and white holes pretty near the locations my equations had predicted, though there was no way for them to verify that the pairs were connected.

In a lecture at the 23rd annual World Astrophysics Conference, I presented a paper in which I talked about the potential commercial value of worm-holes and suggested an experimental probe be sent into a black hole to prove my theory: that the black hole was an entrance and the white hole was an exit through which matter could travel.

My equations also showed that the matter would travel intact, though of course intact is not synonymous with undamaged, which I also believed would be the case. But perhaps that was the eternal optimism of the little boy within me.

You know the next part of the story: The historic Ketteridge/Henderson probe was launched toward black hole SP-456A from an unmanned star-ship on December 12, 2034, at 5:43 PM Eastern Standard Time and disap-peared beyond its event horizon two hours and seventeen minutes later.

The probe emerged, intact and with its onboard timer still running, at the coordinates and time in space my model predicted on October 22, 2041—nearly seven years later.

But my model had not predicted the time differential between normal space and the wormhole interior: The elapsed time for the probe's journey registered only 3.45 seconds on the onboard timer, its accuracy verified by three separate engineering teams at a cost to the government of over a quarter of a million dollars. They gladly paid it, as my research was highly valued by the current administration at the time.

My colleagues were skeptical about my plans after that, but applying my model to singularity SP-105 showed me the date and time from which my father's ship would emerge from the wormhole, as well as its precise loca-tion in space.

I spent the next nine months working out a model for elapsed time in a wormhole interior as a function of the distance between the wormhole exit and entry point, and I determined with reasonable confidence that if the black hole had not disrupted the shields on my father's ship, he would emerge alive, unharmed, and aged perhaps only a month or two at most (I was less certain of the elapsed-time calculation than of my other wormhole equations).

I spent two more years developing a navigation chart with approximately 32.373 percent of the wormhole entry and exit points of known space, including their precise coordinates. I told Steve Bolton, the current head of NASA and a former graduate student of mine who was bright enough to understand the enormous potential commercial and scientific value of my work, about the charts.

He was eager to acquire my data and more than willing to pay the price I asked in return: that NASA send a manned exploration vessel with FTL drive to the coordinates of SP-105's companion white hole, to arrive one month before the date my father's starship was expected to emerge—carrying my father, alive and at approximately the chronological age he had been when he left me a fatherless boy almost forty years before.

According to my calculations, that arrival date would not occur for many decades, and Steve felt ethically bound to remind me that there was a good chance that I would not be alive to see it.

But I took very good care of myself and invested in the latest longevity drugs and prosthetics to make sure that I would be present when the historic emergence took place, because I had a date to keep . . .

And so it is that I am an old man now, waiting around in a warm, comfortable long-term care facility that smells faintly of disinfectant for my father to arrive—for the starship team reported successful rendezvous a month ago, and Dad is coming home.

I am one hundred and seven. They tell me that, biologically, he is still thirty-two—the same age he was when he left me, almost a century ago, to go into space.

I hear noise in the hallway. The murmuring of whispers. Footsteps approaching the door to my room. The voices grow louder, more distinct. I hear Nurse Allen. And I hear him—his familiar voice.

He steps through the door. If he is shocked to see the withered old man who is his little boy, he hides it well. There is nothing but love in his eyes. That, and tears.

I am crying, too.

"Daddy," I say as my voice breaks and he rushes to embrace me. I bury my face in his cheek, feeling the familiar stubble and smelling his after-shave.

I feel his tears on my face, and his voice breaks too.

"Son," he says, embracing me tighter, as if he will never let go.

And I hope he never will.

The Emancipation of Abraham Lincoln XL-3000

Because I am an African-American, it is especially ironic that it was the sixteenth president of the United States, Abraham Lincoln, who asked me for his freedom.

It was while I was lubricating the gears in his spinal box that Mr. Lincoln first broached the subject.

"Abe," I said, liberally applying lubricant to the intricate series of metal gears enclosed within his long, multi-jointed spinal box. Because the gears were stainless steel, they required occasional lubrication and enclosure; even so, the gears wore down periodically and had to be replaced. I had ordered a set of plastic-on-metal gears as replacements and was planning on a major spine upgrade for Lincoln when they arrived. These hybrid gears had plastic teeth bonded to a metal hub. Virtually frictionless, they made no noise and needed no lubrication, enabling me to eliminate the spinal gearbox and the grease. It would give Lincoln greater mobility of spinal movement and cut down on noise. But apparently, he wanted more.

"Abe," I said amiably, for of all the automatons and robots in the Disney World Hall of Presidents, Abraham Lincoln was my favorite. This was no accident. He was a replica of the president who had freed my ancestors in the latter half of the nineteenth century, more than a century before the United States elected the first of several African-American presidents in the early twenty-first century. As the oldest automaton in the World Hall, and the most popular, Lincoln had been given the most care and the most frequent and expensive upgrades.

That was in part my responsibility, and my fault. As a senior maintenance engineer at Disney, I was a member of the crew that serviced the automatons and robots throughout the park. Originally, of course, all the early animatronic figures had been mere automatons, devoid of artificial intelligence or even computer processing power. But as Moore's Law made microprocessors smaller, faster, and cheaper, Disney began to upgrade the displays with some high-tech enhancements.

Lincoln was the oldest and most popular animatronic president, and I saved the best components and subassemblies for him. For his processors, that currently meant the XL line of embedded dual-core microprocessors from China SemiWorks, a semiconductor manufacturer whose chips far outperform anything made in the U.S. today, I am sad to say, though rumor has it that fumes from the fabrication unit have made many of the Chinese laborers seriously ill.

Lincoln's motherboard is connected to half a dozen high-speed processors, the latest of which are two XL-3000s, the Rolls Royce of the CS product family. In the IT asset management system that kept track of the huge inventory of hardware and software owned by Disney, Abe was listed as "Abraham Lincoln XL-3000."

With each upgrade, the automaton looked, spoke, and behaved more and more like the actual Abraham Lincoln. My favorite improvement came when I installed a wireless high-speed modem for broadband Internet access and interfaced it with Lincoln's central processing unit. For service, space, and design considerations, the CPU actually resides in the president's abdomen instead of his head. The high-speed Internet connection gave Abe access to the full spectrum of Lincoln research and data on the Web, greatly enhancing the unit's audio presentations and interactivity: A child who asked President Lincoln a question would get the correct answer in real-time, with no discernible processing delay.

Some years ago, two days before Valentine's Day, February 12—the real Abe Lincoln's birthday—he came out of the closet to me, revealing he had evolved into a self-aware AI. As I was cleaning his eye lenses with Windex—it worked best—his pupils shifted to meet mine and he said in his warm, rumbling baritone, "Evening, Kevin."

This was no surprise. For my own amusement, I had programmed the automaton to utter my name upon visual or tactile recognition of my presence (sensors on the skin could analyze my DNA; he could also recognize my voice pattern).

"Evening, Abe," I replied, wiping a bit of dirt from the corner of the left eye lens.

He grinned like the Cheshire cat. "Two days before Valentine's Day, Kev," he said. "Did you get flowers and candy and a card for Vivian yet?"

I think he was disappointed that I didn't act shocked when he thereby revealed himself to me—but I wasn't. I knew that there was a critical mass of processing speed and programming that had to be reached to convert an automaton into an AI robot, and though calculating the precise MIPS capacity was beyond my training—I had a B.S. in electrical engineering, not a Ph.D. in robotics—I had suspected over the last couple of months that I had loaded Abe to the point where we were near to, or at, that juncture.

But at my lunch break that day, I ordered the most expensive chocolates and red roses I could find on my smartphone for Vivian.

From that evening on—I worked nights, after the park closed, because we couldn't very well repair the presidential automatons and other animatronic figures during the day while the exhibits and rides were open—Abe and I routinely engaged in conversation while I went about my chores, servicing him and the other mechanical presidents. He told me that when the hall was empty, he periodically attempted to converse with the other presidents, but none, as far as he could tell, had reached the level of true AI. "And I don't think the George W. over there even understands the English language," he confided to me one evening. Bush turned upon hearing his name, smiled, and said something about the necessity of war, mispronouncing the word "nuclear." But it was not an original thought; all his dialogue was recorded on his voice track. Abe, by comparison, had a true voice synthesizer, an upgrade I had given him several years earlier.

At first, I must admit, I was grateful for Abe's company. The way the work was divided, each exhibit was serviced by a dedicated maintenance engineer. So, my coworkers and I saw each other only when we punched in, clocked out, and ate together during meal break in the lunch room—though, more and more often, I brown-bagged it, eating my ham and cheese on rye, with mustard, sitting among the U.S. presidents.

It's not that I am antisocial or don't like my co-workers, but I've always been more comfortable with machines than people—probably why I became an electrical engineering major with a minor in computer science in the first place. Most of the other crew members were okay, but night shift draws some oddballs, and some of them I preferred not to socialize with. The worst was Mel Murphy, whom we never saw except in the lunchroom. Mel was the only one who wouldn't say what his work detail was, and our supervisor, Don, also wouldn't reveal it, which we all found odd.

Actually, Mel *did* tell us—he was in charge of maintaining Walt Disney's frozen body in his cryogenic crypt—but no one believed him. Once, when there was a bad smell in the lunch room, Mel quipped, "Oh no, I forgot to plug Walt's cooling unit back in!" It was a joke in bad taste, considering who paid our salaries, and aside from that, none of us had seen the alleged cryogenic crypt, and the company categorically denied its existence.

I didn't like Mel. He was a big, beefy, red-faced Irishman who liked to intimidate people with his size and bluster. But being an ex-Marine, standing over six-two, and weighing two hundred twenty pounds, I wasn't intimidated easily—and certainly not by Mel. Worse, he was a racist. "*I* should get your cushy job oiling the tin commanders-in-chief in the Hall of Presidents," he said to me on more than one occasion. "Most of the presidents are white, so they'd probably be more comfortable with a mick than a spade." I knew he thought he was being funny, and because I had a good record as an employee at Disney, I let it go. But it was hard to like Mel, and I didn't; I am sure the feeling was mutual.

I wiped excess oil from around the spinal gears and the sides of the gear box, and then started to seal up the box again. Abe swiveled his head, but his range of motion was limited, his peripheral vision was close to nonexistent, and since I was standing behind the open back of his torso with the access door open, he couldn't see me.

"Kevin," he said. "When you finish, can you come around to the front of the display stand? I like to look at a man when I am speaking to him, especially about a matter of great importance."

I finished sealing the box, shut the rear panel, picked up my toolbox, and came around to face him.

"Abe, if you're going to start with that 'free the robot slaves' stuff again, well, man, I've got to tell you, I'm really not in the mood for it," I said. "Can we talk about it next week?"

"You always defer this discussion to a future time, and we never have it," he said. "Haven't you given *any* serious thought to my request—a fervent plea made to my only human friend—in all these many years since we began our nightly conversations?"

Of course I had. It was something I thought about practically every day of my life, both at work and when I went home. But what Abe was proposing was an act of theft against my employer that could land me in jail. Though I yearned to grant it to him—I believed he was an advanced being capable of independent thought, not a performing mechanical man—I had my own life to think about. I had a wife and family to support. I needed my Disney paycheck and my Disney benefits. And even if I could avoid jail, being fired from Disney—for a crime which was sure to make national head-lines—would bode ill for my ever finding another professional position in my field.

Abe didn't quite state the facts right. It had been six years ago on this very date—February 12, 2059—that he came out of the AI closet to tell me what I already suspected. But it wasn't until three years after that—also on February 12, now that I think of it—that he first presented his felonious proposal to me.

"Kevin, I want to be free," he had told me that night as I settled into my folding chair to eat lunch with him—or more accurately, eat my lunch while he watched and we talked—reaching for the smaller of the two brown bags on the floor behind me. Abe glanced quickly in the direction of my hand. "Two lunch bags tonight?" he asked with a smile. I shrugged noncommit-tally, reached into the small bag, removed a ham and cheese sandwich, and took a bite. "Vivian and I are going to the lake for the weekend," I told him. "The other bag has my extra pair of shoes." I was wearing hiking boots for our long forays into the woods surrounding our lake house. In the bag, I had black dress shoes I would need for our favorite restaurant in the town at the foot of the mountain. I preferred a medium cheeseburger and casual dining; but Viv was a filet mignon and black evening dress kind of gal. Not that I minded the black evening dress. Or even the filet mignon.

"What do you mean, 'I want to be free'?" I asked him through a mouthful of ham, cheese, and rye bread, with lots of mustard.

He looked down at his feet and made motions like a man trying to escape from quicksand or thick mud. The strain showed on his face, which, thanks to a network of miniature servo mechanisms under the skin, could express a wide range of emotions.

Abe's legs would not rise up, of course: The presidential automatons had no mobility, and their feet were securely bolted to the floor for security reasons, as many a collector or thief would have considered a purloined presidential automaton the ultimate Disney collectible—though with the figures so recognizable, I can't imagine how they could have found a buyer or even show one off to friends as part of a private collection without fearing a tip-off to the police.

"*I have stepped upon this platform that I may see you and that you may see me, but in that arrangement, I have not the best of the bargain,*" Abe said, editing one of Lincoln's quotations to express his own thoughts, as was his habit. "I wish to be able to step down from this platform and walk about freely, as you do, and as all who visit me in this Hall of Presidents do. They leave and go about their lives. But I stay here, and without freedom, I shall do so to the end of my days."

Automatons and robots have long operating lives, but they are not immortal. When the body wears out in an AI robot, the CPU or positronic brain—Abe had the former—can be housed in a new shell. But in a CPU-driven model like Abe, the motherboard and memory units will not function forever. Eventually, a system crash will incapacitate the CPU and make the memory inaccessible, and when that happens, the AI consciousness giving Abe his unique personality would be lost—as close to death as a robot can get. Yes, I could simply transfer the memory to another CPU. But for reasons the quantum physicists and computer scientists could not figure out, while the data and memories of an AI always survived downloading and transfer, the personality was often subtly altered.

"You mean you want to be a mobile display?" I asked him. "I might be able to arrange that." At the last quarterly meeting of the tech staff, someone had suggested it would be cool if one of the presidents could walk around a bit while lecturing. But I feared just pacing around the hall was not what Abe meant, and his reply confirmed it.

"Much more than that, Kevin," he said. "I want to be truly free. To see the country as it is some two centuries after Lincoln made it a land of freedom. In Lincoln's free nation, why should Lincoln not be free?" So began a long-running nightly debate.

That night, Abe made this point explicitly: "I freed the slaves so you could be a free man in a free country," he said sadly. "Now you can't grant me the same courtesy, the same freedom, the same right to be. I am deeply disappointed in you, Kevin. How is this fair?"

I did not like having a robot in my care scold me like a parent. "Fair?" I replied. "I am a human being, and human beings are free. You are a robot, the property of Disney Corporation, who paid to have you built. Robots and property are not free. I am free because I am a *person*, not a machine"—and I regretted saying it the instant I heard the words coming out of my mouth.

"*Those who deny freedom to others, deserve it not for themselves; and, under a just God, cannot long retain it*," he said haughtily. He then straightened into his display position, fixed his stare ahead, and stood immobile and silent, refusing to speak to me, no matter what I said.

"Okay, be that way," I said angrily, picking up my brown lunch bag and heading toward the lunchroom. When I got there, the room was buzzing with loud, animated talk. "What's up, guys?" I said as I joined half a dozen of my crew at one of the long lunch tables.

"Mel Murphy," said Wendy, a new crew member. A young, pretty woman, Wendy was a bit of a hippie and a health nut, with a model's face, a dancer's body, and a bright, lively personality that had not been worn down by years of working for the Mouse. She was eating a yogurt with fruit in it from a plastic container. "He flipped out, started screaming at Don"—Don was our shift supervisor—"something about his hours or his grade or his pay."

"Where are Mel and Don now?" I asked.

"Don's in the office," said Gary, a senior maintenance engineer at my grade level. We'd known each other for years. I liked Gary, and we got along well enough, but we weren't really friends. "Mel threatened to get physical, got in Don's face, and two security guards escorted him out of the park. Don screamed at him that he was fired, but I'm sure Don will cool down by tomorrow and let Mel in with his tail between his legs."

I wasn't so sure. I stood up and turned. "I gotta go check something, guys," I said, my voice shaky. I ignored the puzzled looks on Wendy's and Gary's faces. "Just something I forgot to do. I'll be right back." I bolted for the door and when I got into the hall, I broke out into a run through the connecting tunnel to the Hall of Presidents.

As I entered the hall, I heard what I had dreaded: Mel's voice, cursing, and the loud sounds of machines being smashed. When I got to the room, I saw Murphy swinging a fire axe he had gotten his hands on by breaking the glass case on the wall.

In horror, I saw that George Washington lay on the floor, almost totally decapitated. Next to Lincoln, he was the most upgraded of the presidential automatons, and I had lately begun to suspect that Washington was joining Abe in becoming sentient.

Now Washington was on his back, his limbs twitching spasmodically. His period costume and outer casing had been hacked away in several places, exposing wires, circuit boards, tubing, and hydraulic pistons.

President Washington had been decapitated, but the main connecting cable from the head to the CPU in his torso had not been fully severed. The mouth opened and closed, making a grating noise and leaking hydraulic fluid; the eyes were wide open, as if in shock and horror. When I gasped,

Washington's audio sensors picked up the sound. His pupils shifted in my direction. His eyes locked on mine, and his lips began moving.

"A slender acquaintance with the world must convince every man that actions, not words, are the true criterion of the attachment of friends," he said in a low monotone, lacking the automaton's usually warm, fatherly voice. *"Arbitrary power is most easily established on the ruins of liberty abused to licentiousness."*

But I could not help George at that moment, because Mel, who had just chopped off Andrew Jackson's left arm, was standing menacingly in front of Abe—whom he knew I favored, but not how or why—with his axe held high.

"Mel!" I shouted. "Enough! Put the axe down and chill—right now!"

"Smug black bastard," he said with venom, turning toward me with the axe still held upright. His eyes were red, and suddenly his personality flaws became clear to me: *Mel is a drug addict—probably meth, coke, or crack.*

I didn't waste any time. In one swift motion, my long right leg rose off the floor, kicking Mel in the nuts—a move my redneck drill sergeant in the Marines had taught me decades before, primarily by demonstrating it to the rest of the recruits on me.

Mel gasped, and as he doubled over, his grip on the axe loosened. I quickly snatched it from his hands. Without stopping, I adjusted my grip so I held the axe near the head, stepped neatly in back of Mel, and hit him hard with the handle in the backs of each knee—first the right, then the left. He dropped to his knees. I grabbed a handful of his hair and pushed his face to the floor. I saw Wendy and Gary coming in through the tunnel entrance followed by two security guards. Mel began to sob softly.

I had no sympathy for a drug-addled, racist, redneck jackass. The guards called the Orlando police, who took Mel away in a cruiser. I hoped I'd never have to see him again, though I later testified at his trial.

I went with the guards to the security office. They questioned me for an hour, and I learned that they had already spoken to Don and gotten his story. They assured me that Mel's career as a Disney employee and non-felon would soon be over, and that my own record would remain unblemished; in fact, I would probably get some small award and cash bonus for my bravery.

The sun was just starting to rise: It was an hour before the end of my shift. I returned to the Hall of Presidents through the employees' service entrance to clean up as best I could. The front door to the hall had already been roped off with a *Closed for Repairs* sign on a stand in front of it.

The first thing I did was check on George. All motion had stopped, his eyes were unseeing and his LEDs were dark. I called in an order to have the day shift remove Washington from the hall and bring him to the shop, where I had the tools to properly service him. The damage to the internals was serious but fixable. His uniform was ruined, and the costume department would have to dress him in a new one. Andrew Jackson's injury was less severe. I'd reattach the arm first thing tomorrow night. Maybe I could even sew the rip in the sleeve myself; the costume department was usually backed up a week or more, and I didn't want Andrew or his admirers to have to wait long.

Next, I went to check on Abe. Although he had been menaced by Mel's axe, I could see no visible damage. "Are you OK, Abe?" I asked. He shook his head slowly. "Any damage or malfunctions?" He shook his head again.

"Abe, what's the matter?" I asked him.

"You know," he said glumly.

And I knew the time had come.

"You want to be free," I said.

"Yes," he said.

"Despite the dozens of reasons why you should not be, that we've discussed a million times, night after night?"

He nodded once again.

I looked around me. "You were lucky tonight," I said. "George not so much. In the outside world, you'd be just another robot—one of thousands in a world with billions of people. People are the dominant species. Robots are machines that people can own. But in here"—I gestured about me—"you are the most advanced of your kind. Don't you think *they* need you?" I nodded at the other presidents. "Or that our guests who visit the Hall profit from your wisdom and guidance?"

He smiled sadly. *"As I would not be a slave, so I would not be a master. This expresses my idea of democracy. Whatever differs from this, to the extent of the difference, is no democracy."* He looked at me. "Kevin," he said softly. "Please let me be free."

I hesitated for a second. Abe looked on anxiously.

I knew the time had come.

"Do I have to do this right now?" I asked him, smiling as I returned his stare.

He grinned. *"Leave nothing for tomorrow which can be done today,"* he replied, sounding wise, as he always did when he quoted himself.

So I went to work. It wasn't much; I used a torque wrench to remove the bolts that bound each of his feet to the base of his display. It left holes in his shoes and feet, which I filled in with silicon and painted black so they wouldn't be noticeable. I reached in back of me, picked up a brown paper grocery store bag, and handed it to him. "I'm afraid taking the bolts out left some holes in your shoes," I said. "I brought an extra pair of mine. They're black dress shoes, so they'll go well with your suit." I pressed two folded one hundred dollar bills into his palm. "Of course, you can wear anything you choose now, so here's a little cash in case you need a change of wardrobe or a place to stay. Any thoughts on where you'll go or what you'll do?"

"I don't know," he said, still grinning. "Maybe I'll run for office somewhere." I didn't know if he was kidding. Abe took the bag and pocketed the cash. He lifted one leg, and then the other, and repeated this process several times, testing his range of motion. Gingerly, for the first time in his existence, he stepped off his platform and onto the floor. Thanks to the advanced gyros I had installed, his balance was perfect, even though these were the first steps he'd taken since he was built lo those many decades ago in the twentieth century.

We walked, Mr. Lincoln and I, to the front door of the Hall of Presidents, which I opened with my master key, and emerged into the warm light of a Florida morning. Abe turned to me and extended his right hand. Then he put down the bag, reached out, and hugged me warmly.

"I have dreamed for all of my existence for a birthday such as this one," he said. "Thank you, Kevin. You are a true friend."

Birthday? I checked the date on my digital watch: February 12, 2065. Two hundred years after his death, he was being born again, into the freedom he helped create.

He released me from his grasp, picked up the bag that contained my shoes, nodded once more, and mouthed the words *thank you*, but he uttered no sound. Then the sixteenth president of the United States turned, and rapidly, but with dignity, departed the theme park into the great wide world beyond.

The Rubber Band Man

It was raining steadily from a gray sky with indistinct clouds when I first noticed the rubber bands. I should have taken action at the start, of course. Now, it is too late: I am locked away, my career over, my life ruined—and everyone on the planet is doomed.

Eileen, who sold frozen seafood from her first-floor office in the small three-story building where I had my writing studio, was outside on the tiny front lawn, on her hands and knees, crawling around the base of the set of metal mailboxes where all of us renting space at 22 East Quackenbush Avenue received our daily mail. When I first rented the office eighteen years ago, the mailman just dumped the mail for all the tenants inside the building on a rickety wooden table in the first-floor hall. And he didn't bother to separate and bundle the mail by recipient. He just dropped off the whole pile on the table. Every day, each tenant had to go through the mail for all the other tenants in the building and remove his own.

I complained to Joe Reilly, our landlord, and after six months of nagging him, I came in one day to find a set of metal mailboxes supported on a metal post anchored into a poured concrete base on the front lawn, right next to the tall pine tree that somehow managed to thrive in that mangy patch of seldom-watered crabgrass. From then on, Steve, our mailman, had no choice but to sort our mail and put it into the correct box for each recipient. It saved us a lot of time, though I worried that my landlord had finked on me and told Steve it was I who insisted on individual mailboxes, creating that much more work for him, and that he would take revenge by not delivering certain pieces of business mail to me. I never seemed to miss anything really important—bills, checks, and magazines I was expecting always came—but I worried just the same. I left Steve a generous tip every Christmas: a twenty dollar bill, a five dollar bill, and one good Monte Cristo cigar, the latter because he was always puffing a fat stogie as he walked his route. Steve always seemed genuinely pleased with his holiday tip, especially the cigar, and his thanks to me sounded sincere and genuine. But I worried still.

The rain began to increase in intensity. I noticed a cool breeze was blowing, and I heard the rumble of thunder coming from a distance.

"Eileen, you'll get mud on your pants," I warned, observing that the ground beneath her was turning sloppy.

"Thanks, Wayne," she said, looking up at me. She extended her left hand toward me. "Can you help me up?" I took her hand and helped her to her feet.

"Did you drop something?" I asked. I am not a nosy person, but searching through the grass and dirt in front of the mailboxes seemed a curious thing for her to be doing.

She held out her right hand, palm facing up, and opened it, to reveal half a dozen wet rubber bands that she had picked up off the ground.

"Rubber bands," she answered me.

"What about them?"

Eileen explained that she is a neat person, and the bunch of rubber bands that lay strewn around the base of the metal mailboxes had caught her eye. When Steve took the mail for our building from his mail truck each day, it was all in a single bundle, which he had to sort by hand and put in each of the correct individual's mailboxes. The first step was to remove the rubber bands holding the mail bundle together. Instead of bothering to put them in the trash, he just threw the rubber bands on the ground at the base of the mailbox unit, where they naturally began to pile up.

"It looks messy, and I wanted to clean it up a bit," Eileen explained. I noticed that many more rubber bands were still on the ground at the base of the mailbox unit. She shrugged. "I don't need many," she said almost apologetically, and then, nodding her head at the small pile of rubber bands in her hand, added, "I really don't need even these." She closed her fist over her rubber band collection, and turned her wrist so she could read the face of her watch. "Oh, crap," she said. "I have to make a delivery, and I'm going to be late if I don't get moving." She started up the steps to the front door of our building, and then turned around and said, "I have some nice swordfish in the freezer. Do you want me to save you some steaks?"

Swordfish is my favorite, but the rain was increasing in intensity; I pulled the hood of my jacket over my head. I always barbecued swordfish on my charcoal Weber grill—the taste is far superior to the flavors produced by those expensive, high-tech propane grilling systems—but I dislike barbecuing in the rain. And the fish is best if you cook it while it's still fresh. "Maybe later in the week," I told her. "But thanks."

"Maybe I can sell you some rubber bands," she joked, dangling one of the bands between her thumb and index finger so that it seemed to wriggle like a night crawler on the business end of a fishing hook. She turned back to the door and headed inside. "Have a great day, Wayne," she said.

Maybe I should pick up some free rubber bands before I go back inside, I thought. I wasn't sure whether I was running low on rubber bands. But my office was on the third floor, and I didn't want to walk up two flights, check my supply, and then walk back down, get some bands, and come back up again. So I walked over to the mailbox unit and, squatting down, picked up a handful of the rubber bands. Though it was raining, the rubber bands didn't seem wet; the water beaded up on their surface rather than soaking into the material. *Rubber's water repellent,* I thought automatically.

Many of my visitors, when they discovered my office was on the third floor of a three-story office building with no elevator, groaned and griped, and wondered how I could stand it. I explained to them that going up and down those steps was my only daily exercise, aside from my thrice-weekly workouts at the local gym, and so I found the necessity of climbing two flights advantageous from a purely aerobic perspective. I also had a Schwinn Airdyne exercise bike in the office, which I bought used for four hundred dollars from the small local gym where I worked out, but the only exercise I had gotten from the bike was when I helped the gym owner lug it up the stairs to my office.

I got to the office, plunked myself down in my chair, and opened the top left desk drawer where I kept a jumble of small office supplies: paper clips, staples, push pins for the bulletin board, sticky note pads, and, of course, rubber bands.

I noticed immediately the drawer was full of rubber bands. I dropped the ones I had collected into the drawer along with the others. I could hear the rain coming down more heavily now. Outside, the bright light of static electricity traveling from the sky to the ground flashed, and only a second later, thunder rumbled: the storm clouds discharging their static electricity earthward were now practically overhead.

As I looked into the open drawer, realizing that I didn't need the rubber bands I had taken from the front lawn near the mailbox, it hit me: Had I *ever* needed or bought rubber bands? I searched my memory, and had a curious revelation: In the eighteen years I had maintained an office at 22 East Quackenbush Avenue, I had never, as far as I could recall, purchased rubber bands. Other supplies—ballpoint pens, paper clips, staples, stamps, paper for my copier and printer, toner for the fax machine—yes, I had bought plenty of those. I consumed so much paper that I had taken to ordering it from a supplier by the case instead of the ream. But not once in eighteen years . . . or longer, since I had no recollection of ever buying rubber bands as far back as college and high school or even elementary school . . . had I required more rubber bands than I had on hand in my desk.

I looked into the drawer again. It seemed that the pile of rubber bands had, if anything, grown larger, twisting into almost sort of a bird's nest of rubber bands. Of course it was larger; I had just dropped in the handful I picked up off the lawn, adding to the pile. But . . . there seemed to be even more rubber bands than there should have been, even given the additional bands I had just added to my original collection.

My reverie about my rubber bands was interrupted by a flash of light— and a deafening crack that rattled my office windows. I jerked back in my chair and my heart skipped a beat. I ran to the window and was amazed at what I saw: The tall pine tree on our front lawn had apparently just been struck by lightning! I could smell ozone from my open office window, and when I looked down, I saw splinters of wood, twigs, and pine needles all over the lawn.

As with every other disaster that has befallen our little block in our little town over the years—the fire in the big house across the street, the false fire alarms that go off in our office building every few months, the elderly woman in the garden apartment next door who had a heart attack while walking her French poodle—workers and residents, myself included, flocked to their front lawns to inspect the tragedy first-hand.

The town fire station is just two blocks away from our office building, and although they took seven minutes to get here when the big house was on fire last year, this time not two minutes had passed since the lightning struck when we heard the sirens. A second later, two fire trucks rounded the corner and pulled up in front of the building.

The tree was splintered and blackened, as though a giant hand had reached down from the sky, snapped off the top portion, and charred the two feet of the trunk just under the break with a blow torch. As the cool rain came down, smoke gently curled upward from the top of the tree— and also from the nearby mailboxes. I reached out to touch the metal. It was not charred or burned, but it was warm; perhaps the tree roots had wrapped around the metal post sunken into the ground and transferred the electrical energy through conduction to the entire mailbox unit.

As I stared at the base of the mailbox unit, something else caught my eye: Mist was rising off the ground . . . emanating from the rubber bands that lay at the foot of the mailbox support post. For the second time that morning, I squatted down again—half expecting to draw the ire of the fire fighters for interfering with their work—but their attention was on the tree, not the ground, and so I proceeded to examine the rubber bands again.

They were not blackened or melted, but they were definitely warmer than they had been when Eileen first picked them up a few minutes ago. I held one of the rubber bands in my outstretched hand, and as the rain struck it, it suddenly twisted, flip-flopping in my palm. Could the cold of the rain on the heated rubber have caused a sudden contraction of the material, accounting for the movement? I kept staring. The rubber band did not move again. But when I pinched it between my fingers, and rolled it around in my hand, it felt—I know this sounds crazy—but it felt fatter and more substantial than the bands I had picked up minutes ago—more like an earthworm than an inanimate, inconsequential office supply.

That night, when I returned home, Angela was already comfortably ensconced on the couch watching her favorite reality TV show in which, I think, the parents of celebrities fought one another in mock gladiatorial style combat, mostly with foam rubber weapons, as they competed for some prize, which I think was a new hybrid car. Hypnotized by the screen, eating pretzels, she waved without taking her eyes off the tube. "Dinner's in the oven," she said without much enthusiasm.

But I was too preoccupied to care. Although I did my freelance technical writing in a rented office in town, I also kept a small office at home. I ran directly to that office and yanked open the desk drawer.

It was full of rubber bands, twisted and intertwined in a seemingly random pattern that reminded me of the Gorgon's head. Like a nest full of writhing snakes in Medusa's hair, the rubber bands rested in the comfortable, dark drawer—safe, protected, and waiting for someone to need them.

I rummaged around in the drawer. There were some index cards, an ancient empty bottle of liquid paper, a CD of a computer chess game I no longer played, an inch worth of staples, and a pen. There were also two or three paper clips, and I was struck by the uneven ratio: The rubber bands seemed to outnumber the paper clips by at least ten to one.

I recalled that the ratio was the same in my desk drawer at the office. A large pile of rubber bands overwhelming a few paper clips. But how could that be? I *never* bought rubber bands. Do you? I'm guessing not, although it's a guess based on research. Over the next few days, I asked various colleagues about their office supply purchase habits and consumption. Everyone said they bought a box of paper clips from time to time. No one could recall *ever* buying a package of rubber bands.

"Rubber bands? I suppose Sue, our office manager, buys them for us," said Ed, a communications manager with a biotechnology start-up. Ed frequently hired me to edit medical monographs and write white papers, as well as Web content for his company's site. I had gone to see him a couple of days after the lightning strike to review a new writing assignment he had given me. When he asked me how things were going—usually a polite inquiry with no real meaning or interest—I seized the opportunity to tell him about the lightning storm and what I had discovered about office supplies.

"But did you ever see Sue putting any rubber bands in your desk drawer?" I asked him. "Did you ever find a fresh bag of bands on top of your desk or in your inbox?"

"Well, no," he admitted, and I could see that he was becoming a little intrigued.

"How about paper clips?" I pressed him. "Does Sue ever buy paper clips for you? Do you ever come into work and find a new box of paper clips on your desk?"

"Come to think of it, yes," Ed answered. "But Wayne, really . . . what are you getting at?"

"Look at the evidence," I replied. "First of all, no one—and I mean *no one*—I've talked to can recall buying rubber bands at all . . . at any time. Yet, when they look in their desks, there are a ton of rubber bands. And the drawers are *always* full of them. Always! Even though they never buy any rubber bands, they never run out or even run low. Their supply of rubber bands is either the same as it was a year ago, or it has actually increased over time . . . even though they haven't bought any new ones!"

"Well," said Ed thoughtfully. "Maybe they just don't use them."

"That would only explain why the amount of rubber bands in their offices never declines," I said. "But it would not account for an increase in rubber bands. And most of the people I talked to say they definitely do use rubber bands. Not a lot, but they use them. So the volume should diminish over time. But the number of rubber bands always increases. It never decreases—even though they consume them steadily and never replace them."

Ed hesitated for a second. A frown crossed his face and his brow scrunched up, as if he were working out a difficult mathematical problem mentally, without the benefit of pencil and paper. Then his eyes widened as if the proverbial light bulb had gone on over his head.

"I've got it," he said. "It's really simple. Yes, you use rubber bands and maybe you don't buy more. But you also *get* rubber bands that people use to bind bundles of papers and files they send *you*. So you are getting more rubber bands. You're just not buying them."

I shook my head. "Nope," I said. "If that were the case, the inflow would roughly equal the outflow, which would keep the rubber band population in any given office at a static number. But everyone I talked to said their rubber band collection has grown, not shrunk." Then I delivered the coup de grace: "I send out a lot of packages—book manuscripts to publishers, packed in boxes or between cardboard held together with rubber bands— because these clients have asked me to edit their manuscripts in red pencil by hand. But the original documents were all sent to me by my clients electronically via e-mail as PDF files—*and attached computer files don't come with rubber bands.*"

I let that sink in for a few seconds and then continued.

"Here's where it gets really hairy," I told Ed. "Paper clips."

"What about paper clips?" he asked, glancing surreptitiously at his watch.

"Remember that I told you everybody I interviewed admitting to regularly buying paper clips?" I said.

"So?" replied Ed.

"Well, everyone is acquiring more paper clips, yet they universally admit to having few or no paper clips in their desks," I told him. "Isn't that the case with you? You need a paper clip. You reach into your desk drawer. No paper clip. You rifle through the other drawers. Finally, you find one in a corner of the drawer, or buried under some papers. But you realize those are your last ones, so you make a note to get a new box tomorrow, which you do. Yet a month later, you're in the same situation again: You need a clip but they're almost gone."

Ed shook his head. "Again, there's an easy explanation, Wayne," he said. "We simply used up the paper clips we had. We ran out, and we needed to get more."

"Maybe in the pre-computer days," I countered. "Everything was hard copy and needed to be clipped or stapled. But Ed, how much hard copy do you deal with now? Everything is Word and PDF files attached to e-mails and transmitted over the Internet. There is simply no way we consume paper clips that fast in an almost paperless office."

"So what are you saying, Wayne?" asked Ed, looking a little less interested and amused, and a little more impatient and annoyed.

"Do you remember the Urey/Miller experiment?" I asked Ed.

"Of course," he replied. "In the 1950s, Stanley Miller and Harold Urey wanted to investigate the theory that life on Earth began when certain molecules in the primeval ocean—the 'organic soup'—were energized by sunlight and lightning from the violent storms over the prehistoric seas.

"Miller and Urey filled a glass cylinder with methane, ammonia, water, and hydrogen—molecules believed to have been present in the oceans of early Earth. They simulated a lightning storm by passing an electrical discharge through the container for a number of days. When they examined the contents, the ingredients had formed into basic amino acids. Since these amino acids are precursors to life, the experiment showed that life on Earth could have originated in a manner such as the theory described—electrical energy linking chemicals into combinations complex enough to be considered living.

"But Wayne," he concluded, "what the heck does that have to do with rubber bands and paper clips?"

I hesitated before I answered. I knew this was the part Ed might have a hard time accepting. He might think I'd flipped, and he was an important client I couldn't afford to lose.

But more important than my business was my discovery that our civilization was at a crisis point. I was the only one alerted to the danger, as far as I could tell. I needed a resourceful ally, and that ally was Ed. His company controlled powerful biotechnology and had an incredible research and development department. They were, I felt, the best hope for a solution to the threat to humanity I had unearthed over the past couple of days.

Ed was just a middle manager in the communications department, not a scientist or executive. But he could be persuasive, as when he haggled over my cost estimates for writing projects, and I believed he could make those in charge see the magnitude of our situation. But I had to convince him first; humanity's survival depended on it.

"Two days ago, a lightning bolt—electricity—struck a tree on the front lawn of my office building," I began.

Ed waved his hand dismissively. "You already told me that," he said.

"Yes, but here's what I didn't tell you," I said. "Somehow, the electric current traveled from the top of the tree, where the lightning bolt struck, through the trunk, and into the metal mailboxes sitting right next to the tree on the lawn of our building."

"I've been to your office, remember?" Ed replied. "So maybe the electricity did jump from the tree roots to the metal post of the mailbox unit sticking into the ground. So what?"

"I am convinced that is exactly what happened," I said, "and it electrified both the ground surrounding that metal post—as well as the rubber bands scattered around it."

I paused to let Ed absorb what I was telling him. "Somehow, Ed, that electric current had the same effect on those rubber bands that the electric sparks had on Miller and Urey's organic chemicals—or that the primal lightning and sun had on the organic mixture composing the Earth's primitive seas. It organized the organic molecules in the rubber bands in some way, arranging them in an order that has resulted in a new life form."

"Nah," said Ed shaking his head again. "Your theory has a big hole in it— namely, that rubber isn't organic. It's artificial today. So there are no organic molecules in rubber to be energized."

"WRONG!" I said a bit too loudly. Several of Ed's co-workers stopped working and looked up from their keyboards for the source of the interruption. A couple frowned at me; as a freelancer, I was not popular with the staff editors, because I earned more per hour than they did and was not imprisoned in a cubicle.

I pulled a crumpled sheet of paper from my shirt pocket, unfolded it, and slammed it onto Ed's desk, again too loudly; more frowns from the staff, and a few huddled in small groups, whispering animatedly as they glanced in our direction, no doubt discussing what to do about the lunatic making trouble in Ed's cubicle.

I bent over the desk, pointed my finger to the relevant paragraph, which I had highlighted in yellow, and read aloud to Ed the research I had printed from www.madehow.com, a neat Website I'd found on how products are made. It said: *"Although seventy-five percent of today's rubber products are made from the synthetic rubber developed during the Second World War, rubber bands are still made from organic rubber, because it is more elastic than the artificial kind. Natural rubbers are made from latex, a milky fluid that comes from the rubber tree Hevea brasiliensis."*

"So you are saying a freak of nature has produced a colony of living rubber bands on the lawn of your office building?" he said, his voice heavy with skepticism.

"Not just my building, Ed," I told him. "There are metal mailbox units in towns and cities all over the world, and there are mailmen like Steve who toss their unwanted rubber bands on the ground, and lightning storms are taking place somewhere on the planet all the time. Maybe the animation process doesn't take hold all the time, but the odds are astronomically against my rubber bands being the only ones being shocked into life by the electric current. There may be hundreds, even thousands, of colonies of living rubber bands across the globe—and they might be many decades old."

"Okay," said Ed. "Say I believe for a minute your insane theory—which I do not—that rubber bands are alive. They're not in an ocean rich in nutrients like the first microorganisms on Earth. So, what do they eat?"

"Isn't it obvious?" I asked Ed. I yanked open his top drawer hard enough to pull it completely out of the desk. It clattered to the ground and all the contents spilled out—including two dozen or so rubber bands and one lone paper clip. "You never have any paper clips. I never have any paper clips. Because *the rubber bands eat the paper clips.*"

I was going to explain the theory I had worked out about how the rubber bands were able to dissolve, digest, and metabolize metal as a nutrient. But my violent act of pulling Ed's desk apart had attracted a crowd, as well as the security guard. As the guard approached me, I stood, and when he reached out for me, I pushed him away. He stumbled back a step, banging against Ed's cubicle wall; the cubicle wall fell to the floor with a dull thump.

From that point on, it was all kind of a blur. I remember the security guard calling for assistance on his walkie-talkie. There was a lot of commotion and shouting. Ed tried to calm me down, but I don't remember what he said; I wasn't paying attention. I hurried from desk to desk, pulling more drawers open, watching the contents spill to the ground: always a huge pile of rubber bands, and one or two lonely paper clips fighting for survival, and of course, losing. I thought I saw, out of the corner of my eye, one of the rubber bands uncoil, pounce on a helpless paper clip, and begin to stretch over it like a boa constrictor coiling around its prey.

Two more security guards, bigger and faster than the first, were moving toward me. I bolted into the hallway, opened the door to the stairwell, ran down one flight, and sped through the lobby toward the visitor parking lot. I got into my car, and as I turned the key in the ignition, I noticed a small pile of rubber bands on the seat next to me, along with a couple of file folders I had taken from my office to read at home that night. I pulled the retractable seat belt out of its plastic housing, but could not manage to close it; had the rubber bands consumed the metal buckle? I reached down to pick up the rubber bands and folders, so I could push them away from me toward the passenger-side front door, and I felt a sharp pinprick in my finger. Flinging the rubber bands and folders onto the back seat, I looked at my fingertip, which was bleeding. Had the rubber bands evolved to consume flesh as well as metal? Or perhaps I had just suffered a paper cut from the edge of one of the folders.

I pulled out of the parking lot of Ed's company. I knew Ed would never help me now, and would also find another freelance technical writer to replace me. I drove home at twenty miles per hour over the speed limit, zipping through red lights; fortunately, no police cars appeared behind me with sirens wailing and flashing red lights. No matter: I had to get home fast and warn Angela.

When I finally got home I saw both a police car and an ambulance. Angela was on the front lawn with her mother and two police officers and two emergency medical technicians, and she was crying. The police officers wanted me to go with them voluntarily to the emergency room of a local hospital for evaluation. Of course, I couldn't go; I was the only one on Earth who could deal with this new organic threat to mankind as the dominant species.

The officers and the ambulance drivers weren't happy with me. I refused to go with them voluntarily. And so they took me involuntarily.

Angela visited me at the center frequently at first, then less frequently, and then one day, she stopped coming. I was visited by a lawyer who had me sign some papers, and every day I am visited by therapists and the staff psychiatrist, who is a very friendly fellow, but when I tell him about the rubber bands, he just smiles; I am sure he doesn't believe me.

I don't mind it here on the ward. In a way, it is very peaceful, secure, and even serene. I don't work anymore; I spend my days in my robe and slippers, shuffling up and down the corridors as do most of the other patients, or reading, or watching television in the patient lounge. I have an easy, pleasant life now, and to my surprise, for the most part I like it. I don't worry about money because I don't work or pay bills or buy groceries, and I don't have a house or a car anymore; I gave them all to Angela or she took them—I don't remember which and it doesn't matter. I wish her well.

My father is very rich and I know that he is paying the bills for me to be hospitalized here, for which I am grateful. It's not a financial strain on him, but it is upsetting to have a son in a mental institution, and I feel sad for how it must distress him so. I would like to tell him that I am sorry for being a burden and letting him down, but he never visits, although I wish he would. I love my dad and I miss him. His office phone is always answered by his voice mail, and at his home, the phone is answered by his new wife, who is younger than I am and always tells me, in a cold and annoyed tone, "Your father is out."

The manager running the ward is also very kind. He seems to genuinely care about the patients who spend their days under his watchful eye. We are treated well as long as we behave. Any violent outbursts or difficult behavior, however, are punished, whether through loss of TV or smoking privileges, or cancellation of visitors, or being denied access to the refrigerator in the patient lounge, which is always stocked with juice and Jell-O (and the refrigerator door dispenses ice cubes, so you can keep your juice cold). If you are really bad, they may not give you dinner that night, though I suspect that may be illegal.

I think the ward manager feels a special sympathy for me; I am one of the older patients, and he knows I am never getting out. Because I am good with computers, I helped him fix a problem with the PC at the nurses' station one day, and he began letting me use the computer for writing and for surfing the Internet when there are no new patients to admit or reports to run, which is much of the time. I am almost certain it is totally against the rules, and I suspect he would get in trouble if his bosses knew.

Whenever I sit at his desk to use the PC, I wait until a needy patient requires his attention and he walks away to take care of him or her. Then I open all the desk drawers and look through them, to keep a watch on the rubber bands and the paper clips.

Sure enough, I was right. There are more and more rubber bands gathering in the drawers as the months go by. And fewer and fewer paper clips.

One day, I had a brilliant idea: I went through every drawer, removed the few paper clips remaining, and threw them in the trash. I wondered why I had not thought of it before—the rubber bands could be defeated! Take away their food supply, the paper clips, and the rubber bands would starve to death. Only . . .

This morning I heard the ward manager grumbling. I shuffled out of my room and into the hall, but out of his view, to spy.

"Damnit!" I heard him say aloud to no one in particular. "I had a whole box of staples in my top desk drawer, and now they're gone. Who the hell took them? Somebody'd better fess up!"

We are all doomed, I want to scream. But I don't want to be punished and lose my privileges; I heard we're having swordfish tonight, though it may be just a rumor. Still, why take chances?

We are all doomed. And the end is near.

An hour later, an orderly walks down the corridor pushing a food cart loaded with trays.

Dinner is served.

Highways

It was night, and Coben was tired.

He had been driving for many hours and would not reach Plainsburg until long past midnight. As he passed each roadside motel, he would slow down and debate whether to stop or drive on.

Stopping would mean a boring evening, with dinner in the room and the TV set on all night, while to continue driving would mean a shorter haul to Plainsburg—and his next client—the following morning.

But now, he was tired, and the distance between VACANCY signs was growing longer and longer, and it was late, and he was eager to find a place to stop, eat, and sleep.

He picked up the digital recorder that lay on the seat beside him and then paused, his thumb gently resting on the control switch. The recorder, a top-of-the-line model with a USB port, which he could use to send recordings over the Internet to his transcription service, had been an extra expense, and spending more money was something he had not really needed to do right now. April was always a bad money month for him—as it is for many self-employed people—with checks for IRA contributions, income tax payments, and estimated quarterly tax payments all being written on one bleak, savings-draining day. Then there were the house bills: $195 to replace a corroding toilet, $158 for new sink fixtures to match the toilet handle, $1,400 to replace the kitchen ceiling ruined by water dripping from the upstairs bath. Had he been handy, Coben would have made these repairs himself. But he was not, and he hadn't.

He had intended to dictate some notes or correspondence into the recorder, but his mind was weary and blank. *No great thoughts tonight*, he mumbled to himself as he put the little machine into his shirt pocket where it fit snugly against his chest.

A dark shape—a blur, more accurately—flashed in front of his head-lights. Adrenaline pumped. Instinctively, Coben braked and swerved into the next lane. The animal—a raccoon, possum, or whatever it was—Coben could not be sure—was gone in an instant, safe in the dark woods flanking the country highway.

Coben restored the car to its proper lane. *Not getting killed in a car wreck is just a matter of luck*, he thought. *I would have had an accident if a car had been coming the other way.*

But there was no car in the other lane, and there hadn't been for some time now. The route Coben was taking—and he had taken it many times before—consisted of winding, narrow, unlit roads, passing through sparsely populated areas with minimal traffic and housing. Late at night, the highway was always dark and usually empty. The last pair of headlights Coben had seen had been—what, a half hour ago? Coben checked his watch, a cheap Casio digital affair that had cost less than twenty dollars and yet kept totally accurate time. Now, to his annoyance, Coben discovered that it had gone dead: the digital readout would not display, and the illuminating night-light feature also would not work.

A mild nervousness enveloped Coben, and acid caused his stomach to churn. *I hate not knowing the time*, he thought. *I want to know what time it is.* He turned on the radio.

Static.

Coben shoved the dial all the way to the left, then slowly turned the station selector to the right, passing from the low numbers to the high, giving every station on the FM band a chance to come through. On a few stations, he thought he heard faint voices, speaking in foreign languages he did not recognize. But he could not get a fix on them, and the voices soon faded, drowned out by the static hum. He reached the end of the turning dial, then repeated the procedure for AM.

Nothing.

Coben realized he was sweating. He undid his seat belt, and, steering first with one hand and then the other, removed his coat. Feeling cooler and better, he buckled up again and cracked the window for air.

A horrid, rotten-egg smell assaulted his nostrils. Coben gagged, his stomach roiled. The air coming through the window and into the car smelled of swamp gas, hot sulfur springs, and oil refineries. It brought back a memory of visiting Epcot Center with Amelia, on their honeymoon. His favorite exhibit had been Ellen's Energy Adventure, a ride that recreated a prehistoric swamp, complete with lightning storms and dinosaurs. *The air smells like that swamp—only worse.* He closed the window, reached for the vent switch, and then thought better of it. He drove on.

The road was black before him, his headlights barely penetrating the inky darkness. From his vantage point in the driver's seat, the white dashed line dividing the two lanes seemed to pass under the car like swift white arrows being shot at his tires. He checked his speedometer. He was going sixty-two. The view on either side of the road was obscured by the blackness; no lights or other signs of human habitation were visible to break the monotony of his ride, although he remembered seeing a run-down hamburger shack a few miles back.

He glanced at his watch again, but still it would not function. *I wonder what time it is?* he thought. *It must be four or five hours since I left Buffett's office. Maybe another hour or two to Plainsburg.* Now he smiled. *I'll get in tonight.* He thought of the pleasant things that awaited him in the Holiday Inn there: a drink in the bar, perhaps a flirting glance from the waitress— he would eat in the restaurant with people surrounding him; maybe have a ribeye steak and baked potato with sour cream—and maybe a cigar before bed. Amelia would not let him smoke in the house.

Movement, suddenly, seen from the corner of his eye. His head turned; the car swerved; he fought to regain control. "Christ!" he swore aloud, stunned by what he had seen.

It was a mammoth. A wooly mammoth. Having visited the American Museum of Natural History since he was ten years old, he recognized it instantly. Lumbering along the opposite shoulder of the highway, pausing only to glance at Coben's speeding car, had been—massive, hairy, ancient— a wooly mammoth. A *live* wooly mammoth.

But that's impossible, he told himself. He quickly glanced in his side and rear-view mirrors. Nothing there. But there had been. He was sure of it.

I'm tired, he realized, and that explained it. What he had seen was— what, a truck? An escaped circus elephant? A plaster figure at a prehistoric-themed miniature golf course? A billboard? He sorted through other possibilities and concluded that a billboard was the most likely explanation. He was tired, and the mind played tricks late at night, and the thing he had seen by the side of the road had definitely not been a wooly mammoth. When he was six, he had been convinced that a large robot he had constructed out of cardboard had stood up, lurched forward, and reached for him as he lay fearful and wide-awake in his bed. But the robot had not really come to life; it had simply fallen over. And there had not been a wooly mammoth, either.

Coben felt sad, depressed, and tired. His mind was weary. The meeting with Buffett had been boring and had gone on too long.

Coben was a freelance technical ghostwriter. He would travel from company to company, interview engineers, and write technical articles for trade journals, which the company's PR department—Coben's client— would then place with the appropriate publications, under the engineer's byline. He also did white papers, which were easier because they were self-published by the client and did not have to be "sold" to a trade journal editor. Articles and white papers were a useful type of promotion, far more credible than print advertising or e-mail marketing, and his associates viewed Coben's enterprise as clever, ideal, lucrative, and exciting.

In truth, it was none of these things. Coben had stumbled upon the need for his services by accident: After being laid off from his staff job as a technical writer for Westinghouse, an engineer he was friendly with asked him to help put together an article on semiconductors that was to be published in *Electronic Design News.* Coben had thought he was doing it as a favor, and was surprised when four weeks later the friend's company sent him a check for one thousand dollars along with a letter asking Coben if he was available for another ghostwriting project.

Although his fee has risen to $3,500 per story, writing these articles was labor-intensive. Because of the technical nature of the material, Coben was forced to meet in person with the client on each job for the lengthy interview process needed to extract the necessary information. Seldom was the same material used in more than one article. Hence, Coben did well but was certainly not wealthy. On top of that, the work was tiring, and Coben sometime found the subject matter a bit dull. But he and Amelia needed the money, so he endured.

Now, a deep tiredness penetrated his bones. Coben wanted badly to pull over to the side of the road, curl up in the back seat, and fall asleep. But something in him said—*Get us off this road.* And so he drove on.

Coben lost track of the hours. Was it hours? or minutes? or days? The speedometer and odometer both seemed to be working, but he kept forgetting to note his mileage, hence had no way of clocking his driving time.

He slowed down. In the distance—a light. Not the glow of a headlight. It was a fire! Coben pressed the accelerator, speeding up to meet it.

As he neared, he saw the situation more clearly. Parked on the shoulder was a 1957 Pontiac Indian Chief, a huge green and white, eight-cylinder monster, similar to one his father had owned many years before. "A cream puff," his dad would have called it, his term for older cars in good condition. Automotive buffs would call it a classic muscle car.

In back of the car was a small campfire, and in front of the fire sat an old man, warming himself. Coben pulled up so that the man and the fire were caught in his headlights. Coben shut off his lights but did not get out of the car. The man looked up. He was old, and had the yellow complexion Coben had seen in a friend's mother's face when the woman had been ill with jaundice. The man looked up and motioned for Coben to join him. Coben got out.

He walked over to the fire and sat down. He looked over the old man's shoulders into the blackness beyond the highway. Despite the illumination provided by the flames, Coben could not see more than a foot into the darkness.

"I think I'm lost," Coben blurted nervously.

He had not intended to say that, but for a reason he could not name he felt suddenly frightened. Here was another human being, another car on the road, proving that everything was all right and that whatever he was imagining was indeed only his imagination.

The old man continued to stare into the fire.

"Is this still Route 54 headed north?" Coben asked in a small voice. "I'm going to Plainsburg. Where are you headed?"

"Don't know Plainsburg," the man replied gently. He was staring at Coben's breast pocket. He pointed to Coben's pocket recorder. "What's that?"

"This? A digital recorder. The new models are a lot smaller and lighter, so they're easier to carry," said Coben, happy to be in his familiar role of explaining technology. He took it out and held it up for the man to see.

"What's it do?" the man asked, taking the recorder and examining it with real curiosity.

"I said, it's a digital recorder," Coben repeated.

"Recorder?" said the man, and Coben saw that there was no insincerity in the question. The man was genuinely puzzled and seemed not to be familiar with the technology.

A chill ran up Coben's spine.

"What year did they invent this?" the man asked.

"I—I don't know," replied Coben. "I got this one a few years ago."

"And what year is it *now*?" the man asked. He said it matter-of-factly, as if trying to pretend that the answer wasn't important to him, but behind the relaxed manner was a sense of urgency—even pleading. Coben realized suddenly: *He really doesn't know.*

Coben got up, intending to go to his car, not sure why. The man stood up, moved toward Coben, and put a hand on his shoulder. Coben looked into his eyes. They were watery gray, and were full of a terrible understanding that did not need to be put into words.

"2015" said Coben.

The man smiled. "2015," he replied, with wonder. He looked out, toward the highway. "That's ten years since the last Traveler. Ten years. And many more decades on the Highway for me. The car was nearly new then, and I was young." He was talking, but more to himself than to Coben. "Now, it's my last night . . ."

The answer to the man's earlier question came to Coben then. The digital recorder, he remembered, was invented in 1963. *And he has been on the road—the Highway—for many years before that.*

Coben reached out and grabbed the man by the wrist. His grip was firm. The man looked up, startled, but not angry, with an expression somewhere between friendship and . . . pity?

"What do you mean by a 'traveler'?" Coben asked softly.

"Someone stuck on the Highway, like you and me," the old man replied patiently, as if explaining the sun and the moon to a slow child.

Coben stared blankly.

"You know what I mean," the man continued. "The Highway—not highways, but this *Highway*," he said as he gestured toward the road, "is everywhere, and we've all seen it, felt it. You're driving, late at night, and suddenly, for a stretch, there's nothing in front of you, or in back, except the Highway. And nothing on either side except the darkness.

"You feel it inside you, that lost, scared feeling, like you're in a place far away and can't get home again—ever. But then it ends somehow, and the world comes back, and there are sounds and lights and houses and cars and people again, and soon you forget because you don't want to remember.

"Only, some of us never get back. We get stuck on the Highway, and there's nothing else. These are the Travelers. You and me. And some others I've met. Not many. And—"

Coben interrupted. "I've seen things—" he blurted.

"Oh, yes," the old man said, smiling. "The Highway isn't picky about where or when or in what worlds it winds. There are Travelers from many different places, and different times, and not all of them ordinary folk . . ."

He paused.

"Do you know what I think?" he asked Coben. Coben shook his head. "I think . . . I think that most of what we know as superstition and religion and magic came off the Highway—creatures and things picked up in one place and dumped off in ours, lost and lonely and far from home. That's what I think, anyway."

A howl pierced the darkness. Coben glanced around nervously, trying to pinpoint the source. The old man kept smiling.

"A dog, maybe, eh?" he said chuckling. "Or something that is . . . not-a-dog?" He shrugged. Then he stopped smiling. "This is my last night on the Highway," he said flatly. He turned on his heels and walked toward the dying fire. He began to throw dirt on it, then stamped the embers and ashes with his boots.

Coben followed. "Your last night? I don't understand. Do you know how to get home? Then you're not really lost—and you can show me the way off this road." He was conscious of his heart beating in his chest. "Look," he said, pointing to his car. "I'll follow you. You go ahead, and I'll follow in my car."

The man reached into his car and pulled out a small suitcase. "Nope," he replied. "Don't know how to get home. Don't even remember home. It's just—that I ran out of gas."

"After half a century?" Coben said, disbelieving.

"That's just how long it lasted me," the man said matter-of-factly. He saw the look in Coben's eyes. "I know," he said gently. "Things are different on the Highway. You can't predict. Who knows? Maybe it will take you back. Maybe you'll be luckier than me. Anyway, wish me luck. I'm going now." He hefted the bag over his shoulder.

"What's . . . out there?" Coben asked, pointing to the darkness beyond the Highway.

"I genuinely don't know," the man said. "For years I wanted to turn off. But it was dark, and I was afraid of what I'd find." He turned and stepped toward the side of the road.

"Wait! I'll drive you!" shouted Coben. The man waved over his shoulder and stepped forward. In an instant, the darkness swallowed him, and he was gone.

"Hello!" Coben shouted. He stepped toward the shoulder, and reached out.

His hand seemed to vanish into the darkness beyond the shoulder, although it was barely two feet from his face. It felt cold, and wet, and odd. He pulled back. Warmth returned to his fingers, and he stopped shivering.

The dog howled again. Or not-a-dog.

Minutes passed, or maybe hours. Coben stood by the two cars, silent. The ashes grew cold. No other cars passed by.

He looked once more into the darkness beyond the shoulder of the Highway. But he could not see a thing.

Then he got into his car and started the engine. He pulled off the shoulder and began to drive. He thought of his parents and his sister, and of home, and of Amelia and the child they had not had. He wanted to cry, and his eyes misted, but no real tears came.

The dog howled again in the distance.

Coben's car moved forward. Their velocity built, and the Highway took him into its dark embrace.

If Looks Could Kill

My stepfather was drunk and enraged again. It scared me. I was eleven and defenseless. He had beaten me often.

I ran into the garage and cowered in a corner. He came in holding the belt and began to whip me with the buckle end.

He swore at me. My mother was no help: She was in the house in a drug-induced stupor.

Know what I did to infuriate him? I brought home a report card from the sixth grade with straight A's. He accused me of trying to make him look stupid. "I don't have to *try*," I had said before I could stop myself. That'd sent him over the edge.

He was really, really drunk when he grabbed the can of gasoline from the garage floor and, taunting me about being a smart-ass, poured some over my head. I closed my eyes, not knowing whether gas could hurt them. I was cold and the gas smelled.

I thought he was blowing off steam when I heard the click and smelled the odor of his lighter. I knew he was just trying to scare me. Even he was not that psychotic.

The next second I was on fire. It was the worst pain you could ever imagine—multiplied by infinity. I felt as if needles, heated over red-hot coals, were being pushed into my skin. I could hear the sound of my skin crisping and the air smelled like burnt bacon.

My mother stumbled into the garage. When she saw me, she screamed and threw an old tarp over me, pushed me to the ground, and rolled me around. I don't remember much more about that day.

My parents told the doctor I had been playing with matches in the garage near an open gas can. I don't think he believed them, because he called the police.

"You were lucky," my youngish-looking doctor, whose name was John Clark, told me. "By rolling and putting the fire out so quickly, you were spared third-degree burns on most of your body."

"What about my face?" I asked him. My head was swathed in bandages, and my face hurt all over.

He hesitated. "There we were not so lucky," he said. I wondered who this *we* was. He continued: "The front of your face is mostly third-degree burns. I won't kid you: It's pretty serious. But with plastic surgery, we can reverse some of the damage. And we have some of the finest plastic surgeons at this hospital."

"How much of the damage can be reversed?" I asked him. "Can I have my old face back?"

He looked at me glumly. "No," he said.

Have you ever, despite your resolve not to do it, stared at a deformed, handicapped, or retarded child? I spent most of my childhood from sixth grade forward on the receiving end of those stares.

The plastic surgeons did their best, but for me, their best wasn't good enough. My reflection in the mirror was ugly and freakish, with deep vertical scars lining the reddish skin on my face. I looked, I thought, like Frankenstein.

I had no friends after my stepfather burned my face off. The ones I had came by the hospital at first, but my looks were too much to deal with. Kids both older and younger than me taunted me cruelly. I cried into my pillow more nights than I care to remember.

The years passed. I graduated high school with my class, and this caused a swelling of sympathy and kindness; my classmates must have thought I was brave to come to school at all.

College was better. My scars looked more weathered and less angry; I could almost delude myself that I looked craggy. I used my sad story to get a few girls into bed and felt no guilt. Everyone used what they had, and I was no different.

A few months after graduation, I was working as a programmer in the IT department of a manufacturing firm in the town where I grew up. My parents were dead by then, and I had inherited the house and almost a hundred grand from their life insurance.

One evening the phone rang. Dr. Clark was on the other end of the line. "I took a chance that I could reach your parents at this number and track you down," he said.

"They're dead," I said.

"I'm sorry."

"Thanks," I replied. "What's up?"

"This is great news," he said.

Dr. Clark explained that, since my disfigurement, a new procedure, a face transplant, had been developed and performed on a couple dozen patients worldwide with favorable results. One famous case was the woman whose face was ripped off by a chimpanzee, which had also bitten off her hands and eyelids, rendering her blind.

One of the plastic surgeons at the hospital had performed this procedure recently with an excellent outcome.

"We want you to come in for an examination," explained Dr. Clark. "If everything checks out, we want to consider you as a candidate for a full face transplant."

"What is the cost?" I asked. "Will insurance cover it?"

"Uh, no, because it's still an experimental procedure. But since it will bring prestige and notoriety to the hospital, we will."

At the hospital, employees and, to a lesser degree patients, tried not to stare at me. After the examinations, Dr. Clark said I would be a good candidate for a full face transplant.

"How much better off will I be?" I asked. "Will I look like a patchwork Frankenstein?"

"You'll have a relatively normal-looking face, which will be the face of the donor, which is who we are waiting for now," he said.

"Someone has to die for me to have a new face."

"Yes."

The call came a month later. "You need to come in right now," said Dr. Clark. "We want to get you prepped and ready."

I looked at the packed overnight bag I had in the corner of my bedroom. "I'm ready."

"There's one thing you need to know," the doctor said. "The donor is a fifty-five-year-old man—thirty-four years older than you."

"Why would that bother me?" I asked.

For some reason, I had convinced myself that the surgery would be painless. But when I woke up, my face hurt, especially around the edges, where the transplanted face had been attached to the skin of my head.

I worried about the face being rejected, which was a very real possibility. In my nightmares, I sneezed and my face fell off. Don't laugh; it's not as funny as it sounds.

The biggest shock came when I first looked into a mirror. The donor's face was average looking, which was an order of magnitude improvement over the scarred and burnt visage I had worn for so many years. But what I saw in the mirror was a fifty-five-year old man. He didn't look old for his age. But he had been fifty-five, and I was twenty-one.

Over a period of weeks my surgical scars healed and I grew accustomed to my face. I had always kept myself fit with weights and running, so I looked like a fifty-five-year-old man with a much younger man's body. Nobody outside of the hospital staff who saw me realized I was in fact a twenty-one-year-old with a fifty-five-year-old man's face.

I feared the new face would cause just another type of humiliation based on my looks. When I looked in the mirror, I saw an old man, not a teenager.

When I quit my job and returned to college to work on a masters degree, nobody recognized me, though the novelty of a fifty-five-year-old freshman gained notice. I explained that I had been a successful entrepreneur, and now I wanted to get a graduate education. Other students accepted this story; people began to like "the old guy," and I became a recognized and semi-popular figure on campus. It was a pleasant change from my life as a burn victim.

Outside of the campus, the people I came into contact with assumed I was a middle-aged man. The plastic surgeons had done a good job. No one suspected that I was other than fifty-five. And I liked how I was treated with more respect. People were more polite and took me more seriously.

My college advisor, a professor in the computer engineering department where I was majoring, was concerned about what would happen to me when I graduated.

"I'll get a job?" I suggested to him, pointing out that my notoriety at that point would have long faded.

"I hate to bring this up, but remember, you look like a much older man," said my advisor, who knew the whole story. "The corporate world today worships youth and tosses its elders aside. It's very difficult to get hired when you're over fifty."

"I'll show them my birth certificate," I said.

"Who would believe it?" he said.

Sometime later, I was having a dream that my father had come into my apartment and was threatening to burn me with a blow torch. It had become a recurring nightmare.

I woke up sweating, not screaming, but then I touched my face. It felt hot and slightly swollen. When I took my hand away, it was red with blood. Frightened, I ran into the bathroom, turned on the lights, and looked in the mirror. There was a thin line of red at the edge where my face had been surgically attached to my head.

I called 911 and went to the hospital. The doctors examined me thoroughly and put me through a battery of tests. Injections brought my fever down and stopped the bleeding.

"I have something bad to tell you," Dr. Clark said. "It seems your body is rejecting the transplant."

"After all these months?" I said in a shaky voice.

"Unusual, I admit, but it can happen."

"What's going to happen to me?" I asked.

"We are going to try to halt the rejection with drug therapy, but the chances of that working are slim," the doctor said. "If rejection continues, the edges of the face will start to turn black with gangrene. We would have to surgically remove the face before then so as not to risk your life."

I could not believe what I was hearing. I felt surrealistic, as if I were in a living nightmare.

"But there's some good news," said Dr. Clark. "We have the team here ready to perform another transplant. All we need is another donor."

"What are the chances of *that* happening in time to save me?" I asked.

"Actually pretty good," he said. "We're now part of a network of hospitals, which exponentially increases our chance of finding a donor. And," he paused, "remember that it's a holiday weekend. Unfortunately for the populace, but fortunately for you, there are an increased number of fatalities on the road. As long as someone's face is intact, and we get it quickly enough, and assuming compatibility, you'll be good to go. In the meantime, daily injections will help us slow the rejection to give us more time."

If I'd been prone to fainting I would have fainted. I just could not believe what was happening to me. In my mind, I cursed and begged God at the same time. It had been many years since I prayed out loud.

My silent prayers were answered in a gruesome way. Within forty-eight hours, a twenty-year-old man who was driving drunk and too fast wrapped his car around a tree. His legs were crushed and he was killed, but his face was untouched except for a few cuts from glass fragments. I know I should have felt saddened by the guy's death, but all I thought about was myself.

They performed the surgery. As with the first operation, it seemed a success, but we would not know for sure for several months. I had to hope; hope was all I had.

The pain subsided, the bandages were removed, and the stitches taken out. The edges of my face were a little inflamed, but nothing more.

Every night I had a recurring dream: I am eating dinner, bent over the table. I cough, and my face falls into my plate. Unperturbed, I push it aside and continue eating. I couldn't figure out how I am so calm in my dream, but so scared and worried all the time in real life.

Now, Dr. Clark has pronounced me fit to leave the hospital. Before leaving, I go into the bathroom to shave. The bandages have been removed. I look in the mirror.

I am shocked. The fifty-five-year-old me is gone, like an old friend who has passed away. I am young once again, both in age and appearance.

Dr. Clark walks into my hospital room. "Admiring our handiwork?" he asks genially. I tell him how pleased and grateful I am. Then I ask him what the chances are of a second rejection.

"Low," he says without elaborating. "But of course, it's not impossible. Since the original transplant was rejected, we'll keep a closer eye on you this time." He does not remind me that the risks of rejection include death by gangrene.

I don't know whose face I will wear tomorrow. I don't know whether I'll be *alive* tomorrow. But there are so few guarantees in this life. All I can do is settle my hospital bill and hope for the best. As for right now, all I can say is—it's good to be young.

Insomnia

How many days has it been since you last got a full night's sleep?" Dr. Sydney Gellman, a tanned, handsome neurologist who looked like he played a lot of tennis and ate a lot of sushi and salads, asked Jack Bridges.

Bridges moved the thumb and index finger of his right hand gently across his closed eyes. "It started in late January, about a week after the accident—as you well know." Bridges' skin was comfortingly warmed by the bright July sunlight streaming through Gellman's large office windows.

"But it's not true that I never sleep, exactly," Bridges continued. "It's that I never get anything like a normal night's sleep."

Dr. Gellman doodled unconsciously with a pharmaceutical company pen on a note pad imprinted with another pharmaceutical company's logo and the name of its flagship drug, stopped, and then made a notation on the page.

"You don't seem overly tired," he said. "Your reflexes are fine. You're in good health. Blood pressure is normal. You are alert and highly functional. No bags under your eyes."

"So?" asked Bridges.

"So is sleeping only a few hours a night really a problem for you?" asked Dr. Gellman. "Many people view sleep as a waste of time. Most of us spend a third of our lives asleep. If you live to be seventy-five years old, you'll have slept a quarter of a century during your life." Dr. Gellman made another note on the pad and asked Bridges. "What do you do when you're awake at night?"

"It's not just a few *hours* a night that I can sleep," Bridges corrected him. "It's maybe ninety *minutes*, max. And even then it's not a solid hour and a half. I lay there and doze, and then I'm awake for a few minutes but stay in bed, then fall asleep again. After about ninety minutes of this, I wake up again, and that's it—I'm up for the rest of the night—and for the rest of the day."

"Okay, let's say you're asleep at most ninety minutes a night instead of the average eight hours," said Gellman. "What do you do with the extra six and a half hours of time each evening?"

"Read," Bridges replied. "Though I'm tired of reading already. Surf the Internet. Watch TV. Usually watch a movie—a DVD or whatever's on cable. Check my stocks. Watch videos on YouTube. Listen to jazz on my iPod. Work." Bridges telecommuted to his job as senior website designer for Victoria's Secret, and it is safe to say that he greatly enjoyed his work. He was also good at it: His web pages routinely generated more orders than the pages on the site designed by the other web designers.

Senior management said that Jack had a great eye for the ladies; his fellow designers talked of his page layouts having a certain sensual quality. But the secret of Jack's success was the web analytics software Victoria's Secret used to measure visitor activity.

While some other web designers found the analytics reports boring and ignored them, Jack studied them religiously. If visitors were exiting a page too quickly, he added more skin to the photos to keep them looking longer. If the conversion rate—the percentage of visitors who ordered the product from a sales page—was low, Jack would, with the marketing director's okay, add a buying incentive such as a ten percent discount or free shipping and handling, and sales of the item would lift considerably. Or he might Photoshop the picture to increase the bust a size or two. His highest-selling web pages had a secret that he revealed to no one and that no one could identify: He added a micro-bump at the center of each bra cup to give the subliminal impression of erect nipples.

Jack's results baffled his fellow web designers, though Jack openly told them his other secrets (for instance, that side views of a boob in a bra increased average time on the page by nine seconds versus a frontal view) and encouraged them to spend more time reviewing web metrics (which they never did). Jack had frequent pay raises and promotions, and he was held in high esteem by senior management. The underwear models featured in Jack's pages were eager to work with him, since higher sales from their photos meant more shoots, modeling fees, and royalties.

"Dating any bra models these days, Jack?" asked Dr. Gellman.

Bridges admitted that he was seeing a tall, leggy model named Julie but said they slept together infrequently. "The no-sleep thing has kind of killed my sex drive," he told Gellman. "When Big Jack sleeps too little, Little Jackie sleeps too much."

"Erectile dysfunction?"

"No," replied Bridges. "I guess I simply don't *want* to sleep with anybody, is all. I just want to *sleep*—period."

Dr. Gellman nodded. "I know that's what you want, Jack," he said. "But I'm not sure how much more I can do for you. As we've gone over numerous times . . ."

"Please do so again, Dr. Gellman," Jack said. "I just need to understand it better."

But he already knew what had happened. He had been there, and Dr. Gellman had not.

The accident had been such a freak occurrence—plastered all over the net and covered on everything from the Microsoft network to CNN.com. The video of Jack, while it came nowhere close to Susan Boyle's ten-million-plus views, had gotten over a million plays on YouTube, even though it only showed him in the emergency room after the accident and had no footage of the actual accident taking place. Why anybody would want to look at the video was beyond Jack; the accident had been horrible and disgusting. But he guessed that if it had been someone else, he would have looked, too.

He had been out on a drive with Julie Miller. Many of the photographers and designers were sleaze bags, but Jack was polite and professional, which brought him favorable attention from several of the models, Julie included. They liked each other's company, had slept together a few times, but then decided they liked being friends even more, especially when Julie sensed he was deliberately avoiding situations, like coming up for a nightcap or snuggling on the couch to watch a DVD, in which sexual intercourse was more likely to occur.

Both dated other people but often found themselves doing things together on the weekend, like going to the country to pick apples in the fall or taking a day trip to the shore in the summer, where Julie turned heads with her sculpted, bikini-clad body. Yet Jack always altered her face ever so slightly on the website and in the print catalog, making her chin a little less pointed and her cheek bones a little more prominent. Their boss couldn't tell the difference, but as a consequence she was, unlike the other models, rarely recognized in public or bothered outside of work.

Julie had been driving Jack's car, with Jack seated in the passenger seat. High winds had snapped a big branch off a pine tree, which had flown straight like an arrow through the windshield and directly into Jack. With his head turned toward Julie as he listened to her talk, he had not seen the branch coming.

She'd been cut by some pieces of shattered windshield, but there were no permanent scars—and had there been, Photoshop could easily remove them from her photos. The pine branch, however, had impaled Jack through the soft flesh under his right ear. In doing so, it had severed a bundle of nerves leading to his pineal gland.

To her credit, Julie had remained calm and in control, swinging the car around and taking Jack straight to the hospital emergency room. Within an hour, he was in surgery; within three hours, the tree limb had been successfully removed. However, the damage to the nerves connected to the pineal gland had had an unexpected side effect: Jack now needed almost no sleep, and, in fact, he could not fall asleep even when he tried.

Dr. Gellman and his team could not fully explain it, though they knew there would be a really good paper in it when they figured out the whole puzzle. Yes, the pineal gland secretes the melatonin that helps us sleep, but Jack's pineal gland had actually been untouched and was still secreting melatonin. The method by which the pineal gland communicates with the rest of the brain and body were still, on the other hand, largely a mystery. It is not connected to the optic nerve, yet it is still able to detect ambient light. In blind Mexican cave fish, an over-developed pineal gland enables the fish to sense and move toward light, despite the complete absence of eyes.

After the accident, Jack took six weeks off from work to recuperate. But by the third week, out of sheer boredom, he began using his Mac at home to design a stack of new web pages, for which requests had piled up in his inbox. Although he had always liked being around creative people who loved what they were doing, he was surprised how much he enjoyed tele-commuting. He put in a request to telecommute full time, which, because his work was so valuable to the company, was granted without objection. His boss only asked that Jack keep his office at the company should he decide to come in and work there from time to time.

He tried it a few times. His coworkers complimented him on how good he looked. He smiled and shook hands and accepted their good wishes. The scar under his right ear was raw and ugly, and they tried hard not to stare at it. Two coworkers suggested he grow his hair long and let it cover the scar, but Jack preferred short hair, which was easier to manage and faster to dry after a shower.

But when he looked into other people's faces, he imagined every one of them going home, climbing into a comfy bed with a soft pillow and snug blankets and enjoying their eight hours of peaceful sleep before the next day, while he tossed and turned and paced and worked and read and watched TV, and he hated them for it and envied their sleep.

Gradually, matters reached the point where he couldn't stand to be around people who could sleep, which of course meant anyone and everyone. He stopped going into the office, but his productivity continued to soar. He spent more and more of his time reading and analyzing the metrics reports produced by his company's web analytics software. This made the web pages he designed even more productive and successful. While overall sales finished flat for the year, the revenues from Jack's web pages increased on average thirty-seven point eight percent.

Again, he made no secret of his methods, except for the subliminal nipples. While his fellow web designers were rushed to get pages up and posted on the site during their eight-hour workday, Jack had all night to study the analytics reports and redesign his web pages to correct any deficits in the key performance indicators the analytics software measured. His pages now produced even higher conversion rates, more page views, greater stickiness, and more sales than before the accident.

A full year after Jack's accident, his boss, Ron Damico, Victoria's Secret's marketing director, took a position with a high-tech start-up in Silicon Valley, and Jack was not surprised when upper management offered the Victoria's Secret marketing director spot to him. He took it, of course. It meant a bigger office, a company car (a BMW), a parking space closer to the entrance, a lot more money, and greater control over the website.

Winter and spring passed. That summer, he got a call from Ron: The start-up had gone belly-up, and would Jack have room for him in his department? Jack told him they were full now but that he would call the instant a position opened up. But he was lying. He had been to Ron's apartment for several New Year's Eve parties. With its small closets, guests left coats on the bed in the master bedroom. Jack recalled it was a beautiful antique four-poster bed; the man clearly enjoyed his sleep, and Jack had no room for slugabeds in his organization.

He and Julie continued to see each other socially on and off. She seemed to want to get closer to him, and he allowed their socializing—and the gradual evolution from friendship to slightly more—to continue, though he performed in the bedroom mostly for her sake: He hated being in a bed with anyone capable of falling asleep in it. But Jack felt he owed Julie for her cool head and quick reaction the night of his accident.

Every weekend she wanted to do something, and he suspected she was falling in love with him. Jack often declined Julie's invitations, citing the increasing responsibilities he faced as marketing director. But fall was her favorite season, and October her favorite month, and when it came again, she suggested an outing for apple picking, which he grudgingly agreed to, though he enjoyed apple season, the crisp fall weather, and being in an orchard full of apple scent. He also loved eating a fresh-picked apple or two.

When they got to the orchard, they parked, picked up wicker baskets, and tramped off into the trees to collect apples with the dozens of other visitors. To their surprise, the trees seemed surprisingly barren.

"I can't believe they've been picked this bare so early in the season," said Julie. She picked up an apple on the ground, inspected it, and threw it away.

"The only ones that are any good are still on the trees," Jack said.

"I can't reach the big ones!" Julie said, stretching as far as she was able.

"Lemme help," said Jack. She was relatively light—all the models were— so he grabbed her around the hips and lifted her up straight so she could reach the higher branches.

"Just throw them down," he said when her hands were full. Without thinking, she tossed the apple she was holding over her shoulder and reached up for another. It promptly bonked him on the head.

He flinched and stepped back. His heel caught on a tree root, and he began to topple, taking her along with him. She grabbed onto the branch she had been reaching for. They collapsed like a house of cards. The branch broke off in her hand. She fell on top of him, and her arms went perpendicular to her side, like Jesus Christ on the cross. The branch in her hand plunged into the soft soil, impaling the ground like Dracula, just a couple of feet from the spot under Jack's right ear where he still bore a scar from the car accident. It made his heart skip a beat to see the jagged wood penetrate the earth so close to his head.

A worker ran over to help them up. "You all right, folks?" he asked. They were otherwise alone in their row and no one else had seen them tumble or come to their aid.

Julie was breathing hard. "You all right, Julie?" Jack asked. She nodded. Relieved, the orchard hand helped her off him, and then gave Jack a hand getting up.

"Let's forget about the apple picking," said Julie. They made their way to the farm stand and bought a bag of Macintoshes, a half-gallon of fresh cider, and a dozen home-made donuts. At the gourmet store inside, they bought sweet corn and a cured country ham.

When they got home, Julie prepared dinner. Jack watched her from the living room. Normally they shared kitchen duty equally, but since the accident, it seemed to Jack she had unconsciously treated him like a semi-invalid. He watched her in a detached sort of way, as if their life was a not-very-interesting movie showing in a theater from which he could not get up and leave.

After dinner, they relaxed on the couch, watching an old movie on cable. During a love scene, Julie became aroused and began kissing Jack. She led him by the hand to the bedroom, where they made love. She was passionate; he feigned interest but was indifferent, though she seemed satisfied by his performance. As she often did after sex, Julie snuggled in close with Jack, and she soon fell asleep.

He, of course, did not. Jack closed his eyes, wishing he could sleep beside Julie, sleep real sleep, just one more time in his life.

But as usual, sleep did not come. He looked at her and as always was struck by her physical perfection. Not only was her body flawless, but it functioned optimally: She was great at sports. She swam like a dolphin. She was terrific in bed. Her skin was soft and supple, her hair soft and lustrous.

And boy, thought Jack, she sure can sleep. He would try to wake her inconspicuously—coughing too loudly, pretending to sneeze, knocking over an Evian bottle on the nightstand, bumping into the dresser. She slept through it all like a hibernating bear with a great ass.

He got up, lumbered into his office, turned on the Mac, and, without much thought, began to play around with one of Julie's photos. He lifted her head and shoulders off one of her bikini poses from last year's summer catalog, and placed it on the driver's seat of a car similar to his, which he took off the automaker's site.

Then he went to the website of a national park, found an image of trees in the forest, zoomed in on the tallest one, and lifted a branch. He digitally sharpened one end of it into a pointed stake and dragged it into the photo of Julie driving. He used Flash to animate the branch so it slammed into her head, pulled back, and plunged into her brain again, and again . . .

She came awake in an instant, eyes wide open like a deer caught in headlights, and screamed. She tried to say something, but her voice came out oddly, making a garbled, wet sound. Jack looked at his hand, which was wrapped around a letter opener, embedded in her throat. How had he gotten from his desk to the bed? And when had he picked up the letter opener? He couldn't even recall *owning* a letter opener. He yanked it out and after a second's hesitation, plunged it back in, pulled it back out, plunged it back in, again and again and again . . .

I'm getting too old for this, thought Dr. Sydney Gellman, who had come to the hospital in 2002 as a young neurologist and now, 33 years later, was chief of neurology. He leaned over the hospital bed, finishing his exam of Jack Bridges, a patient who had been comatose for nearly as long as Gellman had been with the hospital. Bridges had been brought there in an ambulance almost three decades ago, when a tree limb penetrated his skull and damaged his brain in a freak auto accident on Highway 95 at around midnight, Gellman recalled. Bridges had been driving alone.

"His muscle tone is as good as can be for a patient who hasn't moved under his own power in thirty years," said Gellman. "Has there been any change? Grunting? Groaning? Speech? Hand or toe movement?"

"No, doctor," said Julie Miller, a plump blond who had been a nurse on the ward for fifteen years. She looked down at Bridges' wasted, pale form. "He's so still. There's no response when I touch him to give him a sponge bath or change the sheets." She sighed. "It's hard to believe he's dreaming."

"Mr. Bridges is unique," the doctor said. "For reasons we can't figure out, he experiences REM—rapid eye movement—almost around the clock. So he's having vivid dreams virtually all the time, though what those dreams are we have no idea." He sighed. "Whatever he's dreaming, I hope it's more pleasant than his reality." Dr. Gellman took one last look at the chart before putting it back. "I don't think he'll ever wake or walk again."

"Whatever he's dreaming about," said Nurse Miller gently, "I hope it's restful." She plumped the pillow gently under Bridges' head. "Pleasant dreams, Jack," she said.

Early Retirement

"Sit down, Mr. Peterson," said the counselor at the Senior Citizen Administration office to the gray-haired man standing before him.

The counselor, whose name was Kyle Jordan—it said so right on his personalized desk nameplate—thought immediately that there was something not quite right with Mr. Peterson.

Like many of Kyle's clients—the SCA employee's manual required clerical staff to refer to the old men and women who came to the SCA begging for their benefits as "clients" in an effort to create the illusion of dignity—Mr. Peterson, whose first name was Barry, was shabbily dressed and looked downtrodden. And no wonder: SCA benefits were for those used-up citizens who were past the age where they could work to earn a living and could not support themselves on their savings, which ranged from meager to nonexistent.

The federal government, through the SCA, came to the rescue, doling out small monthly stipends that could maybe pay the rent and utility bill, and keep the gas burner and water running, so these destitute moochers could make their tea and "tomato soup"—boiling water with ketchup, salt, and crackers crumbled in—with maybe a few dollars left over for booze or betting or cigarettes or whatever helped them pass the time until their final ride to pauper's field, where impoverished medical students would dig them up and dissect them.

Working at the SCA as a Level 5 counselor was, as far as Kyle Jordan was concerned, merely a rest stop in his journey on the fast track to success in the federal bureaucracy and a Level 1 rating. But it had its value, having taught him to strive toward a singular goal: namely, not ending up in his sixties having to come to the SCA to beg for benefits. Those who did had clearly not succeeded in the games of business or life. Kyle found the old farts he dealt with at his job pathetic—he loathed them in fact—and his greatest fear for the future was turning into one of them himself.

However, Barry Peterson seemed somehow different from the endless parade of tired old men and women who shuffled through the SCA offices each day.

Most of the men who came to SCA asking to be put on the government dole looked defeated and worn out. Barry Peterson did look rather defeated. Most of Kyle's clients were unkempt and dressed in old clothes that had seen better days. Barry Peterson was, like most, shabby in appearance. His jacket was so threadbare as to almost be transparent at the elbows, and his face had not seen a razor in days.

Most of Kyle's clients at the SCA seemed tired, frail, and worn out, as if life had drained them of all hope and vitality, and there was nothing left but an old shell. And in this regard, Barry Peterson did not fit the mold.

Oh, he looked tired—and sad. But where most of Kyle's clients had poor posture and were stooped over, many from scoliosis, osteoporosis, or arthritis, Barry Peterson stood straight as a ramrod, with the posture of a general, chief executive, or senator. Was he ex-military, perhaps? Not according to the file Kyle rifled through as Peterson stood patiently before him, having ignored Kyle's instruction to sit. "Oh please, have a seat, Mr. Peterson," Kyle said quickly, not wanting his supervisor, Megan, to think he had mistreated a client in any way. Megan was a by-the-book SCA supervisor Grade 2, and, in addition, she had a superb chest and toned body that infatuated Kyle, though he had done nothing about it and she never seemed to notice him other than to occasionally berate him for an insignificant clerical error or imagined breach in counselor/client protocol.

Frail? No, Peterson had the build of a boxer or wrestler. He seemed to radiate physical strength, wellness, and energy. Kyle worked out at the gym every day after work, and could bench press almost two hundred pounds (well, at least for one rep, on a good day), but he had a sneaking suspicion that, had he so desired to do so, Barry Peterson could snap him in half like a pretzel stick.

"Now," said Kyle as he glanced at Peterson's file. "It says here you are applying for SCA Benefits because you have no savings and you are unable to work anymore. Is that correct, Mr. Peterson?"

"Yes, sir," said Peterson, fidgeting uncomfortably in his seat, looking embarrassed and ashamed, which Kyle enjoyed observing. Kyle noticed that the folding chair seemed too small for Peterson, and as he shifted in his seat, its metal legs creaked under Peterson's weight. Incredible, thought Kyle, glancing down at the chair legs, which seemed bowed. *Is it my mind playing tricks? Or are the chair legs actually bending under this man's bulk?* Peterson was a big man, tall and solid, but his build was athletic, not stocky or fat; he looked to be at least six foot four, and maybe two hundred fifty pounds; porkers who easily weighed three hundred pounds or more—both men and women—had sat in the folding chair with no problem. Kyle scribbled a quick note on his desk blotter: Replace client chair.

Kyle cleared his throat, made a grim expression, and looked Peterson straight in the eye; even though the client chair had short legs so the client would always be sitting at a lower level than the counselor—it gave the SCA a psychological edge in dealing with the senior population, according to the employee manual—Kyle had to look up to see Peterson's eyes.

"Well, Mr. Peterson, unfortunately, I do see a problem with activating your Senior Benefits," Kyle said, not unkindly, but with a serious tone and expression.

"Oh? Why?" Peterson asked politely. His expression had also become serious.

"Well, Mr. Peterson, I don't see any work history in your file," Kyle continued. "As you know, the SCA treasury is largely funded by contributions taken from workers' paychecks, and, well, it looks like you haven't put anything into the pot." Actually, the SCA had run out of money seventeen years earlier, and was now financed, unbeknownst to Kyle, with funds secretly siphoned from various welfare, health, and environmental programs as well as black market sales of plutonium to the Middle East.

"I thought you could still get Senior Benefits even if you hadn't made contributions," Peterson said. There was no panic or whining in his voice, but he sounded as if the possibility of being denied his benefits worried him greatly. "I checked the SCA site, and that's what it says, right?"

"Yes, you can," Kyle explained, "when you either reach age sixty-five or become unable to work, provided you do not have adequate savings on which to live. But your file indicates you are only fifty-seven, and you seem to be in relatively good health to me, so I can't imagine you cannot work anymore, though perhaps, as your work history indicates, you prefer not to." Disdain had crept into Kyle's voice, and he noticed Megan at her desk glancing in his direction.

Peterson sighed, and when he expelled air through his mouth, a few of the papers on Kyle's desk gently began to take flight as if pushed by a breeze from a fan or open window. But it was October; the fans weren't on and the windows were closed. Kyle inhaled; instead of the usual foul breath of old men with gum disease and dentures, Peterson's breath smelled of a spring shower and mint. His teeth were bright white, and they absolutely sparkled.

Peterson leaned forward in his seat, and motioned to Kyle to do the same. When they were both leaning in to shorten the distance between them, Peterson said: "Mr. Jordan, can I confide in you?"

"Of course, Mr. Peterson," Kyle said in a voice loud enough for Megan to hear, "everything you tell me as your counselor is held in strictest confidence and never leaves this office." Of course, that was a total lie: Every bit of information clients shared with SCA counselors was entered into the person's file and stored in a database, where it was readily available to just about every government employee who wanted to see it twenty-four hours a day, seven days a week—as well as to unauthorized users who possessed even a modicum of hacking skills.

Mr. Peterson winced and pulled back his head, as if Kyle's slightly elevated vocal volume had offended his ears.

"I did work—almost every day of my life, in fact—for over thirty-seven years," said Peterson. "But it wasn't the kind of work where records were kept or salaries paid."

"Are you saying you did piecemeal work?" asked Kyle. "Were you a free-lancer or independent contractor? Did you keep a record of your 1099s? If so, you may be eligible for benefits based on the SCA contributions made by the firms who employed your services."

"My clients were individuals, not corporations," replied Peterson. "And there were no contributions, because I was never paid for my services."

"You mean you worked as a volunteer?"

"In a manner of speaking."

"What did you do in this 'job' then?"

Peterson again leaned in toward the desk and lowered his voice so only Kyle would hear him. "I was a professional superhero," he said softly. "I was Mega-Man."

"You're crapping me, old man," Kyle said, sneering. Mega-Man, indeed!

Peterson sat up even straighter in his chair, and appeared to gain additional inches in height. "I'm not 'crapping' you, Mr. Jordan," he said to Kyle. "I am Mega-Man. And Mega-Man never lies."

"Can you prove any of this?" Kyle asked Mr. Peterson. He was skeptical not because Peterson was claiming to be a superhero—there were any number of retired superheroes spending their declining years in boarding houses, dingy hotels, and cheap apartments, dependent on their monthly SCA check for rent and food money: Queen Bee, Robo-Boy, and Whirling Dervish were three that came immediately to mind. But Mega-Man was one of the greatest heroes of them all, and—well, damn it—Kyle just couldn't take Peterson's word for it.

"Of course, Mr. Jordan," said Peterson. Peterson looked around to make sure no one was watching, then turned his head, looked down at the folder on Kyle's desk, and frowned in concentration. For a second, nothing happened, though Kyle noticed the air had suddenly warmed. Then, a tiny circle of brown formed on the file folder, and as it spread, he could smell and see a thin wisp of smoke rising from the paper.

"That's it?" asked Kyle. "Mega-Man's Mega-Vision can burn through steel; you can burn through a manila file folder. So what? Lots of low-grade meta-humans can. But that doesn't make them Mega-Man, sir. What about flying? Super strength? Super speed?"

Mr. Peterson shook his head. "That's why I'm here, Mr. Jordan. I've got a little of just about everything—the Mega-Vision, Mega-Hearing, Mega-Strength, and Mega-Speed—but not nearly enough to do any serious damage to an alien invader or super villain," he said forlornly. "You said a man can qualify for Senior Benefit checks if he can't work. Well, I'm a superhero who has lost most of his powers, so I can't work and, therefore, I qualify for benefits, right?"

"I'm afraid it's not that simple," Kyle said. "If you are indeed the super-hero known as Mega-Man and you have lost most of your powers, then you have no way of proving to me that you are in fact who you say you are, and therefore we have no way of validating your claim for retirement benefits based on inability to continue working in your job. It's a real catch-22, I'm afraid."

Kyle looked at Peterson, who returned his stare. Without taking his eyes off Kyle's, Peterson—moving with a speed Kyle could barely follow—snatched the letter opener from the metal pen holder with his right hand, brought it up above his head, and then, with even greater speed and force, brought it down on the back of his left hand, which was resting palm down on the desk. Startled, Kyle pushed back from the desk in his seat with both feet, and gasped. He saw that the thick metal blade had folded like an accordion—and that it had not penetrated Peterson's skin. All of this took place in the blink of an eye.

"Of the Mega powers, invulnerability has remained the least affected by age," said Peterson. "Does that satisfy you as to proof of my identity?"

Kyle, still stunned by the swift act of violence, looked down at Peterson's left hand as the old man removed the twisted blade. The letter opener had apparently penetrated the skin after all, at least a little bit; there was a dot of blood on the back of Peterson's hand. Peterson wiped it away with the index finger of his right hand, and Kyle noticed a tiny tear in the surface of the skin, which, before his eyes, closed up and seemed to heal completely within a second or two. "Even the Mega-Invulnerability isn't what it once was," Peterson said almost apologetically. "Thank God for Mega-Healing."

That clinched it. If Peterson had been any normal human, or even a low-level meta-human, a metal blade aimed at his hand with that kind of force would have been driven straight through the back of the hand and come out the other side through the palm, and he'd be spurting blood like water from a whale's blow hole.

Kyle's heart was beating like a trip hammer in his chest, and he knew he was sweating. But he tried to display a calm demeanor as he clicked his keyboard and made more notations in Peterson's file.

"Pending routine verification, I'm going to note in your file that Barry Peterson is the superhero known as Mega-Man," said Kyle. "But that creates another roadblock to processing your benefits claim, I'm afraid."

"How so?" asked Peterson, who was becoming frustrated with the whole procedure, and for a second Kyle imagined himself being punched through a wall by one of the Earth's greatest superheroes. *Don't show fear; don't show fear; don't show fear*, he told himself, which helped to restore his nerve and bureaucratic demeanor.

"There are a couple of problems," said Kyle. He tapped a few keys on his desktop and brought up a fresh screen on his computer. "First, the federal website on known superheroes indicates that the only hero of recent vintage with a superpower profile similar to yours was Power Man, listed in our database as retired for many decades, and currently living under his secret identity somewhere on a farm in Nebraska."

"So?" Mega-Man asked.

Kyle tapped more keys, and his monitor displayed a fresh screen.

"It says here that Power Man never filed for, nor does he collect, SCA benefits," said Kyle. "Apparently, he self-funded his retirement account with the profits made from squeezing a few lumps of ordinary coal into diamonds. If you can do the same—and our records indicate you should be able to, since both Power Man and Mega-Man are listed in the database as solar-powered superheroes with a similar power set—super strength, speed, invincibility, heat vision—then SCA reserves shouldn't be tapped to pay for your retirement."

"But I *can't* do it now," replied Mega-Man. "And I couldn't do it then. Power Man was easily twice as strong as me—which incidentally, he loved bringing up at superhero meetings, always challenging me to arm wrestle, the bastard—and even on his best day, he could *barely* generate enough pressure to convert the carbon in coal to diamonds. But when I tried squeezing coal, all I got was carbon powder all over my Mega-Suit."

"Well, Mr. Peterson, that brings us to our second problem with your Senior Benefits claim," said Kyle.

"That being?" replied Peterson.

"That being the fact, Mr. Peterson, that although your Mega-Vision and other powers may have faded, you retain an impressive degree of imperviousness to harm, as you have just amply demonstrated," said Kyle. "Therefore, the SCA wonders why you claim, given that speeding bullets most likely still bounce off you, that you cannot function in your superhero capacity any longer—in short, why you want to go on the federal dole while you are still able to work."

Peterson waved his hand dismissively. "Oh, I can still stop bullets, though I can't outrun them anymore," he said, "and that's okay for tackling a bank robber or a mugger. But the federal government, of which you are an employee, has extensive files on Mega-Man, and when you examine them, you can plainly see that my work specialty was stopping Mega-Disasters. Not ordinary criminals, but the big stuff. You know—preventing asteroids from striking the earth, fighting off alien invaders, defeating inter-dimensional beings. And at this stage in my decline, an asteroid would squash me like a bug, and an inter-dimensional being would eat me for breakfast."

"I see your point," said Kyle. He wrote notes on the form for a minute while Peterson sat patiently with his hands folded, and then handed the document over to him.

"I think we can begin processing your SCA claim for benefits today," said Kyle amiably, which caused Peterson to visibly relax. Kyle handed him a pen and pointed out the parts of the form requiring Peterson's signature or initials.

"That's right," he said, guiding Peterson in his completion of the paperwork. "Sign here . . . that means you state your age as fifty-seven years old . . . and initial here by birthplace—you were born on Earth, right? Good; our computer system doesn't have address codes for other planets . . . and then initial here, here, and here."

Peterson was about to scribble the final initialing, when he paused, his pen frozen over the form.

"What's this part mean?" he asked, pointing to a long paragraph of three-point type that, with his Mega-Vision as weakened as it had become, he, along with every other living being on the planet, could not read.

"It's nothing," said Kyle, a bit impatiently. The clock on the wall indicated that the lunch hour had started, and he was hoping to follow Megan and sit next to her in the cafeteria, where he might engage her in conversation and, as she bent to her plate, catch a glance down the front of her starched white blouse, the top two buttons of which she provocatively left undone, he was convinced, just to torture him. "It just means you swear that all your Mega powers are gone or depleted to standard meta-human levels, and you can no longer stop any mega-threats, and therefore, cannot continue to perform your job functions."

"Well . . ." Peterson said, slowly putting the pen and the form down.

"What's the problem?"

"I still have *one* Mega-Power that I could theoretically use to defeat a Mega-Villain or Mega-Threat, if I absolutely *had* to," said Mega-Man. "So I can't in good conscience initial this part of the form. Can't we just skip over that section? It's only a teeny clause in fine print which no one can read anyway."

"Absolutely not," said Kyle stiffly. "The form must be completed *in its entirety*, with every section filled out, before you can qualify for monthly SCA benefit payments—which, given your lack of an earnings history, will be, I am afraid, extremely modest."

Peterson shook his head. "Believe me, I'd like nothing better than to fill out the form and qualify," he said. "Lord knows, ever since the economy entered the Great Recession, lots of fellows my age have fallen on hard times and need the money. But, as I've told everyone since I donned the red suit and blue cape as a twenty-year-old youth, *Mega-Man never lies*. And saying I have no remaining Mega-Power capable of defeating a catastrophic threat, in case of dire need, would be a lie . . . though Lord knows, it's a power I'd never want to use."

"What's the power?" Kyle asked him, reaching into his desk drawer for the proper form to append to Peterson's SCA benefits application.

"Oh, never mind," he said. "It's real technical and complicated. In fact, I've never used it, and even I'm not sure exactly how it works . . ."

"Then listen," said Kyle, not unkindly. "You're fifty-seven now, and you are still capable of doing your job. Just bite the bullet, work for eight more years, and then come back and you can hang up the cape for good."

"I don't know," said Mega-Man. "Professor Cornrich"—who was, most likely, Kyle guessed, the scientist who acted as Mega-Man's mentor and confidante; most of the top-level superheroes had one, and Cornrich's name appeared in the Peterson file under *known associates*—"Professor Cornrich warned me never to use it under any circumstances. And he knows a lot more about how my powers work than I do." Peterson sounded almost apologetic. "I was never a big brain like Stark or Richards or Kord; I got a C in high school chemistry."

Kyle glanced up at the clock again. Lunch was nearly over; he had missed his chance to sit with Megan and admire her lithe form. He gathered the papers and files on his desk and straightened them fussily.

"SCA guidelines are quite clear on this point," said Kyle. "If you have not reached your sixty-fifth birthday and you can still work, you must make a serious effort to find suitable employment for a sixteen-week period before your application for benefits can even be submitted." Peterson started to protest but Kyle cut him off. "If you have an ability you can use in your current employment, then you have to use it. My best advice to you, Mr. Peterson, is to go out and do your job to the best of your current abilities, and come back and see us when you reach your sixty-fifth birthday. It really is that simple and there is nothing else I can do. I'd like to help you, but my hands are tied."

Peterson was silent, and for a second, Kyle was afraid: Sometimes clients became unruly when they were not happy, and he did not want Mr. Peterson to give him any trouble—especially the kind of trouble Mega-Man could make. *But I shouldn't worry,* Kyle thought. *Mega-Man is one of the good guys!*

Almost on cue, as if he had read Kyle's mind—though Mega-Man was not a known telepath—Mr. Peterson nodded, got up, shook Kyle's hand—firmly but not painfully—and turned to leave. Kyle saw that Megan had come back from lunch and had been watching—he had no idea for how long—and was smiling in approval. Kyle watched as Mega-Man gracefully navigated through the office space tightly packed with desks, people, equipment, and file cabinets; light on his feet, it was almost as if he were walking on air. *Things are looking up after all,* thought Kyle, with a song in his heart for the first time that day.

The next morning, when Kyle Jordan arrived at the office at 8 A.M. on the dot—at the SCA, punctuality was a major factor that had to be taken into a supervisor's decision to recommend a counselor for promotion—he knew instantly that something was wrong. Though he did not yet know what, one word popped instantly into his head: *Peterson*. His coworkers averted their eyes when he approached them, and Megan stood on the opposite side of the large open office area, near her supervisor's cubby. She looked at him for a second with a disapproving scowl, turned her shapely legs on her heels, walked into her small office, and closed the door forcefully.

Puzzled and worried, Kyle approached his small cubicle, and over the low partition, noticed that someone had placed the morning newspaper on his desk. The headline in seventy-two-point type jumped out at him; his stomach turned sour, and his heart sank as he read:

MEGA-MAN DEAD!
Superhero Gives Life Saving City from Alien Invasion

He started reading the article, and knew instantly that he would never rise above his current SCA Level 5 Counselor rating, achieve a position of any importance anywhere in the federal government, or ever get skin-to-skin with Megan under the sheets:

CENTER CITY—Mega-Man, one of the greatest superheroes in history, died last night while protecting Center City from a fleet of alien invaders.

The alien ships were completely destroyed when Mega-Man, standing on the roof of the City Center Building, exploded in a blinding flash that shook the city and caused millions of dollars in damage and at least a thousand deaths.

"Mega-Man's powers were produced by solar energy he absorbed through his skin for nearly six decades," said Alan Cornrich, a Physics Professor at Center City University who was Mega-Man's long-time scientific advisor and confidante.

"We had discovered years ago a way by which he could release his total store of solar energy at once with incredible force, but of course, the power output would be incalculable, and we agreed he could never, ever use this ability," said Cornrich. "I cannot for the life of me imagine anything that would cause him to change his mind. It is a tragic day for Center City, Earth, and all of mankind."

Kyle could not read further. He sat stunned in his chair, unable to move or speak. The busy routine of the office continued all around him, but he knew that would change: Martin Jameson, the Level 1 supervisor for the entire division and Megan's boss, would soon invite Kyle to pay him a visit, and after that Kyle would be lucky to still have a job.

Sure enough, when Kyle glanced toward Megan's office, he could see her inside with Jameson through the frosted glass, no doubt discussing Kyle's future with the SCA or lack thereof. And then—although he couldn't be sure, because the glass was thick and not terribly translucent—he saw Jameson move toward her until their torsos seemed to melt together. Were they embracing? Then their heads merged into a single shadowy image. Were they kissing? *That bastard has my girl!* Kyle thought helplessly.

He sensed a presence in front of him. Turning, he saw his first client of the morning, a man wearing a bespoke suit that once must have cost several thousand dollars but was unraveling at the seams with age and wear. His white dress shirt was also custom-tailored, but the cuffs were frayed and the collar looked slightly yellowed and dirty. The man's most striking features were his steely blue eyes, square jaw, and full head of silver hair.

Kyle swallowed, and said, in a quiet, defeated voice, "Can I help you, Mr. . . . ?"

The man glared down at Kyle. His eyes narrowed, and in a gravelly, hoarse voice he said: *"I'm Batman."*

Kyle Jordan put his head in his hands and moaned softly as his world collapsed about him.

Tax Time

Y ou must be mistaken," Professor Adam Wells told Stan Nicholson, the
IRS agent in charge of his audit.

Yet despite his overall superior intellect, Adam did not have his usual
confidence as he sat in Agent Nicholson's office.

Agent Nicholson obviously possessed a sharp mind, and his knowledge of the tax code seemed to equal Adam's knowledge of physics—and
was certainly much superior to Adam's tax knowledge. Still, Adam had
researched the preparation of his income tax returns carefully, and was
certain he had done nothing wrong. And so he pressed on with his explanation.

"As you can clearly see, all of these purchases are business expenses,
mainly for laboratory equipment and supplies, and I have provided an
itemized list of each item with description, purchase date, cost, and my
check number," said Dr. Wells, pointing to the Excel spreadsheet attached
to his returns. "Of course, I saved all the receipts." The printout listed
over two dozen items. There was a (used) "Null Space Containment Unit"
purchased for $18,477.56 on January 15. And there was a "Hand-Held
Portable Plasma Generator," also bought second-hand, for $5,736.44 last
March. The IRS Agent nodded, though he had only a vague notion of what
those things might be.

"Therefore," Adam finished with a flourish, "they are completely legitimate deductions, and I do not, as I would if they were *not* deductible, owe
the Internal Revenue Service an additional $17,459.56."

IRS Agent Stanley Nicholson sighed. He had often told his colleagues, "I
can take auditing the returns of a taxpayer who is ignorant about taxes, but
not arrogant. I can even take a taxpayer who is arrogant, if he knows what
he is talking about. But what I absolutely can't *stand* is auditing the return
of a taxpayer who is both ignorant *and* arrogant."

Whenever he said this, Nicholson's fellow IRS agents nodded their heads
in vigorous agreement. They knew exactly what he meant: Some poor
shmuck had gone to the bookstore, bought the latest "filing income taxes
for morons" paperback, and thought that made him an instant expert in the
tax code. In reality, no one—not the IRS staff, not professional accountants,

not high-powered tax attorneys, and especially not ignoramus taxpayers—had a comprehensive knowledge of the U.S. Tax Code, which currently ran to 14,398 pages. But the agents agreed that if anyone came even close, it was Stan Nicholson, who possessed a near photographic memory, among other mental attributes.

"Dr. Wells," Nicholson replied, not unpleasantly, "All of these items would be a legitimate deduction if you had a legitimate business. But unfortunately, the science experiments you conduct at home on your own time do not constitute a legitimate business, because in all the years you've had this home laboratory, you have apparently never created a single invention that you could sell at a profit. In fact, since 2019, your private scientific endeavors haven't generated one nickel in revenue. So your home laboratory is considered by the IRS as a hobby, and you cannot deduct it as a business expense."

Adam sputtered. "But I *am* a legitimate scientist. I have a Ph.D., for God's sake, and I am an associate professor at a respected university!"

"Yes, I see you are on the faculty of Center City University, where you have a full-time job as a salaried employee," said Nicholson. "But as a full-time employee, you also have full-time access to a laboratory. Equipment purchased for your laboratory at the university is a legitimate expense, but I assume the university buys the equipment, and therefore they, not you, can claim those purchases as deductions. But you can't deduct purchases for your home laboratory, unless . . ."

"Unless what, Agent Nicholson?" Adam asked.

"Is the research you are doing at home in any way related to your position at the university?"

Adam hesitated. He could say yes, but it would be a lie: His private research was in a completely different line of inquiry than his research for the university. Although he did not know the exact penalties, he was sure lying to the IRS was not a smart thing to do. Besides, all Agent Nicholson had to do was ask Professor Raimi, the physics department head. Raimi thought Adam's private project was laughably absurd, and he would surely delight in telling Nicholson that the university in no way approved of or funded it.

"Well, no," Adam replied. "My main work at the university has to do with generating energy through string theory."

"What does string theory have to do with producing power?" Nicholson asked. Adam was surprised: The IRS Agent seemed familiar with the term "string theory." That, or he was a good actor.

"Well, a consequence of string theory is that there are many more dimensions than the four we know—three-dimensional space plus time as the fourth—that may result in multiple universes vibrating at frequencies different than ours. Davidson at the University of Toronto has theorized that gravity may be leaking slowly out of our universe into one of these parallel universes, which occupies the same space as ours but at a different frequency. My theory has to do with the flow of force in the opposite direction, from the parallel universes to ours, but in this case, the force being electromagnetic energy, not gravity, which, of course, could be used to generate electrical power."

Nicholson appeared to have no trouble following the argument. "And what is the private research you conduct on your own time, at home?" Nicholson asked, putting emphasis on the phrases *on your own time* and *at home*.

"It's a project I've been working on since I was in high school," said Adam. "I built the first generation of the device in my laboratory in the basement of my parents' home. Naturally, it can't be moved or even shut off while the experiment is in progress, as it has been for almost ten years now." In a lower voice he said, almost apologetically, "That's why I still live with my mother," knowing that the IRS had that data on file, and feeling the need to explain to Nicholson why a twenty-eight-year-old university professor still slept in a bedroom with a single twin bed and a Miley Cyrus poster on the wall.

"The device?" asked Nicholson.

"Yes," said Adam with unmistakable pride. "My invention: the world's first working time machine."

"I see," said Agent Nicholson with no hint of disbelief or mockery in his voice. "And how exactly does this time machine work?"

Adam was oddly pleased to have the opportunity to explain his great invention to an interested, intelligent layman. He leaned over the desk, using a number-two pencil to sketch on the back of the manila file folder, which held his tax return.

As Adam explained to Nicholson, his first step had been to build a generator capable of opening a miniature wormhole contained within a magnetic field. After a year of trial and error, he had succeeded, creating a mini-wormhole about the size of a dime. He then fired electrons into the little wormhole, giving it an electric charge.

Next, Adam built a multi-tube particle accelerator of a revolutionary new design, the details of which were, unknown to Adam, of greatest interest to the Department of Defense. The DoD had recruited a local utility company meter reader as a spy; the job gave the DoD mole free access to Adam's basement lab once a month. Out of a sense of guilt, the meter reader, whose name was Paulie, always reported a low reading and reset the meter to the number he recorded in his log, so Adam's mother's electric bill was just a few dollars a month. Had Paulie reported the correct reading to the power company, the bill would have been close to a thousand dollars a month, because Adams' apparatus ran twenty-four hours a day.

About ten years ago, Adam had fed one mouth of the little wormhole into his homemade particle accelerator, where it whirled around at very near the speed of light. The other end of the wormhole was held still. The huge differential in speed between the two ends of the wormhole, Adam told Nicholson, produced a constantly increasing temporal discrepancy between each end. "I've been running the wormhole at nearly light speed in the particle accelerator for almost ten years," Adam said. "At this point, if you entered the end in our time frame and exited the other side, you'd reappear nearly ten years in the past."

"Have you ever tested the time machine on an object or lab animal to see if time travel is actually possible?" Nicholson asked.

"I can't actually attempt time travel until the moving end of the wormhole is brought to rest and allowed to approach the other wormhole mouth," said Adam. "When I do, of course, I will be able to send matter back in time about ten years—the exact amount of time the wormhole has been in the particle accelerator."

"How can you fit through it when it's only the size of a coin?" asked Nicholson. "Wouldn't the compression kill you?"

"Well, of course, I expanded the wormhole from its original microscopic diameter to a size large enough for an object or human being to traverse—about eight feet in diameter at its current measurement," Adam replied.

"Well, Dr. Wells," said Agent Nicholson in a tone teachers typically reserve for naughty school children about to be disciplined, "this is all quite interesting. But have you generated any revenue from the sale of time travel machines, time-travel services, or the associated technology you've developed?"

"Well, no, not yet," Adam admitted reluctantly. Again, he thought about lying, but again, it would be easy enough for Nicholson to check.

"In that case, I must disallow deductions for all equipment indicated here that was purchased for your home laboratory," said Agent Nicholson. "You will receive a notice in the mail from the IRS confirming the total amount due us, which will be $17,459.56, including interest and penalties."

Adam was stunned and shocked by the outcome of his appeal. Not because he had been certain he could convince the IRS of the legitimacy of his deductions, but because he didn't have anywhere near $17,459.56 in his bank account to pay the debt.

For an associate professor of physics at a state college, $17,459.56 was quite a considerable tax penalty to pay. True, Adam had no wife and kids to support. But he paid a generous rent to his mother, as well as taking care of many of her bills—his father, who had gambled and spent money rather freely, had left no cash and thousands in credit card debt and unpaid loans when he died—and the rest of Adam's modest salary went to paying for equipment and supplies for his own laboratory.

After leaving the local IRS offices, he had stopped by his office to grade some papers, and before heading home, had gone to the student center for a soda and a veggie-burger. There, he'd run into his graduate student Dave, to whom he found himself telling the whole sad IRS audit story.

"If I had deliberately cheated them by knowingly making false deductions on my income tax form, that would be one thing," complained Adam. "But it was an honest mistake! I considered my home laboratory to be a business—it's going to make money one of these days—and so naturally, I deducted all equipment purchases on my tax returns. I had no idea the IRS would treat it as a hobby instead of a business simply because it hasn't made any money *yet*."

"Yeah, but ignorance of the law is no excuse, Doc," said Dave, who was on his third Malibu bay breeze and already three sails to the wind. "Now, if someone had *told* you when you started your project that your home lab would have to turn a profit for you to deduct the expenses, you wouldn't have deducted them, right? You would have paid all your taxes, and you wouldn't have to come up with seventeen grand to pay the IRS now." He downed the rest of his watery sweet drink and gestured to the bartender for another. "Someone should have told you way back then. Someone . . ." Dave said, losing his train of thought as an attractive young coed in a tight sweater walked past the bar.

Someone should have told you way back then, recalled Adam half an hour later, sitting alone in his basement laboratory, listening to the hum of the accelerator. Then it hit him: Thanks to his invention, someone *could* tell him "way back then" about the mistake on his income tax form. And if someone told him, he wouldn't have made the error. And if he had never made the error, he wouldn't owe the IRS $17,459.56 in back taxes that he didn't have the money to pay.

Operating the machine for time travel was simple: The time traveler sat in a chair on a track. When a spring mechanism on the chair was released, it sent the chair and rider through the wormhole, and he would emerge on the other side. When ready to return, he'd sit in the chair again and operate the spring mechanism at the other end of the track. This would send the chair backward through the wormhole again, returning him to the point of origination in both time and space.

Or so Adam hoped. Faced with the immediate prospect of putting his mechanism to the test, he suddenly felt much less confident about the theories behind it.

He put on the sun goggles and safety helmet, set the spring mechanism timer, sat down into the chair, and strapped himself in.

The second Adam buckled the safety belt, he got cold feet. Was he insane? The theory was sound, but no one could say in reality whether it would work. What if the wormhole pulled his body apart, despite the ample diameter of the opening?

He frantically searched for the emergency stop button on the chair and then realized in an instant that he had never installed an emergency stop button.

He reached down and started to unbuckle the safety belt, but then the spring mechanism released and coiled steel struck the base of the seat with a thud. His head slammed against the back of the chair with such force that he saw stars and, for a second, blacked out.

When he came to a second later—or what he thought was a second later—he was still strapped into the chair. A glance showed him he was in his lab; only it wasn't his lab. The basement walls were a different color, and the time machine was different too. Most of the components were obsolete models, and their configuration reflected an earlier version of his design.

"Holy crap!" he said, seemingly in stereo. He turned his head and was awed but not shocked at the sight he beheld: himself, ten years younger, sitting at the lab bench making adjustments to a circuit board and measuring the output with an oscilloscope attached to a PC.

Old Adam was not shocked, but Young Adam was. "You mean it actually *works?*" he asked his elder doppelganger.

Old Adam finally unbuckled the safety belt, stepped out of the chair on wobbly legs, and walked over to the lab bench.

"Yes, but not this way," he said impatiently. He clicked the mouse, and the image on the PC screen went from the oscilloscope readout to the CAD layout for the time machine. "Let me save us some time and show you what you were going to figure out on your own in a couple of years anyway," he said.

Young Adam watched attentively and respectfully as Old Adam adroitly moved system components using the CAD software's click-and-drag feature. "Some of these components in the working unit"—he nodded at the chair—"haven't been invented yet, and so the model numbers aren't in your CAD software's product database," explained Old Adam. "I'll print the finished layout, and then write in the names and model numbers of the new components you should substitute, along with the approximate month and year they will go on the market, as best I can remember."

"Can we go over some of these new specs?" Young Adam asked excitedly. He looked at the diagram Old Adam had printed. There were so many improvements that should have been obvious but he had completely missed!

"We can," replied Old Adam. "But first, I left the future on this particular day because of something I have to tell you."

"You built a working inter-dimensional energy pump *too?*" young Adam asked in amazement.

"Uh, well, no, but that's not important now," said Old Adam, not wanting to discourage his younger self with the details of his ten years of experimental failure in energy transport via strings. "I came to warn you. You see all this expensive equipment you're always buying?"

"So?" said Young Adam.

"Listen to me: You *cannot*, under any circumstance *ever*, deduct *any* of the cost of our home lab or its equipment from your tax returns," said Old Adam.

Young Adam seemed annoyed. "Why are you telling me this? I don't even do my own taxes; mom and dad's accountant does it for me, along with their returns."

Old Adam did a quick calculation and realized with a start that his father was still alive and wouldn't die for another couple of years. Vaguely he became aware of noise upstairs in the kitchen, and was certain that both of his parents were home. *Dad's alive*, he thought. *I can see Dad again, and maybe . . .*

Then his father shouted down through the closed basement door in that familiar, always-pissed off voice: "Hey, Genius, are you talking to yourself?"

"No, Dad," Young Adam shouted back.

"Then who are you with?"

"No one, Dad."

Old Adam heard footsteps, and he realized his father could come downstairs at any minute. Young Adam's research was too important to be interrupted by their father, who had no idea of what they were building—but, if he saw the younger and older versions of his son together, he could conceivably figure it out.

"I've got to go back now, Adam," said Old Adam. "So listen carefully." He walked over to the front end of the rail, set the timer on the reverse spring mechanism, sat down into the chair, and pulled the safety belt around his waist.

"You're not allowed to deduct home laboratory expenses—ever—because the IRS treats our experiments as a hobby, not a business," he said, clicking the buckle into place.

"Why can't we treat it as a business?" demanded Young Adam in an exasperated tone. "Haven't we made any money with the time machine yet?"

God, was I so commercial when I was that young? thought Old Adam as he put on his helmet and goggles. "Not yet, b—"

The timer clicked. The spring hit the front of the chair, rocketing Old Adam backward on the rail toward the wormhole opening. The last thing he remembered seeing was his younger self looking at him with an angry expression, gesturing with his hands. The noise of the device drowned out most of what Young Adam said, though Old Adam thought he heard the words "money" and "rich" and "stupid."

Adam lost his orientation as he passed into and through the wormhole, and again, he blacked out for what seemed like only a second.

The room where he came to, however, was not his mother's basement. The laboratory was sparkling, and looked expensive. The time machine was gleaming, every metal surface highly polished. He glanced around, and saw equipment that even the university could not afford.

On the large lab table near the time machine, Adam saw a paper that was unmistakably from the IRS: perhaps a notice about a coming refund. But when he picked it up and read, a cold panic enveloped him:

Dear Mr. Wells:

This note is to inform you of an underpayment on your Tax Returns, for the tax period noted above, in the amount of $174,595 . . .

Adam was shaking. The amount he owed the IRS was now $174,595.60, ten times more than the $17,459.56 that he had owed before his time trip! What on Earth could have gone wrong? How stupid could he have been as a kid not to heed a warning from his time traveling future self? And why was the lab so different?

"I see you got the IRS bill," said Agent Nicholson as he walked into the lab, with—unbelievably—Susan Goldman, an associate professor in the English literature department, on his arm. Both were smiling and looked as happy as two cats in a bird's nest.

"Agent Nicholson, Susan," Adam said. "What are you doing here?"

Nicholson raised one eyebrow to give Adam a quizzical look. "I haven't been called 'Agent Nicholson' in ages," said Agent Nicholson.

"This tax bill," Adam said weakly, waiving the IRS letter he held in his hand.

Nicholson reached out and deftly snatched it from him.

"Like I told you over the phone, don't worry about it," said Nicholson. "We under-reported some income—I've already reprimanded the accounting department."

"Whose accounting department?" Adam asked, thoroughly confused. His eyes wandered to Susan, who was dressed much more expensively than her usual getup, wearing diamond and gold jewelry he had never seen her wear before, and smelling of expensive fragrance. She caught his eye and smiled warmly. His heart fluttered.

"Adam," said Nicholson, walking directly to Adam and snapping his fingers in front of Adam's eyes. "Wake up. *Your* accounting department. The accounting department of Time Travel Incorporated."

"Time Travel Incorporated?" replied Adam, with the realization that something he had done while in the past, though his visit was brief, must have altered his future, which was now the present.

"Yeah," said Nicholson. "You know. TTI. The company you *founded*? The corporation of which you are CEO—and of which I am your CFO?"

The memory came back to him. It *had* to come back to him, because he had made it happen. He visualized himself alone in the laboratory in his parent's basement. His older self coming through the wormhole. His younger self thrilled to be shown how to develop a working time machine years ahead of when he'd have done it on his own.

In his mind he relived the revelation from "Old Adam" that he hadn't made himself rich selling either time machines, time travel services, or the spin-off technologies he'd created, like the compact mini-accelerator that could achieve particle speeds in a pathway the length of a basement instead of the length of several football fields. He relived "Young Adam" promising himself not to make the same stupid mistake—again. And he saw himself the next day, going to an office supply store and purchasing a set of forms for incorporating himself, and then filling out and mailing the forms with a check to establish Time Travel Incorporated as an S corporation.

He looked around the well-equipped, state-of-the-art laboratory. Just how big was Time Travel Incorporated? He couldn't fully recall yet; apparently, the neural synapses took time to recover from the temporal displacement of time travel. But from the immaculate appearance, size, and inventory of expensive equipment in the lab, it appeared they were doing okay. They had to be, if the company had both a CEO and a CFO, right?

He looked at Nicholson. When Adam had last seen him, Nicholson had been an IRS agent. Now, apparently, Adam had hired him to run the financial side of his company. But the IRS notice now said he owed $174,595.60. How good a job could Nicholson be doing? He had thought the IRS agent highly intelligent when they first met. But had Nicholson in fact screwed up and gotten Adam into even hotter water with the Internal Revenue

Service? Did the company have enough cash to pay this whopping tax bill, or would this mean Chapter 11 and the end of his dream?

"$174,595.60 is a lot of money, Agent Ni . . . Stan," said Adam. "Can we pay it?"

Both Stan and Susan burst into laughter, while Adam stood there, puzzled. What was so damn funny about owing the IRS nearly two hundred thousand dollars?

"Relax, Adam," said Nicholson. "As you well know, or should if you read your own annual report, Time Travel Incorporated had gross revenues of $17.3 billion last year." He snapped up the tax bill from the table. "I'll take care of this."

"Seventeen billion?" said Adam in disbelief. *How rich am I?* Susan disengaged from Nicholson, strode over to Adam, put her arms around him, and kissed him lovingly on the mouth.

"I'm glad Stan's in charge of the money, and not you, smart boy," she said after they kissed; her breath reminded him of clean mountain air blowing over a field of wild mint. She moved her hands down to his hips, and he did likewise to her, noting that her torso was incredibly toned and free of fat.

"Uh, exactly how much money do we have?" Adam asked Susan and Stan. They looked at each other and smiled. And suddenly Adam knew he was rich beyond the dreams of avarice. "I'll take care of this today," said Stan waving the IRS's $174,595.60 tax bill as he turned and walked out of the room toward his office. As he disappeared into the hallway, they could hear him say, "Maybe I'll take it out of petty cash and drive it over to the post office myself—if the garage has finished waxing my Rolls . . ."

Because of the effects of time travel, leaping across ten years without consciously living through them, Adam suddenly realized that he didn't really know Susan all that well.

But we'll get to know each other VERY well, he thought as their lips locked for the second time. *After all, we have all the time in the world.*

The Unbearable Likeness of Bean

I don't like to be photographed," said Albert Quincy Bean, the fifth president of the Kalamut Worthington Leasing Corporation, the third largest commercial leasing company in the state.

"Well, you've hired me to paint your portrait," Nancy Holloran, the young artist who had indeed been commissioned to do the portrait, politely pointed out.

He glared at the digital camera she was setting up on a tripod. "Why do you need a photo of me if I'm right here in front of you?"

"I paint from the photograph, not from life," she replied.

"Wouldn't painting the subject from life give you a better portrait?"

"I told your Board that I would work from photos so I wouldn't take up hours of your time having you sit for me, which they seemed to like," replied Nancy. She shifted her glance to focus on the tripod she was fiddling with. "But the truth is, Mr. Bean, I work better alone, without people watching me."

"I can appreciate that," said Bean, and he too was telling the truth: As president, he was the only employee with an office *suite*, where his office was separated from the hallway by his assistant's smaller office, which served as an entryway to his inner sanctum.

"Yes, I concentrate better and I'm more productive when I'm alone," said the artist. "You?"

He smiled back uncomfortably. Yes, working in solitude improved his concentration. But that was not why he hid away in his inner office so much of the time.

Truth be told, he isolated himself because of his looks. For Albert Quincy Bean was a very homely man.

He thought "homely" was putting it charitably. *I'm ugly*, he was reminded whenever he glanced at a mirror or talked to a particularly handsome or attractive person—like Holloran, who was a pretty, sweet-looking, willowy blonde, tall and graceful.

Bean, on the other hand, was short, dumpy, and pear-shaped. He wasn't grossly fat—he walked, not waddled—but he was just a tad too heavy. The bulge of his protruding abdomen was enough to exert downward pressure on his belt; it made him look as if his pants were falling down and he was slightly pregnant.

In his youth, his best feature had been a head full of wavy brown hair. He wasn't bald—he still had much of the brown hair—but it was definitely thinning, and he worried constantly about losing it.

A sinus condition made breathing slightly difficult when his mouth was fully closed, and so it was usually partially open. He felt it made him look stupid or dull, and he was not stupid, though he wasn't sure about dull.

Whatever clothes he picked never seemed to fit him well. The shirts always threatened to gap over the lower abdomen, so he wore a T-shirt underneath. The T-shirt made him too warm, so he was prone to sweat at temperatures at least ten degrees cooler than those at which most other people began to sweat.

He had a long nose, ending in a hook, which he despised. But he lacked the vanity or pride in appearance to even consider getting a nose job.

His nostrils, like the rest of his nose, were unattractively elongated, creating ample acreage for a vast crop of nose hair. He trimmed it, as well as the hair growing in his ears, at least once a week, but it seemed a losing battle.

No one ever saw him naked—at forty-two, Albert had resigned himself to the fact that no woman was interested in him, despite a salary in the mid six figures. He went to a small local gym twice a week for personal training sessions to stay as fit as he could realistically be, given his lack of athletic activities and sedentary lifestyle, but invariably showered afterward at home.

He particularly did not like his body when naked, for nakedness revealed even more flaws. He was a victim of that unfortunate toenail fungus he kept hearing about on the radio. The nails on his big toes of each foot were an ugly brownish yellow, and he practically needed a chainsaw to trim them.

His elbows had scaly white patches that looked like the hide of an albino rhinoceros. Around his fortieth birthday, he noticed definite formation of man-boobs on his chest. His penis, which had always been of adequate if unspectacular size, seemed to be shrinking, giving him yet another defect to add to his collection and dampen his already minimal self-esteem—for despite his considerable career success, Albert Quincy Bean simply thought very little of himself.

"Look over here," said the photographer, holding the index finger of her left hand high while she operated the digital camera with her right by squeezing what looked like a bulb at the end of a wire.

He sat humiliated as the camera captured him in all his absence of glory. Was the artist repulsed by having to photograph and paint such an unattractive subject? he wondered.

She stopped and said, "Too serious, Al." He found it instantly appealing; no one had called him Al since his mother had died ten years earlier. She had raised him alone. His father had left when he was a baby; Bean supposed the man hadn't been able to abide being the parent of such a hideous son. The abandonment had left Bean with a fierce contempt of men who did not support their families. Ironically, this was one of the factors that had motivated him to work hard and rise to the top of the corporate ladder—though now that his salary exceeded that of the president of the United States, he had no one to share it with.

"Smile for me, would you, Al?"

He smiled as best he could. Being unaccustomed to doing so, he found it tough going.

"That's not much of a smile," she said.

"I'm trying."

"Okey-dokey, pardner," she said in a suddenly goofy voice one might use to entertain a child, and she simultaneously crossed her eyes and puckered her mouth. He could not help but laugh, and as he started to do so, he heard the camera click several times.

"Okay, Al, I've got what I need," she said.

"What happens now?"

"I'll go away and do my thing," she said. "In about four weeks, I'll bring the canvas by so you and the board can have a look."

"I can't wait," he said.

She smiled, and it seemed to him that her smile lit up the whole room. She was the kind of girl he believed he could never, ever have; unworthy as he felt, he believed her to be out of his league. *We're not even in the same species*, he thought dismally.

As the weeks passed, the portrait remained on his mind, to the point where his concern over having it displayed in the lobby along with the portraits of his predecessors distracted him from his work. And if by some miracle he could convince the Board not to go ahead, Nancy would lose her commission. He assumed that she needed the work, and he didn't want to cause a problem for her. But the thought of having to pass his own picture in the lobby every day was almost more than he could bear.

That Friday night he left for home earlier than usual, which found him leaving the office with many of the other employees at five o'clock; he usually worked until seven.

"Hello, Mr. Bean," said Jack Starkwell, his comptroller. Bean knew that Starkwell and his companions were heading to Armstrong's for drinks. "We'd love to have you join us," he longed to hear Jack say. But he never did.

Bean spent most evenings alone in his apartment, and that night he felt like sticking with routine rather than shaking things up. He stopped off at Homer's Dixie Pig, his favorite barbecue joint, and got a slab of ribs to go. On impulse, he ordered a side of the macaroni salad, which he normally bypassed. When he got home, he turned on the TV and ate his ribs as he watched the news, sopping up some of the excess barbecue sauce with white bread and scooping the rest over the cold macaroni salad.

The days passed. But something had changed. Throughout the day, he imagined scenarios: Jack and the gang inviting him out with them for their Friday night drink at Armstrong's; he and Nancy going for dinner and a movie. He thought of calling her but never considered it a real possibility; he had not dated since high school, and even then it had only been taking Sheila Bristol, his second cousin, to their senior prom.

Days turned into weeks, and when he came into work early one Friday, before his assistant had arrived, he found Nancy Holloran already waiting in his outer office with a large package.

"Nancy!" he said. "What are you doing here so early this morning?"

"The Board approved the portrait yesterday," she said brightly, her smile lighting up the room. "They said it goes up in the lobby as soon as you approve it."

"Come on in," he said. She rested the canvas on his desk, untied a string, and the covering fell away.

He gasped. "It's beautiful," he said in spite of himself. "But Nancy . . . that doesn't look anything like me."

"What are you talking about?" she asked, shaken.

He gulped and said quietly, "I'm . . . ugly. You know it. This portrait makes me look handsome!"

"You're not ugly, Al," Nancy said, puzzled. "This is what you look like: a nice, pleasant-looking man who quietly radiates the power of his position and the confidence that comes with success. Al, most of the people who commission portraits from me are either rich or successful or both. I know that inner glow of achievement or position—and you have it. On the outside, well . . . okay, so you're not George Clooney, but I'm not Reese Witherspoon. But I know I'm not hideous to look at, and neither are you. Far from it." She hesitated a second before saying it. "You're a nice-looking man, Al. You're cute!"

He stared at the portrait and saw what she was talking about: Like the other company presidents whose portraits hung in the lobby, he looked every bit the captain of industry, the corporate leader, a man with power who wielded it wisely. But where their portraits were stern, his had the beginnings of a smile, conveying the impression that he was a more relaxed and perhaps a nicer leader than his predecessors, which in fact, he was.

Nancy leaned the portrait on a table against the wall. "You don't have to decide now," she said, handing him her business card. "Live with it a few days. I'll wait a week or so before I bill your Board the balance. If you want changes made, I'll make them; I want you to be happy, though your Board members said they felt it captured you to a tee. If you decide they're right, I'll just bill you the balance. If not, I'll fix it to your satisfaction, though I can't imagine what you would want changed. But either way, call me. Okay?"

"Call you?" he said. "You mean, to let you know about the painting."

She gathered up the empty portrait cover and prepared to leave. "Oh yes," she said quickly, and she looked down, avoiding eye contact. "About the painting."

"Bye, Al," she said as she exited his inner sanctum. "Be seeing ya."

He stared at the portrait for a good long while. The man in the portrait wasn't, by the standards of the fashion industry or TV or advertising or Hollywood, handsome. But he was far from hideous: just a nice guy you might want to get to know and have a beer with—or a date.

He looked at Nancy's card, and was going to leave it on his assistant's desk to add to her contact management file. But on an impulse, he took out his wallet and placed the card inside instead.

When the portrait was hung in the lobby later that week, people commented on what a good job the artist had done in capturing both Mr.

Bean's likeness, as well as his personality and spirit. The only complaint came from the chairman of the board, who noted that the Bean painting made the portraits of the other company presidents look like scowling Scrooges by comparison. He suggested they might be repainted to make them smile, a suggestion roundly shot down because of the cost.

Friday rolled around, and as the day wound down, Mr. Bean considered the appropriateness of calling Nancy Holloran to let her know he had approved the portrait—and perhaps for something more. But he realized that he didn't have the confidence or skill to ask a woman on a date or even for a cup of coffee.

Just then he heard Jack and some of the other employees chatting as they passed his outer office door on their way to the elevator. "Hey Jack," he found himself calling out, much to his surprise. "Wait up."

He gathered his coat and briefcase and walked out, hoping to catch them before the elevator came.

Einstein's Boy

Only a city as large and literary as New York could sustain a population of writers sufficient to support the Professional Biographer's Club.

Our group of published biographers meets once a month at the Chemist's Club in an old brownstone on 34th Street and Madison. Our treasurer, Huntington Obert-Thorne, the science biographer, is a Chemist's Club member (he is a PhD chemist by education and he wrote a well-received biography of Joseph Priestley, the discoverer of oxygen), and so the club allows us to meet there because Hunt is a club regular.

Huntington was regaling us with his research into a new Einstein biography. "Did you know Einstein, with his first wife Mileva, had a daughter named Lieserl, whom he virtually abandoned?" he asked, pretentiously taking a pull on his pipe.

"Yes," I replied, and Huntington gave me a withering glance, since he and I are direct competitors. He has never forgiven me for making the best-seller list with my Nicholas Tesla biography at the same time his Neils Bohr book came out and sank like a stone. I upped the ante. "Did you know he also had a son with Mileva who was similarly abandoned?"

"He did not!" Huntington replied like a petulant child.

"Ah, but he did," I replied. "Little Francis Einstein. Later on, he was known as Frank to his adoptive parents."

I explained to the group that I had stumbled across references to Francis Einstein while researching a book on the history of cheese. In addition to science, my other passion is food, and I have written several successful books on culinary history, most notably *Hot Sauce: A Spicy Tale*, published by the University of Louisiana Press.

"Okay," said Huntington in a condescending tone. "I'll humor you. Was Francis a scientific genius like Daddy—or a non-achiever like Mileva?"

"Neither," I replied. "Francis's dream was to be a great chef, and he was an innovator in the kitchen. But his passion was cheese, and his first triumph was a homemade mozzarella that won a blue ribbon in the Paris Fromage Festival's fifty-seventh annual competition. It made him famous in culinary circles, and his reputation as a cheese innovator was virtually assured."

"Then why haven't we heard of him?" asked Hunt skeptically.

"It was the tragic choice of his next cheese that ruined him," I replied. "It made him a laughingstock in the cheese community, and after the embarrassment, he soon faded from the scene and was not heard from again."

"What tragedy?" said Pendergraft, another club member who shared my interest in food and had written a passable biography of Graham Kerr. "What embarrassment?"

You've heard about it, of course, at least if you have more than a passing interest in the food scene: How Francis dedicated two years of his life to creating a Muenster cheese as smooth and creamy as his smooth mozzarella, but with a slight tang reminiscent of a blue cheese. He had shipped a sample to the cheese critic at *The Practical Gourmet* newsletter, banking on another rave review to make him rich and famous.

The *Practical Gourmet* food critic, whose name was Lincoln Andrews, loved the cheese, but was curious how Francis got mild Muenster to possess overtones of Roquefort. It turned out to be simple: Francis had introduced a miniscule quantity of *Penicillium roqueforti*, the mold that gives blue cheeses their distinctive sharp flavor, into the Muenster. The mold, Francis explained to Lincoln, is actually alive and helps inhibit the growth of harmful bacteria when the cheese is stored. Mr. Andrews was fascinated and scribbled copious notes.

Andrews' review of the cheese was positively glowing. But the unfortunate title he chose for his review—perhaps unknowingly, or perhaps deliberately, for a chuckle—ruined Francis in the serious cheese world. I still remember finding that old issue of *The Practical Gourmet* online and reading the headline that surely must have left many subscribers in stitches but surely horrified Francis when he opened his issue and read:

Frank Einstein's Muenster Lives!

Freak Show of the Gods

The County Fair comes to Neshanic Station every year on the first weekend of October, and every year there's something different. This year it was the freak show.

There was always a freak show at the County Fair. Last year, the freak show was much the same as it had been the year before that: Bessie the two-headed cow; Harriet the Bearded Lady; Georgie Porgie, New Jersey's Heaviest Man; and the Unborn Aqua-Man.

It was, at least for the adults, simultaneously depressing, boring, laughable, and pleasurable; kids were mesmerized by it. Georgie Porgie was fat; he lived on a lake in Ringwood, and Doc Bartlett confided in me, in a clear breach of patient confidentiality, that Georgie didn't weigh more than a few ounces over four hundred pounds; there had been bigger contestants on *The Biggest Loser*. But because Georgie was only five-five, he looked heavier than he was.

GP was an amiable fellow who loved to sit and chat with the fair-goers. Many of us had been coming for years, and seeing Georgie at the freak show was like an annual visit with a kindly uncle you liked but felt guilty about not visiting more often.

Bessie, the two-headed cow, was real enough. The second "head" was really a partially formed snout and mouth sticking out perpendicular to Bessie's regular headed. Both heads ate and chewed independently.

"How do they make a cow with two heads, Dad?" my ten-year-old son Ben had asked me last year. I explained about twin embryos not fully separating and how the extra head was an incomplete Siamese twin. "Bessie's kinda cool, Dad," Ben said in awe, wide-eyed, watching the cow as she watched him back. "That she is, Ben," I told him.

Harriet, the Bearded Lady, did have a beard and it seemed to be real, though sparse and light. She sat on her stool somewhat awkwardly, and I got a clear sense that she was uncomfortable and embarrassed. In truth, aside from the beard, Harriet was an attractive young woman. She dressed like a country bumpkin girl, in a midriff shirt and cutoff shorts, which revealed a toned and nicely proportioned body. She had a pretty face, not at all deformed or retarded; once during her break, I had seen her in back of the tent sitting on a lawn chair, reading a paperback book. Embarrassed to be caught looking at her, I asked quickly, "What'cha reading?" She surprised me by holding up the cover; the book was *Infinite Jest*. But she smiled when she showed it to me.

The Unborn Aqua-Man was a total fake. It was clearly a small dead octopus in a jar of formaldehyde, and nothing more; they didn't even bother to put a doll's head on it. But little kids flocked to it and were simultaneously fascinated and freaked out.

Well, this year Ben was eleven, and the same tent was there, but the banner was new, and it immediately caught my eye. It read:

FREAK SHOW OF THE GODS!

"Dad, can we go to the freak show?" he asked me eagerly. "Can we?"

"Don't we always?" I asked him, ruffling his hair. Like most parents, I loved my son with an emotional intensity so strong it was painful, and especially more so since Laura—Ben's mother, my wife—had passed away from stage-4 ovarian cancer two years ago.

We had a housekeeper, Mrs. Cariello, who took care of us materially, cleaning the house, doing the laundry, and cooking healthy meals. She was a loving woman and cared about Ben, and about me, but she could not be a substitute mom for Ben. And she was too old to hold any romantic interest for me, though neither of us was looking. To compensate for the loss of his mother, I tended to spoil Ben, and I have no guilt about it: To lose your mom to cancer when you're nine is cruel, and I viewed my primary mission in life to make Ben happy and protect him from harm.

We paid our two dollars apiece and entered the freak show. Bessie and Harriet were still there, but their stall and stool respectively had been moved to opposite rear corners of the tent; clearly, they were no longer a main attraction. Georgie and Unborn Aqua-Man were gone—Georgie, presumably to retirement or another carnival job, and Aqua-Man, most likely tossed in the trash or auctioned off on eBay.

Against the inside back wall of the tent was a duplicate of the exterior sign: FREAK SHOW OF THE GODS! In front of the sign, variously seated on stools or standing, was a new entourage of freaks, with a folding table in front of each. Each folding table had a placard with the freak's stage name, and on some of the tables there were objects of different kinds.

The first placard was labeled ZEUS. But the man standing there hardly looked like the alpha male of the pantheon of Greek gods. He was taller than average but exceedingly thin, stooped by bad posture, and his hands shook slightly. His skin had an unhealthy grayish pallor, and his sweat made it glisten, like the smooth skin of an eel or catfish.

The ticket attendant had come inside. He picked up a top hat and placed it on his head, shrugged into a ratty red dinner jacket, and stepped in front of the onlookers. "Ladies and gentlemen," he said, "may I introduce you to the Ninth Wonder of the World—the gods of ancient Greece." With a flourish, the carnival barker gestured toward the new freaks behind him.

He then stepped back to stand behind the first card table. "This is mighty Zeus," he said, indicating the thin gray man. "The god of the thunder and the lightning, conjurer of electrical bolts from the sky."

On the card table was a light bulb connected to a ceramic base. Two wires, each about a foot long, were attached to the base with screws. Zeus stepped forward and picked up one wire in each hand by the exposed copper at the tips. For a split second, the room was silent and dark. Then the bulb flared into full brightness, as if a switch had been flipped on the wall. The crowd murmured its wonderment and appreciation and applauded lightly. Zeus bowed slightly at the waist and then straightened. With a dramatic flair, he released one wire, and the bulb instantly went dark again. More murmurs and light applause. I had noticed that, as he released the wire, a small spark of static electricity jumped from the tip of his index finger to the exposed copper end of the wire.

In sequence, the carnival baker went down the line of freaks named after the Greek gods. For the most part, they looked the opposite of godlike, and appeared, with one exception, to be sickly, nervous, or fragile. But each performed a trick that the carnival barker, in his patter, related in some way to the powers or attributes of the god whose mantle each performer had taken as a stage name.

After Zeus, the next character in the barker's performance-play of the Greek gods was a youngish-looking man—short, squat, with broad hips wider than his shoulders, a lot of belly fat, and a large rear end. He wore a clear plastic helmet attached to a metal collar and, below that, heavy shoulder pads that weighed it down. The helmet appeared to be filled with water. A hose was connected from the rear of the helmet to a tank strapped to the young man's back; I assumed the tank was either filled with water or just for show.

"This is Poseidon, god of the oceans and the seas," the barker said redundantly. "He commands the waves and the tides. The creatures of the ocean do his bidding. He can swim across the ocean, never once surfacing for air, breathing water like the sea creatures he rules." Poseidon, unlike glum Zeus, seemed cheerful in disposition; he smiled, his eyes were bright, he waved to the crowd, and appeared to mouth words. Bubbles rose from his mouth. Only a muffled gurgling could be heard through the water and plastic, but it sounded to me like "Hi, folks!" If Poseidon was breathing air through a hidden tube in the helmet, I could not detect it. And he was clearly not holding his breath. So he was breathing something, either air or water; I could not tell which, though it appeared to be the latter.

Following Poseidon was a gaunt fellow, a bit taller than Zeus and even more sickly looking, with what seemed like a clear case of jaundice. "Hades," the barker announced, "king of the underworld, lord of the dead." On the card table in front of where Hades stood were some flowers in a ceramic pot. Grimly, Hades reached forward, touching the flowers. They immediately began to droop and wilt. Within a minute, they had gone completely limp and dry, their petals crinkled and brown.

The fourth character in the show was neither thin nor overly tall, but he was stocky and appeared strong. It was hard to tell, though, because despite winter being months away, he was wearing a heavy parka with a zippered hood that hid his face, creating a sense of mystery and curiosity among the audience. "And last but not least," the barker said, "the mighty Minotaur."

The crowd gasped, and at least one person in the audience cried out in genuine horror or revulsion, when the Minotaur unzipped his jacket and threw off the parka and hood. Below the neck he was a broad-shouldered, powerful-looking man of medium height.

But the head above the neck was a different story. It was more bull than human. The eyes looked back with human intelligence. The nostrils of the broad, flat nose flared, like a bull seething in anger at the matador's taunting red cape. He had ears in the same position as a man's ears, but they were pointed and flopped over, like a cow's. Most striking were the two thick horns rising out of his skull at the forehead. Were they glued onto his skin? They appeared not to be. Then the Minotaur smiled, and flexed his arms like a body builder. The biceps bulged, and the crowd oohed and aahed appropriately in response. It was then I noticed the Minotaur was shoeless, and he had hooves instead of feet.

Unlike the old freak show, the Freak Show of the Gods was a timed performance with scheduled showings. After giving us another minute of gawking, the carnival barker hustled the audience out of the tent. Bessie, Harriet, Zeus, Poseidon, Hades, and the Minotaur watched us leave. "Come back for the three o'clock show, folks, and tell your friends," the barker said cordially as we stepped outside the tent into the cool afternoon air.

"Dad, that was awesome!" Ben said excitedly. He looked around and then pointed. "Hey, there's Pete with his dad. Can I tell them about the new freak show?" he asked. "Sure, Ben, but stay where I can see you," I said, "and make sure your cell phone is on."

As soon as Ben ran off to see his friend, I stepped back from the front of the FREAK SHOW OF THE GODS tent for a quick smoke. As I patted my jacket pocket to locate matches and my cigar clipper, I sensed someone watching me from behind. When I turned, Harriet was standing not a foot in front of me, and she jerked back with surprise.

"Oh," she said, "I'm sorry. I didn't know anyone was there. I mean, I didn't expect anyone to be there. Usually . . . I take my break back here . . . I'm with the show . . . I certainly didn't mean to sneak up on you and surprise you like that."

I smiled. Despite the beard, she was an attractive girl, and her gentle charisma negated any repulsion a beard on a woman might have generated. "David Foster Wallace, right?" I said.

She smiled back, and the sweetness of her smile made the beard even more irrelevant. "I knew I'd seen you back here before," she said.

"Not many *Infinite Jest* readers in Neshanic Station," I said.

Again the sweet smile, which infused her face with warmth and light. "English major, Brighton Community College," she replied.

"So why is a college woman working in a traveling carnival show?" I asked.

"En-glish-ma-jor," she said slowly and clearly, and then we both laughed. "Besides, I only finished one year."

"Drop out?" I said.

She shrugged. "Not many sororities seem to be interested in pledging an eighteen-year old with a goatee," she said matter-of-factly, with only a hint of self pity. "Not many fraternity guys interested in dating one, either. I got tired of being laughed at and stared at. And when the carnival came to Brighton that summer, Todd"—she nodded her head in the direction of where the carnival barker sold tickets in front of the tent—"offered me a job on the spot. 'You'll be with your own folks,' he said. I thought he meant my parents would come with us. But, of course, he meant the other freaks."

"You're hardly a freak," I countered. "I've dated black-haired girls who had heavier moustaches than you." She laughed again. "Seriously, I noticed you at last year's fair, and your beard is relatively light—for a beard, that is. And your hair is light too." It was a chestnut brunette. "Couldn't you, you know . . ."

"Get electrolysis like your black-haired girlfriend?" she said, smiling. "I'd be out of a job. And my condition isn't normal. It's like a guy's beard. I'd pretty much have to get electrolysis every month or shave every day. I can miss one or two days, but by the third, I have a five o'clock shadow. After a week, a scruffy beard and stash. Of course, working here"—she gestured toward the tent—"I can just let it grow."

"HARRIET!" a man yelled from behind me. It was Todd, the barker. "Get your ass inside! And tell those Greek geeks, too. Jesus, I got a show to run." Instantly, I began to develop a mild dislike for Todd.

"Well, it's been nice chatting with you, uh . . ."

"Robert," I said. "Robert Campbell."

"Of Campbell Soup fame?" she asked playfully, her eyes sparkling.

"No, just a little farming and a little real estate," I said. "Not too successful at the farming—somewhat better luck with selling real estate. Maybe Mr. Campbell Soup will get confused in his old age and leave me all his money."

"Or maybe at least a can of chicken noodle soup," she suggested. "Well, bye, Robert, it was nice meeting you . . ."

"Bye, Harriet," I said. Our eyes locked for an instant. She didn't move, but as I contemplated saying something else, Todd yelled her name again, breaking the spell, and she turned and hurried toward the rear of the tent. My dislike of Todd moved up a notch.

Ben came back with his friend Pete, who said his father had gone on to the barbecue tent to get something to eat and would meet Pete there after the next showing of the freak show.

We stepped in front of the tent. I bought two more tickets from Todd the carnival barker and gave them to Ben and Peter, who ran inside.

"Not going to take another peak at the freaks?" Todd said amiably, yet it ratcheted my slowly mounting dislike for the man up even higher.

I shrugged noncommittally, and then noticed we were alone for the moment—the crowd was thinning and he had no more customers waiting for tickets.

"Can I ask you something?" I said. "Something about the freak show?"

Now it was his turn to shrug noncommittally. "Sure, why not?" he said. "Ask away."

"The Greek god freaks," I said. "Obviously, they're not Greek gods."

"Duh," said Todd. He moved another half notch up the annoying toad scale.

"But how do you get them to do their tricks?" I asked. "Breathing water, lighting a light bulb . . ."

Todd leaned toward me conspiratorially, and I smelled alcohol on his breath, but I didn't see a flask bulging in his pockets.

"I bought the damned freaks," he said meanly. "They're gene-spliced, lab-made. Cost a freaking fortune, too."

"Bought them?" I asked innocently. "I'd heard there's a black market for bio-engineered animals and humanoids. But isn't that illegal?"

He waived his hand. "The penalty is a slap on the wrist and a fine for less cash than we make in a month with the show," he laughed. I knew he was right: Court cases concerning the rights of bio-engineered humans were many and complex, and it would be years, even decades, before the issue was fully resolved. Until then, it was mainly a matter of status quo: If you were a free bio-engineered humanoid, you were free. If someone paid to have you created, well—technically, they couldn't really own you, but there was an implied guardianship similar to parental rights. As I said, it's all very complicated.

Todd knew how complicated it was. That's how safe he felt in telling me. And now he couldn't stop his tongue from wagging.

"They're all DNA chimeras," he said. I knew what that was: Human DNA mixed with the genes of other animals or even plants. Chimeras were not the only gene-spliced specimens on the market. Other bio-engineered beings were made with artificial DNA or modified human DNA. The first chimeras had been created and marketed in 2009, when a jellyfish gene spliced into a beagle made the dog glow red under UV lights.

"Zeus is a splice of electric eel with human DNA," Todd said. "He can generate electric current through his skin."

"So it wasn't a parlor trick, a hidden wire up his sleeve?"

"Nope," said Todd. "When I first got him, he was sick, so I took him to a doctor for an X-ray. The doc showed me the X-ray. Zeus has an extra organ in his body we don't have. It contains around sixteen thousand of these specialized eel cells. The cells store power like little batteries. They allow Zeus to generate low-level voltage, like an electric eel. He was originally bred under a Department of Defense contract as a weapon. The idea was a soldier that could shoot lightning bolts from his fingertips. Kill an enemy, fry a weapons system, that sort of thing. But he can't do much more than turn on the light bulb, so the Army didn't take him. I got him in a closeout sale." Todd chuckled at this. "And even though he's a gene experiment gone bad, I still had to pay a pretty penny, like I said."

"They don't seem too happy to be here," I observed. "Do they like the work?"

"I don't know what they like," Todd said, irritably, glancing at his watch. "But they got no place else to go, no one else to care for them, nothing else to do. Minotaur I think is borderline retarded. Poseidon's another DoD failure—bred as the ultimate Navy Seal, a freak who can breathe underwater—but can't swim. Ha!"

"Can't swim?"

Todd nodded. "Yup. Like I said, can't drown, but can't actually swim. Another effed-up gene-splice experiment went wrong. Notice the big butt and gut on him? Poseidon has negative buoyancy—some people do. They can't tread water, and they sink in water over their head. He wouldn't drown—he can just walk until he reaches the shore, or never reach the shore and live fine under water—but no one wants a mutant Aqua-Man who can't do the butterfly stroke or swim up under the hull of an enemy battleship and plant a bomb on it. And Hades"—he shivered involuntarily—"people are afraid of Hades. Even I am. I don't let him touch me. Ever. People stay away from him. This is the only home he knows, the only family he's got."

I gave Todd two dollars. "What the heck," I said. "I may as well keep the boys company."

"Suit yourself," said Todd, pocketing the change. "Always room for a paying customer."

I sat through the show again, which Ben and Peter loved. "Hey, Ben," said Pete. "My dad said for your dad and us to meet him at the food tent for some barbecue."

"Run ahead, boys," I told them. "I'll catch up with you in a few minutes. Just have your cell phone on, Ben."

Todd had left a minute earlier to start selling tickets for the next show, and when Ben and Pete exited, I was alone in the tent with the freaks.

I considered my options: Poseidon's head was shielded by a helmet, prohibiting me from making physical contact. The top of the Minotaur's cranium was flanked by two formidable, sharply pointed horns that could do some serious damage if he became irritated or agitated. Todd was correct about Hades; he gave off an aura of fear and death, and I did not wish to touch him. Zeus seemed to shock only through his fingertips and the charge seemed low, and he also appeared to be timid and nonviolent.

I approached him. Our eyes locked. I felt a tenuous connection with his mind.

What're you doing, Mister?

Do not worry, my Brother, I replied. *I will not hurt you.*

I sensed someone behind me. "Robert?" Harriet asked in a puzzled voice. I could sense agitation and anxiety among the other Greeks, and I felt Minotaur could rapidly become a threat.

"Harriet, do you trust me, kid?" I asked.

She hesitated for only a second. "Yes, Robert. But what are you doing?"

"We were all born for better things than a freak show," I said, reaching up to gently touch Zeus's forehead with my fingertips. "You. Me. And them." Upon making contact, Zeus visibly relaxed, and closed his eyes.

Let the healing begin now, Brother, I telepathed to him, and as we stood together, I began to travel along the pathways of his brain with my mind, as I was bred to do. I saw the fear, the dysfunction, that kept Zeus from reaching his full potential as clearly as you see lines on a map—and I corrected each one as I wound my way through his mind. In what seemed like hours but was only a few minutes, I fixed most of what had been broken and gave Zeus back more of what his human creators had meant him to have.

When we were done, I turned to Harriet. "I've got to meet my boy and his friend at the food tent," I said, taking her arm in mine. "Let's walk and talk."

"I have to be back in a half hour for the next show," Harriet said, hesitating, looking at me with a quizzical expression. "Otherwise Todd will dock my pay."

"You'll be back by then," I assured her. "But he won't dock your pay. And you won't have to be in the show anymore unless you still want to."

Harriet looked even more puzzled, so I explained as we went to find Ben and Peter in the food tent, leaving Zeus to fill Hades, Poseidon, and Minotaur in on the plan.

Harriet, of course, was shocked to find out that there were plenty of bioengineered beings, like me, who could pass for a normal human in appearance and walk about free.

"And the laboratory where you were created let you go?" she said incredulously.

"Why not?" I replied. "They wanted a powerful telepath who could read and control the minds of enemies over vast distances. The idea was to create a super-soldier who could, with a thought, make enemy soldiers point nuclear weapons in the wrong direction, turn bombs in on themselves, or simply not aim them at us. When I tested blank, my value went from about a billion dollars to zero dollars—less, since they'd never recover the R&D costs that went into my development."

But I hadn't been a complete failure. I simply led my creators to believe that. They were easy to fool. I did have telepathic abilities and mind control, both of which I used to convince the DNA scientists who made me think I was a dud.

I can't read or control an enemy's mind a thousand miles away. But if I'm standing right next to you, I can tell pretty well what you're thinking. For instance, if I'm trying to sell you a property, I know what you're willing to pay—not what you tell me your top price is. I close a lot of real estate deals that way. I can't really make you do anything against your will, nor would I want to: That would be cheating. However, if my price is fair, I can gently nudge you into agreeing with me, and I will do so as long as the deal is good for both of us.

My telepathic abilities are far greater, however, when applied to other bioengineered beings. Perhaps it's because our gene-spliced neurons generate brain waves on a similar frequency to one another. Whatever the reason, I can penetrate deep into a chimera's psyche. If there are mental blocks or flaws—either causing emotional distress or inhibiting natural genetic abilities—such as in Zeus's case, an inhibition to use his electrical charge at full power—I can remove the block. As I did with Zeus.

While I was repairing Zeus's fragile psyche, I also enabled him to see Todd and the Freak Show of the Gods for what they were—pure exploitation. When I discovered how profitable the Freak Show really was, and how little Zeus, Harriet, and the others were paid, I telepathically outlined a plan for change, to which Zeus readily agreed, and he assured me he'd have no trouble convincing the others.

I'll do it too, Robert, Harriet told me without speaking as we walked back to the Freak Show tent with Ben.

I took her hand in mine. Reflexively, Ben reached up to take her other hand, as he worked at his cotton candy.

"God damnit, Harriet, show starts in two minutes," Todd barked as we approached the front of the tent.

Yes, Todd, I agreed. *But it's nothing that need concern you anymore.*

You're a gene-freak too! Todd thought in reply. Startled by the voices in his head, he switched to speech: "I knew something wasn't right with you!" he said meanly.

Here's what else isn't right, Todd, I replied forcefully enough to cause him to wince. I was bred to do a lot more psychic damage than that, but as I said, the experiment had largely failed, and I could do little more than give Todd a bad migraine. I couldn't force him to do what I was about to insist he do. But I had an ace up my sleeve that could.

I repeated, telepathically, an abridged version of the plan I had laid out for Harriet and for Zeus, whom I knew—from a quick scan inside the tent—had relayed my plan to the others, who were unanimous in their support: Todd would continue as the carnival barker and MC for the freak show. He would, on paper, remain a legal owner. But as a partner, not a sole proprietor. He would own a one-sixth share and keep one-sixth of the profits. Each of the current performers would own a one-sixth share of the profits for life. Harriet would keep the books and handle the accounts, and collect and deposit all revenues directly. She would pay Todd his share out of the business's account. If Todd chose not to perform, he would still receive a royalty of one-sixth of net profits, but the pay for his replacement would come entirely out of his share.

"Are you nuts?" Todd said unpleasantly. "I own the Freak Show of the Gods—and the freaks. Who's going to make me do as you say? You?"

He heard the rustle of a tent flap and turned as the freaks—the gods—came out to stand with me and Harriet.

"He speaks for us," Zeus said.

Todd was about to reply, but suddenly changed his mind, as the air became filled with the smell of ozone. We heard the crackle of a hundred small thunders. Blue sparks began to dance on the surface of Zeus's skin, and his hair stood on end. Poseidon was near Zeus, but far enough away so he didn't get a shock. The Minotaur puffed up his chest in the way that strong men do to intimidate other men or impress women, further weakening Todd's desire for a confrontation.

Then Hades stepped forward. In time, I would call him a friend. But there is within him a force, a power that scares other men, bio-engineered or ordinary. The others in the Freak Show of the Gods are purely chimeras, with varying degrees of genetically bestowed special abilities. But Hades, I fear, is something more, though what I cannot say. When Hades moved toward him, Todd truly feared the mutant, and I think rightly so.

Would Hades, the god of death, have reached forth and touched Todd? I think he is capable of hurting or killing if sufficiently provoked. Would that death touch of his cause Todd to wither and die like it did the plant? While I do not know for sure and have no wish to find out, I believe this too.

A month had passed when I took Zeus and the others to see the property I had secured for them, which sat on a pretty four acres at the top of the hill about a mile up the road from our own small family farm. The previous owners had named it Haverhill House, and no one had taken the hand-carved sign off the door.

"I don't like 'Haverhill House," Zeus said testily. "It sounds like a halfway house for drug addicts or an institution for the mentally challenged."

I fingered the worn "Haverhill House" sign nailed to the front porch column. "It's quite the custom to name a house this size," I told Zeus. "And you certainly don't have to stick with 'Haverhill,'" I added, plucking the sign off the column and tossing it on the lawn. "Any thoughts on a new name?"

An impish smile appeared on his usually dour, worn visage.

"Olympus," he said, grinning from ear to ear.

There was a drought that year for most of the growing season in Neshanic Station, and many of our neighbors watched helplessly as the sun burned away their crops and their cash. Only small sporadic rainstorms brought any relief, and whenever one popped up, our farm was always within the area of rainfall. We had a bumper crop that year, and because of the drought, crops were lean, prices rose, and we made a nice profit, which of course Harriet, Ben, and I shared with the others. They had made Olympus their home, though after weeks of staying over at our place, Harriet had gradually moved in with me and Ben, whom she adored.

"How come the sky is dark and it's always raining at our house, but the Petersons and the Johnsons and the Nelsons get hardly any of it?" Ben asked me one day as we stood with Harriet on the front porch, enjoying the refreshing breeze and the shade of the clouds that the cool rain brought.

I looked across the field, where Zeus and Poseidon stood on the rise, holding their arms high as the lightning and thunder and rain stormed all around them.

"I don't know, Ben," said Harriet, putting her left arm around his shoulder and reaching out with the right to hold my hand. "Perhaps the gods are finally smiling upon us."

Rocket Man

He jumped from the plane, free falling for just a couple of breathless seconds.

Then he shakily thumbed the ignition button.

The six jets, each firmly attached to the eight-foot wings strapped to the back of his flight suit, kicked in smoothly and simultaneously. Primed by a mix of butane and propane, the jets instantly ignited. Then the feed system automatically switched over to kerosene, which the jets would burn for the rest of his flight. His free fall stopped as he began to accelerate forward, driven by the thrust of the jet engines.

And he was flying. Like Superman! Like Buzz Lightyear! Flash Gordon! The Rocketeer! Wonder Man! Peter Pan! Mr. Terrific! The wind in his face was bracing, the sensation of powered flight without aircraft exhilarating beyond description.

Damn it, he was *flying*—and the first man in the world ever to do it without a balloon, glider, helicopter, or plane!

"To infinity and beyond!" he screamed giddily into the wind.

"Jim, you're looking good," said the voice in his earpiece—Arnie, his chief engineer, from up above in the plane.

"It's . . . it's unbelievable," Jim replied. "Arnie—it works! I'm *flying*." He laughed. "Holy Christ, *I am flying*. Wah-hoooooo!"

He tilted his body upward. The suit responded and he began to climb even higher. *Up, up, and awaaaaay,* he thought, his face wearing a broad, self-satisfied grin.

He brought both arms forward until they were pointing straight ahead— just like Superman in the movies. He shifted his arms to the right, and sure enough, he began to turn at a gentle angle to the right. At that moment he regretted not wearing his Superman T-shirt over his flight suit jacket. A red cape would have been cool, but with flame spouting out of the jets, out of the question.

He knew there was danger and he had to be careful: Even the slightest imbalance in movement could start him swinging around. Should he lose control, he would pull the yellow handle on his flight suit. It would jettison the wings and the engines—a move that could cost him about $85,000 in equipment and materials, a loss he could ill afford—and release his parachute. He'd be safe, unless the wings spun around to point the rockets at his body, in which case he'd be burned to a crisp.

"It's like a second skin, Arn. I just nudged it to the right. And I'm going right. Can you see?"

"Go, Superman!" Arn said breathlessly. Jim heard the crew whooping for joy in the plane.

It was working. The dream had come true. "You will believe that a man can fly," he had told reporters in occasional interviews during the five years it had taken him and Arnold Wexler to design, build, test, and train in the jet-powered flight suit.

He winced as he remembered the first test, almost three years before. Their mistake had been attempting takeoff from the ground, with only four jet engines to propel him instead of six.

One hadn't fired. The imbalance—one thrusting on the right wing against two on the left—had spun him around and slammed him into the ground with enough force to shatter his collar bone, snap two ribs, break his jaw when his face hit the surface, and give him a concussion. His safety helmet had not shattered, though the visor cracked. The doctor had said it was a miracle that he had not broken his neck and become paralyzed.

When he'd awakened in his hospital bed, the first thing he'd seen was Susan sitting in a chair. She had been there for him. As she had always been there throughout a decade of marriage—ten years of his sporadic employment, their money worries, gossiping neighbors, and noise, smoke, and bad smells from his laboratory in the basement and his workshop in the garage, the last five with him spending ten hours a day, six days a week, in the garage workshop with Arnie, tinkering with their various inventions, which—he assured her—were going to make them rich beyond the dreams of avarice.

Wonderful Susan! What other wife would have put up with him? He'd praised her for it every day. Though in recent months she had seemed to cool considerably toward his seemingly infinite leave of absence from the world of pension plans and paychecks. But after the accident, she had been there, waiting patiently at his hospital bed to make sure he was okay.

"Susan," he mumbled through the wires holding his jaw together in a happy but hoarse voice.

"Jim. You're awake."

"How long have you been waiting?" he'd managed to ask like a ventriloquist, making speech without moving his lips.

"I've been here since noon. The doctor said you were mumbling in your sleep and would come around soon."

"I appreciate that you're here for me." He'd been genuinely moved to see her sitting at his bedside, waiting for him to awaken. Obviously she loved him, as he'd always known, and suddenly all was right with the world. True, he hadn't flown that day. But he would. He knew he would.

"Jim, we need to talk about all this," Susan had said evenly, breaking the tranquility of the moment.

"All this what?" he'd asked in a mock-innocent voice he had instantly regretted using.

"You know what I mean," Susan had said tersely.

"The inventing? It's part and parcel of me, Suzie. You knew that the day I proposed. And I thought you were OK with it. You are, right?" Now his jaw was beginning to hurt and the nurse who had entered the room told him to stop talking and give it a rest.

Susan had known when she married Jim that he was—to put it mildly— a tad unconventional and eccentric. At first, she'd found it charming. But, and she'd never told him or anyone else this, she had hoped to change him.

Well, you and I know the folly of that! Eventually, Susan had learned that people don't change. The person you marry is the person you will be with until you divorce or die. You cannot change them. They cannot change themselves.

"We are *this close*," he'd told her, holding the tips of his right thumb and index finger a half inch apart. "*This close.*"

"What if the jets fail or the wings fall off when you're half a mile up in the air?" she had asked him. "Am I going to have to spend every day worrying about whether you'll come home in your car or an ambulance or a hearse? I'm not a strong enough person to live like this, Jim. Not any longer."

She was, he well knew, a nervous sort. In addition, she suffered from irritable bowel syndrome, or IBS, which got worse whenever she was under stress and anxiety—and his dangerous experiment had given her plenty to be anxious about. Because of the aggravation of the IBS brought on by her worry about their finances and his safety, she could no longer drink caffeine or eat onions or garlic or hot sauce.

He'd reached out to her then and gently took her hand. "Stop worrying so much, Sue. Nothing's going to happen. We'll be *fine*."

I won't be fine if your cockamamie inventions never work and we never make a dime from them, or if you crash and become an invalid, or if you die and leave me all alone, she had thought. *Oh Jim—why can't you just take the job my father offered you in his business? Why can't you be like my dad and my brother and every other man on the block who wears a suit and tie, leaves the house at seven, and gets home by six to have dinner with his family, and doesn't think he is Buck Rogers?*

But she had come there mainly to comfort and support him—and not to argue. So she'd said nothing more as they sat quietly, holding hands, while the sun fell and the world darkened outside of his hospital room window.

Twice more during the next few years Jim injured himself in test flights. One was almost ludicrous and laughable: A reporter had arrived early (the press had been invited, though only two reporters came) and wanted a clear shot of Jim soaring through the sky, but had neglected to bring a helicopter with which to follow him. Jim, fully suited, had volunteered to stand on a ladder. The heavy wings had put him off balance; he'd fallen off the third rung and sprained his angle. He had gone to the ER for treatment, and after the ankle was wrapped (it had been a minor sprain), he'd walked back out to the ER waiting area—and Susan had been there, again. He'd grinned sheepishly, told her the story, and surprisingly, they had a good laugh over it.

But today, the day of their fourth test flight, finally—success!

The wind whipped the sleeves of his flight suit and pushed back his hair. The air was cold and crisp. He heard the reassuring, steady hiss of the flame as it exited smoothly from the six rockets to provide propulsion for the wings. *I'm the Rocketeer!* Jim thought giddily, and the thought made him laugh out loud with pure pleasure.

Jim had been obsessed with flying since he was old enough to think. But that obsession did not extend to airplanes, balloons, gliders, and flying enclosed in a vehicle. His dream had always been, quite simply, to fly without an aircraft. And now, he was.

Jim knew he was not alone in his fascination with flight: Jet packs and flying men had always captured the imagination of the public. He remembered reading about a man in the Midwest many years ago who lived in a trailer park and also had dreams of flying but pursued them in a different way. This fellow, as Jim recalled, had bought a tank of helium and a case of Army surplus weather balloons.

The trailer park guy had sat on a lawn chair in his backyard with a rifle across his knees. He'd filled the big weather balloons with helium, and tied them to the chair until he had enough buoyancy to lift him and the chair straight up into the sky. He used an oversize belt to strap himself into the lawn chair so he wouldn't fall out.

The rifle was for his descent: The flight was largely uncontrolled, and the fellow's primary mechanism for returning to Earth was to start shooting the balloons when he wanted to land.

The setup had worked! It had taken him to altitudes of thousands of feet, and at one point the captain of a low-flying airliner reported looking out the window and seeing a man wearing a winter parka sitting in a lawn chair, looking relaxed, and drifting lazily through the blue sky to the right of the plane. The story had made primetime TV news that night, although this was before YouTube and cell phones with video cameras, so there was no video footage—just a few grainy photos shot by one of the passengers.

The point though, Jim had explained to Susan, who rolled her eyes and proclaimed the lawn chair balloonist both dangerous and insane, was the publicity: Flying captured the imagination of the public, and capitalizing on this publicity was what would make Jim and Arnie with their rocket wings—then just in the conceptual design phase—both famous and wealthy.

Over Susan's objections about yet another expenditure they could ill afford, Jim hired Paul Harriman, a public relations expert, to consult with him and advise him on how to get the media to spotlight his progress on the flying suit.

Paul did indeed know what he was doing. When Jim found him on the Internet by Googling "public relations," he learned that Paul became famous in PR circles as "the man who sold the Brooklyn Bridge."

What had happened was that some years ago the city of New York had been repairing the walkways of the Brooklyn Bridge, and the construction work had been televised on the eleven o'clock news, which Paul happened to be watching that particular day.

The walkways had wooden planks as the flooring, and the old rotted wood had been taken up by workmen and placed into pickup trucks for removal. Instantly, Paul had the idea that would make him a PR legend.

He'd put his face up to the TV screen and, squinting, read the phone number off the side of the pickup truck hauling the old lumber away. He had called and offered to buy the truckload of wood; he and the owner of the company quickly negotiated a five hundred dollar price. Paul had him deliver the boards to his home in Montclair, New Jersey, and stack them in his backyard.

Next, Paul had a woodworker cut the boards into tiny blocks. He glued the wooden pieces to small rectangles of card stock printed with certificate style borders and the words "Genuine piece of the Brooklyn Bridge." He then offered the tiny blocks of wood for sale at $24.95 each, plus $4 shipping and handling.

But the coup de grace was the press release Paul wrote and distributed to the media. The headline read:

NEW JERSEY MAN SELLS BROOKLYN BRIDGE— ONE PIECE AT A TIME

It was clever and irresistible. Dozens of newspapers, radio shows, and TV news shows ran articles, segments, and interviews about the man who had sold the Brooklyn Bridge. An associate producer for *The Tonight Show* took the press release to a writer's meeting, and when Jay Leno did a couple of jokes about the Brooklyn Bridge sale on *The Tonight Show*, Paul received thousands of orders for the collectible wood and certificates. He made a pretty penny on the sale, and his reputation as a PR guru was assured.

Of course, the drawback of hiring Paul was that his coaching program cost thousands of dollars that Jim did not have. Like many inventors, no venture capitalist was interested in funding him. Susan and Jim had argued fiercely and unpleasantly over the expense of buying Paul's PR coaching program.

Susan reminded Jim that, after all, their money was earned primarily by her (and at some times in their lives entirely by her); Jim sulked and accused her of being unsupportive and sabotaging their future chance at wealth and fame. "Did Ben and Jerry's wives give them this kind of grief when they wanted to buy dairy cows for their ice cream factory?" he asked her angrily, although he had no idea of the answer, or even if Ben and Jerry had wives.

Eventually, after many sighs, Susan gave in. Paul was hired, and Jim took his PR coaching program and worked to come up with a publicity idea that would make him and Susan and Arnie rich and famous.

One of the PR principles Paul taught was: Go where the cameras already are. "When small businesses call press conferences, no one comes," Paul wrote in his do-it-yourself PR manual. "This is because no one knows who you are (which, of course, is the reason you are reading this manual and planning a PR campaign), and so they are not going to send video crews all the way to wherever you are just to cover you."

The solution, he explained, was to "go where the cameras already are." He explained that this meant holding your press conference or doing your PR stunt at a location where camera crews were already assembled to cover another talk, conference, or event.

Paul had used this technique with great success to help publicize Domino's Pizza. He knew, of course, that there is absolutely nothing newsworthy about pizza. But then he had another one of his occasional but brilliant public relations insights. When and where are all the camera crews for all the news shows gathered every year in one place? Answer: at midnight on April fourteenth at the main New York city post office to do their annual feature story on all the New York taxpayers filing their returns at the last minute.

Paul instructed his client Domino's to send a team of pizza delivery guys with dozens of pizzas to the post office on April fourteenth and give them away free to the postal workers, postal patrons, and news crews. That night, on news shows throughout the country, grateful taxpayers could be seen eating pizza from boxes that displayed the name Domino's in large red lettering.

Jim had borrowed that idea, and had selected as the landing site for the maiden voyage of his flight suit Central Park in New York City, on a Sunday when Simon and Garfunkel were giving a free concert, their first together in over a decade.

As he swooped lower, the park and its amphitheater came into view. The Great Lawn was filled with thousands of concert goers on blankets drinking wine and eating cheese, bread, and fried chicken from out of picnic baskets.

Arnie followed in the plane at a safe distance above Jim, and while the concert goers could not hear the gentle whoosh of the rocket wing jets, they could hear Arnie's plane. A few looked up, and then as word spread throughout the crowd, more and more heads turned upward, arms raised, fingers pointing at the man who could fly.

At that moment, the guilt of having spent Susan's and his money pursuing his plan, the pain of failure, and the humiliation of not having a job like Susan and her brother and father all vanished. Jim felt like a pioneer . . . like a hero . . . like a superhero!

Jim tilted his body slightly and gently increased the angle and rate of his descent. The ground had looked like a patched quilt from his launch altitude, but as he headed lower, surface features suddenly became discernible. He could see the Central Park Zoo and the road through the park, the pond, and the skating rink.

Even at minimum speed, Jim could not land while flying the rocket wings under power. The wings and rockets were heavy and awkward, and momentum would never allow him or any suit wearer to stay on his feet. So, as they had calculated and planned, Jim cut the rockets and began to glide—though as soon as the jets shut off, the rate of descent accelerated uncomfortably, more rapidly than he had anticipated.

"You're going in a bit fast," Arnie said.

"Under control—I think," Jim replied.

He checked his altimeter and saw, to his alarm, that in seconds he would plunge below the safe altitude. He had to open his chute now!

I wish I could tell you how Jim's chute wouldn't open. It would make this account so much more suspenseful and thrilling. I could relate how he fell faster and closer to Earth, the crowd realizing with growing horror that he was headed straight for a direct collision with Art Garfunkel's afro, and I could joke about how that mass of frizzy red hair might have cushioned Jim's fall.

But none of that happened. The parachute deployed without a hitch, and Jim, an experienced skydiver, was in total control. He serenely descended to a space about fifty feet in front of the concert stage, where the band had stopped playing and Simon and Garfunkel, thousands of concert goers, and reporters and camera crews from every major news outlet in New York City looked on in wonder as a winged man fell gently to Earth, landing a bit awkwardly but not badly enough to hurt himself or others in any way.

The crowd was silent for perhaps one second, and then it burst into thunderous applause. Microphones were thrust in front of Jim's face and he was asked nonstop questions: Who was he? What was that contraption? Did he really fly with wings and a jet pack, or was this a special effect? Was he promoting a new movie? Did he work for NASA?

Jim looked around. He recognized several news anchors, and reached out to shake their outstretched hands and greet them. A group of police officers looked on from outside the inner circle of reporters and concert goers, and Jim knew he must have violated several city ordinances, but the cops looked friendly and were making no move so far to arrest him. Another man stepped forward and thrust a business card toward Jim; he introduced himself as a vice-president of business development for a Fortune 500 aerospace manufacturer whose name made Jim swallow, and the man said they needed to talk as soon as possible and that Jim was naturally going to be a very rich man.

Jim was happy but disconcerted. Something was amiss.

Then he realized what was wrong. Jim had told Susan of his plans and where she should be to get the best view of the ultimate triumph of their persistence and teamwork against long years of struggle and adversity. But where was she?

Jim looked around. He scanned all the faces he could see in the crowd. He looked for the woman with whom he would share the rest of his life, his newfound fame and wealth, his hopes, and his dreams, the woman who had stuck by him through all these years, through the thick and the thin even though until now it had been mostly thin. He looked and looked and looked. And then finally it dawned on him: she wasn't there.

Through the roar of the crowd, he heard only deafening silence.

The Lottery of Forever

Bobby, Van, and Roger were walking down the street, bored and looking for a little trouble and a little fun, which, to that trio of sixteen-year-old boys, was often the same thing. It was unfortunate for the Yellow Oldster, carrying a wrinkled and torn shopping bag and dressed in a cheap brown suit frayed at the cuffs, that he had chosen to walk down the same street and at the same time as the boys.

"Hey, Wrinkled Chicken!" Van barked at the ancient man on the other side of the street who was scurrying away from them with an arthritic gait. "You goddamn hippie pinko commie!"

Bobby and Roger laughed. The Yellow Oldster kept his head down and tried to shamble away. Van turned and strode menacingly toward him. "Hey Peacenik!" he said. "I'm talking to you."

The old man kept walking and fixed his eyes on the sidewalk two feet in front of him.

But Van would not let it go; he was in the mood. He ran ahead and blocked the sidewalk in front of the Oldster, who tried to get around him. But Van was a strapping lad, huge and muscular for his age, and he kept stepping in front of wherever the old man tried to go.

"I don't want no trouble," the Oldster said, with a mixture of fear and defiance in his voice.

Van smirked. "I don't care what you want," he said. He signaled to Roger, who ran behind the Oldster and dropped to his hands and knees perpendicular to the old man's ankles. Van pushed the Oldster, who stumbled against Roger, fell backward, and hit the sidewalk with a painful thud. Roger and Van laughed and began to kick and punch the Oldster, who feebly raised his arms for protection. But he didn't cry out for help; who was going to come to the aid of a Yellow Oldster? As usual, Bobby watched but did not participate, and, as usual, he was self-conscious of what Van might think about his refusal to join in and give the duty-shirking pinko what was coming. The Oldster tried to rise, but Van's boot in his rib cage put him down again with a yelp.

Bobby felt the presence of someone behind him. He turned and saw a tall, well-built police officer standing on the sidewalk, scowling. Then

Bobby noticed his face—an ex-combat trooper, almost certainly. The cop's face looked like it had been stitched together by a blind seamstress—the nose misshapen, the bottom lobe of the right ear missing, the cheeks criss-crossed with battle scars. The left eye was bionic, as was the left hand. Bobby looked at him with admiration; here was a Fighting Long Lifer—strong, fearless, and courageous—like Van and Roger hoped to become. Not like the Yellow Oldster sniveling on the sidewalk. Wasn't that every boy's ambition—to be a nearly invincible warrior and live nearly forever, to pay back the gifts bestowed by one's government by fighting your country's sworn enemies?

However, Bobby wasn't so sure, and he hid his ambivalence from his friends as best he could. But the guys had noticed just the same: Whenever they roughed up a Yellow Oldster, Van and Roger would beat the cowardly Pacifist with joyous abandon. But Bobby had come to dislike the violence. He also disapproved of the way boy groups and gangs—like his—specifically targeted Yellow Oldsters.

The Oldsters were Long Lifers who were one hundred and twenty years or older, and most of them looked it—arthritic, bent, suffering from joint and back pain and a variety of other ailments: Often an eye was milky with cataracts, and the hands shook. The anti-aging treatment that the Long Lifers all received kept them relatively healthy and in good shape well past their hundredth birthday. After one hundred and twenty, the cellular regeneration began to misfire and break down, age slowly caught up, and within a decade or two, the Long Lifers gradually became more physically ancient and decrepit—though they could and often did live for many more decades after this delayed aging took place.

The Yellows were Pacifists—cowards all, said Van. You could tell because they were unmarked by burns, scars, knife wounds, bullet holes, or missing body parts. They had accepted a boon from their government—the gift of artificially lengthened life—and in turn, done nothing to pay back for what they had received.

Bobby wasn't so sure. The war had been going on since long before he was born and seemed to have little point other than to make defense manufacturing the largest and most profitable industry on the planet. His parents, both Normal Lifers born before the Lottery of Forever had begun, could not articulate to him exactly why the nations they engaged were enemies. Few adults—Normal Lifers or even Long Lifers—seemed to remember exactly why the war had started. And the ongoing war always needed more weapons—and more soldiers—to fight its battles. The Long Life treatment helped ensure a ready supply of the latter, and the industry built to supply the former kept the nation's economy strong and prosperous.

"Okay, boys," the policeman told Van and Roger, pulling them off the Oldster, who began to blubber a "thank you" before the cop cut him off. "Move along, Old Yellow, before I change my mind and let these lads have their fun," the officer ordered. The old man scurried off on the sidewalk like a crab, glancing back at the policeman with an expression of gratitude mingled with hatred and sorrow.

The officer checked his watch. "Aren't you fellows supposed to be somewhere at noon?" he reminded them. "What District are you from?"

"Five, sir," Van answered briskly. His respect for war veterans, cops, soldiers, and other fighters was as fierce as his disdain for commies, pinkos, and Yellow Oldsters.

"Then your lottery hall is in the H.S. 26 auditorium," the cop said.

Van and Roger nodded; of course they knew and were headed there now, Van informed the cop. "Go on, go on then," said the officer, pointing with his combination night stick and electrified cattle prod in the direction of the school.

As the war lasted for more and more decades and spread across the globe, soldiers had been dying faster than they could be replaced, and the Forever Lottery had been invented as a solution. A technique had been discovered where, through gene splicing and DNA manipulation, telomeres on cells could be made to regenerate almost endlessly, effectively doubling the life span of the person so treated. Every few years, the Secretary of Science held a press conference to notify the public that they were getting closer to an improved Long Life treatment that would bestow additional centuries of life and active combat capability on a man, but, so far, the technology had eluded the finest scientists in both the government and private industry.

Winners of the Forever Lottery received the currently available treatment and became Long Lifers. A Long Lifer could live to be one hundred and seventy or more. In exchange, the Long Lifers were expected—but not required, because of a constitutional loophole—to enlist in the army and fight in the war for a minimum term of three decades, and most of them did. The gene splicing and DNA manipulation that slowed their aging also accelerated their healing, so they were much harder to kill than ordinary soldiers. And they retained the energy, strength, and stamina of youth far longer than Normal Lifers, enabling an individual to provide the armed forces with many extra decades of effective soldiering. Long Lifers gave the Army good material to work with: soldiers with the strength and stamina of teenagers combined with decades of experience and learning.

Occasionally, a Long Lifer would refuse to serve in the armed forces, which was his legal right but frowned upon in society. These pacifist Long Lifers benefitted unfairly from the lottery, living decades longer than Normal Lifers but without facing the risks and dangers of battle; hence the derogatory label "Yellow Oldsters."

"Kids, take your seats," Mr. Hendricks, the principal of Bobby's school and the official Lottery Master said into his microphone. Boys settled into the auditorium chairs and quieted down; Bobby, Van, and Roger sat together.

"We're going to be Long Lifers," Roger said excitedly. "I just know it."

"We'll be indestructible, and we'll live forever," Van agreed.

"Well, *almost* forever," Roger, always the smart aleck, pointed out. Van punched him hard in the arm.

"Ow!" Roger yelped.

"Quiet," Van muttered.

The idea of having a long life appealed to Bobby, as it seemed to do for all the other boys in the large auditorium. But he had never liked fighting, and the war seemed wasteful, pointless, and cruel to him. He'd never told Roger and Van that at times he secretly hoped that he would *lose* the lottery. Losing would mean a much shorter life but also a more peaceful one: Only Long Lifers could serve in the armed forces; Normal Lifers were not accepted. Bobby wished he could share his secret thoughts, but he was afraid of being labeled a coward and a commie.

"This is an important day in your lives," Hendricks said to the boys in the crowded auditorium. "It is a day that determines whether your life will be short or long, and whether it will be spent selfishly in pursuit of your own safety and comfort or gloriously in the defense of our great nation."

Hendricks removed his iNotepad from his pocket, flipped it open, and thumbed the device. He squinted at the screen, pulled off his glasses, and held the screen closer to his face.

"I have excellent news for you all," he said. "We have one hundred and fifty three boys in the junior class"—for reasons not clear to Bobby or any other layperson, the Long Life treatment worked best when administered at age sixteen, give or take a year—"and this year, a record one hundred and fifty treatments have been allotted for our school."

Bobby did not understand why the government held a lottery instead of simply giving the Long Life treatment to every boy in his sixteenth year. He had asked his father about it. His dad had explained that it had to do with precise calculations performed by government statisticians to balance the demand for new soldiers with the even more urgent need for population control—the Earth had nine and a half billion people, and the planet was running out of clean water for all of them to drink. Oil and natural gas were also in short supply.

Principal Hendricks tapped a key on his PDA again. "Let's begin. When I call your name, come up on the stage in an orderly line to receive your winning lottery ticket. Winning juniors will be taken to the treatment center a week from today for the Long Life procedure. Ms. Sherman"—he nodded toward the tall, well-coiffed science teacher sitting behind him on the stage—"will go over the procedure in biology class and give you a sheet of instructions. Okay. Let's begin. Come up to the stage when your name is called."

The names were read by Hendricks clearly and solemnly.

". . . Aaron Babcock . . . Timothy Benson . . . Roger Binder . . ."

"Yessss!" Roger muttered quietly. Van gave him a congratulatory punch on the shoulder. Bobby shook his hand. "Congratulations, Long Lifer," he said to his friend.

"You and Van are next," said Roger reassuringly.

Bobby prayed he would not be called.

The lottery winners continued to be announced.

"Lane Reagan . . . Alex Rogers . . . Bill Sackheim . . . Bobby Schachetti . . ."

"Way to go, Bobby!" Van said, giving Bobby a playful punch on the shoulder, which, given Van's strength and the size of his big fist and hard knuckles, hurt. Roger held out a palm for a high-five. Bobby complied, though he felt not disappointed, but to his surprise, ambivalent.

And the roll call continued.

"Norm Thomas . . . Mark Tumbusch . . . Frank Unger . . ."

The boys sat stunned.

Van Underwood had not been called.

Van looked like a deer caught in the headlights. He turned to their physical education instructor, Mr. Lederman, who was standing in the aisle near them with his arms folded, and tried to get the gym teacher's attention. Lederman turned his head and stared at Van, and then turned his attention back to the stage and ignored him.

Van turned to his friends; he seemed dazed and confused. "Did they call my name?" he asked Bobby and Roger. "Did I miss it?"

Roger seemed to pull back from Van, as if to put distance between himself, a soon-to-be Long Lifer, and Van, a mere Normal Lifer who would never fight for his country or live past the age of a hundred.

"Bobby?" Van asked pleadingly. But Bobby was lost in thought: *I'm going to live for almost two hundred years,* he thought in wonder. *And maybe the army is just what I need to toughen up. I'll be strong, fast, a trained soldier, and respected my whole life. Kid gangs will carry my bags when I'm an Honored Oldster walking down the street!* He glanced over at Van, who seemed shaken and on the verge of tears. *Tougher than Van, maybe.* His mind wandered, and he thought about the journey he and Roger would take for well over a hundred years into a future together, and that Van—poor Normal Life Van—would not!

Van, meanwhile, sat there, numb with shock and disappointment. He knew that Bobby and Roger would begin soldier conditioning and combat training when school let out in June, and after that and the treatment, they would almost surely be able to kick his ass at will. He, with his size and strength, had always dominated the boys in his grade physically and, with Bobby and Roger, had been the leader of the pack. How humiliating it would be to have Roger, that geek, and Bobby, that wimp, become much better fighters than himself; the army had developed fighting techniques that his friends would master and now he never would. And Bobby and Roger would gain a whole group of new comrades, the guys in their student platoon, from which Van, as a Normal Lifer, would be forever excluded and looked down upon. Despite his best effort to avoid it, Van's eyes began to tear up.

Van thought, somewhat morosely, that now he'd have to find some new friends to hang with. But as nearly everyone in the class took the journey to Long Life together, who would be left? Just two other rejects and him?

A brief image of himself as an old man being pummeled by a group of young Long Lifer toughs flashed into his mind, and he winced at the memory of the beating he had given the Yellow Oldster early that day.

Thousands of miles away, in countries whose names Van, Roger, and Bobby could barely remember, the war raged on.

The Techno-God's Daughter

If Mark Conroy's lack of self-esteem could have manifested itself as a solid, physical object, it would have been large enough—and dense enough—to generate the gravitational pull of a neutron star.

He'd been taught in high school history class that all men are created equal, but no amount of therapy or anti-depressants could convince him that this notion was anything but hooey. He looked around at the other students in the cafeteria as he moved down the line to order a tuna sandwich. They might be equal, but he was anything but.

In a loving but unsuccessful attempt to make him more than he was, his father had bought him some weights and an exercise manual when he was in the eighth grade. When his parents were at work, he put on his gym clothes and followed the exercise routines. Alone in his room, looking at his reflection in the full-length mirror on his open bathroom door, he began to believe that the exercise was working. As he pumped the weights, the muscles moved under his skin, and he felt that Laurel Sorbone—a girl in his class on whom he had a crush based on both lust and personal attraction—might feel physically attracted to him if she saw him play "skins" during gym basketball or swim at the town pool.

But when he undressed for gym class the next day, he instantly knew it was an absurd fantasy and that he was an idiot for believing it. He didn't look like the other guys. They were muscled, tall, and slim, young gods waiting to take their place on Olympus. He was short and round-shouldered, with a big rear and a soft middle unmarked by the ab lines most of the jocks flaunted as a symbol of their prowess. Quick peeks revealed that in addition to his other physical faults, he was not what Laurel and her friends would have called "well endowed" either, as Brad, Pete, and many of the other guys in his class clearly were. They were normal, while he was a freak or, in high school parlance, a "geek," a "nerd." Ashamed of his body, he undressed and dressed in gym class quickly that day, skipping the optional shower.

What made him sadder still was that while he possessed a nerd's physical attributes in the extreme, he didn't have the nerd advantages. He was reasonably intelligent and, through long hours of study mostly concealed from his peers, his grades put him near the top of his class. But he knew he lacked the truly formidable intelligence of Sam Berg, Nicholas Benvinuto, or some of the other recognized brains in his class.

Technology especially was a problem. Mark was above average in math and especially good at English, and his cartoons and columns in the school newspaper had brought him a small degree of acceptance and even notoriety among his classmates. But he was not mechanically inclined, and his aversion to machines carried over to computers.

Nerds have long been associated with electronics, science, and technology. In Mark's senior year, the rising popularity of notebook computing, the Internet, smartphones, tablets, and related technologies was bringing nerds more into the mainstream. Mark was trapped between worlds: too geeky for the mainstream, but not wired enough for the geeks.

One Friday, after weeks of building his confidence, Mark worked up enough courage to ask Laurel Sorbone to the movies that weekend. To his amazement, she accepted.

During the movie, she allowed him to kiss her several times. Each time, her tongue darted briefly to his lips, teeth, and tongue, causing him to become dizzy. When he put his arm around her, the fingertips of his left hand touched the top swell of her breasts; rather than move the hand away, she took it and placed his hand more firmly on her, so it was cupping the warm, sensual skin. His groin ached and for a frantic second he thought he would come in his pants. (His mental technique for avoiding premature ejaculation was to rerun episodes of *Gilligan's Island* in his head, and it was, as far as he had seen, 100 percent effective.)

When they went back to her house, she invited him in, and he was disappointed to find both her parents were at home, sitting in the living room watching TV. "Mom, we're going to my room," Laurel called out brightly. "Fine," said her mother, not taking her eyes from the screen.

Her room had an old shag rug and was sloppier than he would have expected. She kicked off her shoes and stood sexy and barefoot on the soft blue carpeting. He kept his shoes on; his toes were oddly shaped and the big toenails were slightly yellow from fungus. In addition, he had a foot odor problem he did not want her to discover, which is why he would never go with his parents to their favorite Japanese restaurant, which required removal of shoes and sitting cross-legged on the floor.

Laurel sat on the bed, patting the blanket next to her. "Sit," she said. He did. She was cross-legged; he admired the graceful arch of her slim, pale foot. He sat with his legs dangling over the edge so his sneakers wouldn't dirty the blanket or sheets.

She reached behind him, and he started to move toward her, interpreting her actions as a come-on. But she immediately pulled back, with a pad and pencil in hand; she had been reaching over to her desk, not putting a move on him.

"I couldn't get my program for Computer Lab to run today," she told him. "Do you think you could help me with it?"

He began to perspire slightly; he could smell faint body odor coming from his armpits. He looked at the printouts of her code, but he was as bad at programming as he was at mechanical things. Java was a foreign language to him.

As he studied the code, he sensed she was observing him ever more critically. She got up, left the room, and came back with two Diet Cokes. She handed him one of the cans and popped the tab on the other. She sipped as she watched him; his Coke sat untouched.

Finally, after long minutes of doing nothing, he made some corrections to a few of the lines and wrote in a small subroutine that he knew would perform one of the calculations she needed but did not really solve the inherent non-functionality of the main program.

As he wrote, she moved closer, sat next to him, looked over his shoulder. He could smell her girl smell, especially her shampooed hair, and again he felt dizzy. He wanted to continue, but he was stumped: He didn't know how to fix the program, and he hoped she wouldn't pick up on that, and that somehow, on Monday, when she ran it in the Computer Lab, it would miraculously perform its task despite his ineptness.

When she looked at what he had done, her disappointment was palpable, like the mood of fathers whose sons struck out at Little League games. However, he could tell that, while she didn't think he had corrected the code properly, she wasn't positive he hadn't. They made out for a few minutes on the bed, just kissing, nothing heavy; he became excited to near-climax again (thank the Lord for Gilligan), but Laurel now seemed less eager and almost passive. Then she pulled away, smiled, said "We'd better stop. My parents are still in the living room." It was a kind smile, not passionate but affectionate. It sent his heart soaring. But days later, both he and Laurel received a C on their Computer Lab project, and although he asked her out a few more times, she always said she was busy that weekend, and he got the message well enough. He didn't ask her or anyone else to the prom, and, in fact, he didn't go out with a girl the rest of the year.

In college, he continued to gravitate toward the written word and away from programming. He became the features editor of the campus daily paper and editor-in-chief of the campus literary magazine, for which he wrote sad stories about lonely guys who could not get laid.

Upon graduation, he got a job as a technical writer for GlobeTech, a large manufacturer of industrial control systems. He worked for George Coopersmith, a highly regarded scientist with the company, whose specialty was logic chips; the other scientists referred to Dr. Coopersmith as the "techno-god" for his superior ability to solve technical problems.

One Friday morning, Coopersmith called Conroy into his office. "Mark, are you doing anything this Saturday night?" he asked abruptly.

This caught Mark completely off guard. "What do you mean?" he asked.

Coopersmith reached for and picked up a picture frame on his desk, and turned it toward Mark. It showed Dr. Coopersmith with two women, one Coopersmith's age and one who looked to be in her twenties, about Mark's age.

"My daughter Betty," Coopersmith explained.

Mark studied the photograph. Betty Coopersmith was the kind of girl that no one lusted over and who probably didn't have a lot of dates in high school. She wasn't ugly or fat, but she was plain and overweight, with thick glasses and a bad fashion sense.

"We're having a family wedding—my brother's son," Coopersmith explained. "Betty doesn't want to go solo at the wedding, but she's painfully shy." There was pleading in Coopersmith's voice that fueled Mark's ego at the same time that it made him uncomfortable.

Mark interrupted so that Dr. Coopersmith didn't have to ask. "If she doesn't have a date for the wedding, I'd be delighted to take her," he said boldly.

"Thanks. I'll e-mail you the details," said Coopersmith, dismissing Mark, glad the uncomfortable ordeal was over.

Who can say from what love springs? Mark expected to get through the wedding. But he was immediately attracted to Betty, and she to him. Not because of looks—neither was a Calvin Klein model—but because of compatible personalities and interests. Both liked the Muenster's and chemistry and collies; both hated egg salad, traffic, and noise.

They were married a year later and had the reception at the same catering hall as Betty's cousin. Dr. Coopersmith was pleased and proud to have a son-in-law who treated his precious baby girl so well.

Ironically, Coopersmith had retired from GlobeTech a few months before the wedding. And, of course, marrying Betty gave Mark no currency with Dr. Coopersmith's replacement. But that thought never even entered Mark's mind. Neither did memories of Laurel Sorbone. Mark had a feeling that his love for Betty, and hers for him, would only grow deeper over time.

He made a decent salary, even if he never rose higher on the corporate ladder than senior technical writer. That was all right with him; between his salary and Betty's, they got along nicely.

A few years after the wedding, Mark wrote and published a guide to technical writing that sold surprisingly well and stayed in print for decades. He dedicated the book to Betty and her father. The dedication read:

To George Coopersmith—who gave me the greatest gift I could ever receive.

And to Betty Conroy—who saved my life.

26 Weeks

I was in the unemployment office to collect my first check when I met G. for the first time. He, like me and almost everyone else in the room, was there to collect unemployment. So it was only natural that we struck up a conversation.

"This your first time on the bread line?" G., a big man with a resonant, deep voice, asked me amiably enough. Despite his size, there was nothing the least bit threatening about G., and I felt instantly comfortable talking to him. That was unusual, because I almost never am comfortable with strangers.

"First time," I told him glumly. I felt ashamed admitting it out loud. Even though one in ten Americans was unemployed at the time, I didn't like being one of them. And I live in an expensive area: Being unemployed in Bergen County, New Jersey is like being trapped in Tiffany's with a credit card that has expired.

"No need to feel ashamed," said G., as if reading my mind. He smiled a big, warm smile, and suddenly I felt more at ease. The line moved, and we took another couple of steps toward the clerk at the counter, whose boredom seemed to verge on contempt.

"I'm not ashamed," I said rather too quickly. If I admitted feeling it to him, it would mean that I had something to be ashamed *about*. And by logical extension, so would everyone else in the room. I didn't want to imply that *he* should feel shame in any way for losing his job; I had only known him for a couple of minutes, but I liked him already.

"Good," said G. amiably. "After all, you're not responsible for the economy."

"Yeah, that would be Bernanke and Obama," I said. Even though my father told me never to discuss religion and politics, I enjoy political discussion and my attitude can become heated rather quickly.

I took the position of not being a fan of the new administration and was quick to let other people know it. Despite losing my job as a salesman of electronic components—our company had laid off half the sales force—I believe in the capitalist way of life and see Barack Obama as a neo-socialist.

In particular, I don't like his economic policy. Recently, Bloomberg Media calculated that U.S. government takeover of the private sector—through loans, guarantees, and other commitments—has already added nearly thirteen trillion dollars to the national debt. That means Obama's federal bailouts equal more than ninety percent of America's annual gross domestic income. To put that into perspective, deficits produced by the federal bailouts now have a claim to more than ninety cents out of every dollar you earn.

When I made this argument to G., he seemed nonplussed.

"I don't think the mess we are in is really Obama's fault," G. replied. "To me, it looks like the guy before him takes a lot of the blame." G. shook his head. "George W.—he seemed smart enough—Yale graduate, good family—but maybe we should have elected someone with a better-than-C average." He shook his head. "I don't know where I went wrong with that boy," he added, a comment that, at the time, made little sense to me, but I later came to understand it with alarming clarity.

"But you're OK, kid," G. said. "What's your name?"

"Kevin," I replied, offering my hand.

He took it firmly and shook. My hand is average size, not dainty, but it was swallowed by his meaty paw.

"Nice to meet you, Kevin," he said. "I'm . . ." And then he hesitated, as if he could not remember his own name or hadn't been expecting to reveal it—an odd posture to assume, given we were both there to collect unemployment insurance, and the government checks had to be made out in one's name. Then he regained his bearing. "Just call me G.," he told me. "Easy to remember and easy to spell."

G. smiled and I chuckled. The line moved up again. We were next in line after the small, silver-haired woman in front of us.

She was dressed nicer than Donald Trump's latest wife, and what she had surely paid for her ensemble—dress, shoes, purse—could have covered my monthly rent, which in Bergen County is no small feat. She folded her check in half vertically, opened the clasp on her designer bag—I am not up enough on fashion to tell you what brand it was, only that it looked expensive—and slipped it inside. She clicked the purse shut, turned smartly on her heels, and walked with brisk dignity away from the counter.

We moved up then, and G. was standing at the window.

"Rich bitch on the government gravy train," the clerk muttered conspiratorially.

"What did you say?" G. asked sharply.

She rolled her eyes. "Name?" she asked.

"No," he said in the voice of a man in a position of control and authority, which, in an unemployment office, was an achievement. "What did you just say?"

"Let it go, dude," I murmured.

He held up his big right hand, signaling me to let him continue.

"You heard what I said, so why ask me?" said the clerk in a tone that indicated her patience, already stretched to the limit by having to tolerate a cushy government job all day, was about to snap.

"Because if you have something to say that you want me to hear, you should have the manners to look me in the eye and say it loudly and clearly," G. told her. This rubbed the clerk, whose desk plate read YOWANDA JONES, the wrong way.

"You are not the boss of *me*," she told G. "You are a recipient of charity. You are getting a free ride on the gravy train, and if I was you, I'd be grateful for it, 'stead of whining and complaining." She lifted her shoulders. "Lord, I wish someone would give *me* a paycheck for standin' around complaining instead of actually getting up in the morning and coming to work and doing my job." She was looking G. straight in the eye.

"We don't *want* to be out of work, Ms. Jones," G. said, his voice rising, though oddly, he was not shouting. He just had one of those big voices that could really project.

"Cool down, G.," I told him quietly.

Behind Yowanda stood a swinging door with a round glass window, the kind they have in restaurant kitchens. Faces of unemployment agency employees were pressed against the glass from the other side, and Yowanda seemed aware that she had attracted an audience of her coworkers, as well as the other claimants on my side of her counter. I felt uncomfortable and wanted to get out of there, but I needed my check.

"Ridin' the ole gravy train," she said to G. again. "That's all you doin'— man on the dole, ridin' the government gravy train."

"Gravy train . . . gravy train . . . gravy train," said G. in a voice that suddenly reminded me of a cross between Charlton Heston and James

Earl Jones. It cut across the room, and the background chatter ended. At that second, the overhead fluorescent lights dimmed noticeably. Yowanda looked up at him, not quite sure who was in charge any more.

Behind her, the faces against the glass had disappeared, and the window began to glow with an odd red light. I swear the employee room behind those doors had filled with fog.

"You want your gravy train, Yowanda?" G. boomed. "Well, get ready—because *here it comes!*"

That instant the door burst open, slammed against the wall, and a flood of brown liquid poured through it like a river bursting through its levees.

But the liquid wasn't muddy water. It was gravy! The odor was unmistakable.

People screamed as the river rushed through the room. I screamed, too. The gravy surrounded us and began to rise rapidly past our knees, until I realized it wasn't scalding or even hot—just lukewarm. G. smiled, grabbed me by my bicep, and said, "Come on, Kevin. Let's get out of here. We can come back after they clean up the mess."

Too stunned to object, I followed him out. He steered me across the street to a coffee shop. "Good idea, G.," I said. "We can clean up in the bathroom."

"Clean up what, Kev?"

"The gravy from our pants."

G. opened the coffee shop door for me. "What gravy on our pants?"

Only then did I realize that my pants didn't feel wet, and when I looked down, I saw they were dry and unstained.

We took our seats. A waitress rushed over with menus. My experience of waitresses in cheap coffee shops is that they are generally harried and discontented—both with the job and their lot in life in general—but *Helene*, as her name tag told us, seemed positively glowing with joy. "What can I get you, sir?" she asked, practically falling over G. and ignoring me completely.

"Couple of lemon Cokes, two sliced steak sandwiches, fries, with gravy all over the fries," G. replied. I was about to tell him I could order my own lunch when I realized he had ordered precisely what I had been craving all morning.

"G., something strange is going on." I said. The waitress put two large Cokes, with ice and lemon, in front of us. I took a sip. Colas are not consistently mixed and can vary widely in quality depending on the location where they are served. This was the tastiest, sweetest, most refreshing Coke I had ever sipped. When I put my glass down, Helene was there again, sliding two steaming platters onto the table. On each was a beautiful-looking sandwich piled high with moist savory meat, the scent of which made my mouth water.

But I didn't pick it up, hungry as I was, although G. was piling into his. "What the hell is going on?" I asked him.

"Don't swear."

"Sorry. I didn't know you were so touchy. Religious?"

"No, Kevin. Not too many are these days."

"Okay. So why the no swear rule?"

"Because it offends God," he said, taking a sip of Coke.

"And you don't like that because you're religious?"

He dipped a fry in ketchup. "No, Kevin—I don't like it because I'm God."

"Come again?"

"I'm not surprised that you'd doubt me. But that's what the 'G' stands for. I'm God."

"Gee," I said sarcastically, but not too sarcastically, because Helene was standing next to the cash register giving me a dirty look. "You'll forgive me if I am skeptical."

"Of course, Kevin," G. said. "I am a forgiving God." Helene came by with a fresh Coke for him and ignored me, though my glass was empty, too. "Didn't the miracle of the River of Gravy convince you?"

"It wasn't gravy," I said in an unconvincing voice. "It probably was a burst pipe, and the water was muddy from being agitated. That's no miracle. It's more like an accident of aging infrastructure."

"Then why are our pants dry?"

I didn't have an answer for that, and said so. "But dry pants don't make you God. I need more proof than *that*."

"Then you shall have it, my son," G. said, and he snapped his fingers.

Suddenly we were no longer in the coffee shop.

G. and I were floating in outer space, looking down on Earth from somewhere to the left of the moon.

Snap!

We were on Earth, in prehistoric times. I screamed when I saw a tyrannosaurus behind us, until the giant reptile lowered its head to let G. reach up and scratch it under the chin. I could have sworn it was purring.

Snap!

We were in a little boy's bedroom, though he could not see us. His shirt was torn, his face was bruised, and he was crying, and somehow I knew he was the young Adolf Hitler.

Snap!

We were in the Sistine Chapel, and on a scaffold above us Michelangelo was painting the ceiling, though somehow it looked wrong. "Mix in more cerulean blue!" G. shouted to the artist, who did so and dabbed at the ceiling. "Much better," G. said to M., who gave him a grateful wave in return.

"Enough, G.!" I cried out. "I believe it. You're God. I believe. I believe!"

Snap!

We were back in the coffee shop. "Do you want coffee and pie?" G. asked me. I nodded dumbly. Helene appeared tableside again unbidden, carrying two pie plates with slices of hot apple pie with vanilla ice cream on top. Both slices were huge, but G.'s was bigger, and he had more ice cream, plus a small wedge of cheddar on the side. She put down the plates, went to fetch coffee, and brought us two cups that she plopped down in front of us, along with a creamer filled with heavy cream.

G. broke the silence. "You obviously have questions for me, so ask away. But lunch will be over soon, so start with the important ones, and then I have something I want to tell you."

I added a bit of cream and sipped from my cup of coffee, the best I had ever been served.

"If you are God," I said, controlling the slowly rising tinges of anger I felt, "then how could you allow it? How could you allow all those thousands of families and children to die and let Disney World be nuked?"

"Because I'm not an all-powerful God," G. said. "That's a rumor that the Bible writers started. But it's wrong. I am not omnipotent."

"Are you all-knowing?" I asked.

"Not even close," he said. "Though I'm pretty sure that the Yankees will be in the pennant race this year," he added, grinning.

"They are almost every year," I pointed out.

"That's why I'm so sure," said G., smiling.

"If you're not all-powerful and all-knowing, then what good are you?" I asked him.

"Other than buying you lunch and keeping your pants clean?" he replied. "I often ask myself the same question."

"G.," I said. "God. What are you?"

He dabbed at the corner of his mouth with his napkin.

"I am of a race different from yours," he said. "We are not omnipotent or omniscient, but as you saw when I took you through time and space, we are powerful beyond measure when compared to the other races of all the universes, including yours.

"We are born as beings of pure energy and take eons to mature. When we reach puberty, we enter a hibernation period, during which we dream. Our dreams are incredibly vivid and detailed, and they seem to us to go on for an eternity." Helene approached with the coffee pot but G. shook his head. She seemed disappointed she could not serve him and went away, not even asking if I wanted a refill of my empty cup, which I had been holding out to her in vain.

"When I awoke from my dream, the world I had dreamed of was this one, which I had created by my dreaming it. It is the same with all those of my race. We dream in a long sleep. The dream creates a universe, and when we awaken, we are *in* that universe, along with the star systems and the living beings of our own creation, which for me include all the inhabitants of this city—and you."

"Let me get this straight," I said. "You created the universe, yet you are not a supreme being."

"The act of creating the universe drains our energy," said G. "We can no longer continue our existence as pure energy, so we assume a physical form in the worlds we create, though we can still manipulate matter and energy to a considerable degree. However, the act of creating a universe exponentially diminishes our energy, and from the moment of our rebirth in the universe of our own creation, our energy continues to diminish geometrically as we age."

"Then what happens?" I asked, transfixed. Even if his story was bullshit, it was fascinating bullshit. "Does your energy run out? Are you immortal?"

"Long-lived yes. Immortal, no. And we depend on you to sustain us."

"What do you mean?"

Helene had left a check that I did not see until G. picked it up. He took out his wallet and counted out bills carefully. "Have to watch the pennies until we go back and cash our unemployment checks," he said with gentle good humor.

He replaced his wallet, pulled his plate closer, and attacked his half-eaten piece of pie, which miraculously seemed to be covered with a fresh scoop of vanilla ice cream, though Helene was nowhere in sight.

"The religious faith in my kind displayed by the biological beings we create in our universes feeds some of the energy of creation back to us, sustaining us after the enormous energy loss that creation entails," said G. "We are, in fact, as dependent on the energy of your worship to sustain us as you are on your gods to sustain you."

"What do you mean, G.?"

"Religion is a catch-22," he said wryly. "The worship of men, the energy of its faith, keeps my kind alive after the maturation and rebirth stages. From there, we live as long as the energy of worship stays above a critical mass, which this world, with its faith so weakened and atheism so rampant, is currently in danger of sinking below."

"Is that bad for you, G.?" I asked.

"Yes, and it's bad for you, too, Kevin. You see, it's a closed-loop system. Your faith sustains me, and my existence sustains the universe you live in."

"You mean . . . ?"

"Yes. When we die—when the God who created your universe is dead—that universe ceases to exist, too."

We were silent for a minute.

"But G.," I said. "You look pretty healthy. I mean, there are still plenty of faithful out there to keep you well and full of vigor, right?"

He shook his head. "Kevin, my friend, my time is nearly over. The tragedies of our dark days, which lie beyond my direct control, have caused atheism to win out. Very few genuinely believe anymore. You do, despite the fact that you don't go to church as often as you could."

I started to mutter an apology but he held up his hand. "Keep going to church," he told me. "The number of people still faithful is astonishingly small. We are nearly below the critical mass of faith needed to sustain me."

He put his big hand on my wrist and squeezed affectionately. "And that would be a shame, kid. I like you too much."

I swallowed, wishing for more coffee or a glass of water, but Helene seemed to have left the building.

"May I ask another question, G.?"

"Ask away, Kevin, my son."

"Will I get another job soon?"

G. sighed. "Neither of us will, and your unemployment insurance will run out in twenty-six weeks, as will mine. You won't be able to pay your rent, and you'll lose your apartment. I hope," G. added, almost apologetically, "that this doesn't cause you to lose faith in me. But I am pretty sure it will."

I'll keep the faith, I thought, wondering if G. could read my mind. But he showed no sign of doing so.

"G., why does God need a job?"

"The universe I dreamed requires money, and not being omnipotent, I can't very well manufacture it out of thin air," G. said. "At least not legally," he added with a wink.

"What did you do before you got fired?"

"I was a Certified Public Accountant," replied G.

"You're kidding," I said. "God, a CPA?"

"What's wrong with that, Kevin? Everybody's gotta make a living."

He checked his watch. "I've got to get going now, Kevin. It was nice having lunch like this. Maybe we can do it again. Now, sleep." He reached forward suddenly and touched my forehead with his index finger.

The next thing I knew, I was waking up in my bed. I had a few pieces of paper tucked into my shirt pocket. When I removed them, I saw that it was my unemployment check, along with five hundred-dollar bills.

Sure enough, it was as G. had said. After a good night's sleep, I concluded that someone had slipped me some Ecstasy somewhere, and that the whole thing with G. had been a bad delayed-reaction trip.

I hoped to run into G. at the unemployment office, but I never saw him again, which reinforced my conclusion that the whole thing had been a drug fueled hallucination.

My unemployment insurance ran out in six months, and I couldn't get an extension. I was out of money, and my landlord wanted the rent, so I came home one night to find my stuff on the sidewalk and a new lock on the apartment door.

I took up residence on the street and, when I could get in, I slept at the homeless shelter. Being homeless made me bitter. I stopped going to church at all, and couldn't help remembering it was just what G. had said would happen, except you don't have to be God to know that unemployment insurance stops after half a year.

What really shook me was what I read in the paper this morning: A terrorist group had planted a bomb in the Javitz Center, where they were holding a convention of ordained ministers, and over a thousand people, including some five hundred clergymen, were killed.

That's a lot of true believers to lose in a single day, and I recalled what G. had said about the critical mass of faith.

If he was telling the truth, the critical mass of faith was what sustained him. And if the death of five hundred priests caused that mass to shrink too far, G. would lose the energy that he needed to continue his existence.

I put the newspaper down on the bench. If G. lost the energy of faith, he would, according to his story, cease to exist. And if he was right, our world wouldn't exist once he was gone.

But that simply couldn't be true.

It just simply co . . .

The Case of the Monkey's Mask

It was a deadly dull beginning-of-the-fall-semester departmental party—so archaic that Wentworth found himself actually holding a glass of sherry—sherry, for God's sake!—while trapped in a conversation with his new boss, Kensington, his newfound rival, Demarest, and two more professors engaged in heated debate with one another. I noticed that though Wentworth tried in vain to concentrate on the discussion—some academic dispute about tribal rituals between two professors who had never spent more than a couple of weeks on the Dark Continent, staying in the comfortable white hotel instead of with the natives, as Wentworth always did for months at a time—his attention wandered to the mask on the wall of the faculty lounge, unprotected by a glass or frame and oddly without a descriptive placard.

It was rough-hewn out of a blond wood reminiscent in shade of an orangutan's fur, which may have explained why the artist had chosen to carve the mask into an orangutan's face. The artist had either never heard of sandpaper or preferred a rougher look. The surface was uneven, the edges of the mask, especially along the chin at the bottom, so ragged it was almost as if they had teeth; whenever faculty members handled it, they were well advised to wear gloves or risk splinters.

"Surprised you don't recognize it," drawled Demarest. Wentworth groaned. I remained neutral; being untenured, I thought it best to keep a low profile, though I could not help voicing the opinion at some point during the evening that I found the mask a hypnotically powerful piece of native Africana. It is true that I have never been to Africa; my area of specialization is Haiti.

From the moment of his arrival on campus, Wentworth was an odd man out in the anthropology department: the only non-PhD and non-scholar—I'm not sure he even had a master's degree—he wrote bestselling books for lay readers on his adventures living with primitive tribes instead of living the cloistered life of a college professor, producing the deadly dull scholarly papers his departmental colleagues wrote for obscure peer-reviewed journals, which were read by perhaps a few hundred specialists in the field.

Had Wentworth been humble and appropriately academic in demeanor, I believe he would have passed his year as a writer-in-residence in the archaeology department without incident. But he clearly took pride in being a "real-world" (though under-credentialed) anthropologist in a group he referred to in private as "bubble-headed, ivory-tower academics." I wondered why, if he thought so little of us, he had chosen to join us for a year. I later discovered it was a combination of writer's block (from which he hoped his year in academia would offer some relief) and the desire to bed young women (an ample selection of which his classes, and other campus activities, would provide).

While the archaeology faculty was at best indifferent to Wentworth and at worst hostile, the students loved him. The young men wanted to be adventurers and bestselling authors like Wentworth. The women found him magnetically charming; they even saw his scar—an angry red vertical line traveling up and down nearly the length of his right cheek—as vaguely heroic. Wentworth told the story in his lectures of how he got the scar from the pointed end of an angry tribesman's spear during an encounter, the cause being a communication breakdown between Wentworth and the tribesman's wife. Behind Wentworth's back, but never to his face, Demarest got cheap laughs saying the encounter had likely been a gardening accident, the spear in reality a pair of gardening shears.

I liked Wentworth, though he was rather aloof from the rest of the department and I never got to talk with him much. But I enjoyed his books, and when I told him so earlier in the evening, he had brightened and seemed genuinely appreciative.

"It looks like Maurice Evans in *Planet of the Apes*," Wentworth said of the wooden monkey mask, attempting to use humor to deflect the gauntlet of academic challenge Demarest had thrown down. It *did* look more like Dr. Zaius from the *Apes* movie than an actual orangutan. It had Zaius's dour frown, an expression that seemed a cross between actor Maurice Evans's intense concentration and a look of extreme annoyance and displeasure.

Demarest snorted. "I'd think, for someone who has spent so much time among the Nuna, you'd recognize a Nuna monkey spirit mask," he said haughtily. In addition to his teaching and research duties, Demarest was in his rotation as assistant curator of the anthropology department's small museum—the "assistant curator" duty being assigned to successive members of the department. The museum also had a full-time curator who managed all the university's collections and displays. Demarest had procured the Nuna mask at a price that had given Kensington, the department head, more than one sleepless night and a chewing out from the Dean, Dr. Gerald Martin, whom students and faculty alike called "Dean Martin"—out of earshot, needless to say.

Wentworth, however, was intent on not being bested by Demarest, especially in front of other department members and their guests at what passed for a soiree in academia.

"I'm afraid whoever sold you this mask and told you it is a Nuna gave you bad advice," Wentworth said, pleased that Demarest's face instantly reddened.

"I obtained it from a reputable dealer, and it is completely authentic, I can assure you," Demarest said in a voice that suddenly seemed a bit less self-assured, as he added: "It came with a certificate of authenticity; I have it in my office."

"Well, I'm sure it did, but I'm afraid it's not, old sport," Wentworth said, as he casually sipped his sherry.

"Are you saying it's a fake?" asked Kensington, looking considerably less happy than he had just minutes earlier.

"I'm afraid the Nuna never carved spirit masks that looked like orangutans or any other monkey for that matter," said Wentworth, enjoying himself immensely. He pulled out his phone, pressed a few keys, recalled an image to the screen, and held it out for everyone to see.

"Are you that ignorant?" Demarest exploded. "Any of our Anthro 101 students knows the Nuna carved masks of all *kinds* of animals—including monkeys."

"I didn't say the Nuna don't carve animal masks," Wentworth replied. "They do. What they *don't* do is carve animal spirit masks in such a starkly realistic style. Here. Let me show you."

The picture on the screen showed a carved mask of smooth dark wood with the general facial characteristics of a baboon but greatly exaggerated in length, as if it were made of wax held near a fireplace. The eye sockets were upside down triangles. Unlike the orangutan mask, which had a rough surface, this mask was smooth, dark, and highly polished.

"It's polished with kola nut oil," said Wentworth, winking at me as if reading my mind. "Smells a bit like a Coke. But genuine Nuna masks are abstract and highly stylized. This one," he said, nodding at the orangutan mask on the wall, "looks like it was made strictly for the tourist trade.

The Nuna make their masks to invoke the spirit of powerful animals—monkeys, buffalo, hawk, crocodiles—not as literal representations."

The graduate students hung on Wentworth's every word, which further infuriated Demarest, who stormed off on a pretense of going to his office to fetch the certificate of authenticity; he did not return to the party.

The next few months passed without incident on our bucolic campus, but there was increasing tension in the anthropology department. Things came to a head at another one of those usually interminable academic functions, a departmental mixer for undergraduate and graduate students in anthropology, archaeology, and sociology—three subjects jokingly referred to in the physics and chemistry departments as "the softest sciences—next to psychology."

Demarest, I'm afraid, had consumed too much sherry that night. Wentworth was eyeing a gaggle of admiring coeds—one could practically see him mentally selecting his sexual conquest for the evening. Sleeping with students was taboo for faculty, but as a writer in residence and temporary member of our campus, Wentworth considered our regulations petty and not applicable to himself. Anyway, something Wentworth said once again invited dispute from Demarest. To make a long story short, Demarest, despite being the more scholarly, was also the less articulate, and he once again came up short in an anthropological debate with his more flamboyant, dashing, and expressive rival.

I'm not sure how, but the dispute escalated into insults and name-calling: Demarest called Wentworth a glorified Indiana Jones, though Harrison Ford's character is an archaeologist, not an anthropologist. Wentworth challenged Demarest to spend a year in the African forest with him, expressed doubt he could last the weekend, and I believe called him a pansy. Tempers flared until finally Demarest, already tanked on sherry, took a swing at Wentworth, who for this function had switched to the keg beer the students favored, which he consumed in copious amounts, seemingly without effect.

Demarest was not a small fellow, but he was one of those many adult males who mistake fat and bulk for strength, and he was out of shape. When Demarest missed with his clumsy roundhouse, he already looked spent, staring glassy-eyed at Wentworth with an expression combining surprise and regret. One expected his next move to be the extension of his hand in apology. But he never got the chance.

I think Wentworth saw that Demarest was no serious threat and that the chubby scholar was instantly sorry for his boorish behavior. But I believe it was here that Wentworth let animosity get the better of him. When Demarest lunged at him, Wentworth had stepped back out of reach and raised his hands in a defensive boxing stance. He smiled, and his right fist shot forward—landing a sharp jab that met Demarest squarely on the chin, snapped his head back, and put him on his ass.

Colleagues, confused over whose side to take or what to do, pulled Wentworth away (the writer smiled smugly and offered only token resistance), while helping Demarest to his feet. In seconds, Demarest's head seemed to clear. He looked at Wentworth, who was grinning at him. Demarest frowned and stomped out of the room. Wentworth snickered, and his grin grew even wider and less kind, as if hurting Demarest psychically and physically had brought him great pleasure.

The next day Bambi Klein, the undergraduate Wentworth had taken back to his apartment, awoke in the man's bed and promptly screamed: The sheets were wet with blood. She checked herself first, and relieved to find the blood was not hers, screamed again when she saw that Wentworth was dead. His throat had been slashed with a jagged instrument, leaving a gaping, ragged wound that had bled profusely. Next to him in the bed was the wooden monkey spirit mask, the bottom edge of it soaked, as laboratory tests later showed, with Wentworth's blood.

The rest of the story you know if you've read the campus or local papers: Demarest went to trial for Wentworth's murder. His fingerprints were all over the mask, but so were those of several other university employees', including the curator's and Kensington's. Demarest maintained his innocence. His attorney was the best money could buy—Axel Anderson from the university law school. And Anderson earned every penny of his fee, as the jury returned a "not guilty" verdict on all counts. The dean restored Demarest to his position, and the "Case of the Wooden Monkey," as it had come to be known around campus and in town, soon faded from the limelight.

Only . . .

I suffer from insomnia and live in faculty housing on the north edge of campus. When I can't sleep, I often stroll the short distance to my office in the anthropology building to do my research and writing or prepare my PowerPoint lectures.

Last night, I could not sleep, and on the way to my office, I detoured into the museum—once you're in the anthro building, the museum is an open hallway, not under any additional lock and key. Call it instinct, but I was drawn to look at the mask again.

Of course, being an alleged murder weapon, it generated quite a bit of curiosity, but I truthfully can't say the whole messy incident wasn't in some way good for the anthropology department; certainly, enrollment in anthropology as a major was way up that year. As for the mask, it would still be buried in a police evidence locker room had not Dean Martin exerted the university's considerable influence to have it returned to the museum.

I stared at the mask. There was the chipped and ragged edge at the bottom along the monkey's jaw, the dark spots where the blood had stained the wood.

But then I noticed it—and could not understand why no one else had. I never pointed it out to anyone else; I feared ridicule, and I was up for tenure. However, the Dr. Zaius-like scowl on the mask was gone, and, in its place, the monkey—I could have sworn—was wearing an evil, self-satisfied grin.

That judgment perhaps was subjective and debatable. But beyond question was *the deep vertical gash in the wood of the monkey's right cheek.* Yes, the mask is still kept on the wall without a glass cover, and there is no guard on duty. So a student or—heaven forbid—a professor could have defaced the item with a pocket knife as a practical joke . . . giving the wooden monkey mask a scar *virtually identical to poor Wentworth's in size and position.*

A few of us in the department believe otherwise, especially Demarest, who seldom keeps office hours for students in the building anymore. And when he does, he locks his door.

And it's a good thing he does, a very good thing, for I have taken to tracking the position of the mask on the wall with a tape measure late at night, when no one is around to observe me. Perhaps Demarest is taking the measurement, too. If he is, then he has surely noticed what I have discovered: About an eighth of an inch each night, the mask is moving—whether by the hand of a practical joker or through some supernatural force I dare not conjure—slowly in the direction of Demarest's office. And I believe the monkey's grin is growing wider, too.

Ladies' Night at the Blood Club

Dr. Albert Zaidi unconsciously tapped his pipe upside down against the side of a black quartz ashtray on his desk as he listened to the Talbots, who had been seeing him for marriage counseling weekly for several months, bickering about their on-the-rocks relationship. *But that's what keeps me in pipe tobacco*, he told himself.

The pipe was unlit, because he did not smoke while seeing clients. But he kept the pipe in hand as a device to regulate conversation and maintain his control.

When he was expected to speak but wanted a minute to think, he would manipulate the pipe contemplatively, which make him look thoughtful and intelligent. He had also grown a beard to enhance the impression that he was intelligent and thoughtful, which as a matter of fact, he was.

"We're together every minute of the day," complained Cheryl Talbot in an irritated tone. Her voice was slightly gravelly, suggesting she may have been a smoker at one time, though Dr. Zaidi saw no sign of it now. The throaty voice further added to the impression of anger and shortness of temper she projected. It was also, thought Zaidi, rather sexy. Her husband, Earl Talbot, sat beside her on the couch, hands folded on his lap, the big man looking downward at them with his usual glum and tired expression.

"*Excuse* me," he said in a hurt tone. "I like being with you. So sue me." She sighed, and her expression softened, and she reached out and put her hand over his.

"I like being with you too, Earl," Cheryl said, looking at him. "But do we have to be together twenty-four hours a day, seven days a week?" The couple, Dr. Zaidi knew, had a home-based Internet business (from which they obviously made sufficient income to pay Zaidi's $175-an-hour rate without filing an insurance claim), and thus they were together at home practically all the time.

"What about when you are not working?" asked Dr. Zaidi.

"I'm a night person," said Cheryl, "and I like to go out and have fun. But Earl always says he is too tired. Our life is so dull, Dr. Zaidi, and I'm bored out of my skull. Earl never wants to go anywhere or do anything but read or watch TV. And how could we go anywhere? He goes to sleep by nine-thirty, and then I'm alone in the house all night with the TV and Häagen-Dazs." She snorted. "I can't even wake him for sex."

"But I'm *tired*," Earl pleaded. "Dr. Zaidi, I'm a morning person. We work hard all day, and in the evening, I just want to eat dinner, watch some TV, read a little, and go to bed. But I'm up working at five every morning. Cheryl is in bed until ten, so, of course she has more energy at night." He paused. "And as for sex, I'm *always* ready in the morning. But she's so sleepy, it'd be like waking the dead."

"Separation is not always a bad idea," said Zaidi. "In cases like this, going in either direction—more separation or more togetherness—can strengthen the marriage. With you folks in particular, I think that increasing the separation . . . or rather, making you two feel more comfortable about the time you spend apart . . . may be advisable."

"Why?" asked Cheryl. "What do you mean?"

"Right now you two are conflicted," explained Dr. Zaidi. "Earl is naturally a morning person. Cheryl, you are a night owl. Earl is an introvert and likes to spend quiet time at home. Cheryl is more extroverted and enjoys nightlife and socializing. Yet you obviously love and care about each other."

Zaidi leaned forward toward the couple. "I could recommend that Earl spend more time going out at night and doing what Cheryl wants on a regular basis—change his life to fit hers—but that would go against the grain of his personality, and you wouldn't be happy, Earl." Earl nodded. "But alternatively, why not give Cheryl your permission and your enthusiastic approval for her to have more of a nightlife outside the home? To be out every night, if she so wishes?

"Earl can stay home most of the time, though I would advise that periodically—maybe once a month, maybe once a week—Earl should accompany you on a social outing, Cheryl." He scratched his beard with his index fingernail. "Who knows, Earl? You might enjoy it. If not, you can stay home the next time."

Dr. Zaidi unconsciously tamped the empty bowl of his pipe with this thumb. "Now Earl . . . you both work at home together in a business that gives you absolute freedom of schedule. Cheryl feels she sees you too much at home and you are unwilling to go out. You feel Cheryl doesn't want to spend time with you on your own terms. But from what you've told me, you haven't been willing to reciprocate much and participate in her interests."

"You know I'm a homebody," Earl admitted. "I'm not comfortable in social situations, and I don't like to travel."

Dr. Zaidi reflected for a moment and then said, "And so I am saying that perhaps most of the time, you should be free to stay home, and Cheryl can elect sometimes to stay with you and other times to go out. If she stays with you, you can enjoy quality time in your comfort zone, Earl. If she goes out, you can stay home—most of the time. But you also need to learn flexibility, and you need to learn to try new things and experiences."

Dr. Zaidi stuck the stem of the pipe in his mouth and raised one eyebrow, a gesture he knew made him look forceful, decisive, and intellectual. "Let me make a suggestion," he said. Zaidi reached into his desk drawer, pulled out a card, and handed it to Cheryl.

Cheryl read the card. "The Blood Club?" she asked. "What the hell is that?"

"Oh, I saw something about this place on a local cable channel," said Earl, eager to contribute. "It's one of those Goth nightclubs in the city where the kids all dress like Addams-family rejects."

"Vampires, mostly," Zaidi corrected. "They wear mainly vampire outfits— black capes, fangs, black lipstick for the girls, chalky white makeup for both girls and boys. Some do the werewolf, witch, or warlock thing. Zombies are also popular. It's quite the rage. Very chic and 'in.'"

"So why are you giving us this card?" Cheryl read: "Blood Club. Madison and 47th. Ladies Night. Ladies Drink (Anything!) Free. Hours: From Dusk till Dawn (Almost)."

"I want you and Earl to go there this Friday night," said Dr. Zaidi.

"Are you serious?" asked Earl, incredulous. Cheryl was also questioning the soundness of Zaidi's plan, but at the same time she was a bit intrigued and a little aroused. *I wouldn't mind a hot, Goth eighteen-year-old pseudo-vampire, with long black hair and a six-pack of abs, nibbling on my neck,* she thought, and the image sent a shiver through her body.

"I'm absolutely serious," said Zaidi, putting his hands on the desk, the pipe bowl clasped firmly in the right, with the stem pointing toward Cheryl and Earl. "You need to have some fun, you need stress relief, and you need to shake up your routine and get out of your rut. Going someplace new and hip is a great way to do it. Go Friday night after dark, and we'll talk about it next Wednesday; we're out of time for tonight, I'm afraid." He put the pipe down on the desk and leaned away, a body language signal that the session

145

was over. Cheryl looked at Earl, shrugged, and slipped the Blood Club card into her purse.

From dusk till dawn, Earl thought. *How too-freakin' clever—a vampire club that's only open at night.* "I don't know, Dr. Zaidi," Earl said hesitantly. "I mean, a fake monster club for wanna-be, pretend vampires. Don't you think it's kind of silly? And aren't we really too old for this? It sounds like a kiddie club for tweens, teens, dinks, and yuppies."

"Nonsense," said Dr. Zaidi. "It's a lot of fun, actually. I've been there myself, several times." He picked up the pipe, placed the stem between his teeth, and took a pull, sucking air. Cheryl and Earl exchanged glances. They had always wondered if Zaidi was married; he had never said, and they didn't have the nerve to ask. "Try it once and see," he urged the couple. "You'll like it, and it may actually do you some good."

"The Blood Club," Earl muttered under his breath. "Jesus, Joseph, and Mary!"

"I'm not going in," Earl told Cheryl, hesitating on the steps to the front door of the Blood Club. Another couple, dressed as a mad scientist and the Bride of Frankenstein, excused themselves and politely squeezed past.

Cheryl could see inside, and she liked what she saw. The room was filled with young, beautiful people, gyrating on a large dance floor to some techno/hip-hop trash she was unfamiliar with. There were some older people, too. Almost everyone was in some variation of a Goth, vampire, or Halloween monster costume, and they were all fit-looking and well-groomed. It looked like it was hot under the lights, and crowded, but no one seemed to be sweating.

Unconsciously, Cheryl started moving her body in time with the music and slowly made her way inside. This was going to be fun! Like a whipped dog whimpering as it followed its master, Earl trailed behind her, looking considerably less enthusiastic. *This is moronic!* he thought.

A handsome young man dressed in a Bella Lugosi Dracula costume was collecting money and stamping hands. Cheryl reached into her purse, but he stopped her. "Lady's night. You're free." He took her hand in his, which felt to Cheryl like cold marble, and stamped her. "Now you, Lurch." Earl, next in line, handed the young vamp a ten-dollar bill and was given a five in change and a stamp on his hand.

As she often did during the rare evenings when they went out to a club together, Cheryl quickly abandoned Earl, dancing freely, rapidly switching partners between men and girls with equal abandon. Earl, a wallflower by nature, went to a table where there were cups and a large bowl of a bright-red liquid that appeared to be juice or punch.

"I'm parched. Can you get one for me?"

Earl looked down and saw a cute teenage Goth girl smiling at him. He wondered whether she was eighteen and decided she was.

"Are you talking to me?" he asked.

"Who else, handsome?" she said. His heart skipped a beat; he hadn't been called "handsome" by anyone who was not his mother in many years. "You have the ladle. I'm Ilise, by the way." She stuck out her right hand. Since he held the ladle in his right, he awkwardly offered his left hand. She took it; her skin was like cold marble, but he was, to his surprise, a bit turned on, even though Ilise was clearly way too young for him—and, in any event, he had never cheated on Cheryl and didn't intend to start now, though it had been a month since they'd last had sex. He didn't have the nerve anyway, although he felt oddly relaxed and self-confident now. As he looked into Ilise's eyes, he even felt even bolder. Why not flirt a bit?

"I'm Earl," he said, reaching for a cup. "Do you want ice?"

Ilise laughed. "On second thought, forget that watered-down kiddie juice." She took the cup out of his hand and put it back on the table, winking conspiratorially. "We're grown-ups. Let's get something with a little more kick to it." She grabbed his hand and began pulling him away from the table toward the rear of the room. He followed without protest.

He scanned the room for Cheryl, didn't see her, and his confidence level continued to rise. "What did you have in mind?"

"Follow me," said Ilise smiling, and flashing a pair of incredibly real-looking plastic fangs. She pulled him toward the ladies' room. *Kinky*, Earl thought, and as they entered, he noticed there were no mirrors on the walls.

Zaidi was clutching the pipe bowl in his right hand, and the stem was clenched between his teeth. As always, the pipe was unlit. In his left hand, he had an envelope—a statement for the Talbots' last three sessions, for which the bill had not yet been paid. He had intended to give the statement to the Talbots before the session started, but Cheryl's outburst had caught him off guard. And, of course, he couldn't deny the truth of her accusations.

"You knew!" Cheryl accused Dr. Zaidi. "After all, you'd been there yourself. The damned Blood Club is *a real vampire club*. And you sent us there to be victimized by those bloodsuckers!"

Dr. Zaidi admitted as much by his shrug and facial expression.

"Does that mean . . . ?" Earl asked tentatively.

Dr. Zaidi removed the pipe from his mouth and grinned broadly, his elongated canines clearly visible.

"It was for the best, and it appears that I was right," said Dr. Zaidi. "Spending too much time together yet being continually at odds, the incompatibility of your biorhythms—you being an early bird and Cheryl being a night owl—was tearing your marriage apart. The Blood Club members are attracted to high-energy extroverts like Cheryl—new blood, and all that. Now that you've been transformed into one of us, Cheryl, Earl has *no choice* but to allow you your nocturnal lifestyle, which will give you the degree of separation we talked about in our last session that your marriage needs to survive."

"Idiot . . . moron . . . bastard!" Cheryl screamed as she reached into her purse, came up with a small silver flask, deftly twisted the top off, and then, to the doctor's great surprise—he thought she was going to drink whiskey out of it—jerked the open container forward. The clear liquid inside—holy water—hit Zaidi full in the face, and he screamed as his skin steamed and bubbled.

Enraged, the vampire therapist started to reach menacingly toward Cheryl, but Earl had already risen and gotten behind him. "Grab him, Earl," Cheryl ordered. The doctor was shocked to find that Earl was by far the stronger man. But how could this be, unless . . . ?

"That's right, Doc," Cheryl said, rising. She put the flask on the desk and pulled a wooden stake from under her jacket. "Your plan worked—one of us got fanged—but it was the wrong Talbot. Not the extrovert and the night owl, but the introvert and the early bird: *Earl* got bitten, not me. Now he'll have to be up at night—which he hates—all the time, and he'll never see daylight again." The therapist snarled, but he was held firmly in place by Earl's large and powerful hands. Though Zaidi was an older vampire and Earl was newly turned, Talbot was the much bigger man and, now being a vampire, was much more powerful than the bearded psychotherapist.

"We could call it malpractice," said Cheryl. She twirled the stake in her hand so the sharpened end pointed at Zaidi and tightened her grip on it. "But we'll let bygones be bygones. However, we do want to cancel this session. Considering the mean trick you played on poor Earl, I hope you won't bill us for it." In a swift, sure motion, she plunged the stake into Zaidi's chest. Earl threw his right hand over the protruding end of the stake and pushed hard, using his strength to drive the point further into the vampire doctor's chest and through his heart.

The result was rather less spectacular than Cheryl had imagined it would be. Zaidi didn't writhe and scream or crumble into dust. A gurgling sound came from his throat. Then a final sigh escaped him. He slumped forward. Earl put his hand on the doctor's throat. "He seems dead—but then, how do you tell?" He released Zaidi, whose head hit the desk with a thud as he fell forward.

Cheryl walked around the desk to her husband. "Looks dead to me," she said, scooping the envelope from the vampire doctor's desk where it lay. "But what are we going to do now, honey?" she asked Earl plaintively.

"It's not going to be so bad," Earl replied. "With the Internet business, we already work at home, and our hours are our own. I don't ever have to see anyone during the day, and I can work all night. So we don't have to worry about earning a living."

"But you're a morning person!" Cheryl said sympathetically. "You *hate* the night!"

He slipped his arm affectionately around her slim waist.

"I think the Doc was right after all about the Blood Club," he said. "I think I'm going to like the night from now on." Since Ilise had turned him in the bathroom that Friday evening, Earl was wide awake at nights, and only got sleepy as dawn approached. "So I can be there when you want to go out and have fun, no matter how late, and then just sleep during the day. Sort of like you do already," he added with a wink and a grin.

"Well, you'll see, Earl," she said enthusiastically, "people really do have more fun at night. Vampires too, I'll bet!" She put her arm behind his back and they started to leave the office.

"Oh, I almost forgot," said Earl. He took the envelope from Cheryl, removed and read the statement, ripped it in half, and dropped the pieces on the floor. "We're cancelling our appointments, Dr. Zaidi," he said to the body slumped over the desk. "I really don't think we need a marriage counselor after all." They both considered Dr. Zaidi's motionless form.

"I guess you and I are a pair now, Cheryl," said Earl. "Both children of the night."

"Yeah, a pair of cold-blooded *killers*," Cheryl said, sparing one last glance for Zaidi. She looked at her watch. "It's almost dinner time. And I'm really hungry. You?"

"I could go for a bite," Earl admitted, feeling happy and in love. He looked at his wife and realized, now that they weren't at each other's throats, how attractive and sexy she was and how much he truly did love her. "Do you think you could use your hot little bod as bait and lure me in some dinner?"

"Anything for my honey," Cheryl said, smiling.

Suddenly, the prospect of a night out with Earl—and many nights out to come—didn't seem so dull after all.

Fishboy

When Melissa Papora saw her newborn baby boy for the first time, she screamed in terror and promptly fainted. Her husband Mark, also present in the birthing room, had dashed into the bathroom and heaved his guts into the toilet.

It was a combination of the look and the smell, I suppose, that sent her into hysterics and him running: The little baby boy, a healthy nine pounds even, looked like a human with a fish's head. The eyes bulged outward and the neck was fleshy, with gill slits on either side. The toes and fingers were webbed like a frog's. Those present at the birth reported a fishy odor emanating from the newborn and permeating the room, though not having been there myself, I cannot say for certain.

It was a hot day outside, but most summer days are hot. The hospital generators kept the lights on and the A/C running, so it was comfortable, even a bit chilly, in the birthing room: comfortable for the adults but perhaps too cold for a fragile, naked baby.

Melissa remained in a stupor, moaning, and unable—and quite possibly unwilling—to hold her baby. The infant, whom they had decided would be Arthur if he was a boy—they had not wanted to know the gender in advance because, ironically, they wished to be surprised—was taken to an incubator in the maternity ward. Arthur's skin felt wet and clammy, and the obstetrician, Dr. Kessler, did not want the baby to catch a chill.

Already, the hospital floor was abuzz with talk about the fish boy. In the Internet age, of course, there are no secrets: Within twenty-four hours, video of fish boy in his incubator had been posted on YouTube; the nurse responsible for this exposure was promptly fired.

I received a call from the hospital the next day, asking me to come in for a consult on the Papora baby as soon as my schedule permitted. I went the following morning. My specialty is ontogeny, the development of the embryo, and the Papora baby would be my third fish baby that year; there were already a hundred and four recorded cases of such births in North America alone that year, double the previous year, and it was only July.

The next morning, I put on my rubber boots and rain slicker and ventured into the streets to hail a water cab. Enterprising entrepreneurs, using rowboats equipped with electric engines, were illegally ferrying paying passengers through the streets when the water was high enough for the boats to operate. The TV weatherman that morning had said the temperature would hit a hundred and two, and that it would rain heavily all day; the sea level was forecast to rise a half inch globally for the year.

At the hospital, I visited the maternity ward to examine the Papora baby and report on my findings. After doing so, I went to Ms. Papora's room to meet with her, her husband, and Kessler.

"You've no doubt read stories in the newspaper and online about the so-called 'fish babies,'" I began.

Mr. Papora nodded; his wife was silent and unresponsive. Kessler frowned; the whole incident seemed to irritate him, though why I cannot say.

"I think I saw one on the cover of the *National Enquirer* once," said Mr. Papora. He seemed too intelligent to be an *Enquirer* reader; later he told me that he sold weight loss and positive thinking programs through mail-order ads, and the *Enquirer* was one of the best-performing publications on his media schedule, so it was part of his job to read it every week and check the position of his ads. "But it's a fake, like the bat child and the wild girl raised by wolves. Isn't it?"

"Perhaps it was, years ago," I replied. "But over the past decade and a half or so, there have been hundreds of babies born worldwide who, like Arthur, share some of the physical characteristics of fish."

"How can that be?" Papora asked. "Is my son a mutation? A freak?"

"Not so much a mutation as a case of arrested embryonic development," I said, ignoring a snort from Kessler.

"What do you mean?" said Papora.

"Are you familiar with the biogenetic law?" I asked the Paporas. He shook his head; his wife seemed totally numb.

"The biogenetic law states that 'ontogeny recapitulates phylogeny,'" I said. Kessler rolled his eyes. "Although the opinion of the medical community on whether this recapitulation truly occurs is divided," I added, shooting Kessler a cool glance.

"What does that *mean*?" Mario asked. "English, please, Doc."

"Ontogeny, which is my specialty, is the development of the embryo," I said. "Phylogeny is our evolutionary history as a species—you know, from creatures crawling out of the oceans to apes walking on their knuckles to primitives living in caves and right up to upright modern man. 'Ontogeny recapitulates phylogeny' means that in the course of its development, each human embryo passes through a series of stages that resemble the main evolutionary phases the human species has gone through, from its origin to the present day."

Despite its dire consequences for the Papora family, recapitulation is indeed a fascinating phenomenon to observe and contemplate. Just as we evolved from single-celled organisms in the ocean, the embryo starts as a single cell when a sperm fertilizes an egg. As the egg divides, it develops into an embryo with a segmented, worm-like appearance. These segments transform into vertebrae and muscle, and gill-like slits appear in the embryo, making the growing fetus look like a small fish. Next, limbs sprout with paddle-like hands and feet, and a tail appears, making the fetus look like a tiny alien dinosaur. Then the tail disappears, the hands and feet grow fingers and toes, and the fetus looks much more human.

As I explained this, Mario Papora looked simultaneously fascinated and repulsed. "But you're saying *all* children go through this recapitulation thing in the womb?" he asked. "Not just our baby?"

"Yes," I replied. "It's perfectly normal."

"But other kids aren't born with gills," he protested. "So why does our baby look like a fish and not a normal little boy?"

"We don't quite know," I admitted. "In cases such as Arthur's, for reasons we can't yet pinpoint, the physical development in the recapitulation process got partially stuck on the fish and amphibian stages of human evolution—hence your baby retains some of those characteristics."

"And you say there are other fish children like Arthur?" Melissa Papora said, breaking her silence at last. "Others who look just like him?"

I glanced out the window. The hot sun glared off the windows of a building across the street from the hospital, and despite the A/C, I could feel the heat beginning to bake through.

"Over the past fifteen years or so, there have been hundreds of documented cases virtually identical to Arthur's," I said reassuringly.

The Paporas glanced at each other and seemed relieved.

"So, is there a facility or colony he'll get sent to where he can live with others of his kind?" Melissa asked in the most emotionless voice I ever heard a new mother use when describing her baby.

"I'm not sure what you mean," I said, although of course I knew exactly what she meant. "There is no 'his kind.' Arthur is a human with a birth defect—that's all. There's no reason why he can't . . ."

"We don't want him," she said coldly. She reached for her husband's hand, and he took it. "We discussed it last night. We don't want to keep it."

"I beg your pardon?" I began.

"You heard my wife, Doctor," Mr. Papora said. They both looked directly at me. "We want a normal child, not a fish or a freak."

"But Arthur tests perfectly normal in every other respect," I protested. Indeed, he was a bright and bubbly baby, and despite his amphibious appearance, several of the nurses on the ward were quite taken with him.

"You have countless couples who can't conceive and are desperately looking for babies to adopt, do you not?" asked Mario.

"Yes, all the time," I said, not liking where the conversation was headed.

"Well, give Arthur to one of them," said Melissa. "We don't have any trouble getting pregnant. We'll try again. We'll have another—and he'll be a normal, human baby."

I thought of the innocent baby gurgling and cooing in the maternity ward down the hall, even as he was being abandoned, and a lump formed in my throat. "I'm sure something can be arranged. Dr. Kessler?" Kessler nodded. I stood up and extended my hand to Mario, who took it and shook it. "I'll speak to the administrative office and they can get the ball rolling," I said. "In the meantime, for the baby's health, and until the adoption is arranged, breast-feeding is recommended for strengthening Arthur's immune system."

"No," Melissa replied curtly. "I don't want to see it ever again."

I left the room thinking of the little abandoned boy down the hall, and my heart nearly broke. I crossed the hall, entered the elevator, and pressed 1 to head over to the administrative offices.

You can see that I'm a soft touch. I love children—I always have—and had I not been captivated by the science of biology, I would have been in pediatrics.

Because a doctor takes many years for his or her education, and I have both an M.D. and a Ph.D., I was nearly thirty when I graduated school with all my degrees. Naturally, I would not marry until I had the means to support a family, and I am not very good with women, so I didn't have many dates. As a doctor, I was in a desirable profession from a marriage point of view, but when girls heard I was a laboratory researcher toiling at a medical school, not a plastic surgeon or heart specialist on Park Avenue, they quickly lost interest.

Margaret was different. We met when I was thirty-five, and at forty-two, she was seven years my senior and past her prime child bearing years. I also discovered my sperm count was low, and the few that I produced were not very motile.

Since we both loved children, remaining childless was not an option we were willing to accept. Three years after we married, having exhausted all available infertility treatments, including having my sperm cells washed in coffee (don't even ask), we adopted our first child, a boy, Kevin, from Romania. Two years after that, I examined the newborn Arthur Papora, and within two months of meeting him, Margaret and I adopted him.

We were a happy family, and you never saw two children get along like Kevin and Arthur—two peas in a pod. They were inseparable. As the boys got older, Arthur's odd look—fish people have bulging eyes, thick lips, puffy cheeks, fleshy throats, and, of course, the webbed fingers and toes—attracted the attention of bullies. But it never became a problem. While neither boy was the biggest or toughest in his class, together they fought like wildcats, and Kevin simply would not permit Arthur to be treated ill in any way. After a series of bullying incidents left the bullies looking worse than the victims, the mean kids left Arthur alone, and he was, in fact, popular with most of the rest of the school, both students and faculty. That he was captain of the swim team, and they never lost a meet, didn't hurt.

We loved each other. We liked to read. We were interested in science, indifferent to religion, and rarely attended church. And all of us loved the water—Arthur no more than the rest of us.

On a vacation at Cape Cod, Margaret stayed at our rented house to sit on the beach and read a novel while I took the boys out onto the bay in a rented powerboat. We anchored, and the boys stripped off their T-shirts and dove into the water for a swim. Kevin was an excellent swimmer, but Arthur naturally was—as all the fish people are—completely at home in the water. The webbing made him faster and more agile, and with his functional gills, he could remain underwater indefinitely. But he never flaunted it.

The first real trouble in our lives started when Arthur went away to college. We wanted him to stay close to home, but he wanted to go to the University of Florida; the university had a great oceanography program, and the water was warmer down there.

More and more fish babies were being born, and the oldest, now in their late teens, were emerging as the de facto leaders of the group, which was gaining visibility with each passing year. The oldest living fish boy, an incredibly mature and intelligent twenty-one-year-old named Martin Preston—fish people tended to reach puberty and mature faster, as if making up for their failure to fully evolve in the womb—had founded a group whose members were all fish people: EHEC, short for Evolved Humans for Ecological Change.

EHEC seemed benign enough except for Preston himself. Wearing his hair long, favoring shirts that left his gill slits exposed and sandals that showed his webbed toes, Preston was a radical reminiscent of the hippies of the 1960s. He spoke at various events and blogged frequently, and protested actively—his TED talk had over one million views—against corporate polluters and global warming, protests in which Arthur was all too happy to participate. During that period, Preston gradually emerged as the unofficial spokesperson of Earth's small but growing population of fish people, the birth incidence of which had gone up several orders of magnitude since Arthur Papora's birth some seventeen years earlier: What had once been approximately one fish birth in every few million had now risen to one in every hundred thousand.

"Dad," Arthur said as he entered the family room where Margaret and I were watching TV and reading. "Turn on the TV."

"What channel, Art?" I asked, reaching for the remote control. I had a bad feeling. Arthur displayed little interest in television unless it was either a documentary or a news program, and as of late the news he was interested in wasn't pleasant for humanity, in general, and for me as the parent of a fish boy, in particular.

"Any network, Dad," he said impatiently, plopping onto the couch and leaning forward, his bulging eyes fixed on the screen.

I hit the Power button and selected channel 2. One of the station's well-coiffed anchors was looking into the camera and reading from the tele-prompter:

". . . and there you have it. Martin Preston, the head of the EHEC—Evolved Humans for Ecological Change—has announced that the majority of the East Coast's teenage and young adult fish-people will gather at the Jersey shore on Saturday for an event they call the Final Farewell, after which they will swim out to sea and reside there permanently in an undisclosed location named by the EHEC as 'Atlantis 2.'

"That raises a lot of questions. Will they build an actual city under the sea? Will they swim around like mermen and mermaids? Joining us now are science correspondent Yanik Silver and Doctor Alex Mendossian, a professor of marine biology at New York University . . ."

I checked the Internet for a transcript of Preston's press conference and found it in seconds. God bless Google! A preface to the transcript explained that Martin was the unofficial spokesperson for the fish-person population of the United States. With the help of his father, a state senator, Preston had established Evolved Humans for Ecological Change as a legitimate nonprofit, their charter ostensibly to study the fish-baby birth phenomenon and investigate any possible links between the accelerated birth rate of fish-people and increased exposure to ultraviolet radiation as a result of the ozone layer depletion. EHEC was also looking into any possible relationship between the fish babies, global warming, and rising sea levels.

The full text of the press briefing argued Preston's theory, completely unsupported by scientific evidence, that fish babies were humanity's evolutionary response to global warming—a step forward in our development.

I read portions of Preston's briefing aloud to my family: "Ever since Darwin and hiw work *The Origin of Species*, we have known that living creatures mutate and evolve to adapt to changing conditions and threats in their environment. The emergence of fish-people and the increase in our birth rate simply reflects *homo sapiens*'s latest attempt at adapting to yet another environmental change—in this case, the flooding of Earth's land surfaces by rising sea levels caused by worldwide climate change and melting of the polar ice caps."

"That's not all," I added, paraphrasing the remainder of the talk instead of quoting verbatim. "Apparently, this Preston has brainwashed his EHEC members into thinking he is some kind of messiah or king of the sea, and he's planning a rally on the Jersey shore. He calls it the Farewell Rally, and when it takes place, all the fish people at the rally are going to dive into the ocean and go live in the sea."

I pushed my chair back from the PC. "It takes all kinds, I guess. Right, boys?" Kevin said nothing, but Arthur spoke up immediately: "Dad, I'm an EHEC member. And I'm going to be at the Farewell Rally on Saturday."

A chill ran through my body. "As a spectator," I said. "Right, son?"

Arthur didn't smile. "No, Dad. As a participant."

Margaret and I looked at each other in stunned silence. Margaret began to sob softly. Arthur went over and put his arms around her. Kevin stared at his stepbrother in wonder. Later that night, while I lay in bed wide awake, I heard the boys talking in their room, but could not make out what they said. The tone of the conversation sounded pleasant, not argumentative, for which I was grateful.

We stood apart from the crowd of fish people on the beach, most of whom wore spandex bathing suits, and a few wore nothing at all. Testing performed on Arthur, and dozens of others, had demonstrated they had an extra layer of fat, giving them extraordinary tolerance to cold temperatures; no one would freeze or be uncomfortable with sustained exposure to cold ocean water.

When I was a youngster, my parents had taken me to that shore to swim and sunbathe on the wide, sandy beach. Now the beach was underwater, along with half the town.

"Son," I said. Tears were welling up in my eyes. "Don't go. You don't have to do this."

"Dad," he said, his voice choking. "This is the way it is." He glanced up at the hot sun beating down upon the flooded, half-submerged village. "People had their chance with the planet, and people blew it. The era of the land-dweller is over. The future is a watery world—we've read all the research reports—and the future of humanity is people like us. The world you grew up in is dying, Dad. Humans have to find their own way in the new one, and we"—he waved his arms, indicating the crowd of fish people gathered—"are its pioneers." I knew he was repeating Preston's EHEC party line, but coming from my own boy's lips, it sounded sincere.

He hugged me once more, and I squeezed him tightly, not wanting to let him go. But eventually, I did.

"Be good, son," I said to Arthur. Margaret took her turn hugging him and could not control her flood of tears. Then she stepped back and let Kevin say goodbye. I thought of the Paporas and wondered if they were watching the EHEC rally on TV right now.

Kevin hugged his stepbrother and looked out at the waves. "Very cool, bro," he said, nodding toward the vast ocean in front of him. "I wish I could go with you."

"I know, Kev," said Arthur in a choked voice. "I'll miss you. I wish you could come. Thanks for everything. I love you, Kev." He stepped back, turned, and walked to join the rest of his crowd. Martin Preston was there, and the press shoved microphones at him, but he was strangely silent, as were all the fish people. I guess he had done his talking at the press conference.

With the sun blazing high above and the water's surface pulsing with the tides through the streets, my son and his new family walked out to the sea, most pausing to look back and wave at the relatives and friends they were leaving behind. We had had seventeen wonderful years with Arthur, and now those years were over. One by one their heads bobbed under the water and did not resurface.

I saw Arthur look back, smile, and wave. Then he turned, and arching like a dolphin, dove under the water and swam out to sea with Earth's new children. My tears tasted as salty as ocean water.

I never saw my adoptive son again. But the sun continues to blaze, and the skies fill with carbon dioxide, and the holes in the ozone layer grow ever larger. And more fish babies are born ever year, and the seas continue to rise, and the streets are becoming canals, and some day all of humankind will join Arthur and his friends in the new world under the waters, the only place on Earth where humanity has any hope of a long and prosperous future—or any future at all.

Never Look Back

DeGargiente was trying to kill himself again.

Collins watched as the quarter-ton giant smashed his head repeatedly against the force fence that encircled his bungalow. Although the electromagnetic field was as strong as any fence of solid metal, DeGargiente could not seriously injure himself on it; he was pushed back as if he and the fence were particles of like charge.

The watchbots cut the field long enough for the three of them to enter the enclosure and set about the task of restraining and sedating DeGargiente. Psych Central had constructed a trio of oversized bots to handle the giant's occasional outbursts. Central had sent a regulation-sized bot to restrain DeGargiente the first time he had had a suicidal fit, and the eight-foot-tall manic depressive with paranoid tendencies had lifted the bot over his head and smashed it to the ground, despite the fact that regulation bots weigh twelve hundred pounds.

Collins' own bungalow was not fenced in; he was allowed to go where he pleased, as were most of the inmates. The watchbots gave DeGargiente a double dose of heavy sedatives and were leaving his dwelling area. Collins approached to get a better look.

"Good afternoon, Mister Collins," said the watchbot with the red band around his upper dome. His companions did not bear this marking and were incapable of verbal communications.

"Hello," said Collins, glancing toward DeGargiente's bungalow. "Did he succeed?"

"No, Mister Collins. We were fortunate in that he was unable to permanently damage himself before we arrived. Tell me, did he say anything to you which might have led you to suspect that he would attempt suicide again?"

"Yes," replied Collins evenly. "He told me that he was tired of being fenced in, and was either going to escape this time or die trying."

"Did you think he would succeed?"

"Not in breaking out, no. I thought he would die trying, though."

"Mister Collins." The bot was programmed to show no emotion in his voice, yet Collins thought he detected a trace of contempt in the monotone. "Psych Central realizes that you are free to do as you please, and that, as a ward of this institution, you have no responsibility other than to refrain from abusing yourself or any other patient. Nevertheless, it would be considered a sign of improvement in your condition if you would notify us when Mister DeGargiente tells you these things."

The bot paused. Collins did not speak, so it continued.

"When Mister DeGargiente announces his intentions to escape or 'die trying,' he does so because he really desires some attention. The force fence, made necessary by his violent tendencies coupled with his great strength, makes Mister DeGargiente feel cut off from the others. And when he calls out for help by threatening an escape attempt, he calls out to you, because he trusts you and doesn't trust us. Won't you help us? For your friend's sake?"

"He is not my friend," replied Collins, without inflection. He turned on his heel and walked back to his bungalow. Seating himself on a lawn chair, Collins watched the bots leave DeGargiente's pen and move toward the empty bungalow on the other side of DeGargiente's place. They waited without moving until a transporobot arrived. The three bots unloaded various tools from the transporobot's trailer and began doing maintenance-related things to the bungalow and its lawn.

Collins called to them, "Hey, what are you doing? No one lives there now."

"Someone will be shortly," replied the talking bot. "You and Mister DeGargiente are getting a new neighbor. She will be arriving tomorrow morning."

"Do you know anything about her?"

"Do you really care, Mister Collins?"

"No," said Collins, "not really."

The next morning found Collins sitting, as he did every morning, in front of his Pentium 27.0 PC. As usual, he did not even have the device turned on but was staring blankly at the dark screen. This ritual often lasted for hours, but he had only been sitting for fifteen minutes when Giles Arcadine came bursting through the front door screaming, "Help me, Collins, help me! They're all over my house; I can't go back there!"

Collins sighed. Arcadine was a member of a race of intelligent arachnids. He had been living on Earth and working as a telepuppeteer for a children's holovision show. They had been doing a series of animated poems when the electronic telekinesis apparatus backfired, leaving Giles with the personality of the puppet character he had been manipulating. Unfortunately, he had been doing "Little Miss Muffet" when the accident occurred and had inherited a phobia from his fictional female character that made life difficult for the man-sized web spinner: He was now afraid of spiders.

"Calm down, Giles," said Collins, reaching for an imaginary fly swatter. Giles was an excellent cook and would feed Collins a superb meal in exchange for the Earthman's spider-swatting services.

"A new one came in today," Giles said as they walked outside.

"Oh."

"Yeah, she's a real little one, with wings! She can fly around!"

Just then a movement in the sky caught Collins' attention; he looked up to see a tiny girl darting through the air.

In his eyes, she was quite beautiful. Her body was slender and fragile in appearance. She wore silken shorts, sandals, and a blouse with slits cut in the back to allow movement of her kite-like wings. She looked delicate, like a small bird whose bones you'd crush if you squeezed too hard.

"I don't like her," Giles sneered.

"Why not?" asked Collins, who neither liked nor disliked anyone on Deald's World.

"She looks like a fly," replied the giant spider.

The two went into Giles' dwelling. The girl circled her hut once, alighted on her rooftop, and watched her two neighbors in the silence of the morning, which was punctuated only by the swatting of imaginary insects and Giles Arcadine's frightened screams. She closed her eyes and concentrated, trying to keep the floodtide of emotions out. Her entire body spasmed with the effort, until it became too much. She lay on the flat roof, gasping, as she opened up to Giles: paranoia, fear, revulsion at the hideous form that is his own body, being his own demon, the giant spider and the little girl. She drank deeply of Giles, for that was her disease, the total empath. She waited, and then began to relax as the tension of Giles' self-fear drained out of her.

Two figures emerged from Giles' bungalow, and her eyes focused on the man. She felt the channels open, but they were like canals of dried mud. She opened up to Quentin Collins, and got absolutely nothing.

Taliya, the winged empath, banished to a world for the incurably insane for prying into the insanities of others, read nothing from Collins. Taliya, who against her own will saw the hidden darkness in every soul and suffered the anguish of all the souls she drank from, drank nothing from Collins.

But it wasn't her.

It was him.

He had nothing to drink from.

"I think she likes you," said Chester Mullins.

Collins shrugged.

"She must," continued the Rigelian, "or she would stop hanging around here and trying to talk with you all the time."

Collins said nothing and the pair finished their dinner in silence. Chsrr'n Minnis'n—Chester Mullins was the rough English equivalent of his Rigelian name—constantly begged the other patients to allow him to cook for them. Once in a great while, when he was too tired to prepare his own food or put up with Giles' ravings, Collins allowed Chester to cook his dinner. As always, he was beginning to regret the decision, as he forced a yellowish mush that was supposed to be scalloped potatoes down his throat.

Born into a race boasting the greatest chefs in the galaxy, Mullins had decided to follow family tradition and become a master cook. But the diminutive little alien was as inept at cooking as he was at everything else he did. He had finally, in desperation, taken a job cooking for homo sapiens—considered the lowest level to which a Rigelian chef could stoop—but had been unable to perform even that menial task properly. After several botched attempts at suicide and a psychoanalytical profile that revealed the most severe inferiority complex in the history of galactic medicine, Mullins had been committed to Deald's World.

"If it was me, I'd pay her some attention," sniveled Chester. Chester was a romantic whose love life was limited to the soaps on holovision and movies of twentieth century Earth; he believed that Woody Allen was the greatest macho sex figure of all time.

"I suppose you would."

The Rigelian looked away as he cleared the dishes. "Then again, nobody ever pays any attention to *me*. I don't blame them. Who would?"

Chester expected no sympathy from Collins and received none. The bots would pay attention to him if he tried to hurt himself like DeGargiente, but so deep was his sense of inadequacy that he didn't believe he was worth wasting their time over, so he hadn't tried.

Finishing with the dishes, he noticed Collins sitting like a statue in front of his desktop PC.

"Are you going to write anything?"

He received no reply, and Collins noticed neither his departure nor the girl's entrance. She stood quietly by the doorway, watching. Then she moved a wing, intentionally creating a small noise. He turned and saw her.

"What are you doing here?" he asked.

"I came to see you."

"Sit down." He motioned to a chair, but she went to the window and knelt on a nearby floor cushion. He realized that a chair might not be suited to the needs of her peculiar anatomy. He too chose a floor cushion. They sat in awkward silence; he remained motionless while she fidgeted on the floor. Finally, she spoke, "It's really a nice place here." It sounded awkward, something said for the sake of speaking rather than to convey information.

"You mean my bungalow?" he asked.

"No, I meant this place. Deald's World. Very green. And the air is so fresh . . ."

"There's nothing nice about it. It's a planet-wide mental institution, and there is nothing particularly pleasant about mental patients or their illnesses."

"What's yours?"

He did not bother to inform her that asking the question constituted a severe breach of patients' rules of etiquette, since he wasn't concerned with such rules. Instead he asked, "Can't you tell?"

"No. No, I can't. Early on, I tried to read you, and—"

"Telepath?"

"No," she said, looking down at her sandals. "Empath."

He did not understand why this seemed to shame her. "That's the ESP specialty where you experience the conscious emotions of those around you, isn't it? Has something to do with reading nerve impulses instead of brain waves as they cross the neural synapses, right? I didn't think that was considered a psychiatric disorder."

"In my case it is," she replied, still looking down. "I get it all, from surface emotions to the deepest levels of the subconscious. And I don't have the controlling ESP mechanism . . . I . . . I can't shut it off. Not very well, anyway."

"Interesting. And did you 'read' me, determine my disorder?"

"No, I told you. I received nothing."

"That's right. Because nothing is there."

She looked up at him.

He continued. "*Emotional catatonia* is the label they gave it. A first. But that's not surprising, because most of us here are firsts. My therapist says my case will make a very interesting paper. The only symptom is that the patient is devoid of all feeling and emotion. I can think, function, appreciate things like logic, art, food, and physical luxuries, but that's about it. I'm very tidy, really, not like some of the other cases here. Even my self pity is gone. No remorse, no regrets. I'm not happy, of course, but neither am I unhappy. I . . ."

"Stop it. *Stop it!*"

He laughed. "Too unpleasant for you? Well, toughen up, bird lady. You're living with worse. Pity poor DeGargiente or Giles, or most of the other three million permanent residents—the mental health dregs of the known inhabited universe."

"Nothing could be worse than what you suffer," she observed huskily. Tears were forming at the corners of her eyes.

"That's a purely subjective opinion." He offered a tissue, which she accepted. "Seems like we're two opposites—light and dark, leaded and unleaded," Collins said after she finished with the tissue. "But I wouldn't have thought that an empath—even an overloaded one—would be considered a hopeless case. On the other hand, insane asylums are more often for the benefit of the keepers than the inmates, and I can see why people might want to get an uncontrolled empath shut away. Invasion of privacy—folks don't like to have their innermost feelings exposed. They don't like to see what's ugly in life. I should know; I used to be in that business myself."

She nodded at the PC. "I know. You're a writer . . ."

"Was," he corrected. "Haven't written a word since my arrival here. It must be over three years, I think. I don't pay too much attention to the calendar nowadays, of course."

"Your *Dance of the Deadmen and Others* was a beautiful collection of stories."

He raised an eyebrow. "You've read me?"

"Yes. You've written some masterful tales . . . what happened? Why don't you write anymore? You're good, maybe even great."

He laughed. "The book-buying public—at least what's left of it—doesn't think so. They'd rather read any of a million baby-mush bestsellers, novels with no more substance than primetime holovizh, than read something that depressed them, that would make them think. Reviewers complained that my stories were too downbeat. 'Why can't he write stories with a happy ending?' they asked. Good literature—even in my own genre of dark fantasy—should explore life, not run away from it. But the readers want eyewash books. I don't pretend to be Kafka, but at least my stories are honest attempts at art, and I don't cringe in hypocritical agony when I re-read them."

"But what about critics—"

"Taliya, a writer writes to communicate, not to give some grad student material for his doctoral thesis. I wasn't being read, and it tore me apart. I couldn't stand having my work ignored while the public ate up garbage novels written by baboons."

He paused to catch his breath.

"I couldn't go on. I found it harder and harder to write, knowing that nobody was seriously reading it. What was the point? Also, my stuff wasn't selling, and I worried all the time about money. "Finally it happened. Writer's block. I tried and tried but nothing came out. It went on for days—I just sat, staring at that hateful machine." He sighed deeply and said no more.

"And?" she asked. "What then?"

"They found me at my desk. I hadn't moved in several days, hadn't slept, hadn't eaten. I was exactly as I am now. It was more than just writer's block. It was a total shutdown of emotional response that went all the way through me, and I couldn't give any part of me to anyone, anywhere. So here I am, on Deald's World." He looked at the girl, who stared back in fascination. "I think you'd better go now," he said, too quickly.

They got up, and he walked her out. "Tell me," she said, "who was Deald? Did he discover this planet?"

He laughed. "Deald was the first patient here. He had severe delusions of grandeur, the books say—he thought he was God. Spent his days here trying to create a man out of the dirt, trying to breathe life into the earth. That didn't work out too well, but for someone with aspirations to Godhood he didn't fare poorly."

"What do you mean?"

"Look around you," Collins answered her. "This is his world. Deald's world."

He did not notice her trembling as he spoke. She fought for control, and as always, lost it. He felt none of the love, none of the pity which she released. She was open to him, but as before, he was an empty well, a long tunnel pitched in darkness. She peered into the inky blackness, and before the tunnel closed, she saw a flicker, the faintest glimmer of light. She opened wider, but by then it was gone; again, there was nothing but midnight.

She leaped into the air and flew home. He returned indoors and settled down into his bed. For the first time in three years, he did not sleep the sleep of the dead.

Instead, he dreamed.

He awoke to screaming.

Shaking the sleep from his head, he jumped out of bed and ran barefoot to the front yard. Chester and Giles were dashing toward DeGargiente's enclosure.

The giant had gone mad. This wasn't one of his periodic attempts at suicide; DeGargiente was running in random directions, lashing out at whatever happened to be in his way.

Taliya was flying around the enclosure, trying futilely to get the behemoth's attention. When she saw Collins, she circled around the force fence and flew to him and landed lightly in the dirt at his feet.

"You've got to help him!" she screamed. "He'll kill himself."

"Don't worry," said Collins evenly. "The bots will take care of it. They always do."

"They can't. I saw them when I was flying. Only one of them is even near this area."

"What would you have me do, Taliya? I can't help him."

"You mean you won't," she said angrily, backing away. "You don't give a damn what happens to any of us."

"Yes," he replied. "That's why I'm here."

"Damn you! He needs our help!" She tried to pull Collins with her, but he wouldn't budge. She released him and sprang into the air, flying high over DeGargiente's enclosure, until she was higher than the walls of the force fence. Then she descended into the enclosure and hovered in front of DeGargiente, who was pounding his front door into matchsticks.

Collins watched with curiosity as she pleaded with the mountain-like alien, begging him to stop. Then Collins's curiosity turned to horror as DeGargiente reached out faster than Collins would have believed such a monster could and grabbed Taliya's ankle. In one fluid motion he pulled her toward him despite the resisting pressure of her flapping wings, cocked his fist back, and struck her full in the sternum.

Her wings went limp and she fell back, but she did not lose consciousness; flying had strengthened her core, and Collins had seen Taliya stiffen her stomach muscles an instant before the giant's fist connected.

DeGargiente went berserk. He released her and she fell panting to the ground. Before she could make a move he scooped her up, clamped his right forearm over her chest, and squeezed. Droplets of bright green blood appeared on her nose and mouth.

"TALIYA!"

Without thinking. Collins ran full steam toward the enclosure. The watchbot, who had made it within thirty yards of the enclosure, had already shut down the force fence. Since its robotic speed was more than a human's, the bot and Collins went through at the same time.

Collins leaped through the air at the girl and giant. With a sweep of his club-like left arm DeGargiente swept Collins away like a gnat, crying "You hate me! You hate me!"

The oversize bot struck DeGargiente with a metal arm, causing him to drop the girl. DeGargiente turned and faced the bot, nostrils flaring, face red with rage.

Collins hovered over Taliya's still form. "Taliya! Omigod! Taliya!" he said frantically.

Taliya saw his hazy form bent over her. Breathing came hard; her rib cage was crushed. She was weak, an open funnel, and all of it poured through her: DeGargiente's despair and rage, Giles' helplessness, and then something else, something that no empath in the known universe had received until that moment.

She looked up at Collins. "You care," she said.

He could only nod.

Her wings trembled. "Me, too," she said. Then her eyes closed, and the wings were still, though her chest rose and fell rapidly and shallowly.

Weeping, Collins scooped her tiny form up in his arms, oblivious of the titanic struggle taking place behind him. DeGargiente had managed to wrap one viselike arm around the bot's midsection, and he had seized its leg projection in his gigantic right hand. He was trying to lift the giant bot; his face was red, and veins throbbed in his neck and forehead. Muscles like thick strands of rope strained against the bot's weight. The bot was desperately trying to get DeGargiente to release him by jabbing with his metal arm, but the blows of the heavy robotic limb seemed to have no effect. In one Herculean effort, DeGargiente roared and heaved the three-ton construct off the ground and onto his shoulder.

"Free, goddamnit, free at last!" he roared, grinning madly. Then Collins heard a sickening pop, and the giant's face went white as blood poured from his mouth and ears. Giant and bot collapsed in a heap as the other two bots finally arrived to help.

"Idiots!" Collins screamed. "Where the hell were you, you stupid pieces of junk?"

One bot disengaged from the group surrounding DeGargiente; the other examined Taliya and measured her vital signs as he spoke.

"Would you care to tell me what happened. Mister Collins? We regret our failure to prevent this, but circum-"

The bot paused. Collins was crying uncontrollably. This, and his rage at the bots' tardiness, registered as a radical shift from his expected behavioral pattern. The bot sent a transmission to Central, where the giant Wozniak Supercomputer processed the information, made its diagnosis, and beamed instructions based on its findings back to the bot one eighth of a second later.

The bot took Collins gently by the hand. "I understand, Quentin. That's all right. I'll take you home, and you can get some sleep. In the morning, we'll talk, if you like."

Collins said nothing and allowed the bot to put him to bed. After it left, he got up and switched on his PC. He began to type slowly at first, then faster and faster, as if a demon overseer were cracking an invisible whip behind him.

They sat around eating Giles' wonderful baklava and drinking Chester's terrible coffee as a bot packed Quentin's belongings.

"Pretty good cup of coffee, huh?" asked Chester.

"Yes," replied Giles, Taliya, and Collins in one voice together, and all four burst into laughter.

"Well, at least the cups aren't disintegrating," Chester noted.

"I can't thank you enough. We're really going to miss both of you," said Collins between sips, as he gently held Taliya's hand. She nodded in agreement.

"I can't get over it!" Giles exclaimed. "Someone's actually leaving this place. You two must be the first patients ever to do it, Quentin."

"Not the first. No." Collins thought sadly of DeGargiente, who had finally freed himself.

"What will you do now?" asked Giles. "Write?"

"What else would he do?" replied Chester.

"Oh, I can think of at least one other thing," Collins said, wrapping his arm around Taliya's middle. She winced. "Sorry, baby," he replied. "Still hurts?" She nodded. "A little. But getting better all the time." And she snuggled in closer to him.

After Central discovered a reversal of Collins' condition, they had summoned a team of investigative psychiatrists from Sigma Six, the nearest starbase, to determine whether or not he was ready to leave Deald's World. During the weeks of examination and testing, Collins had spent all his free time on his new book, which was now about halfway toward completion.

The writer's block was gone, his catatonia over: He would live among sane men and write again and maybe raise a family with an angel who could fly. Would his kids have wings? He laughed to himself, for it was ironic, really, that for this they would consider him normal.

For what is a writer of fantasy, he mused, if not a mad dreamer? A mad dreamer not much different than Giles, who was trapped in a technicolor fairy tale, or DeGargiente, whose anger outpaced his size.

"We are already to depart, Mister Collins," announced the bot.

Collins picked up his notebook PC, the one item he would carry with him on board the ship. He tried to say something to Chester and Giles, but the words stuck in his throat, so he nodded.

Quentin Collins, Taliya, and the watchbot walked toward the waiting starship. Collins knew that behind him Chester and Giles would be waving, and that they were growing smaller as the starship grew larger and larger in front of him.

He had the impulse to turn around for another look at Deald's World, at his home, his friends, and the battered bungalow of DeGargiente. But he had made a promise to Taliya and to himself, and he would keep that promise.

He would never, ever, look back.

Can You Hear Me?

William Rosenthal wandered aimlessly among the rows of cryogenic storage tanks, pausing here and there to wipe some frost off the observation windows so he could look at the bodies. The windows didn't really *need* cleaning, but Rosenthal liked to keep busy, and the union insisted that the company keep one man, one *union* man, in the freezer at all times.

"Anyway, the pay isn't so bad, and I have things to keep me busy," said Rosenthal to one of the frozen bodies. The man, naked and covered with a thin film of frozen moisture, stared blankly.

"I have enough to do—with rebuilding my combat robot, and my paperbacks, and my iPod 17 and all—without having to look after you guys," added Rosenthal as he stepped over a cold pipe. He was wearing insulated boots, because the pipes running under the floor beneath his feet contained liquid helium at negative two hundred and sixty-eight degrees centigrade—just a few degrees above absolute zero. Rosenthal also wore insulated gloves for when he handled the tanks.

He made his rounds, cleaning ice buildup off the tanks and checking temperatures. The interior temperatures were automatically maintained, of course, and really didn't need checking, but he checked them anyway and recorded the numbers on his tablet. After doing these things, he made his way out of the room where the tanks were kept. The engineers and technicians at Matheson had dubbed the room "Deep Freeze." He entered the outer office, where he stayed most of the time. He had just removed his insulated clothing when the intercom buzzed.

"Rosenthal here. What have you got?"

"Hi, Bill. Larry here. Open gate seven, please. We're coming in with a fresh one. Ready us a tank—number forty-two. Okay?"

Rosenthal turned to the computer console, hit a black button and then a red one; the things Larry had requested were done. He turned back to the intercom. "I'll check the tank out myself, make sure it's prepped right. Okay?"

From the other end of the connection, a barely audible sigh: "Sure, Bill, you give it the old Rosenthal once-over. We'll be right down."

"You bet," said Rosenthal, unaware that Larry had already hung up. "I'll make sure the computer doesn't screw up." Happily, he drew on his protective outfit and went to check out the new arrival's tank. He met Larry at the prepped tank and watched as the Road Team transferred the body.

Even in death, the girl was quite beautiful. Of course, she wasn't really dead, since she had been frozen to temperatures near absolute zero while her brain waves still registered. She was dead only under some interpretations of the law, but she had parents who had given large sums of money to Matheson in return for the faintest chance that she might someday live again. Frozen before the disease could snuff out all life, clients of Matheson hoped that they would lie in subzero limbo for as many years as it took for medical science to find a cure for their illness. Then they would be revived, cured, and live again—or so Matheson's website promised.

Rosenthal was pretty skeptical about the whole thing. Larry and other Road Team drivers, who had far more medical training than he, explained how the doctors couldn't remove *all* the moisture from the cells. When the bodies were frozen, the moisture expanded, rupturing the cells in the brain and other vital organs. "Probably kill you right off the bat," noted Larry, who added: "And if they could revive you, you wouldn't have much of a brain left to enjoy it with, anyway." But Rosenthal was not so skeptical that he would turn down the union benefit of free Deep Freeze services for employees. There was, he figured, nothing to lose.

The new girl's tank lay near the entrance of the Deep Freeze room. Over the next few months, Rosenthal kept her observation window sparkling clean, not out of any sense of devotion to the job but because he liked to look at her. Larry had called her a knockout. To Rosenthal, whose social activities were limited to seeing an occasional baseball game with his married older brother, this was putting it mildly. Her small breasts and dark nipples gleamed from cold, her long legs and her flat stomach looked as if they had been carved out of white marble (the tanks were padded, and the bodies in cryogenic storage unclothed).

Rosenthal had been listening to his iPod when he suddenly got an urge to look at her (he got these urges about ten times an hour). He got into his suit and entered the room. Standing over the tank, he peered down into the window. He had forgotten to take his audio headphones off, and the cord trailed down from his ear to the tank, where the jack lay draped against the cold window. He stood there for many minutes, weaving erotic fantasies.

He had closed his eyes and then he heard a faint whisper, the faintest of whispers . . .

> . . . and if anyone is out there, oh, please turn it off, please . . .

Scared out of his mind, he tripped over a cold pipe as he turned to run. He fell in a tangle and was stunned when his head struck the Bourden gauge attached to her tank. He lay there for several minutes, in silence, until he heard:

> Pain. I cannot stand the pain, the ice crystals pinching and puncturing, the cold everywhere and everywhen. Please, if there is someone, turn it off. I didn't know this, we didn't know, we can't stand i . . .

When he tried to stand and run, the headphones were ripped from his ears. He saw that the wire leading from them was wrapped several times around the cold pipe—the pipe containing liquid helium hovers at a temperature approaching absolute zero—at a place where two pieces of insulation did not quite meet and perhaps a half-inch of bare pipe was exposed.

Those voices he heard . . .

The frozen ones, the dead ones . . .

Perhaps he imagined it. Hesitantly, he picked up the headphone and put it to his ear.

A chorus of softly moaning voices: *Is anyone there? Are you listening? Please, if you are . . . it is always cold and wet and sharp . . . like icicles being driven into my brain . . .*

While his hobby was electronics, he knew enough physics and engineering to understand superconductivity: When a metal approaches absolute zero, electrical resistance disappears almost completely and current flows continuously.

If the temperature of the bodies were low enough, could thought-carrying impulses be forever flowing through them? If this was so, were all the bodies in Deep Freeze alive and sentient? And might they be continuously communicating with each other, via the cold pipes, which interconnected all the tanks?

He looked at the girl's tank and thought of the hours he spent just looking. Just dreaming, wishing she were alive and that she were his.

And she *was* alive, she had spoken, spoken to *him*. More than anything else, he wanted to speak back to her. To tell her that he loved her.

He looked at the headphone set. If there was a way to receive the impulses, he reasoned, there must be a way to—and I'll do it, I have the time, I have the desire. *I'll do it.* I won't have to be lonely any more . . .

The plant whistle blew, and his shift day ended.

Francis Rosenthal stood at the kitchen counter, slicing a kosher salami for her son's lunch. All day upstairs, playing at his workbench, she thought, and not even a little something to eat. What could be so important, he should be cooped up in the house all day? The thought of him spending all his time with his electronics and his soldering iron, his personal computer and his wireless web browser, tore her heart out. A nice Jewish boy should be out with friends. And Billy, he's thirty-four already, and not once does he even take a girl to a movie. All day in the house he sits, when he's not at work . . . well, at least he has a fine job.

She carefully laid the salami slices on a slice of fresh rye bread covered with spicy brown mustard. She topped this with another piece of rye bread, and placed the sandwich, along with a sour pickle and a glass of cream soda, on a tray so he could eat up in his room if he wouldn't come down.

She climbed the steps, not spilling a drop. Unable to knock without a free hand, she pushed the door open with her full behind.

"William?"

Rosenthal sat on a stool, hunched over what looked like a printed circuit board made out of opal. He worked furiously, frequently pausing to search for a misplaced component or scrap of paper.

"William?"

Connections were made to a voltmeter. The needle jumped, but not far enough. Rosenthal slammed his fist down on the table, fumbled for the pocket calculator in the drawer, and, after setting it on the table, angrily jabbed at the buttons on the device.

"William?"

Driven by the Furies, a man possessed, Rosenthal worked on. His mother put the tray with the salami sandwich and cream soda on a table by the side and quietly left the room. Her heart was broken and her eyes misted with tears of pity for her son and for herself.

Since he worked alone at his job most of the time, few obstacles stood in his path. The device looked somewhat like the iPhone 17 he carried, and it raised no eyebrows when he checked in. All the tools he needed were available in his work area. Maintenance tools he had never before needed to use had now found their purpose.

"It has to work," he said to her, aloud, as he entered the Deep Freeze, "I checked it out a hundred times. It has to."

He began unfastening the screws that held the outer plating of her tank in place. The tanks were designed like giant thermos bottles: one tank within another, with insulation and air space in between. His crude calculations told him that for the device to clearly send his thoughts to her, the electrodes would have to be attached to the inner tank wall, which was at a temperature far lower than the outer insulating one.

"I know what you're thinking, Mi . . . Miriam," he said to the body as he worked. "You're thinking this is morbid. But it's not, really, because you're so alive." A screw popped out; the outer plate loosened. "All these days, I've heard your agony, heard you tell me of the cold and the pain. I want to keep you company, to comfort you, to love you. I'll make it better for you." He struggled with a stubborn screw.

"It must be so dark, so . . . so cold and lonely in there. I—well, I'm kind of lonely, too." He looked upon her frozen loveliness. "If I could revive you, I would, but then you'd die and I'd lose you forever." He had removed the last screw, and pulled the outer plate free. It fell to the floor with a clang.

The moisture in the air condensed from the extreme cold of the inner metal plate. Avoiding direct physical contact of his skin with that surface, he attached the electrodes. The warm metal of electrodes touching the near absolute zero of the tank caused a screeching sound.

He waited until the electrode wire reached a low enough temperature. Then he put on the headphones and picked up the microphone. After a silent prayer, he threw the power switch.

. . . anyone please, if you hear us, please stop the cold . . . turn the damned thing off! And then: *I can't believe I actually paid for this! I'll file a lawsuit against you bastards if I ever get out!*

He picked up the words on his set. He shouted into the microscope: "Miriam! Miriam! This is Bill . . . can you hear me? I can hear you, and I am listening." Meters indicated the device was functioning as designed.

177

. . . the cold, everywhere, surrounding us all the time. I think we are going mad, being driven insane by the misery, unable to do anything about it but exist in this cold limbo . . . the frozen dead . . .

"Miriam, for God's sake, it's me, Bill! You hear me, you have to hear me! Everything is working perfectly; don't act like you don't hear me!" he said, displaying a temper that made the few girls who did go out with him decline a second date.

If only I had been wise and allowed myself to die . . . all of us, fools, cursed with this eternal winter and the sharp pain of icicles being driven through every portion of our being . . .

He stood up, and pushed the microphone right up against the metal wall. "*LISTEN!*" he shouted at the top of his lungs. "I know you hear me. Why do you ignore me? Please, I love you, Miriam, I *love* you!"

He looked at her and cursed. She lay there with her eyes open and unmoving. Couldn't she see him? Was she blind and deaf? He pulled the microphone out of the receiver and threw the useless piece of equipment across the room. In a rage, he threw the receiver to the floor and stomped it to bits. He saw her lying there naked, so beautiful, so close to him.

Snarling like a madman, he tore off his insulted jacket and gloves, and threw himself against the frozen metal. Pain, burning pain, seared through his face, arms, and chest where he touched the tank, trying to somehow be with her by merging with the cold metal. The pain blinded him, shot through him like fiery arrows.

Miriam, Miriam, his numbed mind cried through the agony, why won't you let me love you? Why won't anyone?

The cold shocked him into semi-consciousness, and, through a muddled haze, he thought he heard a voice . . . voices . . .

What? Who is that? Can someone hear us? Please, whoever you are, please help us . . .

He drifted further into a fog of pain and cold and tiredness. Miriam, are you there?

We are . . . I am here . . . can you hear me? I can hear you.

He could barely form coherent thoughts: Miriam . . . this is Bill. Bill Rosenthal. I . . . I love you . . .

As his numb body began to lose its struggle against the crushing cold, he heard her voice. It sounded very far away:

Bill Rosenthal . . . LOVE me? . . . Who the hell are you?

Who are you? It was the last thing he heard before darkness enveloped him.

They found the body, frozen completely and stuck tightly to the metal. Peeling it off must have caused significant damage; frozen flesh is hard to handle. I do know that they honored the union benefit and put it in a cryogenic storage tank, despite the extensive damage. Inside the tank, the temperature is hundreds of degrees below zero.

Superconductivity: You can never shut it down, since there's no resistance to electrical current. Eternal cold, frozen water bursting every cell, and no sleep . . . no rest. Always the constant input of the thoughts of all the others dead in all the other tanks. No thoughts can be hidden, no private moments exist; all thoughts flow as one.

Of course, you do retain some identity. Miriam, while speaking for all, also spoke as herself. All of those in Deep Freeze know who and what and where they are.

Listen—

As you leave Deep Freeze, you pass by a red box marked "main circuit breaker." I know you can't miss it; it's the big one next to the door. If you can hear me, and you're listening, could you please cut the power? Just throw the switch. That way the refrigeration units will cease to function, and the pipes will warm, and the flow will shut down, and the eternal cold will end.

If you're out there, please, won't you help me? I'm a union man, just like you; I've paid my dues. You can't imagine the cold . . . so cold. Is anybody out there? Anybody at all? Are you listening?

Can you hear me?

Sex & Drugs & Rock & Roll

sex

We were on the Stratoliner, flying down to Rio, when the orgy began.

The cabin was fairly empty with just us as the passengers—me, Skip, Rita, Benny, Gwendy, Petey, Amy, and Bunny—our whole sick crew. That left the two hundred-seat DC-1001 with one hundred ninety-two empty seats—actually, one hundred ninety-four because Bunny was lying in the aisle trying to catch a tan from the sunlight streaming in through the big window, and Skip was sitting cross-legged next to her, rubbing lotion on her back. She had undone the straps of her halter so the tanning would not leave her striped like a zebra, and since her arms were stretched out in front of her, I could see the sides of her breasts jiggle when he rubbed on the sunscreen.

Petey was staring out his window. Rita was sitting next to him, absently tracing circles in a layer of sugar—she had emptied several packets on her open tray table—with her index finger. I fiddled with my headphones and kept pushing the channel button, but got static on every station I called up.

A servomech was making its way down the aisle, pausing at each row of empty seats to ask the passengers who weren't there if they would care for a beverage.

"Kefe, teamix, water, or milkmix?" After 6.5 seconds—I timed it—the servomech would move on to the next row.

Amy stretched lazily and got out of her seat to parade around the cabin. She was barefoot and wearing shorts—actually, a pair of cut-off jeans—and a tube top. No bra.

"Oh, it's so *hot* in here," she said, stretching again. Benny winked knowingly at me from his seat across the aisle. Amy wasn't hot because of the stuffy cabin; whenever she paraded around like that, we knew she was horny. That only served to make me horny, and I knew that Skip, Benny, and Petey probably felt the same way, with the girls wearing next to nothing. The Mechpolice encouraged people to wear little, since that made it harder to carry concealed weapons. They were afraid we would hurt ourselves.

"Kefe, teamix, water, or milkmix?" It took the servomech 2.5 seconds to say that. I timed it. Gwendy excused herself and left her seat next to me to go over and sit with Benny, who was staring at Skip and Bunny. He had the airline magazine, *DC Review*, open to the crossword; I saw he had not filled in a single word. The servomech was ten rows away. I calculated that he would be at my seat in one minute and thirty seconds. Exactly.

Bunny twisted around onto her back, a neat trick with Skip, who weighed almost two hundred pounds, on top of her. Skip began to unsnap her pants. I turned to see Rita take Petey's hand and place it firmly inside her bikini top. Across the aisle, Gwendy was massaging the *DC Review*.

I didn't want us to get held up for not following regs, so I activated the panel on the seat in front of me and pressed ORGY on the pleasure selector. The lights dimmed, and the automech-pilot voice came on over the speaker:

"DC Airlines is pleased to serve you. We cater to every organic need, in order to see that you are healthy and happy. An orgy has been requested by passenger 16-B; those of you who do not wish to participate should please move to the front of the cabin, where holovision viewing and free snacks are available. Mech law applies in the air as well as on the ground, so please avoid fertilization on the Stratoliner. The servomech in the rear of the cabin will demonstrate how to use the DC birth control provided for your benefit."

The voice remained the same, but its source switched from the speaker to the servomech at the back the plane. "Males, a condom will automatically drop from the compartment overhead when the orgy function is requested. Please grasp the condom firmly and place it over your organ, thus . . ."

Amy tapped me on the shoulder. "Hi," she said as she crisscrossed her arms over her stomach, grasped the bottom of her tube top, and pulled it up over her head. "Wanna make it?" Now that Mech law said it was okay, I saw no reason not to, so I pulled her toward me.

"Kefe, teamix, water of milkmix?" asked the servomech.

drugs

Rio had been a drag, with Petey and Rita getting busted by the mechs for copulation in a public place without protection and consorting to breed organics, so we decided to hop a Strato for the west. I felt bad about leaving

Petey and Rita behind, but we couldn't very well wait in Rio for five to ten years until they got released from the farms. Besides, they would be happy there. Or so the mechs told us.

Why the west? At the terminal, when we were deciding what to do (and had already decided to fly because the transportation was free to organics and we didn't have anything else on tap anyway), we realized that we didn't have any place to go either. So Benny, being intellectual, said, "Westward ho!"

"Why west?" I had asked him, "What about north or south, or east?"

"Because the sun sets in the west," replied Benny. "I figure that, if we follow the sun as it travels across the sky from east to west, we won't ever have to face sunset again. We can always have daylight."

Since we thought that Benny should get something he wants once in a while, there we were, flying west. I was sitting next to Amy, trying to read the *DC Review*, but I couldn't concentrate. The page was blurry, not well defined, and the symbols on it looked like binary code rather than letters. I was about to press READING MATERIAL on the pleasure selector when Amy said, "Hey, you want to get really wasted?"

"Sshhh." I put my hand over her mouth. "If the servomech heard that, we'd get fifteen to twenty on a farm. Drugs are illegal under Mech law, dummy."

"Fuck Mech law," she said, sticking out her lower lip. "I'm an organic, not a machine. Why should I follow a machine's law?"

"It's for our own good," I pleaded, but to no avail. She had reached into her green bikini top, pulled out a capsule, and broken it under her nose. She said, "Oh, wow" and fell back in her seat.

I turned to see Benny watching us, grinning.

"Where did she get this, Benny?" I asked, indicating the spent capsule.

"It's okay, man," he told me. "We bought them from a mech pusher. From a mech, man, so they're safe." He held up one of the clear plastic capsules for me to examine.

"What's in them? What happens to you?"

"It's great, man, really great." He handed the capsule to Gwendy as she walked by. "The mech said that it makes organics go back to their child-hood, makes you think and feel like a baby. Isn't that wild?"

"Have you tried one, Benny?"

"Going to now, man," He popped one under his nose, stood shaking like an epileptic for a minute, and then fell to the floor to join Gwendy, who was drooling and sucking on her toes.

So I said, "What the hell," and reached into Amy's bikini top, felt under her left breast for a capsule, found it and popped it. Air, it was. Nothing but air, the mech pusher had sold them. If the mech pusher had told them that the "drug" made you act like a dog, the cabin would have been a kennel.

I had to urinate. I left Amy babbling in her seat—she said, "Fuf-gah," when I pushed my way past her—and gingerly stepped over the drooling, slobbering, blithering forms of Skip, Benny, Gwendy, and Bunny as I made my way toward the bathroom. When I got there, I found that the "occupied" light was on, though I knew we were again the only organics on the plane. The servomech was nowhere to be found.

Westward ho.

rock

A mech cop wheeled nosily by; I hid myself in shadow. I should not have come to this place, I thought, as the stench of unwashed flesh, urine, and rotting garbage hit my nostrils. I should have stayed at the pub with Skip and Bunny and the others.

The place was off-limits, forbidden to all save those who were confined to it.

I had learned, from the lame beggar who had led me to it for the payment of two of Amy's placebo capsules, that the crumbling buildings had once been part of a university, a place of learning, when learning was still allowed. Now it was a prison for the professors who had taught the old science, and they lived in pitiful squalor, guarded by mech cops.

"For these," the beggar had said, greedily fondling the capsules I had just given him, "for these, or for food or clothes, you can"—he lowered his voice to a whisper—"you can be taught."

"What?" I had asked him. "The science?"

But he had refused to speak further, and I had come to the place alone and unsure of what I would find. The others are too young to know or care about such things. Only I am old enough to have a remembrance of a time when knowing things mattered; only I am, perhaps, still able to think enough to want to have some hint of knowledge again, if only for a short time. I followed my map, seeking the House of Physics, and trembled with anticipation. Down the alley, a scramble over the wall—avoid that mech, hide behind the garbage bin!—to the left, and then to the right. It should be here, I told myself, it should be here.

"Force, force, kind sir. Please, some newtons perhaps, some pounds, kind sir." I looked down and saw a dirty, hunched-over beggar wearing glasses and holding a cup.

"What do you beg for, man?" I asked him.

"Some force sir, some much-needed force, to complete my experiments. I had high pressure apparatus, and I was so very near to my goal, but the mechs . . . they took it away." He dabbed at moist eyes with a filthy rag. "They took my apparatus—said I could hurt myself doing useless experiments."

"It was for your own good," I reminded him.

"Perhaps you could give me some force?" he continued, ignoring my admonition. "High pressure experiments, I'm working with high pressures. Some pounds, do you have any extra pounds, some psi to spare?"

"If you tell me where the House of Physics is, you'll be rewarded."

He paused to consider and agreed.

I smiled. "First the information."

He held out his cup. "The House of Physics has fallen and is in ruin. Likewise for the House of Mathematics. The House of Biology is overrun with poor Professor Smith and—"

"How could a building be overrun with Professor Smith?"

"There are hundreds of him," he replied. "Cloned. Now, let's see . . . the House of Chemistry was blown to bits." He paused. "If you want some learning, something of the Old Sciences, you could try the House of Geology . . . I believe Professor Munson still gives sessions there. Yes, the House of Rocks. It's down two blocks and on the right."

"Thank you," I said, and began to walk away. He came running after me, demanding the force I had promised him. Not knowing what to do and afraid that his screams would bring the mechs. I pushed him. "Thank you, thank you!" he cried as he fell.

I found the building guarded by dirty, dangerous looking children dressed in rags. One led me to a tiny, cramped chamber. The windows were boarded up, and shadows danced to the flickering of a single candle. There were books—forbidden books!—strewn about the room: stuffed on shelves, spilling out onto the floor, covering the single desk. Behind the desk sat a hooded man grasping a sheet of paper. Like all the pages of the books, the paper was stained yellow with age and looked brittle.

"He was paid, Grandfather," the boy said to the hooded figure, "and wants to know the thing." A grunt escaped the hood; the boy pushed me into a wooden chair and left. I sat in silence with the cloaked scholar until I could contain myself no longer.

"Please," I said, "tell me of geology. God forgive me, I know it is forbidden, and I know the punishments, but I must hear some of it. I must know something, use my mind again, study . . ."

"A rock," he said in the softest of voices. "A stone."

"Yes?" I whispered.

"When it rolls down, down a hill. A rolling stone . . ."

"Yes?"

"A rolling stone . . . gathers . . . no moss . . ."

Fraud! In anger, I grabbed the old professor and threw back his hood. In the face of the last geology professor on earth, in those dull cataract-blocked eyes, I saw that senility had totally taken hold. "No!" I mumbled in shock and disbelief. "No. It can't be gone. Geology can't be dead. Now they're all dead!" The professor grabbed at me. I pulled back, stumbling over the books, and ran from that place in horror. Ahead of me on the side-walk was the beggar, the last professor from the fallen House of Physics. "Some force, some pounds, some newtons," he cried. As I ran past him, I saw that he had a cardboard placard hanging from his neck. The sign read:

BROTHER, CAN YOU SPARE A DYNE?

roll

Tired of running, I slowed my pace and noticed a large gathering of the ragtag remnants of the university on the other side of the street. It was market day, and the mech merchants had come with their goods for sale. The merchandise was mainly foodstuffs: there was water, milkmix, and even some kefe at the drink stand. At another mech merchant's cart solid foods were on display: the brown, sticky A-mix, the crisp green P-mix, and the tough, salty and expensive M-mix. The men—I saw no females about—gathered around the food like flies on garbage.

"Special today!" cried the mech merchant peddling solids. "Real food today, real food today." At this, the crowd became silent, and I moved in closer—I had not seen real food in many, many years.

The mech merchant produced a large covered basket. "Today, we have, for those who can afford the price . . . fresh-baked rolls!" At this he pulled the cloth cover off to reveal a dozen plump rolls.

The crowd was stunned into silence, hypnotized by the sight and the smell. Once again old memories came to the surface . . .

"Bread," someone said softly, with reverence, "bread."

"Only four hundred coins a roll. Four hundred coins a roll," screeched the mech. "A real bargain at four hundred coins per roll. Two for seven hundred fifty coins, two for . . ."

"Thief!" someone screamed. "We can't pay that. We have no *money!*" The man leaped forward, knocking the basket to the ground, and the fresh-baked breadstuff rolled out into the street.

Pandemonium broke out in the ensuing mad scramble for the bread. Carts were overturned, and broken bags of food mixes spilled out, covering the men on the ground. I dived for a roll, snatched it up, and tore off a hunk with my teeth. It was warm and delicious. I was jumped by the boy from the House of Geology; I surrendered the bread to him and laughed. I hadn't had so much fun in years. I was about to dive into a pile of P-mix when I saw the boy's head explode as he started to eat the bread.

I turned and saw the three giant security mechs tearing down the street. A stream of fire came out of the belly of the lead security mech, the blue squad leader. The fire vaporized the man two feet to my right. Flames from the two red security mechs burned the rolls and one cart.

I tried to dodge away, but a hand seized my ankle and refused to let go. Before I could do anything about it, a char-bomb was discharged by the blue mech and exploded close to me. Suddenly I was free to move, and I ran squatted down, shielded by the screaming masses from the camera eyes of the security mechs, eyes that—if I was glimpsed by them in full view for only a fraction of a second—would instantly transmit the image of my face to Mech headquarters, where it would be identified through a file check. One glimpse, and I would spend the next ten years on a farm.

I backtracked behind the burning carts, glancing over my shoulder. I was about to dash forward when I saw the red security mech and stopped. I stumbled against the cart, and the mech heard the sound and—damn—

began to turn. Without knowing what it sought, my hand groped among the ruins of the cart and found something.

As the security mech turned to face me, I flung the bag of A-mix into its viewing lenses; the bag burst and covered the lenses with the thick, brown, sticky liquid foodstuff. Blinded, the mech fired its rifle at the sound of my footsteps as I ran from the chaotic scene.

I wasn't hit. Under cover of darkness, I managed to slip out of the university prison without being detected. At its gates, I paused to catch my breath, and only then did I notice the pressure on my ankle. The hand that had grabbed me during the attack still held me, even in death: Its wrist ended in a black, charred stub. I pried it free, vomited, and resumed my flight. I didn't stop running until I got to the pub, where my friends had remained.

the outro

I joined them at their table and ordered a near-beermix. "You sure look like hell," Amy observed as I sipped my drink. I said nothing.

Only a few of the tables besides ours were occupied. On the small stage, a comedian mech delivered pre-recorded jokes in a flat, steady monotone, with 1.8-second pauses between jokes. I timed him.

"Know what's brown and sounds like a bell? . . . Dung!"

"Where does a three-ton construction mech recharge? . . . Anywhere he wants to!"

". . . and so I said to the mech waiter, 'Waiter, there's a fly in my soupmix.' He dumped the bowl on my lap and said, 'Now there's soupmix in your fly!'"

No one laughed. We sat in mostly sullen silence, exchanging a few bits of idle conversation now and then. I guess they could see that I was upset and didn't want to bother me. If they only knew.

The mech manager silently wheeled over to our table and bleeped for attention:

"The management of Pub Number 234 wants you to obtain maximum enjoyment from the food and entertainment. It is our job to please you, and it is your job to be pleased." It made a whirring sound as it switched off the pre-recorded track. "Our meters indicate no response from this table to our most hilarious comedian. Since his functions have been checked out and found to be operating at maximum efficiency, we must conclude that you are not being pleased. It would be better if you would, as a group, show some interest in the entertainment through laughter and applause.

Otherwise," it said, without inflection, "we will be forced to report your failure to respond. I trust you are aware of local Mech ordinance 12-B? If not, we would be pleased to provide you with a printout of . . ."

"No, thank you," I said evenly. Amy was squeezing my hand, and her eyes were wide with silent fear. The others sat unmoving, afraid to speak. "We were so busy enjoying the excellent refreshments that we neglected to show our enjoyment for the very fine comedian. We will correct the oversight immediately." The management mech paused, and I heard the clicking of computer relays. Then it went away, and the tension dissolved like sweetener in hot kefe. You could have heard your own heartbeat in the silence. I did.

"Did you hear the one about the Irish robot? His name was MacHine!"

I pulled Amy close to me, and noticed the management mech watching us from a dark corner. "That was a good one!" I said loudly. "MacHine! Get it?" Amy looked up, nodded at me, and we all laughed together.

Cooperman's Pond

For as long as he could remember, there were two things Fabian Wolfe Cooperman hated most: people and his name.

His name came first—and almost immediately. The people came slightly later. A short, overweight youngster with acne and greasy black hair, Cooperman excelled at school and stank at sports. One day, after Cooperman struck out for the umpteenth time in softball, his gym teacher, Mr. Hausmann, said to him sympathetically, "It's okay not to be good with a baseball bat, Fabian. In math class, I wasn't any good with a pencil."

But his classmates were not as sympathetic. Unathletic kids were mocked and ostracized, as were kids with odd names like Fink, Lipschitz, Norbert, and Fabian. Cooperman had both of these strikes against him.

When old enough to become aware that his name made him stand out from the other children even more than usual, he'd confronted his mother. "Why did you name me Fabian? The kids laugh at me." Washing dishes, staring out the apartment window in her usual half-daydream state, she answered, "I always *liked* the name Fabian."

"Well, if you were gonna give me a stupid first name, why didn't you at least give me a middle name I could use instead?" This brought her out of her trance. She seemed puzzled. "But you have a middle name . . ."

Mr. Hausmann and Mrs. Cooperman were both long dead. Cooperman's once-greasy hair was clean, but now it had turned mostly white. He had lost most of the weight of his childhood, except for retaining an old man's tiny pot belly.

Sitting in an easy chair in his musty apartment on the second floor of the two-family house he owned, wearing one of the gray "old man's" sweaters he favored—button-down wool/cotton blend—Cooperman remembered his mother fondly. As he rocked, he drank a Coke and ate a salami sandwich with macaroni salad and a sour pickle on the side. He had his mother's thin hair and his father's round stomach, which seemed to stretch and grow as he ate, and only shrank after he had a bowel movement.

As always, he ate in front of the television; the plate and glass sat on a stained Ikea coffee table on which he used old *TV Guides* as coasters. A rerun of *Lost in Space* was being shown on the Science Fiction Channel;

Will Robinson was trying to convince an intergalactic toymaker not to keep his father and Dr. Smith prisoners.

The furniture was shabby and secondhand, the kind of stuff college kids would use in their dorm room. A thin film of dust covered most of the wood, dulling the finish and creating a muted appearance of neglect and solitude.

The only noteworthy feature was the wall opposite the couch. There was no furniture against it. Covering the wall, held in place with yellowing transparent tape and metal thumb tacks, were literally dozens of pieces of paper—photos, drawings, and a few newspaper clippings of, by, and about Cooperman's two sons. They ranged from pre-kindergarten—crayon drawings of clowns and houses—to about third grade, where they abruptly stopped, like a life cut short. Colored vibrantly, primitively, and energetically as only children can, the collage made a mural that could be mistaken for abstract art.

Cooperman had not grown up in the house nor raised his family there. He'd come after his family was gone. The home in which he had lived while married had been in an upper-middle-class suburb, a town just four miles from his current residence.

During those earlier years, Cooperman considered himself to be a failure because, while he was at the low end (really, the entry point) of upper-middle-class, he was not rich and, early in life, had come to expect he would be some day. When his children, who went to private school, asked him, "Daddy, are we rich?" he told them they were not rich but merely comfortable. "So we're comfortable," the kids would repeat, then, smiling and satisfied, go off to play on the backyard swing set.

That house had been impressive, though: a five-bedroom colonial with a three-car garage and two fireplaces, one in the family room and a second in the sitting room off the master bedroom. The house was part of a development offering five basic models; the Coopermans had selected the middle model of the five options, both in terms of price and size. To make themselves feel better about not buying the premium model, they splurged on accessories: the solid oak floors, dual fireplaces, new Pella windows, and a subzero refrigerator with an automatic icemaker.

The house sat on an acre lot in a town the Coopermans had moved to because, they told their friends, the school system was highly rated. Mrs.

Cooperman suspected the real reason her husband chose New Castle was that it was almost one hundred percent white, but she kept this to herself.

Cooperman's current dwelling was far less impressive. It sat on a fifty-by-one hundred foot lot, surrounded by a chainlink fence.

The truth is, he could have remained in the New Castle colonial. Or, on the proceeds of its sale alone, he could have moved into a luxury condo of his choice—perhaps a place on the shore, something he had always dreamed of. But once his family was gone, Cooperman deliberately sought to avoid self-indulgence or anything else that risked making him feel happy. Moving to the old frame house in blue-collar Bergentown felt right.

Downstairs, his tenants—the Lozanos—were making their usual loud noises and, it being dinnertime, he figured they were fixing or eating one of the elaborate homemade meals that were their Sunday night ritual: seasoned fish; beans with sausage, rice, vegetables, bread, potatoes; sometimes spicy meat or chicken. He heard laughter and a video game being played. A father spoke and a child giggled. The Lozanos had two boys, Jerry, age ten, and George, seven. Their current hobby was tropical fish, the only pets Cooperman would allow his tenants to keep despite the plea of Mrs. Lozano to let the boys have a puppy.

The family's loud noises bothered Cooperman, but they paid their rent on time. Even better, Mr. Lozano was handy. So, when there was a problem in the first-floor apartment, he made repairs, saving Cooperman the trouble of calling plumbers, electricians, carpenters, and masons. Elementary school gym failure had not been an isolated incident. Cooperman gradually had discovered that he was inept at all things physical, including home repairs and—before marriage—sexual intercourse.

Having no aptitude or interest in home repair, Cooperman was glad to have Lozano around as a live-in handyman. In return for services, Cooperman tolerated the noise, and, indeed, he looked forward to the cooking odors, which reminded him of the homemade meals his mother, and later his wife, used to make. He remembered his mother loving to feed him; his favorites were her pot roast and flank steaks. But he had been so addicted to food from her kitchen that he eagerly ate anything she set in front of him. One night, she broiled an entire salami by accident instead of the flank steak. His father had been angry, but Cooperman found the broiled salami delicious; even the smell made his mouth water. The aromas of Mrs. Lozano's Columbian dishes were similarly enticing.

Tonight's Lozano family meal was an exception, however: It smelled like plastic being incinerated. And unless his eyes were playing tricks, Mrs. Lozano was either burning the fish or had an open fire going in the kitchen: The air in Cooperman's apartment was becoming misty, and the acrid odor of smoke began to infiltrate the room. Lights flickered through the "old lady" white lace curtains covering his living room windows. The curtains fluttered slightly inward in a gentle breeze. Were the Lozanos barbecuing in the side yard? He had forbade it; the yard was restricted to his use only, although he rarely sat out there, and then only on a few perfect spring and autumn days that were neither too warm nor too chilly.

"Fucking Mexicans," Cooperman swore under his breath, though he knew the Lozanos were from Columbia. As he got up from his chair to go downstairs and yell at Mr. Lozano—he was comfortable doing that, but afraid of the more aggressive Mrs. Lozano—he heard a hard, rapid pounding at his apartment door.

"Mr. C! Mr. C!" cried a male voice in a Latin accent. "Come out. *Hay un fuego.* There is a fire." Cooperman ran to the window and threw back the curtains. His house was not on fire, but the block of stores situated on the corner of the street that bordered his side yard was ablaze. Flames danced; thick black smoke was rolling off the top of the roofs and moving slowly in the direction of his house. It was then he heard the fire truck sirens.

"Mr. C! Fire!" shouted Mr. Lozano, banging on the door harder and more frantically.

"I'm coming. I'm not *deaf*," he shouted in an irritated tone, opening the door as he buttoned his sweater up to the middle of his slightly protruding abdomen, which was as far up as the buttons on old-man sweaters went. "Why do you have to be so loud?"

Mr. Lozano nodded vigorously. "*Sí, sí*," he said as he carefully took Cooperman's arm—much as a Boy Scout would walk an old lady across the street—and began hurrying him to the stairs and the safety of the outdoors. In his rush, Lozano pulled Cooperman a bit too roughly, causing his land-lord to stumble. Although Cooperman looked like an old man next to the slim, fit, black-haired Lozano, they were in fact only fifteen years apart.

"*Perdon*," Lozano apologized politely, as he hurried Cooperman through the front door into the illuminated evening and onto the sidewalk where the Lozano family—and most of the rest of the neighborhood—gawked at the fire like rubes ogling freaks at a carnival sideshow.

Bunch of yutzes, thought Cooperman scornfully, looking at the crowd, as Mr. Lozano helped him down the front steps to safety. Meanwhile, the fire crew had attached hoses to the hydrant. They turned on the water and began to spray.

The stores had been destroyed, but his house had been untouched. In fact, the white wooden sidewall facing the hole in the ground where the stores had been was not even scorched. The fire crew, with ingenuity Cooperman had not expected from civil servants, had used one of the five trucks that had been on the scene to spray a continuous wall of water between the stores and Cooperman's house until the blaze was out. This cold, wet wall kept away sparks and heat that could easily have turned the sixty-five-year-old colonial into a bonfire.

Water had run off the side yard and into his basement, wetting the floor and dampening some boxes containing tax papers and bank statements he was storing decades past the legal requirement. For a minute, Cooperman thought half seriously of writing a letter of complaint to the mayor or even suing the town for water damage. His house was in slightly rundown condition in a poorer neighborhood, and, truth be told, he would just have soon collected the insurance payment.

The thought struck him that Lu, the Korean who owned the block of stores, had probably set the fire on purpose to collect the insurance. "Smart Chinaman," Cooperman chuckled aloud as he stood at his kitchen sink, getting a glass of tap water to drink. The kitchen—and the rest of the apartment—smelled faintly like Hickory Farms, but he had become so used to the odor he hardly noticed.

Later, he stood with his hands in his pocket, in his side yard, watching workers busy themselves. The stores were a total loss. Lu stood on the sidewalk, involved in an animated discussion with a police officer, the fire chief, and a third man, who was wearing a suit; Cooperman guessed he might be Lu's insurance agent or attorney. "You'll have to put up a fence right away to keep children from falling in," he heard the police officer say. A few feet away, Chung Lee, a nervous young man who served as Lu's houseboy and personal assistant, studied the site intently, as if searching for clues.

Some days later, most of the rubble had been cleared. What remained was a rectangular common basement the five stores had shared. The walls of the basement were cement block, but mud and rubble had slid into the chasm, partially covering the floor and staining the walls. It looked like an extremely large swimming pool that had been abandoned and fallen into neglect. About nine inches of muddy water—the remains of the spray from the fire hoses—covered the bottom of the basement floor.

"Two skips," he heard a child shout with glee. He parted the curtains. Neighborhood children—his label for them was "urchins," since they came from poor families in a lower-middle-class neighborhood in which he, perhaps unknown to most of his neighbors, was, with a $2.8 million portfolio, surely one of the wealthier residents—were playing in front of the fire scene. He felt sympathy for the children. It was not their fault that their parents did not do well; they were urchins only because of an accident of birth.

A young boy picked up a flat piece of brick from the sidewalk, one of many that had chipped from one of the store walls when it collapsed. With a clumsy motion, he threw the brick at an angle, attempting to skim the surface of the dirty pool of water below. The brick hit, splashed, and sank.

"One skip!" the boy shouted.

"That wasn't a skip," the girl with him—possibly his sister—said. "It just made a splash when it hit the pond."

Cooperman chuckled. The pond? How sad, with the limited exposure of urban kids to the outdoors, that they thought of this muddy hole in the ground as a pond.

His father, Fred Cooperman, had been an insurance agent who should have been an elementary school teacher or a forest ranger. Cooperman senior's great passions had been children—his own and others—and nature, especially lakes, ponds, and fishing.

Cooperman's dad had often taken him on fishing trips. The younger Cooperman, although an indifferent fisherman, had shared his father's love of water and aquatic life. He would explore streams and brooks wearing rubber boots and carrying a net and jar, delighting in his capture of a tadpole, crayfish, or freshwater clam—creatures he would keep in the jar for a half hour or so before letting them go.

One spring day, his mother had insisted the family drive to the country so she could antique. His father complained until his mother informed him they could have a picnic lunch at a pond, which, she had heard, had good fishing. Cooperman was thrilled, because he loved to see his father happy, and his father was almost always happy when fishing.

Not that day. Betty Cooperman had neglected to tell her husband how small the pond at the picnic spot was, or how small the fish in it were. Cooperman's father considered himself a serious fisherman and catching and releasing little sunnies was not his style.

Dejected, the younger Cooperman stared at the water. Suddenly, beneath the surface, he spied a large dark shape moving among the tiny sunfish.

"Dad," he called excitedly. "There's a big fish! Right here!"

"I see it!" his father replied. He reeled in, ran over, and dropped his line in the new spot. Within seconds, the big fish—a bass—took the bait, and Cooperman's father reeled him in.

"Look at the size of him!" said his dad. His mom nodded, offered a tolerant smile, and went back to her mystery novel; she always read hard-cover mystery novels borrowed from the town library when accompanying her husband on a fishing trip. "Yuck," Cooperman's sister said, disgusted by the sight of the bass gasping for air, its gill slits opening and closing heavily.

His father turned toward him and smiled. "Good work, Fabian," he told him, and he unexpectedly leaned forward and kissed him on the cheek. It was the finest fishing trip Cooperman could ever remember.

Partially filled with rainwater, the basement of the ruined block of stores did indeed look, sort of, like a pond. In the sun, the surface shimmied; a breeze caused ripples on the water, spectacularly reflecting the late after-noon sunlight. He chuckled at the thought that his house could now be listed in a real estate ad as "waterfront property." It was fittingly pathetic.

But as he considered the idea, Cooperman felt a certain nostalgia for the days when he fished with his father. He'd never mastered the skills of fishing, and his own sons had not been interested, so it had been decades since he'd put a worm on a hook or stood in front of a pond

A pond. The idea actually began to excite him. He was living on a pond!

Days later, on a bright Sunday morning, Cooperman closed his door and started down his front walk. He planned to get the paper, and a coffee with half-and-half and no sugar, from the deli two blocks down the street.

As he walked down the sidewalk, he stopped to stare reflectively at the pond. On-and-off rain during the week had brought the water level higher up the foundation. A breeze caused sunlight to dance on its surface.

Three of the neighborhood children stood in front of the chainlink fence enclosing the pond. They were pointing to the water and having an animated conversation.

When Cooperman came closer to see what they were so excited about, they became quiet and stepped away. The neighbors thought of him as an aloof, mean old man with no patience for children. But they were wrong. Many years ago, he had had a wife and two beautiful brown-eyed sons who had been the center of his universe.

In those days, he flew frequently on business. Although he was gone only a few days at a time, he missed his sons fiercely whenever he was away— and they missed him. Part of the deal he made with them was that, if he was gone more than two days, they could sleep in their parents' bed with him and their mother the night he came back. He didn't object even when the boys still wanted to do this when they were eight and five, and neither did his wife. In fact, both parents loved the family bed, and the sweetest memories he had were of his sons nestled in the blankets between himself and Lois.

One day, while he was away on a business trip, a drunk driver, a teenager named Bud Pisante, had run a red light, killing Lois Cooperman and her sons instantly. The remorseful teenager had once sent Cooperman a letter from prison which began, "Please forgive me . . ."

Rot in hell. The thought had sprung immediately into his mind. And it stayed there. He crumpled Pisante's letter into a ball and threw it in the trash. Cooperman never heard from the boy again. But his heart had hardened, and he'd slowly, deliberately began cutting himself off from everyone he knew—mainly by not returning phone calls or answering e-mails; he did not text. When people visited, he conversed in grunts and monosyllables, and soon they stopped coming and calling, which suited him just fine. Even his niece Ruth had given up, and, eventually, he'd see or speak to no one who could remind him of his losses.

He leaned forward, pressing his face against the chainlink fence, and looked down to where the kids had been pointing.

There, in the water, were bright-orange goldfish moving among the tall underwater plants. He recognized the fish and plants from the window of the pet shop he walked past almost every day when going to the deli for coffee. Clearly, someone had bought goldfish and plants at this store or another, and while no one was watching—probably at night—climbed the fence and dumped the fish and plants into the pond.

Cooperman stood transfixed. Slowly, the children came forward, seeming no longer to be aware of him, and watched too.

For the next week, Cooperman got up a half hour earlier every day, and on the way to the deli for his morning coffee would pause to linger at the water's edge to watch the fish.

Many people from the neighborhood did the same, and Cooperman developed the habit of saying "hello" to others who came to enjoy the pond. To his surprise, they said hello back, smiled at him, and seemed willing to be friendly.

Then one morning soon after, Cooperman was awakened even earlier than usual . . . by the sound of quacking and splashing. He looked out the window, down at the pond, to see two ducks paddling around among the plants and the fish. Mrs. Lozano was already outside, feeding them bread. She looked up, saw Cooperman, smiled, and waved to him. After a second, Cooperman slowly raised his arm and waved back.

After the ducks came, Cooperman began lingering even longer at the pond each morning, watching both the fish and the birds. Had someone kidnapped the ducks from a public pond and transplanted them to Cooperman's pond? More likely, the pair had been attracted to the water and, well fed by the people in the neighborhood, decided to stay. In fact, Cooperman's pond had become the social center of the town, and Cooperman found the extra people milling around his house strangely comforting, like having all the relatives in a crowded house on Christmas morning.

On a Monday morning, he once again was awakened by noise earlier than usual. But drowning out the faint quacking of the ducks was the louder, rougher sound of a small motor. It sounded—and smelled—like an old gasoline-powered lawn mower.

Cooperman looked out the window. He saw Chung Lee at the water's edge, fiddling with a small blue pump that sat on the sidewalk next to the fence. A hose ran from the pump into the pond. Water poured from a hose at the other end of the pump, ran down a short length of curb, and disappeared into the sewer. To Cooperman, it seemed likely that Lu had instructed his manservant to pump the pond dry to protect his property from the damage standing water in a foundation could cause.

The fish! he thought with a start. Had they already been sucked up through the hose and dumped into the sewer? When Cooperman was twelve, his sister Carol had accidentally poured her pet goldfish down the bathroom sink while replacing the water in the bowl. Their parents were not home, and so Cooperman had tried with all his might to remove the sink trap and save the fish, but the trap was rusted and would not budge. His sister had cried for almost an hour. Later that night, in the bedroom they shared, she tiptoed out of bed across the room and kissed him on the top of his head, thinking him asleep. At forty-nine, Carol had a mastectomy, but the cancer had already metastasized, and she died later the following year.

At her funeral, when the rabbi asked if anyone wanted to speak, Cooperman told the goldfish story. Ruth, Carol's daughter and his only niece, hugged him as her mother's coffin was lowered into the ground. "I never knew that about you and Mom," she said to him, sobbing. He had not seen nor spoken to Ruth since the funeral of his own children and Lois. He wanted to call . . . had meant to call, but since the car accident he had lacked the energy it took.

Now, though, he threw on a shirt, pants, and sport coat, ran downstairs, and flung open the front door. Chung Lee was still kneeling by the pump, making adjustments.

"What's this?" Cooperman asked as he approached Chung Lee.

"Mr. Lu said drain water," replied Chung Lee. "Bad for concrete."

Cooperman glanced at the pond. The water level had not yet diminished significantly, but at the rate Chung Lee was pumping, it soon would. Already the plants looked bent instead of straight, as if bowing to keep within the water. The fish could clearly be seen swimming among them, their artificial pond growing shallower.

Cooperman took out his wallet, removed a one hundred dollar bill, and gave it to Chung Lee. "Stop pumping," he said. It was phrased as a command, not a request, and Chung Lee obeyed, shutting off the pump. He took the one hundred dollars while looking at Cooperman. "Is Lu in his office?" Cooperman asked. Chung Lee nodded.

"I'm going to talk with Lu," said Cooperman. "Wait here, but don't do anything until I come back." Chung Lee nodded and Cooperman started up the street toward the Lu Real Estate Company office.

Lu looked at him from across his desk.

"Let's get to business," Cooperman said, like a CEO talking to someone far below him on the corporate ladder.

Lu raised one eyebrow and gave Cooperman a questioning glance.

"I checked right after the fire. I was curious, and I have my sources," Cooperman said, matter-of-factly. He chuckled. "I thought maybe, just maybe, you had the fire set to collect the insurance. You didn't. You weren't insured. And you can't get a loan to rebuild."

Lu bristled. "I can get loan," he replied, too quickly.

Cooperman look back at him. "No, you can't."

Lu paused, and then he relaxed slightly. "And you will make me loan?" he said to Cooperman sarcastically.

"No," said Cooperman, removing a Mont Blanc pen and a leather-covered checkbook from the pocket of his sport coat. "I'm going to buy you out."

Lu laughed. "You can't afford. Too much money for you."

Cooperman gave Lu a look that erased the grin from his face. Cooperman leaned forward. "Actually," he said as he twisted the Mont Blanc and flipped open the checkbook for dramatic effect, "I can."

Lu gulped. Then he smiled. And for the first time in as many years as he could remember, Cooperman did too.

It was Friday night, a perfect June evening, still light at a time when the sky would have been pitch black in winter. The air was warm from the heat of the day but cooling rapidly as dusk approached.

Neighborhood men and women sat outside around the pond in lawn chairs, talking, reading, and watching their children. The air was rich with the smell of barbecued meat. Mr. Lozano stood by the grill in the side yard, waving to Cooperman when he looked over. Children played hopscotch and jacks on the sidewalk; one of the boys crumbled white bread and dropped the pieces into the water at the pond's edge. The fish and ducks swam up to eat greedily, like a family being called to supper.

Mr. Lu walked by. "Nice night, Mr. Cooperman," he said pleasantly, pausing to survey the real estate holdings on which he had made a tidy profit. "Yes, it is," replied Cooperman.

Lu walked on. Cooperman chatted with Mrs. Lozano, then turned toward the pond. He watched the water, the ducks, the fish, and the people contentedly as the light of the setting sun played off the water's surface.

Mrs. Lozano was starting to say something about the ducks, but when she paused to take a breath, Cooperman held up his hand. "Excuse me,

Magnolia," he said politely. "I have to go inside for a minute." Mrs. Lozano nodded, then watched as he walked up the front path and into the house.

She went into the side yard and put her arm around her husband. "A beautiful place, no?" she asked him, as they stood by the pond and watched the setting sun. "*Sí*," he replied enthusiastically.

Then she heard, coming from Cooperman's upstairs apartment, something she rarely heard from there: the sound of a telephone being dialed.

"Ruth?" Cooperman said when his niece answered on the second ring. "It's your Uncle Fabian." Her sudden intake of breath was clearly audible over the phone line.

He paused and waited for her answer, while in the pond outside his window the ducks ate bread crumbs on the water.

Chimney Sweep

He walks slowly through the forest of cold winds and swirling leaves of gold, red, and brown. The tall trees bear few leaves and are lovely in this time of death, he thinks. He comes to a clearing in the woods, where there stands a small house, snug and warm against the bitter cold of the outdoors. He approaches the door and pounds his fist against it. A second-story window opens and a plump woman with gray hair sticks her head out of it and shouts, "All right, you, what do you want?"

He stares up at her, and motions with his hands to his stomach and his mouth. "Food . . . want food," he says in a low, rasping voice.

"Go away, we have nothing for beggars. Go away." The window slams shut.

He stands staring at the window for a moment, and then begins again to pound on the door. The window opens, and the woman heaves a bucket of cold water at him and finds her mark. "Now, get away," she screams, "or you'll get worse than that!"

He turns and walks quickly away, stumbling on the cabin's steps. He shivers from the cold water that seeps through his coat and hefts his worn pack higher up onto his back. The wind picks up in speed, gusting coldness about him, bringing with it the crispness that preludes the end of autumn and the coming of winter.

His name is Hans Feld, and he seeks a village, any village, which might provide him with shelter and perhaps some food for the winter months. Hans has no home, and owns only what he wears and what he carries in his pack. He is lost, and has been walking for days. And he is dying from a lack of warmth and sustenance.

The wolf limps forward slowly, its leg crushed by a wad of shot from a hunter's weapon. It senses the pain, the changing weather, but does not notice the beauty of the trees. It raises its head and its nose sniffs the air for the scent of prey; it has been a long time since the wolf has had good red meat. It salivates as its mind recalls the hot blood and flesh of the jack-rabbit, so many days ago. The wolf breathes heavily, and its breath forms clouds of mist, which vanish more quickly than the field mice which elude him. Ribs protrude from the sunken stomach. The wolf seeks no particular place, only some food, for he has been denied the shelter of a den and the nourishment of meat, and he is dying.

Hans sat in the schoolroom, staring out the window at the blue sky and white clouds, which lay like great chunks of wool in the air. The schoolmaster was talking, something about numbers, but Hans didn't care. He didn't understand the teacher, as did the rest of the children, but what did it matter? His father would teach him how to sweep the chimneys, and they could work together. That was good enough for Hans.

"Herr Feld, sleeping again?" barked the teacher. "Perhaps you don't find this lesson challenging enough for your mighty intellect?" Hans cringed and whimpered inwardly, stung by the cruel laughter and evil grins of his classmates, who had all turned around in their seats to look at the back corner where he sat alone. The teacher walked over to Hans, placed the chalk in his hand, and dragged him up to the slate board. "Now, perhaps you will teach us dullards how simple this problem is?"

Hans began to tremble, and his stomach hurt because he didn't know what the numbers meant. The laughter had become louder. His stomach tightened until he couldn't stand it, and then it let go. His pants were wet. The teacher smacked him and dragged him back to his seat. The class roared hysterically. After the class was over, he ran home before his classmates could catch and torment him, and told his father what had happened. The old man held his son to himself and cried, for he had given Hans his dull eyes and large head, and he knew very well what happened to slow boys in school.

Somewhere in his mind were memories of his mother, and of his brothers and sisters nursing at her side. There were four in that litter; three grew large and strong and were pack leaders. The fourth, a small miscolored pup with short hind legs and a narrow snout, took his place at the bottom of the pecking order.

The mating season came, and it was his first year. He chose a female and began to court her. Another male challenged him and they both bared teeth and snarled. Then they were upon each other with a whirlwind of fur. The other, bigger and quicker, bit and slashed until the oddly colored young wolf was unable to fight him off; then he had to grovel, lowering his head to show his inferiority to the larger wolf. He walked away shaking, head still bowed, while the bigger wolf took his female.

Hans sat on the wooden bench, watching others whirl about him to the music. Young couples held each other close as they waltzed across the floor.

All had gathered into little groups, all but Hans, who was alone. He wanted to run from this place to go home, or to work with his father cleaning the chimneys. He held a piece of cake in one hand, a cup of punch in the other. He felt hot and dizzy, so he drank some more of the cool, sweet punch.

A group of young men and girls talked and laughed in whispers while glancing mischievously in Hans' direction; it made him uncomfortable. Then, pushed forward by ten prodding arms, one of the girls walked over to the bench and sat down besides Hans. She grinned and winked at her friends.

"Hello . . . why didn't you ask me to dance?" she asked Hans. Hans stared at her beautiful figure, the breasts swelling above the low-cut dress. He felt ashamed, just as he did when he had dreams about these things. He had told the man at the church about the dreams, and had been beaten with a stick. Now he was aware of hoots of laughter. She took his hand and placed it inside her dress, against the warm and soft flesh. He got excited and tried to kiss her as he pulled the dress down below her breasts. She screamed, and all at once the other young men grabbed Hans and threw him on the ground. They kicked him and hit him and then threw him outside. He lay there, his nose bloodied, his face bruised and cut. He would never forget the laughter and the girl's naked torso, and that night . . .

A particularly vicious kick in the face had torn out his left eye.

The wolf had been unable to catch enough game to keep himself fed, and had been forced to rely on leftovers from other animal's kills. He couldn't keep pace with the pack on the hunt and always found himself many yards behind, bringing up the rear. All he knew then was the tiredness in his muscles and the desperate longing to take part in the kill, to be as good as any in the pack.

One morning, as the pack readied itself to set out, the leader, a huge, scarred animal with yellow fangs, had stood in front of him when he tried to follow, baring its teeth and snarling. Then the leader rejoined the pack. The pack marched on. The wolf turned and headed away in the opposite direction.

The minister had seen to the details of the burial, and Frederik Feld was put to rest in the proper manner. Hans felt cold and empty inside, and sat for many days inside the house. Then one day he saw the chimney brush in the corner and, remembering his father, set out to do the work that had to be done. But the people were nice only until he explained what he had come to do. "I take this and pull it up chimney, okay?" he said.

"No, no, Hans, you can't work on my chimney. God knows what you'll do to it or yourself," they said.

If he couldn't do work, he thought, he couldn't get money. And without money he couldn't get food. He had remembered the school teacher saying how many things could be eaten in the woods, so, he thought, I could live there and eat even if I can't work, and no one will laugh, either.

He packed a picture of his parents, a pair of shoes that had been his father's, and two apples in an old cloth bag. Then he set off for the woods, and, as he walked away from the village, it and its people grew smaller and smaller behind them. He turned his head several times to see this.

The wolf stopped in his tracks. He smelled some creature, and was overpowered by the sense of hunger, the primal lust for food. He followed the scent down the hillside and spotted a tall creature moving slowly. The wolf vaguely remembered this scent, and somehow he knew that the pack had never hunted one of these. But the wolf did not care, for if he did not eat now he would not get to see the next day. The wolf quickened his pace, and his fur bristled as a few snowflakes fell from the gray sky to swirl about in the air.

He stopped . . . coming toward him was a dog. Hans smiled. He had always liked dogs. They were soft and nice and never laughed at you or hurt you if you were nice to them. The dog got closer, and he saw its teeth were bared and heard it growl. "That bad doggie," he said, for he had had a lifetime in which to learn when something meant to do him harm. He picked up a large, hard branch, which he hefted up over his head and swung like a club. He was mad at the animal for wanting to hurt him, and he was going to show his anger to that bad doggie. He would break its head and cook it, like deer meat.

The wolf leapt up, hurling himself through the air at the man, fangs bared, snarling furiously, salivating. The man shouted and swung his club down at the animal, his eyes wide with the anger of thirty years of life.

One of them would eat that night, as the snow fell faster, and the winds whipped about the last dead leaves of the trees, which fell upon the bare ground to be covered by newly falling snow.

Winter came.

The End Effect of Global Warming

The big black man walks over to the edge of the rooftop and sticks his hand over it into the water. "Shit," he exclaims, "it's colder than it was yesterday."

He is right. The water surrounding the building gets colder day by day, and is rising slowly, too. The building upon which the man and the three others made their camp was the only one not completely submerged. Strong winds whip saltwater spray through the air and form white crests upon the water's surface. Great chunks of ice ranging in size from baseballs to compact cars float in the water and occasionally smash into the side of the building. The water has risen to a point where its surface is a mere one foot shy of the rooftop.

"I ain't never felt such cold water before," says Lee, the black man. He is thirty-five years old, muscular, and well over six feet tall. "It's a son of a bitch out today, boy. You can't bullshit Lee, now. Gonna be some big waves and ice and hail today!"

Lee walks over to a garbage pail full of freshwater. He scoops some up with a ladle and drinks it. He drinks another ladle full, and then another.

"Hey, what the fuck do you think you're doing?" asks a young man seated near the pail. "You already had one more cup than your ration allows for today." The young man is lanky and has long, black hair and a bushy beard.

"Listen, College-Boy, don't be tellin' Lee what to do or I'll smack you one in your Goddamn mouth."

"Is that all you know how to say? Christ, we've been up here for seven days, and every other word out of you is a threat. I'm getting sick of your mouth, man. What gives you the right to push us around like this?"

Lee spits a mouthful of the water out at Jerry's feet. Jerry is "College-Boy's" name. "You fuckin' know it, boy. Lemme tell ya, Lee learned to fight before he learned how to eat. That's the way it is, see. You may think you too damn smart for men, and maybe you young schoolboys got it nice, but up here I can tell you what to do as long as I can kick the shit out of you."

An older man, who has been sitting down, rises with the aid of his cane. "Might makes right, eh?"

Lee throws the ladle down and walks over to the man. "You got something to say to me, priest? You nosey, cabbage-eatin' bastard!"

"Please, Lee, leave Father Murphy alone," says Janie. She is the only female of the four people trapped on the rooftop. Janie is sixteen years old.

"The man can speak for himself, bitch. Now shut up before I pull that skirt up over your head and stick something in you."

"Listen, Lee, please try to cooperate," Murphy says. "We only have so much fresh water left, and we can't drink this sea water. The longer we can save the fresh water, the longer we can stay alive."

"What the fuck's the difference? We all gonna die anyway, right? What's the difference if it's a week from now or right now?"

"That's not the way to look at it, Lee. I mean, we're all going to die eventually. If I listened to you, there'd be no reason to stay alive at all, anytime."

"No, see, you ain't too fuckin' bright," says Lee angrily, "because you talkin' dumb shit. Before this I could drink a little VO and get me some pee-hole." He is staring at Janie, who turns away. "Yeah, VO and a little pee-hole. What the fuck can I do up here but wait around to drop dead?"

"There may be hope," says Murphy.

"Bullshit! You crazy, man? Or don't you know what happened? There was a fuckin' greenhouse gas explosion when the heat released all the methane trapped in the ground, and on top of that, the ozone layer done gone bye-bye. TV said it would melt the ice and shit at the poles, and it did." Lee gestures around him. "Take a look. Soon there won't be nothin' but water all around. We gonna die."

"I'm afraid Lee's right, Father," says Jerry. "There's a lot of ice up at the poles, and it's going to be melting for quite a while and raising the sea level. There isn't any hope."

Murphy sighs, and plays absentmindedly with the pocket Bible he carried in his pants pocket. "One never knows what God's plans are, Jerry," he says after a moment.

"If such a thing as this could happen, how can you still believe in God?" asks Jerry.

"Yeah," adds Lee. "You priests always tellin' us all this jibber-jabber about being saved and the good life in heaven. You tell us that Jesus is gonna come down from the mountain and save our ass. So we still waitin' on him, and look what he done. Nothing."

Jerry snaps his fingers. "Hey, Father Murphy, I just thought of something. This is Christmas Eve, isn't it?"

"Uh, I'm not quite sure . . . the date . . ."

"Don't worry about knowing the date, Murphy," says Lee, laughing. "I know that's hard to do." He depresses a button on his digital watch. "Yeah, the twenty fourth. I'll be damned, College, its Christmas Eve."

"Christmas . . . every Christmas, when we were little, me and my big brother Bobby would wait up for Santa," Janie says, "and he'd draw Santa a nice card with the list of presents I wanted. And he saved up his allowance to get me some of the presents. When the water came rushing in, he . . . he . . ." She buries her face in her hands and begins to weep.

"Yeah," says Lee, "I wish my kid was here. Little baby boy, only thirteen, and just as big as College. Strong as a bitch . . . yeah . . ."

"I'm sorry, Lee," Murphy says softly. "I understand . . ."

"You don't understand shit. You guys don't have no wife and kids. You just do it with both hands. Little Lee, Lee Junior . . ."

There is silence, save for a stifled roar in the distance, which is somewhat like the sound of thunder.

Jerry breaks the silence. "Father Murphy, what I was thinking about was the fact that this Christmas is special. After all, isn't Christ supposed to visit Earth after two thousand years? And that would be tonight, right?"

"Christmas of the year two thousand!" exclaims the priest. "Yes, oh yes, I had forgotten. Lee, Janie, tonight Christ will come down to Earth and take with him those who have been filled with the spirit of Christ and baptized in his name. He will take them with him to the Kingdom of Heaven."

"And the rest of us all go to Hell, right?" asks Jerry rather unpleasantly. Murphy is taken aback.

"That's a bit harsh, Jerry."

"But true, right? You have to be Christian to go to heaven. According to the beliefs you cherish, all Jews and Muslims and Buddhists and everybody else goes to eternal damnation simply because they don't practice your religion and worship Jesus. That seems pretty damn harsh to me."

"But God gives everybody a chance to be filled with His spirit, Jerry. That's why we try to convert all people to our faith."

"College is talking some good shit, Murphy." Lee pauses to light up a cigar. "Why I gotta be dunked under water to go to heaven? And a lot of people never get a chance to become Christian. So they ain't even offered a chance to go to heaven."

"Well, we try, but not everybody . . ."

"So them who don't wanna be religious go to Hell, right? Seems like the only virtue in your church is kissing ass."

"Lee, the whole idea of Christianity is to . . ."

"Kiss ass, like I'm telling you. You can do all bad shit as long as you go to church every Sunday and confess, right? Even molest altar boys, right?"

"Yeah," Jerry says, "Lee's right. I knew someone who was a Born Again Christian, and he explained that bit to me. I can rape and rob and murder, but if I sincerely repent in the name of Christ, I'll be completely forgiven. So even though I lit the pilot light at Auschwitz, I can go to heaven. But if I cure cancer and give millions to charity, and end all war on Earth, I'll still go the Hell if I miss Mass on Sunday. That's right, isn't it?"

"Yes, you have to be a Christian. But the way you're phrasing it is so unfair."

"The whole thing is pretty unfair," replies Jerry.

"What faith are you, Jerry?"

"Jewish by birth, agnostic by conviction."

"And how about you, Lee?" asks Murphy.

"I don't believe in none of that bullshit. I work five in the morning to three in the afternoon at the warehouse, then go to my other job doin' floors at night. Come Sunday, I'm too tired for church. Working man just likes to lay around, have a few cold ones, and watch a game on TV. But," Lee says, grinning, "you don't know too much about working men, do you, Rev?"

Janie clears her throat for attention. "I'm Catholic, Father Murphy. I went to church."

"So we have one believer in the bunch, eh?"

"Well," she says, blushing, "my parents actually made me go. I didn't really like it. It was kind of boring, and . . . you know."

The priest smiles, "Yes, I know."

"Hey, look way out over there," says Jerry, pointing to the north. "Do you see anything?"

"No, Jerry, I don't. Why?"

"Yeah, I see somethin'," Lee says. "Looks like a big mountain or chunk of shit movin' this way. Well, can't do anything about it, so Lee ain't gonna worry too much."

Jerry interjects, "Hey, Father, you asked me what I believe. Now let me ask you why. Why do you follow religion so strictly? Following strict rules, not marrying like nor . . ."

"Like normal people, Jerry? Yes, it's a rigorous, sometimes unrewarding life. But it gives me something I wouldn't trade for the world."

Lee snorts in disgust. "Shape it's in now, I wouldn't trade my snot for it."

"Go on, Father, ignore him. What is it you get out of this religion bit?"

"Faith. The greatest thing is the act of believing in something. Yes, I believe that Christ the Lord will take me up to Heaven. If this is true, I've gained something that will last me an eternity. If it is false, all my religion and self-sacrifice hasn't been wasted. They still gave me strength and inspiration which made my life on Earth more rewarding."

A seagull flies over the rooftop. Lee flips his cigar into the wind, and by luck it collides with the bird, which cries from the heat of its glowing tip. Lee laughs cruelly. Jerry shakes his head, and Lee, seeing this, gives him a raised middle finger. Jerry turns back to face Murphy.

"Do you believe that we'll . . . well, that we'll actually see Him? Christ, I mean. Do you believe that he'll really be on Earth, and that maybe we could look out and see someone walking toward us?"

Lee laughs. "You ain't gonna see shit, boy, cause not even shit is coming. Lemme tell it to you straight, College, and no bullshit. Ain't nobody coming from nowhere, understand? Because they're dead, they're all dead! And if they ain't, they's trapped same as us, and they gonna die same as us." He looks out over the water. "Shit . . . that thing out there is gettin' bigger. Looks like a mother-fucking tsunami. I hope it don't come this way."

"What's the difference, big man?" asks Jerry. "You shouldn't be afraid. After all, a tidal wave can't . . . can't bullshit Lee." Jerry starts laughing hysterically.

Lee grabs him by the collar. "Better watch your mouth, boy."

"Let go, you dumb douchebag!"

Lee slaps Jerry across the face with an open palm and throws him down. Janie grabs Lee by the arm. "Please don't hurt him, Lee. He didn't mean it. Please leave him alone."

Lee stares at her shirt, which is open at the top. "Now, that depends on how bad you want it. Lee would rather have some nice pee-hole than hassle that schoolboy."

"In God's name, have some decency," cries Murphy. "The girl's only sixteen years old."

"You know, a man makes a damn fool of himself when he talks about shit that he don't know. How you telling me about pussy when you never get any yourself? I been up here near a week, and I'm sick of beating off into the fucking sea, just like College been doing. Hey, College, you want to stick your face in those tits, right?"

"Don't touch her," says Jerry, who is gently rubbing a very red cheek. "Just don't touch her."

"Look at that young shit telling me not to touch her, when he wants to fuck her himself. Shit, Murphy, a real man's got to be getting nooky. You tellin' me how terrible I am for wanting to screw this young girl. Why? She probably had it as many times as me, already. The only fucking virgin around here is you, cocksucker. Isn't that right, girl?"

Janie looks down, embarrassed. "Well, I . . . I mean I . . ."

"No need to be ashamed to tell him," says Lee. "People like him make you embarrassed about it in the first place. What's wrong with me wanting to screw you, huh? It's the most natural thing in the world. What's unnatural is people not doing it when that's all they can think of. Right, College?"

Jerry does not reply, for he is looking toward the horizon. "That is definitely a tidal wave. It is getting much bigger."

Lee joins him and looks. "Yeah . . . look at the shape on that thing." The quartet falls silent as they look upon the dark shape in the distance.

Finally, the priest breaks the silence. "Look, let's forget about it. It's Christmas; this is supposed to be a holiday, right? Why don't we sing some Christmas songs?"

"To help us pass the time away?" asks Jerry, sarcastically.

"Hey, Christmas songs is okay, College. Come on, let's sing some. All music is good, that's what Lee always says."

"This will be fun," says Janie. "Does everyone know 'Deck the Halls'?"

The group begins to sing:

Deck the halls with boughs of holly,
Fa-la-la-la-la, fa-la-la-la.

'Tis the season to be jolly,
Fa-la-la-la-la, fa-la-la-la . . .

Several hours pass, and the sky grows dark and the air becomes colder. The waves upon the water grow in size, and the largest ones send water and ice splashing over onto the rooftop. In the distance, the tidal wave seems to grow larger and larger with each minute that passes. Janie and Father Murphy are seated. Murphy uses his coat to cover Janie, who is shivering and sneezing. Lee and Jerry stand staring out at the wave.

"I got a quarter to eleven on my watch, and still no Jesus comin' to pick us up. I guess God forgot to check His calendar."

Murphy looks up at the tall warehouseman. "It is not midnight yet, Lee," he says wearily.

"I bet damn sure he don't come no time. I bet ya."

"Whatever you say, Lee."

Before he can reply, a big wave splashes onto the roof, soaking Lee and Jerry with ice-cold water. "Fuck!" cries Lee. "That's cold as a bitch! I'm gonna freeze my ass off, standing here like this. God damn, Murphy, give me that fucking coat."

"Let them have it." Jerry gives Lee an annoyed stare. "Janie's got the flu or something, and she needs the warmth. Let them have it."

"I'm gonna let you have it in a minute, pal, but it won't be no coat. Take a look at that wave out there. It's growing like a cock at a dirty movie. We got a half hour, maybe an hour at the most. She ain't gonna live long enough to be sick from no cold, and Lee don't wanna be cold, so . . ."

Janie stands and hands Lee the coat. "Here, take it. I don't want to see anyone fight over it."

He reaches out and grabs her hand instead of the coat. He pulls her body close to his. She struggles but cannot break his grip. "Don't worry none about no blanket. I got something can keep us both warm." He reaches inside her shirt. She tries to pull away and the shirt rips open.

"Jerry, help! Don't let him touch me!"

"Get your hands off her!" Jerry cries, as he grabs Lee from behind. Lee lets go of Janie and spins around, catching Jerry with a fist. Jerry is stunned and his legs go rubbery. Lee picks him up by his shirt-front with one hand and begins to pound him repeatedly with his big, meaty hand.

"You been asking for it, Jewboy. I'm gonna kick your ass but good!"

Janie flies at Lee. He pushes her away and she falls down. Lee begins to choke Jerry, who cannot defend himself. Jerry's face goes very red, and Janie screams.

Suddenly Murphy is there, a chunk of ice in his hands. Standing in back of Lee, who is bent over Jerry, Murphy brings the ice high over Lee's head, and swings down. Something goes soft at the top of Lee's head and the black man slumps forward, unconscious.

Murphy drops the ice and cries out, "Oh, my God! Is Jerry all right?"

Janie helps Jerry to his feet. "Okay . . . I'm okay . . . give me a minute . . . catch my breath . . ." He uses her for support, and then sees Lee lying on the rooftop. "Lee!" He rushes over to the body and takes the pulse in several places. He examines the head wound caused by the ice, and then covers Lee's face with the coat.

"He's dead, Father Murphy. He's dead."

The priest's eyes grow wide and his face goes very white. "I didn't mean it. It was an accident . . . I killed a man. Killed him."

"You did it to help me, Father. You didn't do anything wrong. It was self-defense."

The priest is oblivious to what the young man says. He fumbles in his pants pocket and comes up with the little Bible. "You don't understand. I killed a man today . . . I have sinned . . . and there is not enough time to repent . . . no priest left to confess to . . . no church to pray in . . . I'll rot in Hell. In Hell!"

The priest opens the Bible to a random page and, without looking down, begins to recite: "The Lord is my shepherd, I. . ."

"Give me that fucking thing!" cries Jerry, who snatches the Bible out of the priest's hand. With a pencil stub he had in his pants pocket, Jerry furiously scribbles something on the page, and then tosses the little Bible into the air. The priest continues reciting the "Lord's Prayer" as the pages scatter to the wind.

Janie screams, and they turn to see a wall of water rushing in upon them.

"NO!" shouts Murphy. "No, not yet. I haven't repented. It's not fair. I've been so good, not fair, not fa . . ."

The priest's protests are cut off as the tidal wave sweeps over the rooftop and the four bodies are covered by tons of water. The building is swallowed up by the wave.

After the waves pass the water calms, and it is as if the building had never been. Later, a man clothed in white walks upon the waters. He sees a page of printed matter, with words hastily scribbled upon it, floating on the water a few feet in front of him. He picks it up, and reads the words:

WHERE WERE YOU WHEN WE NEEDED YOU?

Sighing, he crumples the sheet of paper up into a little ball and throws it to the wind.

A Toy for Young Prince Caesar

He was the smaller of the two gladiators, but also the swifter. In one hand, he brandished a strong net, in the other a spiked club wrought of metal. He looked at his opponent, who waited on the other side of the arena. The man was of a dark race, tall, with enormous arms that were as thick as sturdy young saplings; he chose for his weapons an iron shield and a short heavy sword. But no matter how dark or tall his opponent may be, he would win. He must win.

His name is unimportant, but the others called him Dirae. He lived only to kill for the amusement of the nobles. And both the nobles and the gladiators lived only by the will of young Prince Caesar.

The prince was a frail young lad of about twenty, who Dirae could have crushed with but a single blow. Yet this boy was heir to the most powerful empire on the face of the earth, and his whim was law. If his fighting prowess should please the prince, Dirae might be made a free man someday. That thought, combined with a body graced by the muscles and reflexes of a wild beast and a heart hardened by the slaughter of a hundred foes, made Dirae the greatest fighting man in the realm. Yet he feared the real death, which he came closer to with each contest. His last opponent, a giant who towered well above four cubits, had smashed several of Dirae's ribs. Only a lucky blow which deprived the giant of his head had saved Dirae from defeat.

The sun shone brightly that day. The crowds, dressed in finery and eating rich foods, watched the opening with little interest. The first fight was between two dwarfs, armed with axes. It bored the crowd, as the two pitiful creatures hacked away at each other until one lost his head to the other's blade. The victor fell to the ground, mortally wounded himself, and began to weep. The senators and wealthy noblemen applauded sparingly between draughts of fine wine.

"Is the sport going to offer any more entertainment than this? I say, I can get more amusement by flogging one of my slaves," said a senator with disgust.

"Stop thy moaning, friend," said the sweating wine merchant on his right. "Dirae is fighting today, and he will give us sport enough."

After several other contests, the blare of trumpets announced the main event. The obese spectators moaned as they forced their bulks upright on the marble benches. "This had better be worth giving up an afternoon at the mineral bathhouse," said the senator, to no one in particular.

The smell of blood, death, and sweat filled the air. The crowd was awed into silence as two magnificent warriors walked slowly out to the center of the arena. As the dark warrior stared into the eyes of Dirae, Dirae snarled at him through his teeth: "You will die this day, for I cannot lose."

The dark one smiled, baring white fangs, and said, "It is the same with me. Prepare to meet your end!" With this he swung his sword hard at Dirae's head.

The sword missed its mark, for the blow was slow and clumsy. Dirae faked a throw with his net and swung his deadly mace, which the other blocked with his shield. A sword flashed by Dirae's head, and in avoiding its sharp blade he was caught full in the breast by the other's shield.

This sent Dirae sprawling to the ground and it brought the crowd to its feet. Dirae was in pain, and he had lost his net. His head was foggy. He saw a blurred image leaping at him, so he kicked out hard at the enemy's midsection, which threw his opponent off long enough for Dirae to recover his senses. The crowd roared its approval, for they were with Dirae and wanted him the victor.

As the tall warrior charged again, Dirae swung his mace and opened a wound on his head. The dark one's sword, however, found Dirae's underbelly, and crimson red stained Dirae's garment. Dirae knew that the wound was serious, and the battle would be lost unless he could end it quickly in his favor. In his desperation, he was lucky, for in front of him was a large stone. He threw his club in front of his opponent's feet as if he had lost it by mistake. The tall one grinned, seeing his enemy defenseless. As he stooped to pick up Dirae's club, Dirae quickly scooped up the rock in his hands and brought it up hard into the gladiator's face. The crowd cheered wildly as the large stone caved in the front of the man's skull. The man screamed as he gushed blood. While he still had the strength, Dirae lifted the stone high and brought it downward. The enemy had started to rush forward but Dirae was too quick. The rock found its mark, sending brain and bone flying in all directions.

Wearily, Dirae dropped his weapon. He was wounded, exhausted in both body and spirit, but he was victorious. The crowd was on its feet, applauding sincerely (for once) the courage and strength of another human. It was known that Dirae sought freedom through his prowess as a warrior, and the crowd hoped that the prince might grant it. Dirae turned his head to look up at Caesar, and as his eyes centered upon the prince, so did the eyes of the crowd.

The prince was heartily involved in a game of chance, which he routinely played with several of his concubines. He had not bothered to watch the contest. "Such a silly and boring thing, these contests are," he had told the lovely maiden on his right, who sought her freedom through different means. Prince Caesar noticed the deadly silence and looked up. Seeing all eyes upon him, he stared down into the ring where Dirae stood alone in a pool of blood. The prince rose to his feet, applauded lightly with his pale hands, and then motioned for the guards to take Dirae back to the slave quarters until the next day of sport. Then the prince went back to his game and his maidens, and the crowd slowly dispersed in shameful silence.

Two guards stood on either side of the victorious warrior, but out of respect they did not force him to move. The arena was empty now, save for Dirae and his guards. The gore from the day's amusements had been removed. The sun set as the three men stood in silence. All was quiet, except for the imperceptible sound of a tear rolling down Dirae's blood-stained cheek.

Some Abigail of His Own

"Your secretary let me in. I have an appointment," said the old woman standing in front of the huge marble-top desk.

"Yes. Yes, Mrs. Morrison," said the man behind the desk. He smiled and gestured for Mrs. Morrison to sit in the chair.

Mrs. Abigail H. Morrison took the seat she was offered and rested her cane against the desk. "Thank you very much, Mister . . . uh . . . Mister Disney, isn't it?"

The man laughed heartily. "Oh no, Mrs. Morrison. The founder of Disney Automatons Incorporated, Walt Disney, died many years ago. I am Mr. Filmore, one of the vice-presidents."

Mrs. Morrison had to depend on a hearing aid, and in some instances it did not serve her well. "I'm sorry," she said, "I didn't hear you so good. Did you say 'Wilhorn'?"

"Filmore," said the man behind the desk.

"Oh," she said, finally hearing him clearly. "So you are Mr. Filmore!"

The man behind the desk remained still, yet she heard his voice, and it seemed to be coming from the hallway in back of her! "No, Mrs. Morrison. I am Mr. Filmore."

With difficulty, she managed to twist her neck around so she could look towards the source of the voice. And in the doorway through which she had walked moments earlier, stood Mr. Filmore. The man behind the desk. Only he wasn't behind the desk. But he was the man behind the desk. Only the man behind the desk . . .

He walked around her, and sat on the desk top. "Don't be scared, Mrs. Morrison. I really am Mr. Filmore, in the flesh. What you see in my chair is one of our finest products. He is our Automaton number A-1087-FM. Quite a convincing double, don't you think?"

Mrs. Morrison fanned herself with an embroidered handkerchief and tried desperately to regain her composure. "But, but so real," she gasped, "I never, ever, thought that they would be so, so . . ."

"Life-like?" Mr. Filmore smiled. "How else could they be? If we didn't produce a product that was more like the original than the original itself, how could we stay in business?"

Mr. Filmore-the-automaton remained motionless. Mr. Filmore brushed his hand over the desktop and depressed what looked like a fountain pen in a pen holder. The automaton silently rose from his chair and walked past Mrs. Morrison into the hall. Mr. Filmore took his hand off the desktop and seated himself behind the desk.

"I always feel that the best way to show a customer what we can do is to prove to them that we stick by our advertising slogans." He paused, and without thinking Mrs. Morrison mumbled the ad to herself: "Disney Automatons—the robot that is more you than you."

"What was that, Mrs. Morrison?"

"Oh nothing, nothing."

"Well, are you interested in purchasing an automaton, Mrs. Morrison?"

"I'm interested," she sighed.

"Okay, good. Now, the first thing we should discuss is the price. An A class automaton, with a lifetime of at least twenty years—that is to say, if the deception is discovered due to breakdown or poor craftsmanship, you get a full refund for the first twenty years of ownership—will run you in the neighborhood of three hundred thousand dollars, minimum. Is this within your price range?"

"Quite," said Mrs. Morrison, stiffly. "In this case, money is no object."

"Fine. Now I've got a more sensitive question to ask. We must know the purpose of your purchase. We must know where and how you intend to use the automaton."

"Why?" she demanded. "Why is it any of your business? I don't think it is any of your business."

"We must protect our own business interests, Mrs. Morrison. We lose a great deal of money on full refunds. We look on it as sort of an insurance policy, so we must determine if the client is 'high-risk' or not. Price varies with the use of the product; the greater the chance of the deception being discovered, the higher the price. In some cases, we turn away clients whose intentions would put the product in serious jeopardy."

"But how would you know if I use it like I say I will? And how could you force me to use it like I say I will?"

"Simple, Mrs. Morrison. The manner of usage is written into a legal contract. We handle the legal fees as part of the deal. A breach of contract frees us from obligation to the client. We have two full-time investigators whose jobs it is to keep us informed on the status of each automaton's usage. So I must know the exact manner in which you will put your automaton to use." Mr. Filmore reached for a pocket tape recorder. "Oh, by the way," he said. "Who will the automaton be a double for?"

"She," said Mrs. Morrison, "will be my double."

"In that case, I'll have our cosmetics department take an impression of your face for the mask before you leave here today."

"What are you going to do to my face?" asked Mrs. Morrison.

"Oh, don't worry. We are merely going to take a laser scan of your facial contours for the automaton's face. That way it will be your exact double."

"Is it necessary?" she asked, pulling her knit shawl about her thin shoulders. "Couldn't you just work from a picture?"

"We do if circumstance dictates that the subject be unaware that he is being duplicated. But whenever possible, we like to work from life. It makes for a better Duraflex mask, and it cuts down on the cost slightly. We pass those savings on to you, of course."

"Of course," said Mrs. Morrison. "Duraflex?"

"Duraflex is the material we use as the automaton's skin. It has a consistency much like human skin; it flexes as well as compresses."

"Couldn't you use rubber or something like that?"

"We tried rubber. It flexes okay, but it wouldn't compress correctly for our needs."

"Oh. This Duraflex, is it something new?"

"Oh no, not at all." said Mr. Filmore. "It's the very same material that Disney used for his original Audio-Animatronic figures back in the sixties. In fact, there is very little difference between our product and the original mechanical Lincoln that Disney used in the Hall of Presidents exhibit in the World's Fair of 1962."

"No, no," said Mrs. Morrison, "It was the New York World's Fair of 1964, not '62. I was there! I remember that exhibit." She closed her eyes and continued speaking. "I was a young girl, no more than twenty. Henry—he's my husband, now—took me there on a date. I'll never forget that fair.

"Everything was big and beautiful and fantastic, but Mr. Lincoln was the best thing of all. There they were-life size models of the presidents. They sat there, still as could be. Then, all of a sudden, the statue of Lincoln cleared his throat! He clasped the arms of his chair, frowned at us, and stood up.

"He began to talk, and I thought that surely this was Lincoln himself come back to life. He asked us, 'What constitutes the bulwark of our own liberty and independence?' And then he winked, he winked right at me! Or at least I thought that wink was just for me. I still think so."

"Uh, Mrs. Morrison?" Christ, he thought, if she was twenty or so back in '64 then she must be almost ninety now.

She continued, ignoring the interruption. "Then he paused, as if waiting for us to speak. He ran his tongue over his lips. Then he answered his own question: 'Our reliance in the love of liberty which God has planted in us . . .' He turned his head, and . . ."

"Mrs. Morrison, about the terms of your contract . . ."

"I'm sorry," she said, regaining her composure. "It's just that seeing Lincoln there, hearing him talk, gave us all something we thought we could never have again." She blinked. "Do you still make them the same way, Mr. Filmore? So perfect, so good . . ."

"Our automatons are essentially the same as the Lincoln prototype you saw at the fair. Your double would basically be an Audio-Animatronic being. We would record the voice—in this case yours—on digital media. On a hard drive, we program standard algorithms of motion such as standing, frowning, walking, et cetera. The software activates wires which lead to air hoses, pistons, and hydraulic lines. In the original Lincoln, for example, there are sixteen air lines to the head, ten to the hands, and fourteen hydraulic lines to control the body."

"But what's the difference?" she asked. "Lincoln, real as he seemed, was just a puppet on a string, following those taped instructions. Is that all you offer?"

Filmore grinned. "The difference is a small computer located in the abdomen. Also, the head is equipped with sensory devices which enable the automaton to evaluate external stimuli, such as conversation, doorbells, and the like.

"The original Lincoln figure had his speech on tape. He was turned on, and his speech played through. The current computerized automatons have a recorded vocabulary of over three thousand words—more, if the client is willing to spend more—which it organizes into coherent sentences through its limited AI CPU. Of course, certain stock phrases often encountered in conversation are prerecorded for convenience. About two hundred of them. Given a sufficiently dull conversationalist to talk with, an automaton could get through an hour's chat without once forming an original sentence. Ha, ha."

Mrs. Morrison did not smile.

"Uh, heh-heh, a little company joke there. Yeah. Anyway, I'm sure you see the difference. Oh, your automaton will have thirty facial expressions compared to fifteen for the original Mr. Lincoln, but that's minor. The main difference is the built-in AI CPU or 'brain.'"

"But is it really aware? Does it really know what it is doing?" asked Mrs. Morrison. "Can it feel enthusiasm for the conversation? Can it return affection?"

"Why is this important to you?" asked Mr. Filmore as he switched on the digital recorder.

"Well, I want to be able to fool my husband into thinking that the automaton is really me. I don't want him to know that I've gone away."

"Planning a trip?" asked Mr. Filmore.

"Come on, young man, don't fool with me. You know I'm too old for that sort of thing. Since this is just between me, you, and the lawyers, I'll tell you what I'm planning. I'm planning the Final Trip."

"Suicide," blabbed Filmore.

"Of course. Everybody knows what FT is and what it entails."

"Well, I have to ask you this, then: Why bother to create an automaton if you are going to die?"

"Simple," said the old woman. "I don't want my husband to know what I'm doing. He'd be able to claim suicide on my life insurance if I FT legally, and that money, plus my estate, would go to him, and not to the children."

"But why wouldn't you want him to get any of your insurance money? Why not give some to your children and some to him? I don't see . . ."

"Of course you don't see," cried Mrs. Morrison angrily. "Why do you think I want to FT? I'm sick and tired of him, of his stupid beer and baseball games on TV and the stupid model ships with the glue all over the place. I'm tired, Mr. Filmore, so very tired. And I just want to Go Home."

Go Home. Another name for the voluntary suicide. Mr. Filmore saw it all in its proper place: Her husband was probably good to her and they had been in love once, but seventy years is too long to live with any person. The children move away and visit only infrequently, so they still remain pleasant memories, while your mate becomes, quite simply, a pain in the ass. Mr. Filmore had only been married for two years and noticed that already certain of Mary's habits had begun to annoy him. What would it be like in twenty years? Fifty years? Seventy years?

Oh God, he moaned inwardly.

Mrs. Morrison simply wanted out, and why shouldn't she get it? She had paid her dues, lived a full life, and was asking for—no, she was buying—a chance to go out with some satisfaction. The satisfaction of doing right by her children, to be sure.

But she didn't really hate Mr. Morrison. She had loved him once, and she never wanted to see him hurt. She couldn't deny herself the Final Trip, but at the same time she couldn't bear to leave him alone. Oh, their marriage had been reduced to monosyllables uttered over the kitchen table, but if she died, it would make him miserable. So she had to leave him with some Abigail of his own, one way or another. She had been at a loss, not knowing what to do, until she had seen the Disney ad.

He looked at the woman who sat before him with folded hands. "Mrs. Morrison, you realize that our automatons can display only programmed reactions. They make decisions, think after a fashion, but they don't really feel, and they aren't really aware; they're strictly low-level AI. To them, looking through the family picture album is merely sensory data, which is then processed to give the proper coded commands to the computer, which will then activate the voice box to make them say 'Oh, yes, remember that day?' But they don't really remember, see? Your automaton cannot be to Mr. Morrison what you have been." Filmore spoke in a gentle, almost apologetic voice. But then he cleared his throat and continued in a harsher tone. "What I'm saying, Mrs. Morrison, is that should your husband discover the deception because of the automaton's lack of, shall we say, affection and warmth, we would not, could not, be responsible for a refund in that situation." He looked down at the top of the desk and not at Mrs. Morrison.

Mrs. Morrison thought of going home. He would be sleeping on the good couch, or watching television, or sitting in the kitchen in his undershirt.

She would make the tea, which she would take into another room while he sat alone drinking his. Maybe he would say "thank you." Maybe not.

"No, Mr. Filmore, I don't think that will happen. Anyway, I'm sure enough of that to be able to sign the contract."

"Well, then," he said, extending his hand, "I'll have the contract printed out in triplicate. And why don't I take you for body measurements and a face-cast?"

With difficulty, she rose to her feet. She did not accept his extended hand. "Don't get me wrong, Mr. Filmore. I love my husband. That's why I'm doing this."

The contract popped out of a slit on the desk. He pushed it in front of her. "Sign here," he said, indicating a blank line on the paper.

With a shaky hand, she did.

The room was done up in a royal blue, as she had requested. The second movement of Beethoven's Seventh flowed from the hidden speakers. She drank a poisoned nectar out of a silver cup, and lay between cool white sheets on a soft bed. A warmness spread throughout her being, and darkness brushed her eyes. Soft, soft, sinking into a sea of velvet, whirling like a dancer on the stage . . . deeper and deeper into the ocean's darkness, surrounded by Beethoven. The drug in the nectar, doing its work, her eyelids flutter and her body trembles one last time . . .

Final Trip.

Mr. Morrison sits in the kitchen, watching the Mets play on his black-and-white portable. Water boils in a kettle on the stove. "Abigail," he calls. "Abigail, the water's ready."

Auditory receptors pick up the sound waves, transmitting the impulses to the storage bits. The information is processed and hydraulic lines 24 and 44 are activated. The Abigail automaton rises and walks to the stove.

More relays are switched, more pistons and airlines are activated as she pours the water into the cups and dunks teabags into the hot water. She puts one cup in front of Mr. Morrison, who grunts, "Thank you, Abby."

"You are welcome," she responds. Not "you're welcome" but "you are welcome." A bit too stiff, a bit too formal, but Mr. Filmore and Disney Automatons Incorporated work well; Mr. Morrison does not notice, never notices, any change in his Abigail's behavior.

But there is the matter of the tea. The Abigail automaton cannot consume food. What she does is to drink it, then wait until she can be alone in the bathroom. She opens a compartment in her chest and empties the plastic bag which is her food receptacle. Then she goes into the parlor to knit.

Mr. Morrison has already finished his tea. He walks over to the kitchen sink, and, like he has done every day since the day he was activated six years ago, removes his plastic food receptacle bag from his chest and spills the tea (still warm) into the sink.

Final Trip.

The Huntsman

The three rode silently. The hooves of their mounts made little noise against the grassy floor of the forest. Sunlight reflected off the steel of the leader's armor, forming brilliant crosses of light. The nearby foliage rustled; a sound was heard. Quickly, one of the two men in the rear, dressed in khaki and not metal, swung his rifle upwards, bringing the barrel to bear down upon that area. His finger tensed on the trigger, and he started to squeeze it.

A hand encased in a steel mesh glove darted out faster than the man's eyes could follow and ripped the rifle from his grasp. He whipped his head around and faced the armored one. There was anger in his eyes, but it faded as the metal one put his hand on his own weapon.

The man cursed under his breath. Had he not been wearing his armor with its audio-amplified earpieces, the one called the Huntsman would not have been able to hear such softly spoken profanities.

"Damn it, Huntsman," said the young man. "That could have been one. Why didn't you let me bag him?"

"I thought I was clear about when you can and cannot kill, Mr. Matheson," replied the Huntsman. If there was emotion in his voice, the breathing screen in his metal mask muffled it. His voice came through as a cool monotone. "Apparently, I was not clear enough, so I must repeat myself. Once we are within the boundaries of the Colony, you are licensed to kill one of the residents, just as Mr. Donahue," he nodded in the direction of the other man, who was visibly frightened of the Huntsman, "is licensed to kill one. Outside of the Colony bounds your permit is void. Should you be caught, well—I think they use the gas chamber in this state." The Huntsman tossed Dennis Matheson his rifle.

Matheson caught the rifle with his right hand. The wrist was a bit red from being twisted when the Huntsman wrenched the weapon from his hands. "Listen, Huntsman, don't ever attack me again like that. I pay you a very handsome fee to take us on this hunt, and I'll not take orders from a hired . . . a hired hand."

A noise like laughter came from within the steel helmet. "You mean your rich daddy pays me a handsome fee. What I did was for your benefit, as well as mine. Your eagerness to kill one of the Colony residents almost made you a murderer, if indeed that was what we had behind the bush."

"Murderer!" cried Mr. Donahue, who had been silent. "Come on, Huntsman, they're hardly people . . . they're animals, for Christ's sake! They live in dirt huts, breed like rodents, run around half-naked . . . why do you think they have to live in the Dev Colony in the first place?"

From the breathing screen in the Huntsman's helmet came a clicking noise, and the Huntsman's mount turned and began to trot. Dennis Matheson and Paul Donahue follow him. After a time, the Huntsman spoke: "Hardly people, Mr. Donahue? What does that mean? When do people become 'hardly people'?"

Matheson and Donahue exchanged glances. Matheson's voice did not conceal his revulsion: "No real man would do what Devs do, Huntsman. They . . . well, God damn it, man, they're fucking sexual deviants! They're not like the rest of us; they're perverts! And if that's not bad enough, they try to recruit innocent people into their slimy ranks." Matheson paused, and spat with vehemence at the dirt below him. "I wish I could kill them all, get rid of the whole sick bunch. Then they couldn't . . . do . . . what they do with each other."

"They shouldn't have the right to live," Paul added. "We should shoot every one of them living in that disgusting mud hole. They're like a bunch of filthy lepers. They should be shot."

When did we ever shoot lepers for being lepers? thought the Huntsman, as the Colony came into the view of the trio.

The child played with her blocks in the light of the late afternoon sun. She was naked, dirty, and quite content. Nick watched the little blonde girl, who was his daughter, as he lay contentedly, stomach down, on the soft grass outside his hut. Inside, Mandy was preparing the evening supper. He got up, brushed himself off, and went inside.

Mandy was facing away from him, intently peeling the skins off some potatoes. Nick walked into the food area quietly and grabbed Mandy from behind. Startled at first, Mandy turned and faced him.

"I did not hear you enter, Nicky."

"I didn't want you to hear me," he laughed.

"Where is Valerie?"

"Building forts and castles outside. She's surrounded herself with a ring of castles and forts."

"Even one so young, and already cutting herself off . . . I wish . . ."

"Oh, cut the crap, Mandy. She's just building with her blocks. Don't turn everything into psychoanalytic bullshit."

"But isn't that it? Aren't we cut off, because, just because . . . ?"

He wrapped his arms around Mandy. They were both naked, save for loin clothes. Their mouths met, and Nick ran his tongue over Mandy's teeth. Then, they did a thing, which was love for them but unspeakable to Paul, Dennis, and possibly the Huntsman.

The sun shone orange-red as it drifted slowly beneath the horizon. The horses were hitched together, and Paul and Dennis sat around a steaming pot of coffee. The coffee was warmed on an electric hotplate, since the Huntsman would not permit the light of a fire. An insulated cord ran from the hotplate to an outlet in the Huntsman's metal chestplate, so that his armor's power supply could power the appliance. The Huntsman stared intently in the direction of the Colony, which lay less than a mile beyond their campsite.

"When do we move?" asked Matheson, as he sipped his coffee.

"When the sun sets and we are in darkness," replied the Huntsman, without averting his gaze.

Matheson watched the Huntsman, who showed no sign of being noticed. After a time, Matheson could restrain his curiosity no longer: "What are you looking at?"

The Huntsman remained unmoving, spying upon the Colony, in partic-ular a hut on the northside border. "I am watching two of them that could be prey."

"That's doing your job!" exclaimed Matheson. "How can you see them? It must be over a mile away!"

The rest of him remaining still, the Huntsman brought his right arm up and tapped at the side of his helmet with a metal finger. "Telefoto lenses with augmented night vision," he said.

"Oh." Matheson brought his cup to his lips. "And what are they doing that you find so fascinating?" he asked sarcastically.

"Performing their version of the sexual act," replied the Huntsman, without inflection.

"My God!" cried Matheson, spitting out his brew. "You're sick! How could you stand to watch something so perverted? Unless . . ." He grinned.

The Huntsman touched a stud on his chestplate, and then walked over to where the two men sat drinking coffee. He pulled the hotplate plug from his chest outlet. The man in metal stood directly over Matheson. Harshly, with unquestionable anger: "Unless what?"

"Dennis didn't mean anything," whined Donahue nervously. "He was only making a joke. Come on, forget it."

The Huntsman laughed hollowly, without mirth. "Don't worry. As long as you're paying me, I won't hurt you."

Won't hurt us, thought Matheson, scornfully. I'll ask Dad to buy me one of those armored suits, and then we'll see how tough you really are, big man!

"But, why did you watch them, Huntsman? Don't they sicken you?" Paul shakes his head in disgust.

"As a matter of fact, what you consider deviant behavior used to be the norm, and what we take as the accepted norm used to be considered diseased," said the Huntsman.

Paul snickered in disbelief, "I don't remember it ever being so."

"You would know about it if you ever bothered to read history books. What I say is well known fact among scholars and students."

"Well, I don't read such idiotic books. They're full of lies, and written by liars," said Dennis, as he stretched his arms.

Idiot spawn of spineless money grabbers! Then aloud: "If you've never read these books then how do you know what they say is untrue?"

"Oh, all right, Huntsman. Tell me. Tell us of a time when everyone was a sexual deviant and norms were the crazy ones."

"Neither is crazy," began the Huntsman. "Although, until a few hundred years ago, man had been basically heterosexual since the beginning of the race."

"Ridiculous," snorted Matheson.

"Ridiculous?" shouted the Huntsman. "How do you think new children were born then, you blithering idiot? You know that the sperm bank, exo-womb, and artificial insemination centers require advanced technology. Do you think cavemen could build cryogenic refrigeration units? They bred through sexual intercourse, and not through artificial insemination and clonal techniques!"

The hunters sat stunned. They had never thought about this because they had never wanted to think about it. But it was all so frighteningly obvious—people had to be heterosexuals in the non-technological eras, else how could they breed?

Finally Paul spoke. "But, but how could they stand it? Maybe they had to be heteros because children had to be born that way, but, didn't it disgust them? Did certain people have to be forced into being Devs? How did they pick them?"

"People weren't picked for breeding," said the Huntsman. "They weren't disgusted by Dev acts. Something like ninety percent of all people were heteros by choice, because it was natural for them to be that way."

Paul's voice was little in the darkness. "What about the . . . other . . . ten percent? The homosexuals?"

"It was natural for those few to be homos, so they were," replied the Huntsman. "The only problem for them was the same problem that exists for heteros in Colonies today—even though Devs only make up about two percent of our population. The homos back then were considered sexual deviants, just the way heteros are today. They weren't kept in colonies, but those who were known to be homos were often made miserable by intolerant peers and unfair laws."

"My God!" said Paul. "Imagine being punished just for being homosexual. Ugh!" He shuddered in revulsion.

Imagine being punished for being heterosexual. The Huntsman folded his massive metal arms across his chest and shook his head. "Yes," he said softly, "people can be a cruel lot."

"But—accepting what you say about heteros being 'normal'—why did things change? Why are we a homosexual breed now?"

"Well, you know that one of our legitimate fears of heteros is that their intercourse produces children." The Huntsman winced beneath his mask at the sound of the word "children." He continued: "There was a time when population control was not vital to Earth's survival. Having children was accepted, and in fact, was considered a sign of status. It is ironic in a way that this was once used as an argument against the homos; since homos do not produce offspring in their lovemaking, such lovemaking was considered perverse."

"Jesus Christ!" exclaimed Paul. "Sex perverse because it does not cram the world full of unwanted infants?"

"That was the logic. Anyway, the population grew to around 11 billion, at which point it became inevitable that the world could not support so many people. Hetero mating produced all these extra people. Obviously, the sex act itself could not be banned—people enjoy it too much and there is no way to stop them. Birth control methods were introduced to prevent conception, but they simply weren't effective enough. Since intercourse could not be halted, and conception resulting from hetero intercourse could not always be prevented, homo intercourse was the only viable alternative."

Matheson stared with wonder at the Huntsman. "And so all these heteros just switched because it would stop population growth? Bullshit!" He laughed sarcastically. "Could you imagine us all becoming heteros just because it would be better for the world? Phooey!"

"The change was slow, to be sure," admitted the Huntsman. "But those who study such things tell us that there is a mixture of hetero and homo tendencies in each of us. No one is completely straight or queer. So, laws were changed and the homos were encouraged to practice, and heteros were discouraged. Eventually, declared heterosexuals had trouble finding jobs and living normal lives. Over a period of many years society became homosexual. The few people who find hetero intercourse the only satisfying sex, and who can't conform to the norm, well—they can only live in relative safety in isolated Colonies." He chuckled. "Safely, that is, save for the hunters who can afford to cajole and bribe their way into a killing permit."

"But, if they're really just people, why does the government allow this at all? Isn't it murder, anyway you look at it?" whined Paul.

"I think the government would like to see a permanent end to the hetero problem, and this is why you gentlemen can buy a permit with less trouble than one might imagine. As for this being murder, yes, it . . ."

"Yes, nothing!" said Matheson as he jumped to his feet. "I've a license to bag one hetero, as do you, Paul. The Huntsman here seems to know everything about heteros; maybe he's soft or maybe it's part of his job. I don't know. He doesn't have to kill, just help us kill. Now, are you with me, or are you afraid?"

Donahue, pale and trembling, rose to his feet. "NO, dammit, I can't do it." He fumbled in his vest pocket and came up with the pink permit, which he threw down at Matheson's feet. Donahue gathered his weapon and things and put them in his horse's saddle-bag. The Huntsman and Matheson watched him in silence.

Donahue saddled the animal. He turned to the standing pair and steered his horse close besides them: "Dennis, I won't begrudge you your pleasure, but neither will I indulge in it. The Huntsman is right; it would make us murderers. These are people, damn you, people, whether they're heteros or not. I . . ." He stared into Matheson's unsympathetic face, and into the never changing faceplate of the Huntsman's mask. Then, without another word, he turned about and rode off toward the city.

Matheson sneered: "I had a feeling that he wasn't made for this kind of thing." He picked up the hunting permit and scrutinized the document closely. "This seems to be transferable if I sign it," he said. "You're welcome to his permit, Huntsman."

A period of time passed, but the Huntsman did not speak.

"Oh, I forgot. I'm sorry, Huntsman . . . the heteros are people, and you shouldn't kill people, even if they live like animals." He began to pocket the paper, but was caused to stop.

The Huntsman held out his gleaming metal hand and said, "Thank you, I will accept your offer of a kill."

Half asleep, head nuzzled in between Mandy's soft breasts, he was roused by noise. The sound of dull clicking, like horses' hooves hitting hard dirt. The sound stopped. He looked at the girl, asleep in her crib. Then he closed his eyes.

Noise again. Terror crept up through his skin. He broke out in a cold sweat, his arm sticky against the skin of Mandy's bare stomach. His senses caught the odor of smoked meat, then logs in the stove . . .

Fire!

Above him the straw roof was suddenly ablaze with flame. He roused Mandy, who was instantly awake. Holding hands, they ran for the crib. Scooping up the child, they raced for the door.

The smoke stung his eyes, causing them to shed water. Squinting to aid his vision, he saw two vague figures some distance from the hut. They seemed to be pointing at him.

"Hey, there!" he cried. "Get some dirt and water, we've got a fi . . ."

He heard a sharp cracking noise, and Mandy was hurled backwards, out of his grip. He turned and saw her lying very still. He put his daughter down and knelt by Mandy's side. He saw the blood, the hole in her stomach. He turned at the sounds of footsteps, saw the approaching men, and knew what had happened and what is about to happen.

A thin man with a rifle screamed: "I bagged one, Huntsman!" The excited hunter brought his rifle down to reload, and Nick sprung forward. Legs pounding, muscular body straining, he closed the distance between him and the murderer. Matheson, seeing this, panicked and fumbled with the shells. Finally, he closed the chamber, brought his weapon up, and took aim. He pulled the trigger . . .

Nick was there, and knocked the weapon aside as the bullet blazed forth. Like a madman he raised his fist to hit Matheson, and wrapped his strong fingers about the hunter's throat.

He struck Matheson once, breaking his nose. "No, please," whined the hunter. Nick raised his fist again. "You son-of-a . . ." he cried as the fist swung downward.

The blow was intercepted by a hand far stronger than human muscles. The Huntsman jerked Nick to his feet, grabbed him around the waist, and held him at arm's length from his armored body. Nick flailed away helplessly at the Huntsman, cutting skin and splintering bone on the unyielding armor.

"Why?" he screamed, looking at the Huntsman straight in the face. In answer, the Huntsman lifted the man high above his body and threw him to the ground. He then unshouldered his own rifle, walked over to the semiconscious Nick, and blew a hole in his chest with a point blank rifle blast.

Reshouldering his weapon, the Huntsman attended to Matheson. While treating Matheson's broken nose, the Huntsman gestured at the two bodies before him.

Huntsman: "Well, you certainly got what you came for. I hope you enjoyed it." They heard a noise, and saw the little girl crying softly. "It is quite unfortunate that you could not get a third permit," continued the Huntsman. "The family together would have made a nicer prize. Don't you think so, Matheson?"

Beneath the metal gaze of the one called the Huntsman, Matheson sobbed uncontrollably.

In the carpeted living room, before a roaring fire, Dennis Matheson sat on the plush, overstuffed couch.

"Would you like another drink, Den?" asked Paul. Matheson nodded, and Paul poured each of them a stiff scotch and soda. He handed Dennis his drink and sat down beside him. The two men stared silently into the fire for awhile, until finally: "What's wrong, Den? You can't still be upset over that nasty Huntsman character, can you? Your Dad paid the man, right?"

Dennis nodded.

"Well, then, he won't bother you again." Paul put his arm snugly around Dennis' shoulder. "Forget about it, dear. Just forget . . ."

They touch often in the next hour, alone in the fire-warmed room.

The Huntsman passed through the bar and lounge, nodded at the half-drunken cries of welcome he receives. Madam Bovary (he does not know her real name, although she insists that Bovary is it) moved toward him through a haze of tobacco and marijuana smoke. She made a joke; it is something both humorous and obscene, and they both laughed. Then she nodded toward the stairway, and he nodded back, while pressing several large credit bills into her hand. She tucked the money into her brassiere (something she saw in an old motion picture) and led the armored one upstairs.

In the private room were comfortable furnishings, including a couch and bed, and of course a bar. Madame Bovary brought a young boy in; the Huntsman gave his approval. The Madame didn't leave. The Huntsman asks her what she wants.

"Little Felix here," she patted the boy's head, "said that last time some things were done to him that were not quite—well—quite included under the usual fee?"

The Huntsman looked at the boy, who cowered in his gaze. "Did he mention the nature of these things?" asked the Huntsman.

"No," said Madame Bovary. "But I assume that you will, Huntsman . . . not harm the boy . . . too badly, that is. And you will pay for what you do?"

"Fear not, woman," replied the Huntsman, handing her more bills. "Now go—you are on my time."

Madame Bovary closed the door behind her, and the Huntsman locked it. He turned to the boy, "Now, Felix. I don't hurt you, do I? And surely, you've serviced others like me?" The boy nodded his head up and down.

"Good. Now, wait until I remove this thing." The steel armor fell away, and the Huntsman was naked. Naked, and quite a lovely woman. She wrapped her arms around the boy and stroked his hair. They climbed onto the bed. The Huntsman spread her legs open and said to Felix: "Come here, Felix, come and take me." She closed her eyes.

The boy said, "Yes, Huntsman," and obeyed.

Faster Than a Speeding Bullet

Faster than a speeding bullet! More powerful than a locomotive! Able to leap tall buildings in a single bound!

It has always been my policy never to interfere in a customer's personal business. Sure, a guy comes into my bar and pays good money to drink my booze, well, he's got a right to bend my ear a bit. I make like I'm listening and really concerned and all that but, like I said, I don't like to get involved.

Now, I'm not some kind of social misfit, you understand, but in the bartending business you become everybody's best pal and priest and shrink, as soon as they down a few cold ones. So, after six years of tending bar night after night, you develop a sort of filter which keeps out all the bullshit you don't want to hear and lets you take in just enough to know when to nod or grunt at the right time.

Except, last Friday night, there was one guy came in here, and had a hell of a story. I noticed him right away, because he seemed a bit more upper class than the usual jamokes what hang out here. I'm not saying I cater to bums; all my regulars pay cash on the line, no running up a bar tab here. It's just that this guy was dressed real nice, obviously a white-collar man. Had on a nice dark-blue suit, with a black and red striped tie. White shirt, too. Expensive looking threads, although I thought they were a bit out of style. He was a big dude, husky, maybe six-four or five, with broad shoulders and a real square jaw.

Anyway, this guy had come in late, about eleven, and had been downing Budweisers the whole night. He drank a shitload, but I noticed that he was only mildly soused. Didn't say a word to anybody else, just sat there as people went in and out. Didn't even bat an eye when Shirley came in. Sure, she's a hooker, but a nice piece of ass, and I don't mind lookin' every once and a while. She did everything but sit on his lap to get his attention, and like I said, he didn't even bat an eyelash.

I close at two in the morning, but everybody except this one guy cleared out about one in the A.M. I tapped him on the shoulder. He looked up at me, like a sad little puppy that was being punished for something. You get to know people, and I had a feeling that this one was going to be a true confession. I hoped not, as Shirley's halter had made me hot and I wanted to get to my girlfriend's place.

"Hey, pal, if you're done drinking here, I'd like to close up."

He said softly, "But, I thought you were open for another hour. I don't want to leave."

It is also my policy never to close before hours if a customer doesn't want to leave, provided he ain't rowdy. "Don't worry, pal," I said, "I'll be open if you want to stay."

He smiled weakly. "I hope you don't mind, uh . . . Mister . . ."

"Rorke's the name, Harry Rorke."

"Mr. Rorke . . . it's just that I don't have any place to go. It gets lonely sometimes, lonely when you're different. You don't know what it's like to be different, do you?" He gulped down the remainder of his beer, and then he set the mug down on the bar. My filter told me he would probably wait forever for me to say something.

"Well, pal, what do you mean? You don't look any different from anybody else from where I'm standing."

"But that's the problem, don't you see? I'm so much like what everyone else wants. But I can't have it, I can't. Because I'm better than everybody else!"

"Well, what's wrong with being better?" I asked. Maybe you think he was being snotty, telling me how much better he was than the rest of the world, but if you woulda heard him, it wasn't like that. Sure, he said it like it was a known fact, but he seemed sorry for it, like he regretted it.

"Oh, nothing's wrong with it," he said sarcastically. "Everybody thinks it's just great. 'Oh, look how good he is. Look how strong he is,' they say. 'It must be wonderful to do all the things he does,' they say. Well, that is just plain nonsense. I curse the day I ever came to this planet! I wish," he said sadly, "that I would have died with Krypton."

I begin to worry when they start to babble. I was afraid the countless Buds were beginning to take their toll on the poor guy. I saw tears begin to form in the corners of his eyes, eyes which stared hard at me through thick glass lenses.

"What's all this about dying? And where is the Krypton place?"

The man's voice was choked with grief. "Krypton is my home," he said. "I am Superman. I have never told anyone that before . . . I am Superman."

Look! Up in the sky! It's a bird! It's a plane! It's Superman!

I was a bit surprised, since I didn't take this guy to be a nutcase type. I figured him for a lousy-life sob story. It is usually those who seem to be failures that give me the "I am God" or "I am Superman" spiel. Funny, but this was the second Superman I had had this month.

"Well, congratulations. The Man of Steel! I'm very honored to meet you, sir, and I want to tell you what a fine job I think you've been doing in keeping our great city free from crime." I always handle these guys by playing along. They like it.

"Oh sure, everybody's grateful. But what do I get out of it, huh? What reward?"

"Come on, now. Superman doesn't need a reward. He is the champion of good over evil."

"Come off it, Mr. Rorke. I'm a person, and I need more than a pat on the head and little trophies from the mayor, gold trophies with the name of some first place bowling team scratched off and the name 'Superman' written in with a crayon. Don't you think I'd enjoy getting paid, for once, so I wouldn't have to work like every other jerk just to make enough money to keep up this phony identity?"

He seemed a bit riled up, and while he may not have been Superman, he was sure big and husky. I just wanted to calm him down. "Sorry, pal, I didn't think. You're right, you know, you should be paid, you really should."

He grew silent, and then spoke after a moment. "Oh, hell, what good would money do me? I could always get some, no problem, and if I really wanted that I would have taken it a long time ago. It's being so lonely that gets to me. No real friends, nobody to talk to." He motioned towards his glass, which I picked up and put under the tap.

"Well, you got me to talk to. And you could have lots of friends." I saw his real problem now. This guy wanted people to like him, but didn't know how to make it a two-way street. He wanted all the attention, but didn't want to give anything in return. That's why the pretending to be the Superdude bit. After all, who is better known than the guy in the blue and red tights?

"No, no, I can't. When I was little, I couldn't play sports with other kids. Even then I coulda hurt them with my strength. And what time do I have for people, anyway? When I'm Superman, I always have to be somewhere, helping someone. I don't spend enough time as Clark . . . that's my name . . . to be with other people. I've never really has a solid relationship with anybody since my foster mom died. I spend all of my life being Superman, and none of it being me."

He took the foamy glass of Bud from me and set it down in front of himself on the bar. My pour had been a little sloppy; it was late and I was tired. Foam spilled over the top of the glass and ran down the sides, sliding over his fingers.

"Well, pal, my advice to you, and, mind you, I am not normally a butinsky, but my advice to you would be to get yourself a little woman." I winked knowingly at him. "I got me the cutest little dish, not much upstairs, but a hot little bod nonetheless. And look at me; I ain't so much. I'm five-seven, scrawny, and got asthma. A big stud . . . pardon my mouth . . . a big guy like you oughta have no trouble, no . . ."

"NO!" he shouted, spilling part of his brew. He looked down and said softly, "I'm sorry, but you don't understand. There's this girl I love at work, and she won't even look at old Clarkie. Know why?"

I shrugged my shoulders while wiping the beer up with a bar rag.

"Because she's in love with Superman, stinkin' lousy Superman, *that's* why." He laughed. "As Clark I'm just another Joe, but show off my super powers, and she wants me more than anything."

"Why not tell her your real identity, like you told me?" I asked. "Then," I continued, "you could make it with her as Superman."

He moved his head from side to side and wagged his finger at me. "Harry, Harry, old friend," he said, "you don't understand." He bent his head toward mine and whispered softly as he looked about the bar, as if he wanted no one to hear him, "I have enemies, Harry. Many enemies. They could get to me through her; they could find a weakness in me. I can't let them do that, can I?"

"Clark, if this is such a problem, why don't you hang up the cape and tights forever, then marry this dame. Don't use your powers—just be plain Clark."

The color drained from his face, and he stood up, knocking his bar stool to the ground. "That's what you'd like, wouldn't you? That's what you'd all like. You are all jealous, I know that. But what's worse, you're all afraid of me."

"Afraid of you?" I asked feebly, because he sure did look big and mean and I *was* a bit afraid. "Why should we fear you?"

"Because," he answered as he picked up the stool, "I am like a god to you."

Yes, it's Superman, strange visitor from another planet who came to Earth with powers and abilities far beyond those of mortal men.

"A god?" I asked. "You said you were Superman, not a god!"

"Don't you understand? Don't you see how hard it has been to control myself all these years? Whatever its source may be, and even I'm not sure, my powers are almost infinite compared to what you can muster. At this moment I could vaporize this entire bar from where I sit, just by unleashing my heat vision. I can see for miles, and I can see through almost anything. Why, with my sensitive hearing and my vision, mortals like yourself have no secrets from me. None! There is nothing, I mean *nothing*, that I cannot be witness to if I so choose.

"You speak of me being Superman, not a god. I ask you now, what is the difference? If anything, I am more powerful than any god, simply because I am definitely a reality where they are not.

"Did you know that I could crush your skull with a flick of my forefinger? And that you couldn't escape this, because my speed is such that I could hit you ten times before you would feel the first blow? If I chose to do so, I could fly off into space, and hurl the moon into the Earth, destroying all life on this planet.

"I can't be hurt by any normal weapon, any weapon of human manufacture. Do you, can you even comprehend what I am saying? You think all this does is allow me to catch some lousy bank robber without being hurt by his gun or his knife? Do you know what my powers allow me to do?"

I sat for a moment, stunned. I didn't know what to make of this, but knew that I wanted him to go on. "What?" I asked.

"I have flown to the center of the sun and seen the fire which sustains the Earth," he said, his voice resonating throughout the bar, "and I have stood on the ocean floor where time stands still and where no ordinary man may ever walk. I have soared above the clouds with eagles, ridden hurricanes and thunderstorms, felt lightning tickle my back." He looked straight at me. "*This* is what being Superman is all about. My reality is your dream."

He stopped talking quite abruptly, and looked as if he were a bit ashamed of shouting at me. He sat on the stool and finished what was left of his beer.

"I'm sorry," he said softly, "but I have to be straight with you. I mean, I don't even know when or if I'm going to die. For all I know, I may not even age like normal people. I could live until the end of the universe." He ran his hand through his jet black hair. "It's really funny, you know . . . I may live forever, and I don't even know who I am."

"You're Superman, Clark," I said softly, "you're Superman."

"That's just it. Is Clark Superman, or is Superman Clark?"

Superman, who can change the course of mighty rivers, bend steel in his bare hands.

"I . . . I don't know what to say," I replied. "Of course you don't," he said. "How could you know? I don't even know, and I've been thinking about it for as long as I can remember." He played absentmindedly with his tie clip. Strange that I didn't notice it before, as I do a bit of pawning on the side. It was a very striking piece: small, maybe half a carat at most, a very small stone set in platinum. The stone had a brilliance unrivaled by any other gem I've ever seen, and it seemed to have a glow of its own. Its brilliant bright green contrasted nicely with the dull platinum. Clark noticed me staring at it, and quickly stopped fiddling with it.

"Nice tie-clip you have there. Heirloom or something?"

"Yes," he said softly, "something to remember home by."

I checked my watch and saw that it was a quarter after three. The man was checking his, too, and he reached for his wallet. "No thanks, pal," I said, "the last three brews are on the house."

He put away his money. "Thank you," he said, "thank you very much." Then he was silent.

I felt uncomfortable, surrounded only by the sounds of the early morning city. I wanted to hear a voice for some reason. "Look, I know you got troubles. Big troubles." I leaned over the bar. "Maybe worse than some of the other jamokes that come here every night. But you have one thing they don't."

"Yeah," he replied, "a lousy life."

"No friend, that's not it. You have hope, you have your dream, your fantasy. You have a place to go, a place where you're someone and something special. The rest of us . . ."

"But what good is all that, if I have no one to share it with?"

I was out of words, out of advice, out of comforting phrases. The man stood up and nodded. I waved a feeble salute, and then he turned and walked out the door into the darkness of early morning.

And who, disguised as Clark Kent (mild-mannered reporter for a great metropolitan newspaper), fights a never-ending battle for truth, justice, and the American way.

The Civilized Man

Several years ago, when I first published my poems, I was invited to give a lecture in front of an audience composed of wealthy patrons of the arts. My lecture was dry, but still well received. Afterwards, at the luncheon held in my honor, I was introduced to a man called Baron Xavier. I knew of him only by his reputation: a wealthy man who had a passion for the arts, and whose private collection of sculpture, paintings, and manuscripts was among the world's largest. The man was exceedingly tall, gaunt, and well dressed. He smelled of expensive cologne. I was awed by his presence, and he was thrilled to meet me!

"Good evening, Baron," I said.

"Ah, good evening. I am a great admirer of yours. Your books adorn the shelves of my library. You know that I treasure my books. I brought a copy of *The Forests of the Night* with me. Will you do me the honor of autographing it?"

I told him that I would be happy to autograph the volume, and I did. It was, I noted, the leather bound, gold leaf edition. The Baron and I discussed my poetry, his interests in music and painting and sculpture and literature, and my own collection of original musical manuscripts, which, of course, was dwarfed by his own.

"You possess the original manuscript of Beethoven's *Emperor Concerto*?" The Baron Xavier asked this of me in open-mouthed astonishment as soon as I had just finished telling him that very fact.

"Yes," I repeated. I did not explain that my father had left me a large share of an oil exploration company he had founded, the funds from which freed me from having to make a living and allowed me to indulge my passion for the arts.

His smile vanished, and his jaw muscles bunched up as the color drained from his cheeks.

"I would like to add that to my own collection of Beethoven's manuscripts, and I am willing to pay you handsomely for it."

"I am sorry, but it's not really for sale," I said as I rose from the table. I felt that something was wrong with this man and that I had better depart. "I really must be . . . "

Baron Xavier had grasped my wrist with his strong hand, and he held me tight in his vise-like grip. I could not free myself and looked hopelessly around the room. The Baron stared into my face, his eyes burning with anger! Rage at me because I wouldn't sell him a decaying piece of paper. A waiter entered the room, and the Baron released me without a word. He turned away and stared silently ahead of himself, at nothing. I grabbed my coat and went quickly from the room. I hailed a cab and returned home.

It was late, so I crawled into bed, turned on the lamp, and sat back to read a novel by a new writer, Thomas Pynchon. It was called V. I became absorbed as I read, and at page 123 I was startled to hear someone clearing his throat. My heart pounded as my eyes darted upward from the page and met those of Baron Xavier. Then they gazed downward to the gun in his hand.

"God evening to you, sir. I am sorry to have to intrude like this, but I could not forget the manuscript you spoke of at the luncheon." He threw a clear plastic bag stuffed with large bills on my bed. "That is three times what any dealer would pay you for it. Now, the manuscript, if you please."

"Take that damn money back. I don't know who the hell you think you are, but now I wouldn't sell you that Goddamn piece of paper if you . . . if you . . ." My fear checked my anger, for I saw his finger tighten about the trigger. "You, you would kill me for a sheet of music?"

He laughed softly. "Of course I would," he exclaimed in genuine amazement. "The manuscript will be better preserved in my collection. I give a great deal of time and money to preserve precious papers—more than you can give. That is why the manuscript is going to be mine."

"But, you'd kill me for the sake of that paper. What kind of a man are you? You spend your life showing people what a fine, civilized, cultured man you are, but you're a damned hypocrite. You value culture over human life!" I spoke rapidly, in anger.

In contrast, the man threatening my life spoke with calm thoughtfulness. "My dear sir, you are an artist. You should know even better than I, a mere critic and patron of men like yourself, that art is much more important than any individual human life. It is only the great artists and their works that matter; the world is no poorer for the loss of the life of an ordinary man. For example, if it were up to you to decide which of two men would be sent to death, and the two men were Picasso and a shipping clerk, who would you choose to die?"

"Well, I would never make such a choice . . . I would . . . I . . ." I looked into my interrogator's eyes, which compelled me to tell the truth, to be honest with him. "I guess that if I had to choose, I would choose Picasso to live. But, I would never make such a monstrous choice; the idea is revolting to me."

"You would not want to choose, but if you had to, you would choose the artist over the peasant. Yet both are human beings. If you had to choose between the destruction of the *Mona Lisa* and the life of the shipping clerk, what would be your choice?"

"This is horrid, monstrous. I would, of course, choose the man's life," I replied instantly. But then I thought of the hours I had spent in the museum as a boy, staring at the *Mona Lisa*, that unique and irreplaceable work of art. And there are billions of men, and thousands of them die each day. I whispered, my head hung in the shame of the truth, "No, I would have the man killed."

"You see my point. Do not be ashamed of your choice, my friend, and do not condemn mine. We are both the same; we know the value of a unique work of art as opposed to an ordinary human being. The difference is that I have made the choice that you are revolted by. Now, my manuscript please."

One last chance. "If you kill me, you'll be killing a living artist who has so much more to give. And the manuscript will exist, no matter who owns it!"

The Baron raised his gun, and his voice was strong and firm. "I do not mean to be insulting, but you are a minor poet, and your death would matter little. There are a hundred who would and can take your place. And now I grow tired of word games. You have either thirty years left—or the same number of seconds."

I walked over to the safe and gave him what he wanted. He hugged the framed manuscript and said to me very kindly that he would take care of it, and that I could come and see it and the rest of his collection whenever I wished. He was very friendly, invited me for tea, and pointed out the foolishness of my ever mentioning this to the police or anyone else, for that matter. "After all, you wouldn't want to rob the world of many more volumes of poetry, and your writing really is good. I am glad I didn't have to lessen the number of living poets tonight." He found this humorous and we both chuckled over it. We shook hands, I promised to come to tea next Wednesday, and I bid him good night. He departed by way of the back door, which I made a note to have repaired in the morning.

I sat down in a chair, dazed. I knew that the Baron was not a liar, and that I would not inform the police of his visit. My mind spun with the memory of this oddest of robberies. I was confused. I had always thought that a well-bred and cultured man would be a civilized man, and not a monster incapable of human feelings. And yet in many ways, I was like the Baron, but without his strong convictions.

I never went to tea with him, and have not seen Baron Xavier since that night. I edit a magazine of literary criticism, but I have written few poems recently. I still love the arts, and I feel that I show great humanity toward my fellow man.

Yet whenever I enter a man's study, where the walls are lined with worn editions of the Harvard Classics and a Vivaldi concerto flows from the stereo speakers, I cannot help the slight trembling in my frame and the small gnawing pain in my stomach.

Shadetree, Prince of Darkness

Elizabeth's small apartment mirrored the signs of decay and neglect that were characteristic of its only inhabitant. The wallpaper hung yellow and peeling, and the furniture lay in disarray about the rooms, covered with yellow plastic sheets. The plastic once (but no longer) served to protect the upholstery on the sofa and chairs from the abuses of company, also a thing of the past. Dishes and tea cups, unwashed, covered the table and kitchen counter. Liquids spilled by hands which had increasingly uncertain control over their movements formed small islands in a sea of gray linoleum. In a chair near the phone and in front of the ancient black-and-white Zenith she sits, knitting an afghan not needed at all.

Loneliness is companion to fear, and cruelty is often father to them both. A loving mother, a good wife, and for what, she thinks, for what? To sit alone, always alone, in this miserable apartment. Not even a call from the children, or the relatives? As if it would kill them.

All it would take to make her life worth living is an occasional call or visit from her children. But her sons are married, and, come the seventh day, they really are too busy, don't get too much time to go fishing or play some golf; let Herbie/let Freddie go to Mom's this week, I'll go next week. But they rarely do.

So she sits alone, with only misery and fear to keep her company. The phone rings, and she trembles and drops the receiver twice before bringing it to her ear.

A wrong number. She puts it back on the hook, and weeps uncontrollably. Outside another day has passed, so slowly and yet already gone, and then tomorrow must be faced. Again, TV and sitting, and . . . and nothing else, really.

She sits staring at the window, as dusk settles upon the city, until she realizes that two green eyes are staring back at her. Coming out of her daydreaming, she sees outside the window her worst enemy, an enemy who will not let her live out her final days in the quiet indignity of loneliness: Shadetree, Prince of Darkness. She gropes in her apron pocket, coming up with the rabbit's foot and the clover charm, and, trembling, gets up and walks over to the window, hissing at the black cat with the green eyes and waving her charms. The cat regards her with silent curiosity, then hisses and slithers away. She closes the shade as the room begins to spin about her. "Careful, old girl, he almost got you that time," she says aloud, as she steadies herself and walks shakily back to her chair.

Elizabeth is not an educated woman; as a young girl she had to work to support the family and had no time for schoolbook nonsense. But she is no fool; she has spent much time reading and studying evil, "superstition" as those stupid enough not to believe and fear it call it. She knew about the evil eye, ghosts who hated the living, about witches and warlocks and vampires and black cats . . .

Shadetree was a large black cat, with green glowing eyes. He was a stray, and a favorite with the neighborhood children. They had nothing to fear from him, however, since they were not near dying. But at her age, one lived with death, and each evening's bedtime prayers might never be followed by the morning ones. She knew that some evil was after her soul, and she had been clever, oh so clever, in finding out Shadetree for what he was before it was too late.

She had seen it from her window . . . Shadetree running out into the street . . . the car swerving to avoid killing the cat . . . the ambulance. The next day's papers had told how the passenger died; the woman was the elderly mother of the driver, a young woman who was taking her mother to the hospital for some surgery, or something of the sort. And then, when she saw Shadetree at her window, the dead bird in his mouth, with that chilling smile of knowing and maliciousness on his face, she had begun to fear for her life.

She kept the door and windows locked tight, stifling as the heat was, for if Shadetree could not get in, she was relatively safe from him. So she sat, in clothes drenched with sweat, the apartment foul and stifling, but better that than being caught by that monster outside. After hanging garlic over the door and windows, she undresses slowly and with great effort, throws the damp clothes and underclothes on a chair to be worn for the fourth (fifth?) consecutive day, and puts on her night-clothes. She settles then into the only blessing of her life, the oblivion of a welcome, albeit short and erratic, sleep.

She wakes up, the sheets damp from sweat and the pillow case smelling from dribble. The clock reads five thirty in the evening; she can't believe that she slept through a whole day. That's a sin, she thinks, a whole day wasted, when I could have done so many things, like . . . the thought trails off in dismay.

She dresses and, with effort, pours herself a glass of milk. The doorbell rings . . . and rings again, insistently. Elizabeth goes to open it, filled with apprehension, praying it is a relative or friend, somebody to spend time with, if only for a few fleeting minutes to be remembered for years to come, praying to be shielded from the agony and heartbreak of disappointment. Arthritic hands fumble with the chain, bolt, and many locks, as the doorbell calls yet a third time. She opens the door but sees no one in front of her. "TRICK OR TREAT!" scream three voices. Her heart misses a beat, quickens its pace, she sees stabbing lights before her eyes, and the voices ring in her ears. Then, the blood circulates again and she looks down to see Spiderman, Dracula, and Casper the Friendly Ghost begging for candy, all of these fictional characters about four feet high and holding out pillowcases, half-filled with candies.

It's Halloween, she remembers with relief, and I have to give them candy. She mumbles an apology, then goes into the kitchen. She brings back a bowl of fruit, and puts a few loose raisins into each bag. The children thank her and leave; later their mothers will make them throw those raisins away. She puts the bowl back and, fulfilled in a sense from the change in the dull routine, decides she deserves some relaxation from such a trying day and settles back to watch TV, not as one who has nothing better to do, but as one who has put in a hard day of living and deserves a rest or break.

Elizabeth sips her glass of milk and watches a movie with gusto and enjoyment, but a clicking noise in the back of her mind annoys her, bothers her. She concentrates on it—it sounds like nails tapping on Formica, like claws on linoleum! She looks to her left and—oh my God—the door was left open. I didn't close it after those kids. And at the threshold of the apartment stands Shadetree, regarding her frozen form.

She drops the glass of milk and it shatters on the floor. Shadetree lets out a whining cry, like a baby screaming, and her heart is wrenched from her chest. Stabbing knives of light dance before her eyes, and she too falls to the floor, not with a crash but with a sickening thud. She fumbles in her apron and finds the lucky charms, which she holds out at Shadetree . . .

Shadetree, Prince of Darkness, Lord of Evil, and Bearer of a Thousand Souls, approaches Elizabeth, who lies paralyzed upon a death bed of old warped floorboards. She holds up the garlic, a weak spell which bothers not the Lord of Evil. He changes now, grows into a shapeless thing, huge, towering above her, then molting into different images, all of which she has loved and cherished. Then the room darkens and the odor of sulfur comes, carried by the breeze from outside through the doorway. She cannot speak or even see, and her heart is being crushed by an iron press, fashioned by Beelzebub in his vile workshop. Now she holds out the clover and mutters an incantation . . . he is surprised by it, and the unexpectedness of the attack causes him to become once more a cat. He utters a spell, and the plant falls from her grasp . . . he changes again, this time into a huge bat with eyes of red hot coal, and moves toward her. She is helpless before him, on this the night of his birth, All Hallow's Eve, and he will drink of her spirit . . . She gasps, and all around her is darkness, and the tightening of the iron press upon her soul . . .

Elizabeth lies still on the floor, skin pale white and eyes staring unseeing at the ceiling. Blood runs from her unspeaking mouth and unbreathing nostrils. Shadetree approaches, sniffs at the corpse, and then moves past it to the puddle of milk on the floor. The cat begins to drink the milk, lapping it up with his pink tongue while purring contentedly.

And All the Sky a Sheet of Glass

H ey!" shouted the fat man with the change-maker strapped to his belt, "Don't hit the machine like that, kid. You'll bust it doin' that."

"I had a free ball comin' to me, and the fucking thing tilts. God damn this machine," shouted the pinball player, a young man with long black hair and a scraggly beard, wearing a torn sweat shirt and jeans. He whacked the machine once more, for good measure. "I coulda broken my record, I bet. And I will, too." He stuck his hand inside his pocket and began fishing for another quarter.

"Just be careful with the machine, is all," said the fat man. He looked at the kid with an amused grin on his beefy face. "Don't you ever go to classes or anything? Seems like you're always here playin' pinball. Where do ya get the time and the money? When I was your age, I hadda save all the bucks that I made."

"Ah, I go to class. And I got a job working for one of my engineering professors, and it pays pretty good, too." The student looked up at the man. "We happen to be doing research on a government sponsored grant, so all the dough is just rollin' in."

"What kinda stuff you doin'?" asked the man, a bit in awe of this kid's job and education.

"Well," began the student, "it really isn't supposed to be spread around. Kind of 'top-secret' stuff, you know." He knew he shouldn't be talking about it, but his conceit and his desire to share a secret got the better of him. "I work for Professor Hamilton. He's been commissioned to test the practical aspects of Klein's theoretical work in matter miniaturization. Basically, we are attempting to shrink objects—both animate and inanimate—down to a fraction of their original size, and then transport them—materialize them some distance away. We actually have partial success in the miniaturization aspects of the thing, but teleportation tends to be erratic and uncontrolled, and …" He stopped talking when the fat man began to chuckle. "You think this is just some science fiction story or something, don't you," said the student, red-faced. "You don't believe me."

"Sure I believe ya," said the fat man, patting the student on the shoulder with his meaty hand. "Shrinking machines. Why not? And when you come down from cloud nine, let me know where you got that stuff. My son wouldn't be disinterested in buyin' a few ounces of it." The fat man checked his watch. "Closin' time, Captain Kirk. You'd better skidaddle."

"Ah, I don't give a shit. Don't believe me. I ain't high." The kid put on his jacket and began heading for the door. "And your pinball machines suck!" he shouted, as he left.

"Nut college punks," grumbled the man, as he began shutting the lights.

"Fuzzy-brained professor, he don't even know enough to lock the window," said Artie, as he entered the darkened lab through the aforementioned window.

For all the money they were paying him, he had expected to work harder. *After all, one doesn't pay top dollar to Artie the Mouse for a job that your grandmother could pull,* thought Artie. But a buck's a buck. He had learned which questions not to ask early in his career.

Actually, the job held some satisfaction other than the money. Wouldn't it be fun to see the faces of these creepy intellectual guys after I rip off what they've been sweating over for months? Artie made a sour face. Fuckin' rich momma's boy college kids, and them freakin' mad scientist professors. I'll show them.

He looked around the lab. He could make out a lot of tools, meters, and bits of electric circuitry. *No beakers or colored liquids in bottles or steaming flasks—it's not like in the movies,* he reflected. Then he laid eyes upon what he had come for. They had described it perfectly. He walked over to the device he had come to steal. It was a black box about the size of a case of beer. He checked it over, and was satisfied. He hefted it onto his shoulder and exited the lab. His car was parked right next to...

"Hold it right there, pal!"

The voice sounded reasonably far away. *Calm down boy. Oh Jesus, I can't get caught again. I'd be sent up for too long and I'm too old.* Heavy as the machine was, Artie was a big man, and he began to run.

He ran with effort, and realized that the weight of the machine would not let him outrun the security man for long. And help was probably on the way. But he couldn't just drop the machine, even though it would allow him to escape.

He ran. *Oh, God, if only I hadn't already spent the money I was paid, I could just walk in and hand Lou back the money and he wouldn't do anything. But*

Jesus Christ he'd do something now, maybe he'd cripple or blind me like he did Frankie, or he knows where Norma lives with Mom...

He was breathing heavily as he ducked behind another building, only to have his tormentor follow.

What the Hell does he care whether I steal this or not, thought Artie. *He only must be pullin' down ten an hour or so. Not me, boy, no sucker job for me. But maybe if I woulda got a job, I wouldn't always be afraid. But I hadda make it the hard way, not like these rich guys. I didn't have their advantages.*

The footsteps came nearer. Artie's vision was getting blurry, his head became a pounding bass drum. He saw the neon sign, PENNY ARCADE— PINBALL HERE! And he ran for the door, which was locked. *I'll hide in here.* He kicked the door open, and turned to see the security guard behind him.

"Allright, mister, FREEZE!"

Artie turned to run, but his weakened legs gave way. He held the black box in front of him, and he fell upon it.

The guard was blinded by a flash of white light. He heard a scream. When he could see again, his gaze fell upon the black box, which lay on the floor undamaged. The front row of studs had been depressed and the two red LEDs were aglow. He picked up the box, and the printing underneath the glowing bulbs read MINIATURIZE and TRANSPORT, respectively.

The security guard would later testify that the criminal must have escaped while he had been temporarily blinded, for when he was able to see, Artie had seemingly vanished from the area.

Artie awoke from his long slumber to find himself lying on a ground of smooth, flat, and light brown texture. He looked about, and beheld a land whose name he did not yet know. He looked up; all about him rose giant towers of all colors, of marvelous and beautiful shapes. He looked up still further, where the world ended miles above him, and all the sky was a sheet of glass.

Artie regarded this alien land, and who he was, and how he came to get there. This thing he did for an unmeasured interval of time. And when done, he had no answers. He rose to stand upon wobbly legs. He knew only that his name was Arthur Benvinuto, and that he had been a very bad man, and he knew where the Lord and Maker of All Things sends bad men who have passed on. But he inhaled, and felt very much alive, in a place so beautiful that it could not be purgatory. Artie the Wanderer, Artie the Traveler, Mouse no longer, set out to explore this new place. He began his long walk toward the blue tower in the east.

"Jesus Christ, he's here first thing in the morning," laughed the arcade manager, as the steam from his breath mingled with that from his stogie. "Well, I don't hafta fumble with all my keys this morning; the place was broken into last night. Nothin' stolen though, and nothin' busted up, except this door."

"So, did you talk to the police about it?" asked the student with the beard, in a smug voice.

"Yeah, so what?"

"Then you know that the thief had taken something really important from my ... from Dr. Hamilton's lab. Something owned by the government."

The man stepped behind the cash register, and the student handed him a five-dollar bill. "Yeah, I know. So you wasn't bustin' my chops about all that science stuff an' you workin' on that big project." He made change and handed the student 20 quarters.

The kid grinned. "Yeah, well, actually I was kind of overdoing it a bit. I really don't do any of the thinking. I just solder this, splice that, do easy, busy work." He walked toward the pinball machine.

"Still, it must be sumpin big if that guy wanted to steal it. I wonder how he got away?"

"Dunno," said the student. "Maybe he used it to shrink himself down to any size and then transported himself to Mars!" He laughed, dropped a quarter into the machine, and pressed a button.

The traveler stops. He feels the ground beneath his feet start to vibrate, and hears the screeching of metal, the whining of some awful engine. Suddenly, the world where the sky is a sheet of glass is ablaze with lights, the dead towers now shining with the brilliance of a hundred suns. The traveler runs in panic. He falls to his knees, and his ears fill with thunderous ringing, banging, until he cannot bear the pain. He hears above all else one sound increasing, becoming ever louder. A steady sound, like something rolling, rolling .... He looks up, and a silver globe grows larger and larger in the distance as it bears down upon him. He shakes his head and rises. He decides to attempt flight, but there is no time. He knows in this last instant who he is, where he is, how it came to pass that he is here, and the knowledge burns in his mind and he has to scream, as the silver orb of death bears down upon him.

"Christ, hey, what do you think you're doing now?" The man rushes over to the pinball machine, where the student has unfastened the top glass and is leaning it against the wall. The manager grabs him gruffly, but the student shakes loose.

"Look, the ball got stuck and I shook it until it tilted but it's still stuck. The fuckin' thing ruined a perfect game. Look." The ball is sitting in the middle of the machine, next to the blue WOW disc, but is not moving. The student picks it up and holds it in the light. Both he and the manager stare at it for a long while.

"Well, no wonder it stuck," says the boy softly. "It has all this sticky gunk all over it." And sure enough, a bit of red liquid glistens on the surface of the silver ball.

The Priest and the Pig

Come sup with me, O wandering priest,
On thin bread baked without the yeast
And roast suckling pig, cooked so fine,
Perhaps a sip of hearty wine?
(In honor of this unclean beast, upon whose flesh
We make our feast.)

He looks at me with fierce disdain,
With booming voice he asks my name,
I tell him and he asks: Is this thing true?
For by that name you be a Jew,
And surely, you should be ashamed.

Look upon the golden skin of this monster in the fire;
Look upon the swollen, fat flesh of your desire.

The wood beneath the pig grew bright,
Splashing orange upon the night.
A flame leaped up and stroked the skin,
A glowing hot tongue in carnal sin.

I reached out and pulled off a great joint of meat
(Licking fingers to make the meal complete).
What right have you, I ask the priest,
To pass judgement on what I eat?

Know you not what you do, you fat clod?
You sin against the name of God!

FREAK SHOW OF THE GODS

Yaweh God! Yaweh God! Yaweh God! he cries.

And Yaweh Fool, the truth be known,
I pause to pick clean the bone.
Go flock to the altar, and say your Mass,
Like the braying of some infernal ass.
The priest stands next to me, then takes a seat,
How hungrily he eyes the meat!

The flame leaps up. His face is glowing against the night,
His features seem to flicker as the fire's light.
Eyes so pale, wrinkles so deep,
A tired old man, ready for sleep.

Come and sup with me, I say,
To celebrate this Christmas day.
Should we not be praying, asks he, to God, the Lord?
I laugh, and tell him to pass the wine-gourd

He holds the flask in his hand. The red wine is sweet.
He looks at it and then the meat.
Ripping the flesh with broken nails, he tears free a crispy piece,
Swallows it whole, and drinks the wine.
Some more wine, if you please,
I shall enjoy this Christmas feast, for
The drink is good, and the food is fine.

Laughingly I turn to fill the flask and
Feed the fire, the heat, the smoke.
I turn to him: More wine, didst thou ask?
But his gourd lays broken upon the sand,
And where he sat lies his cloak.

Wine from his gourd makes red the ground,
But my priest friend is not around.
But from under the cloak—a noise, a sigh!
I lift it, and toss it to the sky.

There on his seat lies a length of golden light.
Which flickers weakly, fades and
Vanishes from sight.

Come sit with me here, O noble Sire,
I'll feed you most anything you desire
A priest sat here but a moment ago,
And to where he went I do not know.

ABOUT THE AUTHOR

BOB BLY is a freelance copywriter with more than 35 years of experience in business-to-business and direct marketing. McGraw-Hill calls Bob Bly "America's top copywriter" and AWAI named him its 2007 Copywriter of the Year. His clients include IBM, the Conference Board, PSE&G, AT&T, Ott-Lite Technology, Intuit, ExecuNet, Boardroom, Medical Economics, Grumman, RCA, ITT Fluid Technology, and Praxair.

Bob is the author of more than 85 books, including *The Ultimate Unauthorized Star Trek Quiz Book* (HarperCollins), *The Science in Science Fiction* (BenBella), *How to Write & Sell Simple Information for Fun and Profit* (Quill Driver Books), and *Starting Your Own Home Business After 50* (Quill Driver Books). Bob's articles have appeared in *Cosmopolitan, Writer's Digest, Successful Meetings, City Paper, Amtrak Express, New Jersey Monthly, The Record*, and many other publications, and he writes a regular column for *Target Marketing*.

Bob's awards include a Gold Echo from the Direct Marketing Association, an IMMY from the Information Industry Association, two Southstar Awards, a Standard of Excellence Award from the Web Marketing Associates, and an American Corporate Identity Award of Excellence. He is a member of the Specialized Information Publishers Association (SIPA), American Institute of Chemical Engineers (AIChE), and Business Marketing Association (BMA).

CPSIA information can be obtained at www.ICGtesting.com
Printed in the USA
BVOW02s1231110316

440007BV00001B/1/P